Stat

STATELESS

Mark Collins

Pillar Press

Copyright © 2006 Mark Collins

Stateless
First published 2006
Pillar Press
Ladywell
Thomastown
Co Kilkenny

www.pillarpress.ie

The author has asserted his moral rights.

ISBN 0955082129

All rights reserved. The material in this publication is protected by copyright law.
Except as may be permitted by law, no part of the material may be reproduced
including by storage in a retrieval system) or transmitted in any form or by any
means; adapted; rented or lent without the written permission of the
copyright owners.

All characters in this publication are fictitious and any resemblance to real persons,
living or dead, is purely coincidental.

British Library Cataloguing in Publication Data.
A CIP catalogue record for this book is available
from the British Library.

Printed in Ireland by Betaprint

10 9 8 7 6 5 4 3 2 1

For Clodagh

Acknowledgement

I would like to thank Pia Lauridsen for her help editing drafts of the novel.

*"She knows there's no success like failure
And that failure's no success at all."*
Bob Dylan

PROLOGUE

A handcuffed Sandor Lovas was told the news while in the back of a police car. It came from the bearded guard in the passenger seat who was smoking a pipe. Stalin was dead. It was March, 1953. Sandor, a Hungarian man, had thought about the Russian dictator's death for years; in particular how it would affect Hungary. But as the car drove through Budapest to the headquarters of the ÁVO, the state security police, Sandor's thoughts were not concerned with politics. They were for his own life. Arriving at the station, the bearded guard turned to Sandor, and with irony, quoted the dead dictator, "A single death is a tragedy; a million deaths is a statistic."

Sandor was locked in a basement cell. There was a surgical smell to the room reminiscent of old hospitals, the floor stank of bleach and the walls needed painting. A small window had been bricked over: it once peered on to the pavement of Andrássy Street, and as people walked by, you could see their feet. It was a busy boulevard cutting a straight line through central Pest. Sandor had walked along its wide footpaths many times, he'd sheltered beneath its bushy trees on summer days, sat in its cafes, photographed its buildings, met women in its bars, spent money in its shops and enjoyed its Opera House.

Yet always, he made another association with Andrássy Street: its baths. And two of them were in the centre of his cell, both were large, made of cast iron and their enamel had darkened from scum, shit and skin.

After two hours, three guards entered the cell, the bearded one came in last, the smell of his pipe masking the odour of bleach. They were dressed in the green uniform of the ÁVO, standard issue apparel. Sandor was instructed to sit at a desk, a statement was placed in front of him. It was surreal for him to see his name *Sandor Lovas* placed alongside the phrase *crimes against the Republic*.

The ÁVO considered Sandor an agitator because he had discussed working conditions with colleagues and the idea of striking. Sandor was a mechanical engineer. Recently he'd been concerned with the excessive targets which his factory had been given. Worried about morale, Sandor had discussed this with people he had considered friends, but one of them informed the authorities, which led to his arrest.

Despite Sandor's fear of what might happen to him in this cell, he believed the following: whether he signed his name to the spurious charges or not, he would become a victim of torture, jail or execution. And so, as he thought that he was doomed either way, he decided to be doomed on the side of the innocent and not the guilty.

Sandor was asked to sign the statement by the bearded guard, but folding his hands, he remained silent.

The guard continued. "We have a witness statement. You were talking about striking. Workers aren't allowed to strike."

Sandor said nothing. Outside a tram passed, its wheels engraving the ground.

"Okay," the guard's breath was drenched with smoke. "Fill the baths."

Sandor, aged twenty-six, was six-foot three inches tall. He had black hair, tightly cut on the back and sides and a fringe which hung over his forehead. As ordered by the guards he removed his clothes: a cream-coloured raincoat, dark trousers, matching jacket, white shirt and tie. He placed them on the floor. He stood naked on the tiles. Behind the desk the bearded guard continued smoking.

Looking down at his body, Sandor thought of his parents. He realised that later on they'd start wondering where he was, but unlike the times when he'd arrived home late and his mother had feared the worst, this was the *worst* and she had every reason to fear it. Sandor imagined her staring down from a corner of the cell, watching the ÁVO preparing to torture her only son. It had only been in the latter part of his life that he'd become appreciative of her love for him and how her life had revolved around raising her two children. And how her time, energy, effort and emotion of every colour which she'd spent on them, was the essence of self-sacrifice.

So Sandor directed all his emotion towards her. Ultimately, he felt, he'd have to answer to her and not some divine force, for to disappoint his mother was a far greater sin than to upset any god. However, if there was one aspect of this situation which he took comfort in, it was that she wouldn't witness the torture. For if she could, she'd not only feel it too, but she'd also suffer guilt for not predicting and thus altering the course of her son's twenty-six years.

Years which had come to this: a hose was attached to a tap on the wall, curling along the tiled floor and placed in a bath which was filled with cold water. A guard left the room and returned with a container and a pickaxe. A block of ice was hacked into pieces and added to the water.

Again the bearded guard asked Sandor to sign the statement. He wouldn't. The guard stood up, and from the container which had carried the ice, removed two belts. Sandor offered no resistance as they fastened one around his chest and arms. The strap was cold, so was the belt buckle. Once the guards were satisfied with the position of the belt, Sandor was walked to the bath where the other belt was strapped around his ankles. The guard told Sandor to sit on the front of the bath and as he did, he felt his skin stick to the cold enamel. He kept his knees together and his hands rested by his sides. The hose was placed in the other bath. This time, boiling water. Sandor heard the sound of an immersion heater, the bubbling of water, the rattling of pipes. He felt the warmth of steam.

Sandor felt dizzy as he looked into the bath. It was like the vertigo he'd suffered crossing the Chain Bridge when returning home drunk last week. Cars sped past on his left, while on his right was the silvery flow of the river Danube, scrambling to the end of the bridge where the tunnel sucked cars beneath Buda's hills, he lay on the ground staring at the orange imprint of the city on the night sky.

The bearded guard fetched three pairs of long, protective gloves and a baton. It was black, made of leather and it had a worn and grooved grip.

With the baths filled behind him, Sandor looked at the baton awaiting its impact and he realised that everything was designed to keep him awake as the effects of the cold water would cancel out the hot water and vice versa, and he hoped that a time would come when his consciousness would cut out. It was not death which he looked forward to but an end of sorts, and waiting on the side of the bath he tried to comfort himself by thinking that everything must end, time has to pass. As for pain, he tried to think that it was a function, a chemical reaction, just part of the engineering of the body, and something which could be overcome.

The first blow to his face shattered teeth and he felt the warm taste of blood. The second blow was to his chest. Sandor fell backwards into the bath. Quickly, the cold anaesthetised the pain in his mouth. Blood darkened the water. He felt his hair being pulled as his body was dragged the length of the bath. Ice wedged into his back as the water covered his body; tightening skin, shrinking genitals. Underwater was silent except for the beating of his heart which was being denied oxygen. Water inhaled through his nose was spat out of his mouth and when drawn into his lungs his chest felt unnaturally heavy. Gagging on cold water, he tried to lock his lungs to prevent the intake of more liquid. An attempt to lift his head above water was met with the baton, a feeling of dizziness and momentary unconsciousness before the cold returned.

Sandor was awed by the strength of his body, how it reacted, involuntary movements designed to keep himself alive, his arms and legs attempting to slither out of the leather belts.

Then: hooks attached to the leather belts lifted him out of the water and carried him to the other bath. Plunging him into the boiling water, the guards turned their heads to avoid its splash. Sandor started screaming. As he did he thought about signing the confession, it didn't matter if it was right or wrong, there was something vain and useless about pride; but Sandor was also aware, somewhere beneath the noise he was making, the splashing of the water and the sound of the bearded guard giving orders, that his submersion into the baths of Andrássy Street was inevitable, beyond reason, the power of words, the signing of papers, the will to confess.

And so the boiling water scorched his body, the baton whacked his chest, arms and legs. A gloved hand kept his head down. Boiling water seeped through his eyelids, up his nose, it washed around his tongue, burning his gums. His feet sizzled; his will-to-live tightened every muscle in his body; his toes curled in a savage, spastic grip; arching his back, he managed to push his genitals above the water in a desperate plea for cold air, and as he did, he felt the full force of the baton on his testicles, a spearlike jab into his kidneys.

Then: hooks removed him from the bath. He was placed on the cold tiles. As the guards walked around him, their boots squeaked on the floor like small animals on the deck of a boat.

Sandor felt his consciousness give way. It was like air bubbles streaming upwards from his nose while underwater and unconcerned that this release could be death, his last sensation was his head banging against the tiled floor. And the last idea which came to his mind was an image of himself, not in a photograph but in a cartoon strip, he was floating on a stormy sea and a speech bubble was above his head with the word *help!*

He was carried to a cell where the seconds rolled into minutes, hours and days.

A morning came.

A feeling of lukewarm liquid thundered on his face. It stung. Sandor's eyes opened, an acidic splash on his pupils, and he looked upwards at the bearded guard who was urinating on him. Through pipe-clenched lips, he said, "You're a free man."

CHAPTER ONE

Three years later, Sandor Lovas emerged from a train. The station clock confirmed his suspicion; he was ten minutes early for his meeting with his twin sister, Eva. Once outside the main doors of Budapest's East Station, Sandor stared at the large panes of glass which were part of its façade. Shaped like a fan, he could see both sides of the city in the reflection, the flat sprawl of Pest leading to Buda's rolling hills, below which the sun had set minutes ago. Sandor looked at the glass with the eye of an amateur photographer, it was a simple technique he'd used on many pictures, and when the glass was as clean as the station's, its mirror-like brilliance was always effective. Though Sandor thought it was too dark for photography, darkness had yet to master the sky, the clouds above the hills still carried the sun's last rays and were warmly coloured like the honey-glow behind the station windows.

Standing outside the station exposed him to a chill wind as the building was positioned on a slight elevation viewing central Pest. Autumn had been generous but now it felt like the beginning of winter. A light-coloured raincoat sheltered his upper body and most of his legs though his face met with the cold. People pushed out of the station into the evening rush hour, adding more bodies to the wide footpaths of Rákóczi Street. Sparks flinted on the overhead wires of the yellow trams as they passed cars moving slowly towards bridges over the river Danube and on to suburbia.

At times like this, Sandor was thankful for his height as it enabled him to survey those around him. He scanned the horde though he wasn't looking for his sister. He was staring at the crowd itself, wondering how many of them would attend the demonstration. He was hopeful that many would be there and he broke down what he saw into percentages: if twenty percent from that street, added to thirty percent of each train arriving in the next half-hour, added to half of all those who lived in these neighbouring streets – how many thousand would that be?

What ended this mathematical reverie was the ordinariness of the evening. It was like any other Tuesday, or any day at all. There didn't seem to be anything different in the faces of those who passed. Sandor discerned a mundane purpose in their appearance. They looked like they wanted to go home to their husbands, wives and children. To eat their dinners, walk their dogs. Just like any other evening of any other day.

But Sandor believed that it wasn't like any other day because at 7.37 a.m. on this morning, the 23 October 1956, he'd left his apartment overlooking the river Danube and as he walked along the quays he noticed many posters pasted on walls. As they hadn't been there the day before, he figured that people had been working all night putting them up. Listed on these hastily printed notices were sixteen demands which the Hungarian Federation of University and College Students Association sought from the Russian controlled Hungarian Government.

Eleven years ago the Russians had beaten the German Army in Budapest, and now, the same Russian forces who had liberated Hungary from the Nazis were themselves the object of protest. Since Stalin's death Hungary had slowly become more liberal and people had started to openly criticise Moscow's interference. Although students had organised the demonstration, their demands reflected many people, and they were, as Sandor believed, not the expression of any one political party or individual, but the expression of the country itself.

Hungary was not the only country in the Soviet bloc to air its criticism of Moscow. Less than a week ago news had travelled south from Poland that Russian tanks had appeared in Warsaw as hardliners in the Polish Communist Party requested support from Moscow in order to subdue political hostility there; but instead of violently suppressing the opposition, a Soviet delegation including Chairman Nikita Khrushchev, arrived to discuss a form of socialism acceptable to both the Poles and the Russians. Concessions were made, an agreement was reached and Poland felt victorious.

Sandor was transfixed by the students' demands. Although he was not too surprised that a demonstration had been planned, he was taken aback by the actual demands being made. In summary, Russian withdrawal and Hungarian independence. Sandor had noted the demands on his newspaper, above articles about Hungary's football team and the upcoming Olympics. On the train he'd studied them and had felt himself awaken from a political slumber – a slumber which he'd fallen into over three years ago after his arrest by the ÁVO. Although he'd been released innocent of any charges, the torture had had the desired effect for a time. For the most part, politics had become a personal topic existing within an inner world of thought and solitary debate. It was a subject to be avoided in most people's company and only discussed at home with his father.

When Eva arrived at the station Sandor greeted her with the customary kisses on both cheeks and they proceeded down Rákóczi Street. Sandor was glad that she wanted to attend the demonstration. She, along with their mother, had spent many days and nights watching him recover from being tortured and was blatantly aware of the excesses of the Russian regime. Like him, she wanted it removed. As for their fear of the ÁVO, they felt that by joining a demonstration, by being two individuals among many, they'd be safe.

The crown of Eva's head was two inches short of Sandor's shoulders. Walking down the street, her black hair hung halfway down her back. She was thin and in good shape. Her skin had a healthy colour, like olive. During the summer, when Eva spent as much time outside as possible, she darkened considerably, giving the impression that she was from further east: Romania or Turkey. As twins, they didn't share many physical characteristics.

Glancing at the buildings around him, Sandor saw a person waving a flag from a fifth-storey window. The national colours of green, white and red were visible due to the bright light inside the apartment and the glare from the street. Looking around, Sandor saw more people on their way to join the demonstration. Some started unfurling banners, slogans demanding Hungary's independence from Russia.

At Pushkin Street they veered left. Sandor saw a mass of people moving slowly, and though he couldn't hear anything – no chants, cries or whistles – he sensed power in their movement, in the same way he could sense the strength of the silent slide of the Danube when viewed from behind the closed windows of his apartment. From tributary-like laneways and side streets, other people joined the march. Sandor thought about the amount of people which he'd considered earlier and he figured that he'd underestimated as he couldn't see an end to the masses.

Although it was now dark, the city had enough light to illuminate the crowd. There was a dull uniformity of appearance, a greyscale ranging from Sandor's light-coloured coat to the black leather which warmed Eva. But like the coloured details on some of the dirty bricked buildings which they passed, a burst of yellow paint, the shine of polished gates or the reflection from tiles delicately placed around doorways, the marchers were also speckled with colour. Above the demonstrators' heads many flags flapped, the bright Polish blue, the vivid Hungarian green and the flag of international communism – brilliant red.

Although not yet a part of the main demonstration, the numbers around them had grown and were much greater than those standing in observance. Sandor saw unease in those watchful faces, submission in maternal arms which hung like giant, fleshy necklaces around the bodies of their children. Others seemed hypnotised by the crowd, their motivation for joining a desire to be a part of a gathering, and like small objects on a busy road, were sucked into the slipstream of the march.

Soon, as if a radio dial was being turned up, the sound of the main demonstration came within earshot. The first shouts of support which Sandor heard were not for Hungary, but for Poland. It was political cause and effect; thousands of Hungarian demonstrators cheering Poland's stance against Russia, the guttural choruses sounded like the way a machine might sing, cutting through octaves, not in search of melody, but efficiency.

Sandor was entertained by the cheering crowd though it felt strange to be surrounded by loud, bombastic voices, and for the first couple of minutes he was quiet, not so much fearful of his own voice as embarrassed by it, for it seemed peculiar to be shouting while walking down a street. After walking for forty minutes, their pace gradually slowed down on joining the main demonstration. Sandor held on to Eva as he feared being separated, losing her in the crowd. As he was taller than her and most of the people around them, she asked, "What can you see?"

"People," he replied. "Thousands of people." And not just walking down the street: in the surrounding buildings, faces peered out of apartment windows, waving flags, shouting support, joining the spirit of the march, energy combining the celebratory atmosphere of a festival with the solemnity of political proclamation.

Viewing the march from five or six storeys up, it looked like a seamless flow of people, but on the ground it pushed and shoved its way towards its destination: the Hungarian Radio Building where the students wanted to hear their demands broadcast. As they came closer to the building, the march intensified. At times, Sandor felt his grip loosen on Eva as she nearly slipped away from him and so he walked behind her and not by her side.

Soon, the awkwardness of the crowd became apparent, and those wishing to escape the molten flow of dissent clambered up statues, dangled from lamp-posts and balanced precariously on rubbish bins. Sandor wished that he'd taken his camera with him so that he could capture the crowd on film.

Sandor asked Eva if she wanted to take a break from the marching but she declined. They continued walking to the chant, "Russians Out! Russians Out!"

By now Sandor felt the power of the demonstration, he was awed by its noise and he wondered what would happen. Was it possible that things could change? Would the government listen?

They arrived at the Radio Building. It was a large structure, many storeys high and occupying a block. News spread that the students were being denied access to the airwaves. They were being encouraged to disperse. People continued shouting, "Russians Out! Russians Out!"

A section of the crowd parted allowing a car to pass from a side street to the Radio Building. A student was behind the wheel. Outside the building, he turned the car around and reversed it into the gates. Once, twice, three times, the car revved, smoke gushed from its exhaust as it sped backwards to the crowd's applause.

Sandor watched from one hundred feet away and relayed what he saw to Eva. He was thrilled at the sight of the car smashing down the gates, there was an anarchy to the violence being spurned on by the crowd, the abnormal sight of aggression being directed at an official building. Sandor hoped that the gates would crumble and the car would gain entry.

Then Sandor's attention was cut short by activity on the roof. For a few seconds he thought that the people he saw up there were somehow part of the architecture, and then their silhouettes came into view. Water cannons sprayed the frontline of the demonstrators, then projected far back on the crowd – to Sandor and Eva – and beyond. News spread that it was the ÁVO spraying water. They were defending the building. Sandor strained his eyes staring at the roof above which was a dark sky; unperturbed by the water cannon, the crowd continued chanting, "Russians Out! Russians Out!"

When Sandor heard the sound of gunshot a feeling of anxiety rushed through his chest like heartburn and breathing slowly, he felt the full thrust of fear. The sensation was distinct. It was as if cold bubbles of air had been released into his veins, and on entering the chambers of his heart, they burst, each explosion another spark of fear. Then he realised that the shots were blanks, a familiar sound from his days in compulsory military service and he felt relief. He looked around at thousands of people as their heads ducked. Although Eva pulled fearfully at her brother's arm he felt safe among the demonstrators as he believed that the chances of anything happening to them were next to none; and when the crowd started pushing and shoving as people tried to escape the protest, Sandor made sure that they weren't trampled on.

Sandor was looking at the building when a canister was hurled from the roof and exploded in the air. He pulled Eva to his chest and sheltered his face in her hair as tear gas fumed, rolling like fog across the crowd, and as it did, he heard people screaming as the gas attacked their faces. People pushed through the crowd to escape the tear gas, and in the darkness of his closed eyes, Sandor decided that they should move away from the Radio Building. Slowly, he opened his eyes: streetlights illuminated the tear gas which blew the other way, people tried to leave but were hemmed in by the crowd which continued chanting, "Russians Out! Russians Out!"

Sandor felt Eva's arms loosen around his body as another canister flew through the air. He hoped that the wind would carry the tear gas the other way, but the canister failed to explode in the air. Instead, it exploded on impact with the crowd. Again he pulled Eva closer to him and in doing so he smothered the words coming out of her mouth as he pushed his face into her dark hair. The tear gas stung his neck before the wind blew it away. People screamed and Sandor focused on the spot where the tear gas had exploded. A knot of people loosened, and as it did, a body collapsed on the ground. Sandor stared at the body. It was missing its head. A woman pushed by him, blood marking her face, gristle and bone staining her scarf. It was the first time he'd seen death in eleven years, not since the end of the war, and like those bodies back then, this one repulsed him. As there were too many people around them, Eva was too small to see the dead body, but she asked why people were screaming and he replied, "Someone's been hit."

Quickly, they moved through the crowd to get out of range of the tear gas. Sandor led the way. It was difficult not to stand on people's feet or accidentally push others over. Holding on to Eva with one hand, he used his other to stop the sudden crush of people pushing into them or to help those who had fallen and couldn't get up. When they were nearly out of the crowd more shots were fired. Sandor knew by their sound that they were no longer blanks. He dragged Eva to the ground and they crawled towards a side street. There, he inspected her, looking her body up and down for signs of blood. She was unhurt. Sandor felt the skin tighten on the back of his neck from the tear gas. Spitting on his hand, he rubbed it with saliva; the pain was corrosive like a severe nettle sting. He looked at his body and felt his groin but there was nothing seriously wrong with him either.

Eva was in shock and started hyperventilating. After comforting her, Sandor peered around the corner, back at the Radio Building, mesmerised by what was happening, the randomness of the violence. Being so close to it made it hard not to look, to stare at the people scattering about the street. Some ran towards the Radio Building picking up the wounded while others started to smash its doors down. An ambulance slowed down as it reached the Radio Building and the crowd moved to allow it access, but when the men appeared, instead of tending to the wounded, they unloaded machine guns and ammunition. Beneath their white coats you could see the green uniform of the ÁVO. The crowd surged and the ÁVO opened fire. More bodies fell and the ÁVO retreated inside the building.

Sandor wanted to see what would happen. There were far too many people and far too strong a feeling of resolve for everybody to turn around and go home. He felt excitement, fuelled by adrenaline. Again, he wished that he'd brought his camera with him to record what was happening, to be able to show people later on how the ÁVO had turned on the peaceful demonstration.

Sandor remained with Eva. Soon she started feeling better and her breathing calmed down. When the army arrived some soldiers started talking to the protestors. Then a person appeared on the balcony of the Radio Building and spoke through a megaphone. "Please disperse and return to your homes."

Close by a man fell after being shot in the leg. Sandor pulled him to safety. Eva – now feeling okay – tried to comfort him as Sandor looked for an ambulance, but as he did, the ÁVO opened fire again, this time in the direction of the army and killed some soldiers. Sandor looked at the bodies on the ground: some had died instantly, others were still alive. He became confused; why was the ÁVO shooting at the army? In response, some soldiers gave out weapons to the demonstrators and joined them in attacking the Radio Building.

Sandor looked around at the darkened street, the shine of water on cobblestones, people scuttling in every direction, shocked that soldiers had turned against the ÁVO. Each time a shot was fired from the Radio Building screams rose from the crowd and those with rifles returned fire.

What amazed Sandor was how quickly the demonstration had turned from peaceful to anarchic. He watched as students and armed demonstrators stormed the Radio Building. Soon word spread that certain floors were cleared of ÁVO men, some of whom had been taken hostage. And soon the building, apart from a few ÁVO left on the rooftop, was free.

Outside the building a man started speaking through a megaphone, explaining that the Director of Radio was willing to meet a delegation of protesters, perhaps their demands would be read on air. Students climbed on to the balcony to talk to the director. Minutes later a vehicle stopped outside the building, a truck carrying radio equipment. An official fixed up a microphone and announced that the students' demands would be broadcast without further delay. The crowd cheered. Slowly a woman's voice spoke into the microphone recounting the sixteen demands. The crowd listened to them being read out, the same demands which Sandor had written on the back of his newspaper that morning.

Then a man shouted from an apartment window across the street. "It's not being broadcast! It's rubbish! She's lying!"

People from other apartments confirmed this: on the radio gypsy music was playing and not the woman's voice from the truck. The vehicle was stormed, people grabbed the microphone and its crew quickly dispersed among the crowd.

Sandor stared at the crowd – thinning out in parts due to the fighting – in a state of awe. It was the beginning of the 1956 uprising, the first revolution in Hungary's history in over one hundred years, but seen through Sandor's eyes, it was a spontaneous mess. When ambulances arrived Sandor and Eva helped the medics carry the wounded and put blankets over the dead. Later on word spread that the students had cleared the remaining ÁVO from the Radio Building, but there was one problem; although they had control of the building, they lacked control of the airwaves because the authorities continued broadcasting from a duplicate transmitter elsewhere.

In another part of the city, at the top of Stalin Avenue, stood a statue of the dictator. At sixty feet high, it towered over the expanse of trees being denuded by the coming of winter. It was a bronze structure, resting on a pink plinth. Ropes were attached around the statue's neck and then secured to cars. Tires spun on the wet, cobblestoned streets but Stalin wouldn't give up his view of Pest. Loud cheers were heard with any hint of success. Hungarian flags, with the hammer and sickle now torn from their centres, flapped in the darkness. A man arrived with a blowtorch. He climbed on to the plinth and covered his face. The blue flow of sparks slowly melted the statue's knees. Metal ropes were secured around the neck, arms and waist. Again, they were hooked to cars. The man with the blowtorch jumped down from the plinth. The crowd, guessing where the statue might fall, stood back. Stalin was brought to the ground. A vibration through the streets, a scraping sound like chalk on a giant blackboard as the statue slid along the road. Stalin was dragged through Pest. All that was left on the pink plinth were his boots.

CHAPTER TWO

For most of Sandor and Eva's walk home the city looked as it always did at night: a metropolis whose citizens moved upwards from their ground floor offices and shops to the residential floors of their apartments above. Budapest was a city where people lived in its centre, and most streets, from the run-down to the salubrious, were full of homes. Balconies were packed with flowers and plants, clothes drying, bicycles and junk; while on windowsills sat ornaments, picture frames and decorative pots.

Sandor liked the city at night when darkness seemed to clean the buildings, making them appear fresher than they were. He had often walked around the city in late evening with his camera and tripod, setting up outside buildings or taking in cityscapes from the top of the Buda hills where there was a view of the river Danube and the Chain Bridge lit by thousands of light bulbs draped along its metal wires.

Now, eleven years after the war had ended, the authorities hadn't finished rebuilding the city, apartments were still demolished and one of the bridges across the Danube lay in ruins. Children were warned, but they still liked to play in holes awaiting foundations, amid bricks, dirt and construction machinery. People attempted repairs, wire mesh covered old brickwork trying to keep pillars, posts and statues in place, architectural detail added during more confident times. Sandor liked to think that cities aged well in contrast to humans, the years adding beauty and elegance, but Budapest was like a sick, old aunt being held in place, at times, against her wishes. But corners held a glimpse of what the city could have been, when it was trying to compete with European grandeur.

Budapest was inspired by empire. Not just the grand designs of Vienna, the Austrian Empire Hungary had been a part of, but of Paris and London too. During the latter half of the nineteenth century, city planners had looked to these places among others for inspiration: boulevards ploughed through the city centre; parks were planned with contemporary amenities; a metro was engineered beneath the streets; opera houses and museums were built. And in this turn-of-the-century climate, artistic and civic life had flourished, cafes were open twenty-four hours a day, and the former cities of Buda and Pest – now one and united by the Chain Bridge – looked forward to the twentieth century with confidence.

Then Europe turned into an ocean of death, with Budapest at its centre. And two wars later – from its Golden Age in the latter years of the Austro-Hungarian Empire before the First World War, to its nadir as a satellite state of the Soviet Union after the Second World War – Budapest had started fighting again that night in October 1956.

Sometimes walking, sometimes running, they moved through a city shaking off the signs of Soviet occupation. Russian emblems, such as the red star and the hammer and sickle, had been removed from official buildings leaving holes on their façades. Pictures of Lenin and Stalin had been ripped out of their frames – which less than twenty-four hours ago had hung peacefully above desks – and were now smouldering in street fires, the flaky, charred edges of official portraiture blowing like black snow in the chill, midnight wind. Scorched smiles of Soviet ideologues: Stalin's paternal smirk, Lenin's zealous eyes. And the destruction of all things Russian didn't stop at the symbols of authority; bookshops specialising in Russian literature were ransacked, their windows broken and doors smashed, stock bundled on the street and set ablaze: Chekhov alongside Lenin alongside Tolstoy.

Slowing down outside one shop, Sandor and Eva looked through its window. A tailor's dummy was dangling from a noose, a sign *ERNO* written at its feet. This was an effigy of Erno Gero, First Secretary of the Hungarian Communist Party, a post which had more power than any other in Hungary, including the prime minister. As they continued walking they talked about Gero. Already his tactics had failed. The police hadn't curtailed the demonstrators, the army had been sent in and some soldiers had deserted, even some ÁVO men had rid themselves of their uniform and had run, fearful for their lives. It had only been a week since the Polish protests, and their demonstration was not on the same scale, but still Krushchev had flown in, listened to their demands and reached a compromise.

Surely, this was the least that Hungary could expect?

∞

The uprising lasted thirteen days.

Sandor spent most of this time with his family in their apartment, an old building facing the Danube on the Buda side of the city. As the fighting spread across Budapest and then to other parts of Hungary, Sandor and his father Frank talked endlessly about what might or might not happen. Frank was a tall man with a mop of grey hair and a thin face, his neck covered with folds of skin like a loose sock on a small leg. He smoked a lot and you could hear it in his voice. It seemed as though his lungs weren't made of fleshy tissue but hollowed out of oak, each word sounding like polished wood. Frank and Sandor agreed on many things, especially about the politician Imre Nagy. During the demonstration, marchers had carried portraits of him. Nagy was in his late fifties, with a round head and round glasses, his double chin sat nicely on a chest which extended into a pot belly, and he looked as though he were in a permanent state of postprandiality. He was mentioned in the students' demands, number three:

A new Government must be constituted under the direction of Imre Nagy.

Frank supported Nagy as he represented the acceptable face of communism. Sandor liked Nagy too. Soon after Stalin's death he had become prime minister, and for a time the country had changed. Nagy was a liberal communist. He had released victims of purges from prison, allowed the return of deportees and brought in some land reforms; these went further than in most Soviet satellite states and because of this Nagy was replaced.

On the first night of the uprising, a meeting took place in the Communist Party Headquarters. Erno Gero appointed Nagy as prime minister. It was seen as an offering to the protestors, however, this gesture was short lived as Russian tanks appeared in Budapest and started suppressing the insurgents. So people started questioning Nagy's power. Did he have any? Was his appointment purely tokenistic?

For the first few days of the uprising Nagy had little power, but as the insurgents strengthened so did his position, and the street fighting became a battle for Hungarian autonomy, but under his direction. When the Russians realised the power of his position, talks started. Both sides called for an end to the uprising. Nagy, a forty-year member of the Communist Party, sought a form of political independence from Russia, a balance between the aspirations of the Hungarian people and the *realpolitik* of Russian influence in Central Europe during the Cold War.

∽

Of all the outcomes which Sandor and his father discussed, the variations of political policy and levels of Hungarian economic and military freedom, they never spoke about how the failure of the uprising might affect their family. Nor was it discussed with Sandor's mother, Katie. For most of the uprising she was happy to have her family safe at home, as she felt that Sandor and Eva had had a lucky escape during the demonstration. Katie was tall and hadn't gained much weight since her youth; she was a thin woman of fifty-five with green eyes and black hair. She had been frightened by her children's proximity to death while they had been at the demonstration. Hearing that the ÁVO had opened fire on the crowd proved to her the pointlessness of protesting against any government as in her mind all political action was to be avoided. The uprising reminded her of the war, it was to be survived at home with her family, shy of danger, regardless of how claustrophobic the apartment might become or how safe Budapest might appear at any given time. All of the family had jobs which nobody attended, while Eva's daughter – eleven year old Kristina whose father had died during the war – was taken out of school before it shut down because of the fighting.

∽

After a week of fighting, there was the unprecedented sight of Russian tanks withdrawing from Budapest. Moscow issued a declaration; it spoke of the problems which had been encountered in the course of establishing revolutionary changes in Soviet countries since the end of the Second World War. There had been difficulties and downright mistakes, and due to these mistakes, the principle of equal rights among socialist states had been demeaned. The declaration spoke of the Twentieth Congress of the Communist Party of the Soviet Union which had taken place earlier that year, where these errors of the past had been discussed, and most extraordinarily, Stalin had been condemned by Khrushchev. From now on the Soviet Union had resolved to base itself on the strict principle of equal rights for the people. As Moscow declared that it deeply regretted the recent events which had led to bloodshed and that it was prepared to re-examine its relationship with Hungary – and not to interfere with her national sovereignty – Budapest felt victorious.

But this victory was short, lasting a mere one hundred and fifty hours. A duplicitous Moscow used this time to regroup its force on Hungary's borders, and on the 4 November 1956 the Russian Army launched a massive attack on Budapest. It was all over. Nagy sought political asylum in the Yugoslav embassy; the military leaders of the uprising were arrested. Although some insurgents kept fighting, thousands of people started fleeing the country in order to escape the immediate consequences of the Russian assault and a life of continued Soviet occupation.

∽

And it was a life of continued Soviet occupation which concerned Sandor and Eva. They were both twenty-nine, well educated (a mechanical engineer and a teacher) and they wanted to live in a country which gave them hope for a better life. Sandor foresaw Moscow taking revenge on

Hungary's citizenry, the ÁVO would be given free reign to do as they pleased, and people like him – former 'agitators' – would, no doubt, be singled out. Such was the size of the nationwide uprising, and the might of the Russian Army when re-entering Budapest with its six thousand tanks and one hundred and eighty thousand soldiers, that Sandor believed that it would be years before the political climate would return to one of optimism.

And therefore, he concluded, it was time to leave.

Eva agreed with her brother. She wanted a better life for herself and her daughter. Since Stalin's death Hungary had shifted towards change but now the country was being made an example of, a lesson to other bloc states to toe the Russian line. So the day after Russia attacked Budapest, Sandor and Eva decided to leave, to join the thousands of people already fleeing to unknown countries.

∞

Items were hastily packed in a leather bag; Eva informed her daughter Kristina that they were leaving the apartment; and their parents were told of their plans.

Katie sat crying in a chair by the living room window. Outside shellfire was a dull, muted sound, occasionally getting louder, closer to the apartment. Eva was beside her, also crying. Telling his mother made Sandor feel guilty like when he was younger and tantrums and boyish badness sent her loving face into despair. Katie couldn't understand why they had to go so soon, she questioned whether they understood the consequences of their actions, the finality of leaving your country, the difficulty of establishing yourself elsewhere. "How can you be so sure of Hungary's future? Or that you'll be happy in another country?"

She shouted at Eva, wondering if she had considered the implications of removing Kristina from school at the age of eleven to continue her education in another country and in another language, "Kristina only speaks Hungarian and a little Russian from school."

Eva believed that it would be difficult for a while, but ultimately they would settle elsewhere and that the interruption to her schooling would end.

Katie was dismissive. "It's hard enough bringing up a child in your own country let alone elsewhere and away from your family. And what if Sandor and you separate for whatever reason? What if something happens to him when crossing the border? You'll be left with a child on your own and in a foreign country. Have you thought about that?"

No, Eva hadn't thought about that, nor was she about to. Instead, she said that their minds were made up and that nothing could persuade them to stay.

After wiping her eyes Katie turned them on Sandor and he felt their stare like a firm hand on his shoulder. He defended their decision to leave and said that they would stay together. "This is what we want. It's our choice. And Eva feels that it's the best option for her daughter."

"For her daughter," Katie replied dismissively.

"We all have our reasons," Sandor replied. And he started talking about his experience with the ÁVO three years ago. "Is that going to happen to me again? What are the chances? Fifty to one? Ten to one? Never?" Sandor paused but sensing that an answer was not forthcoming, continued, "This is the problem I have with Hungary. I just don't know what's around the corner. And that's the reason why we're leaving."

Katie couldn't but agree with her son's experience but she pleaded with him to listen to her, to think of their family and how it would affect their lives. "You don't raise children so they can flee their country and never see them again. I can understand why you're worried, but I think that the two of you are panicking. You should calm down. Take time to reflect. It's best not to make any decision, especially one so important when you're in such a state."

But Sandor disagreed. "We have to go quickly or not at all. The Russians will close off all exits from the city, guard the train stations, the roads and the border with Austria." It was therefore important to leave as soon as possible, the longer they left it, the less chance they'd have of escaping and the more dangerous it would become.

Frank questioned the finer details of their plans: how were they getting to the border, how would they cross it, and once in Austria, what were they planning to do?

Sandor's answers, though instinctive and intuitive, were nonetheless vague and unsatisfactory for his father. Sandor wished that the many people leaving Budapest now would support their decision and thus prove their point.

But Frank was as miserable as Katie though his face lacked her surprise and his eyes were not yet scratched by this sudden sadness. Though recognising their decision as final and complete, he was overwhelmed by the urge to counter this cruelty, to salvage his family from events not of their making, the unearthly echo of politics and the furious sound of state. For his children to be carried out of their country in the wake of a failed uprising thus leaving himself and his wife without parental responsibility and the continued immersion in their children's lives was as bad as losing them through an unfortunate illness; but at least that could have been explained through medicine; it could have been understood with a solitary appeal to science; but political episode offered few words of comfort to parents whose children were being taken away by forces man-made and therefore – surely? – avoidable.

Sandor, sticking to their plan of immediate departure, became a man of hurried actions, of instant organisation, and seemingly calm and controlled, he encouraged confidence in Eva. Yet he felt as though he was committing a violent crime against his mother, he felt guilt laden and cruel, as if he'd pillaged his parents for what they were worth and was now moving on.

He remembered Katie's care in the weeks after his torture, an event which had been put behind them though one which had sapped his mother's spirit. She had only recovered from his experience recently and had started to believe in the safety of her family. Sandor was aware of her joyous moods of late, she was no longer filled with subtle pessimism. But now the uprising had changed all that. And she helplessly watched as her children and only grandchild left their home, and to leave on such bad terms, to argue and cry her way through the last hour of their company.

In a final act of protest at her children's decision Katie went to her bedroom denying entrance to all for a few minutes. Upset and confused, Kristina waited with everyone else outside the door. Aged eleven, she was tall, an inch or two shorter than her mother, and like Eva, she too had dark hair and a subtle glow to her skin. She wore a black woollen hat, a scarf and was ready to leave. Her narrow face and dark brown eyes assessed her grandmother's display of emotion, the likes of which she'd never witnessed before, in a state of silent panic.

They waited outside her room. They wondered what to do.

Soon Katie emerged and hugged her twins and Kristina. She didn't say much, just a few words which Sandor couldn't understand due to the low sound of her sobbing. Sandor wished that they weren't leaving in such circumstances. Katie agreed and added that they could change their minds, but she said this, not with the force of argument, but with defeat.

Then she cursed the people who had started the

uprising, revolutionaries, she claimed, who had tampered with the status quo, those whose ambitions were forcing her family apart, pushing her children into exile. "So this is what happens when an uprising fails. You lose your children, your life is turned upside down. And for what?" Katie reflected mournfully. "What if the uprising was successful? Do you think that Hungary would be a better place, that life would suddenly become fantastic? These politicians think that they're the cure for cancer, but do they invent anything new? Does it matter what kind of a country you live in as long as you can eat, work and be around your family? You have that here. What more do you want? What more *is* there?"

Sandor felt a light dusting of shame. Perhaps his vision of life was unrealistic, too selfish, too burdened with youthful ambition and ignorant of the sufferings of previous generations, people who had lived through wars, people who had nearly starved to death, and people who hadn't the pleasure of creating futures and orchestrating lives like they were machines guaranteed to work satisfactorily. Perhaps it was a luxury to have expectations, an indulgence for the few, the decadent whim of a minority.

Sandor hugged his mother knowing that he couldn't answer her, whatever he wanted from life could hardly compensate, in her eyes, for the loss he was inflicting on her, the brute force of their departure, the wicked thrust of separation, a sadness deep and unforgiving.

As they were leaving, Frank asked, "How will we know if you have crossed the border safely? Or that you have settled down in another country?" On the mantelpiece was a photograph of two butterflies perched on a lavender plant. It was taken two years ago, on an overcast day in summer. Sandor never titled his photographs, but Kristina had called it *The Butterflies of Budapest*. Sandor told his father that when they arrive in their country of exile he will contact them, but as the Hungarian authorities might intercept their message, he would use a codename.

Sandor, thinking of the picture, said, "When you hear from us, we'll be The Butterflies of Budapest."

∽

Once at the station, they boarded a train for Györ, a city in the northwest of Hungary. The train was packed, people were sitting on the floor and standing in the aisles. Sandor, Eva and Kristina shared two seats between them. In the claustrophobic carriage you could hear loud conversations between husbands and wives, brothers and sisters, mothers and daughters, fathers and sons. Screaming babies were held in maternal arms. A newborn child no more than four weeks old went from silent to scream in one or two seconds; an explosion of sound, its face dangerously red as if all the blood in its tiny body was throbbing through its head. They were outside Budapest in minutes. Barns were stocked with hay and skeletal trees were sky-high; from the train their naked branches looked like roots and the world was upside down. As they passed through small villages, the train slowed down, its brakes noisily applied, a sound like animals being castrated.

Few words were spoken between Sandor and Eva on the train, Kristina's questions were answered succinctly and without indulgence. As the journey came to an end Eva woke Kristina who had fallen asleep on her lap, while Sandor's mood buoyed slightly as they neared the border, his mind becoming focused on crossing it, surging towards Austria, departing Hungary. Once in Györ, they caught a bus to Ágfalva, a small village four miles from the Austrian border. Here, Austria knifed into Hungary at a sharp angle, like two lines of a triangle, and there was the danger that you could cross from Hungary into Austria and back into Hungary again, unknowingly. At this point, the Einser Canal was the main geographical barrier between the two countries and for a stretch it was the border. Andau, Wallern and Tadten were the first villages inside Austria, while Vienna was two hours northwest by car.

People were cautious about spending time in Ágfalva or other villages nearby as few had good reason for being so close to the border. Single men and women blended in a little better than families with children who should have been in school. As people started fleeing Hungary, local farmers who knew the land around the border made money by leading people across it, while in Austria you could place an order to have people fetched in their homes in Budapest and smuggled back to Vienna. Austrian students, acting as scouts and charging nothing, were making dangerous nightly runs into Hungary to bring people back across the Einser Canal. As the Russians resumed their control of Hungary, it was feared that they would start arresting would-be escapees and send them to prison. So people scattered anywhere they could, hiding in car boots, beneath the tarpaulin of vans, in ditches and barns, awaiting their night-time dash across the border.

Rather than risk crossing the border alone Sandor wanted to hire a guide and when they arrived in Ágfalva a woman approached him after an exchange of conspiratorial glances. She was middle aged and he felt uneasy soliciting something illegal from a woman on the street. To Sandor's eye she looked like a farmer's wife: a wrinkled face from too much sun, her skin leathery brown like worn shoes and deeply grooved like tree bark. Her name was Martha. They agreed that she'd be their guide and she led them to a flat field surrounded by leafless trees, in sight of reedy marshland and ploughed earth. They were wind sheltered by hay stacks, beside a leaky trough. Sandor asked about their chances of getting caught crossing the border. She said that nothing was without risk, and that there were a few theories about crossing it. Some said you needed a guide while others thought you could do it on your own. She spoke of differing accounts of success, its many forms: single men who walked up to the border guards requesting permission to cross, and just like that, the guards allowed it. Or those who approached the guards with their hands full of cash saying, "I don't need this any more," and the guards took it and let them cross. "But that's a risk you take. It might work, then again it might not. But I know the land and the best place to get across," she advised.

Martha explained that she would return later with a few others wishing to escape and then they'd all go to the border just before midnight. She said that it would be wise to rest for the day and eat any food they might have brought. The afternoon passed with a fall of snow which melted when a mild wind swept in from the south-east. From time to time when others passed, Sandor wondered if they were farm labourers working the land or people like him, awaiting their midnight run.

Sandor urged Eva and Kristina to stay still by the hay stacks, blend in if they could, make their bodies appear shadow-like, ghostly, vanished. At sundown Eva wrapped herself and Kristina in her coat, and in a small metal container, Sandor burnt some sticks every now and then, just enough to keep a warm heat glowing in the tin but without a visible flame.

Alone, Martha arrived a few hours before midnight and told them that another couple and a young child would be accompanying them across the border. She requested payment. Sandor took money from his leather wallet and as he counted it his fingers smoothed creases from the cash.

Martha's torch shone on the last transaction he made in his native currency.

Flares were fired once or twice by border guards. Sandor looked around, the light giving him a sense of where the border was among the marshy land. The mushroom of orange colour was followed by gunshot and barking dogs. Sandor knew from his military service that some parts of the border had been heavily mined in the past and other stretches had had their mines removed, but where exactly this activity had taken place he wasn't sure.

As promised Martha returned before midnight with another couple and their child. From her pocket she produced sedatives which a doctor had given her in order to subdue young children before they crossed the border to keep them quiet, as you didn't want a shrill infant's cry to alert the watchtower lights and bring flares to the sky. Martha advised the couple to give their child a tablet and if they were worried that it might last too long, on the Austrian side of the border, doctors were waiting to ensure that sedated children were bounced back to life. The couple declined.

They set off. Sandor felt the freezing soil congeal beneath his feet as they followed Martha. When faced with an open field she turned to them, and in a whisper warned of how they'd have to run quickly across it. Sandor, concerned for Kristina, held her hand as they dashed behind Martha over cold-sharpened land, beneath starlight and with the unnerving feeling of illegality with each step. Sandor felt like a criminal though his crime was unclear. As they ran, their only bag, slung over Sandor's shoulder, squeaked with the sound of ageing leather. A feeling of love and protection for Eva and Kristina rose in Sandor's heart as they arrived at a copse of trees. Martha smiled, acknowledging this success. They huddled for a few minutes, their breath, the warmth of their bodies, rising like a fire without flame, and then they started moving ever closer to the border.

After ten minutes Martha came to a halt by a large bush. She spoke of their proximity to the border. She pointed to three lights in the distance and explained that they were houses in a small Austrian village. "All you do is run in a straight line towards them and then you're in Austria."

It was close to midnight. It was as far as she would take them. She advised them to break up, split in two groups and run towards the lights in two minute intervals. The waterway they'd meet was the Einser Canal, Austria was on the other side, an old bridge would lead them across. The young couple requested that they go first, and without protest from Sandor or Eva, they ran to the border.

Martha departed. Sandor, Eva and Kristina were alone. Sandor counted down the time and when the two minutes had elapsed they started running.

Sandor held on to Kristina's hand and as they ran, he tried to keep one eye on the uneven ground and the other on the lights. Sandor was aware of their breathing, it sounded loud and calamitous, like a pack of animals, and he hoped that it wouldn't draw attention to them. And the sound of their feet too; they trampled on the hard ground like farm machinery. Martha had explained that they were running between two watchtowers but he couldn't see either of them nor could he see any searchlights or hear army vehicles or sirens. The land seemed like an open field anywhere on earth, free of political division and innocent of danger. To ward off anxiety and fear, Sandor concentrated on the swift movement of his legs, the position of his feet, the feel of Kristina's hand, Eva to his right, the bag on his shoulder and the darkness which they cut through in seconds, no more than a minute.

They reached the canal. They crossed the bridge and arrived in Austria. As they did other people came forth from Hungary, running into Austria and dropping their bags to rest on the frozen ground. At different points along the border flares shot upwards and you could hear the sound of guns. Within minutes the Austrian lights which they had been following became clear, one of them turned out to be a clock embedded in a steeple. A perfect sphere, the narrow clock hands hanging in black were like the thin lines you can see on the moon. It read 12.09 a.m.

With the confidence that a gambler has after winning, a feeling of being able of predict the future and the invincibility of that very moment, Sandor rested on the wall beneath the clock tower. Kristina said that she felt hot. She removed her black hat and wiped her sweaty forehead. She smiled at her mother. Eva looked back towards the border, but she couldn't see anything. Relief appeared on their faces and they started to relax. Immediate danger had gone. Austria was safe. Sandor lit a cigarette and his lungs absorbed the smoke with pleasure. He felt that something, a force or energy, had passed through them while running across the border. There was a feral aggression to borders, the essence of division and boundary.

Eva passed a bottle of water around and as she did, a middle-aged couple approached them, their attempt at Hungarian was poor, so Sandor spoke in his school German. They lived close by and offered them accommodation for the night. The man introduced himself as Mr Trost. They walked through the small village, where chimneys pushed smoke into the cold air and a few cars were parked by the roadside. The man told Sandor that they had watched many refugees cross the border and the least that they could do was let some of them stay in their house for a night. Most people in the village were trying to accommodate refugees, but as there were so many of them, they continued walking towards Eisenstadt where a camp had been established. Some of the refugees which Mr Trost had seen were in a bad state, physically ill and anxious. Some were nervous wrecks. But most were young and healthy. There seemed to be very few older men and women.

Mr Trost's house was warm and comfortable. His wife served hot soup and buttered bread. A fire was lit in their small living room. Blankets were spread out on the floor and they fell asleep quickly once their stomachs were full and their bodies warmed. The following day Mr Trost drove them for forty-five minutes to the refugee camp in Eisenstadt. When thanking Mr Trost, Sandor's heart weakened at his compassion; it was as if he had received a valuable gift and he pledged to pass it on.

CHAPTER THREE

Sandor and Eva decided to seek political asylum in Ireland after spending two weeks in the refugee camp in Eisenstadt, one of the principal camps which had been created in Austria since the end of the uprising. Thousands of Hungarians arrived into Austria everyday and Sandor watched with dismay as he realised the difficulty that the authorities – the Austrian Government and the International Red Cross – were having in processing and caring for so many people. Although the day-to-day conditions in the camp were more than adequate – Sandor, Eva and Kristina stayed in warm accommodation and had plenty to eat – they were aware of the difficulty which they now faced trying to leave Austria. The countries which most people wanted to go to were the United States of America and Canada, and this desire manifested itself in long, haggard queues of people outside the respective offices established in the camp.

When they arrived in the camp, Sandor and Eva didn't know what country to apply to and so one day while walking around the camp Sandor heard a loudspeaker announcing *Ireland, Ireland* and on following it he arrived at the Irish Red Cross office. Seated beside an Irish official was a translator who informed Sandor that Ireland was taking in one thousand refugees and that they would be departing in days. As the translator explained this to him, the Irish official, a man with thick-rimmed black glasses, occasionally nodded his head, though Sandor was aware that he didn't understand their conversation. Sandor and Eva wanted to leave the camp as soon as possible, it seemed to them that the longer they stayed, the less likely they'd get out as more people kept arriving each day. People were fearfully speculating about spending months in the camp, precious time when children would be missing school and destinies delayed because of the size of the Hungarian exodus into Austria: a country which had once cloaked Hungary in empire and now kept its border open to accommodate its former subjects.

North America was the most obvious destination, especially the USA, a country which Sandor had thought would come to their defence when the Russian tanks had rolled into Budapest quashing the uprising. But America didn't want to challenge Russia in Eastern Europe and risk world war, and besides, Russia's invasion of Hungary was offset by England, France and Israel attacking Egypt over the Suez Canal. Sandor read the newspapers in Austria, he understood the situation. Hungary's loss was just the balance of European power, the equilibrium of empire.

When Sandor had suggested that they go to Ireland, Eva was surprised as she knew nothing about the country, the only reference which she had ever heard was in school when a teacher had called it the Emerald Isle. Over the years Sandor hadn't heard anything about Ireland either, no radio reports or mentions in newspapers and books. On the map which hung outside the Irish Red Cross office in the camp, the small island looked like a child next to England, while both countries seemed insignificant compared to the sprawling continent of Europe. Sandor had never been on an island or seen the ocean and he liked the idea of giving up landlocked Hungary for such a place. And while he doubted the country as he knew nothing about it, these doubts were dealt with in the following way: the world wasn't North America, France, England or Australia, there were plenty of countries which offered their citizens a comfortable, safe living which rarely appeared in newspapers and as for the countries which did command the world's press, they were generally places that did so for all the wrong reasons, like Hungary at this very moment, a place illuminated by disaster.

Eva's main concern was for Kristina. She had spent two weeks in the shell-shocked city of Budapest only to flee their apartment, exchanging the known and familiar for the rough terrain of the border and the humble conditions of the refugee camp. Eva wanted her daughter to return to a routine as soon as possible; it was November, regardless of where they went, it would still take a couple of weeks or months before they settled down in another country and Kristina found a place in school. Nobody knew how many people would be given asylum in North America or how long it would take to process each refugee; and so Sandor reasoned that being among one thousand refugees bound for Ireland was better than being among ten, twenty, even fifty thousand going to the USA or Canada.

Sandor never questioned why Ireland had decided to admit refugees. Instead, through an interpreter, he asked the Irish Red Cross representative about the opportunities which the country offered and he learned about the budget which the organisation had for the refugees, money which had been raised by the people of Ireland, to help them settle in the country. The Irish Government had also committed itself to helping the refugees during a recent speech to the

United Nations, an organisation which Ireland had joined recently. Although people of all religions were welcome to apply for asylum, the Irish Red Cross was giving preference to professional, Catholic families. As Eva was irreligious and Sandor was a non-believer, though their background was Presbyterian, they applied as Roman Catholics to help their position and explained truthfully that Kristina had spent her eleven years as a child of Soviet atheism.

Being granted asylum by Ireland put an end to the desperation which Sandor had felt since leaving Hungary. Once they had crossed the Austrian border they had not only left behind their parents, jobs, friends and the familiarity of home life but also the citizenship of their country. They had become refugees. When given asylum in Ireland, they were not asked for identification or documents to support who or what they claimed to be, instead they were granted asylum as three people out of the thousands of Hungarians whose presence in Camp Eisenstadt proved to the authorities that they were fleeing Russian persecution. They were not individual asylum seekers forced to make their case, but part of a group whose nationality at that point in time was perceived as persecuted and therefore granted asylum. Sandor, though thankful that they had left Hungary safely and were now leaving Austria, didn't like being a refugee; during his twenty-nine years he had never considered that he'd ever be anything other than a citizen of Hungary. And though he had willingly shed his citizenship by crossing the border, he wanted to assimilate into another culture and become a *citizen* as soon as possible. And so one morning, the sky was a whitened mass of falling snow, a thermometer read minus six degrees celsius, Sandor's breath was everlasting in the still wintry air, they left Austria for Ireland.

On the way to the airport Sandor listened to a couple who had thought they were travelling to Ireland by taking a bus through France, sailing across the English Channel, and flying out of London but now they were relieved to be flying all the way. And another couple spoke about Christmas, it was only a few weeks away, and they never thought that they'd be spending it in Ireland.

Hours later an Aer Lingus Viscount hovered above Shannon Airport, its tail lights flashing against the curve of sable sky like the little dots on a bowl shaped radar. As the plane climbed and turned to face the runway, the engine whine woke Sandor. They had taken off from the flattened earth of Vienna, touched down near the sprawl of London, and as they sped across the purple whip of moon-dyed sea, he went in and out of sleep, the cabin pressure playing with his ears, people passing awkwardly in the aisle, grabbing his seat.

Bounce, screech, the plane touched down. Kristina sat upright as her ears popped. Childish surprise on her face, a countenance Eva recognised as shedding the plumpness of childhood for the geometric lines and length of an adult face, emerging cheekbones stretching the tender puff of puppy skin from around her eyes and above her mouth. Looking out the mist soaked window, her jaw elongated a face which appeared older than eleven years. A draft came from the open cabin doors. It had been bright when they left Vienna, it was dark in Shannon. Sandor had felt ill on the plane: diarrhoea had swollen his stomach, noises ploughed through his abdomen, bubbling up to his mouth, escaping into a fist-concealed belch. He forced a smile but his skin moved slowly like setting concrete, beneath the dim cast of cabin light his complexion looked mottled like the surface of marble. He felt dehydrated as the plane came to a halt near the terminal, outside of which a crowd was gathered, wind lifted coat-tails, fanned scarves, hats were held in gloved hands. First he thought that this crowd was waiting to board the plane, but then he noticed an absence of baggage and people started waving. Sandor noticed an Irish flag: darkness had de-saturated the colours, an awning sheltered it from the wind. Limply, it wrapped around its pole like a tied curtain. Other planes were parked by the runway; rain gave the surface a polished sheen like oil on water.

They entered the airport. Inside, there was a triumphant atmosphere: a couple of hundred people clapped, photographers bent awkwardly, flashes fireworked. Sandor looked around the room and recognised the Red Cross insignia on many people. He was surprised by the reception. In the public dining hall, they were ushered into seats. Menus were written in English and Hungarian. An elderly woman with arms ballooning like zeppelins offered roast potatoes from a metal tray. Sandor nibbled on the golden crust of one in the belief that it could pass undetected through his stomach, like a spy, culinary espionage, and thus avoid sickness. But he felt his stomach turn, its contents rolling like tattered food on a spit. The room temperature soared but his body divined coldness; the slightest draft taunting his skin which itched around his armpits, groin, feet and wrists. Sandor looked forward to leaving the airport and getting into bed.

A man clapped his hands. A woman tapped a spoon against a glass. Like an orchestra tuning up, the room was a discordant mesh of sound. Laughter, conversation, the scrape of metal chair on tiled floor, the scratch of cutlery on crockery. A couple of hundred people stopped their movement of mouth and body and looked at the Lord Mayor of Limerick.

He spoke through a translator, welcoming everybody. There was a round of applause, he smiled. The mayor's speech was translated. "Our sympathy is tinged with profound admiration for the courageous battle for freedom which your people have made against appalling odds. All of my countrymen join with me in hoping that the time will not be too distant when peace and freedom from oppression and all the human rights which we in this country value so highly, will be granted to Hungary. We are glad to support our fellow Christians against the acts of Red Terror we have witnessed over the last couple of weeks. We hope that your stay in Ireland will alleviate the memories of those sufferings and bring comfort and friendship."

The translator introduced the next speaker as being Mr McManus from the Irish Red Cross. A thin man with black glasses and a bushy beard stood up. He was in his late fifties and Sandor recognised him from the Irish Red Cross office in Austria. A cloud of smoke was hurried upwards by a wave of his hand. His words were translated, "Firstly, in agreement with the mayor, we also admire Hungary's great fight for the preservation of Christian ideals and Catholicism. And in doing so I would like to mention the support that we have received throughout Ireland. Many events have been organised to raise money and churches have been donating their collections. There are so many to thank and I'd like to mention some of them: the Golden Vale Creamery Society have donated one thousand pounds worth of cheese. Irish Fruit Juices in Kerry have donated sixty gallons of apple juice and the Chemists' Association of Cork City have given ten million units of penicillin.

"In Dublin, ten thousand pounds was collected over the course of two days. And we have received one thousand pounds from Clonmel. Longford too; they have given four hundred pounds. UCD Dramatic Society put on a show as well for the fund, and so did the Irish Ballet Company. Cadbury has allocated one hundred pounds worth of chocolate to the fund.

"And it's not just the money I'd like to mention. The Marine, Port and General Workers' Union have banned

Russian ships and cargoes in Ireland. Muintir na Tíre has asked the government to support the UN proposals for peace and freedom in Hungary, while Bray Urban Council have observed a minute's silence as a mark of respect. At the commencement of the RGDATA convention in Dublin, members stood in prayer for the Hungarian people.

"A resolution protesting against the savage butchery in Hungary of innocent men, women and children by the Russian Army was unanimously passed at the annual meeting of the Irish Municipal Employees' Trade Union, and it was agreed to impose a levy on each member for the Hungarian Relief Fund.

"And finally, Galway County Council has condemned the Soviet attack and expressed sympathy with the Hungarian people."

A Hungarian soldier was called by the translator, a former captain in the Hungarian Army. He was dressed in military uniform, his right arm ending in a stump of seared flesh, his hand having been lost during the fighting. The soldier said that Ireland had fought for the freedom which she now enjoyed. Europe, he said, had never seen anything like the brutality which the Russians had shown Hungary. After thanking Ireland for her hospitality, his face widened to a smile.

Outside Shannon Airport a man approached Sandor, Eva and Kristina. He pointed to a car, offering them a lift to the camp which they accepted. As they walked to the car, a press photographer took their picture. While driving the man smoked, ash fell on the gear stick and his trousers. The dashboard light showed his clean-cut nails, half moons of calcium white. Rolling down his window, air circulated among the odour of warm bodies and stripped condensation from windows which, when the moon shone, held the colour of unpolished silver. Soon the car stopped outside a house. Sandor saw smoke rising out of a chimney on the darkened roof, while the window light was strong enough to brighten the whitewashed walls. The man opened a small gate and rushed through the garden; narrow trees with trimmed branches surrounded the house like giant feathers. Seconds later he carried a basket back to the car, a cloth covered its contents. The man handed Kristina a bottle of Lucozade, she smiled and then uttered her only English words, "Thank you."

They drove across a dark canvas pinpricked with light from the occasional house. In the distance Limerick blistered the earth four miles away, rising out of the city lights were church steeples which looked like smouldering trees still standing after a forest fire. They were surrounded by dark fields. They turned up a small road. You could feel the surface change to gravel. Sandor thought about the plane, it was the first time he'd been on one, and he was amazed by the distance it had covered, the bold efficiency of transport, being shot through the limitless expanse of sky.

The car lights shone on the heavens, rain fell at a slant. The car slowed down and a soldier stepped out of a small cabin. The man driving the car turned to his passengers, "Here you are now. Knockalisheen Military Camp."

After queuing for a few minutes, the Lovases stood in front of the army quartermaster who ensured that each person had the following supplies: five blankets, one mattress, one pillow, two pillow cases, four sheets and one chair. In a red ledger this information was compiled along with their names (Sandor, Eva, Kristina Lovas); their sex (M,F,F); their religion (Roman Catholic); and their hut number (thirty-three west).

And later: a fully clothed Sandor lay down on his bed after lighting the potbellied stove in the centre of their room. A broom had been left in the hut and Eva swept the floor, though the shadowy electric light revealed clean wooden panels. Eva spoke about getting bleach to scrub the place down, replace the smell of musty damp with the clear sound of hygiene. When the fire started burning, smoke filled the room until Eva shut the stove door. Sandor told her to open the windows but she didn't want to as they looked old and breakable. Outside it was dark. Limerick was in the distance. It was a misty, damp night. Smoke was carried upwards by a thin metal chimney leaving the room evenly heated behind. Eva called it a room, but Sandor knew it as a hut. An army-style Nissen hut, like one he had stayed in during military service.

And later: rolling over in his sleep, Sandor's eyes opened to the sight of the stove. There was a tiny gap in the metal, it was like looking into the heart of a steam train. As a child, Sandor had heard stories of train drivers cooking their breakfast, cracking eggs on to dirty coal shovels, frying them as they sped through the countryside. As if the heat could warm you by looking at it, Sandor stared at the fire, the comfort of the ever changing flames burning behind the metal gate. When smoke escaped into the room, the potbellied stove looked like a fat dwarf smoking a cigarette. Hanging on the backs of chairs, their damp clothes were drying, and their shoes were like petals circling the bulbous stove.

And, later: Sandor checked his watch, it was 4.41 a.m. The fire had gone out. When the wind whipped against the hut you could feel the cold air though Sandor was feeling hot. Sweat glued his trousers to his legs, there were damp patches around his armpits, his lower spine was shining with perspiration. Standing up in the room, suddenly he felt cold and he reached for his coat like he would have grabbed his dressing gown back home. He placed his hands in its pockets.

Sandor felt sick, empty and light-headed. The hut didn't have a toilet. It was a short walk away, by the men's showers.

He shut their door quietly. The number thirty three was painted on the large wooden planks. Puffs of smoke were exhaled from other chimneys in small bursts like a child's breath in winter. He counted down the huts while walking to the toilet: thirty three, thirty two, thirty one, thirty, twenty nine. Most of them were empty, they had been on the first plane to arrive, fewer than two hundred refugees, though more were on their way. The air was so damp Sandor felt as though he was wading through water. The wind beneath the toilet door cleared the air of his foetid smell. Gently, like his anus was an open wound, he swabbed it with the coarse toilet paper. Back in the hut Sandor replenished the stove and sat by the fire and after warming up, he returned to bed.

∽

Ireland revealed itself to Sandor in bright shades of morning sunlight, a light frost on the dirty hut windows. Knockalisheen Camp was perched upon a small hill, viewing the world from a slight elevation. Behind it, further north into County Clare, green and rust coloured fields scaled a hill tumbling towards the sky. Upon these hills, like dirty white flags, low lying clouds were caught in the branches of winter trees. To the south houses were spread out before Limerick City adding smog to the sky.

Sandor walked towards the entrance of the camp and looked at the road which they had travelled on last night, there were fields on either side as it meandered towards Limerick. The entrance to the camp was positioned a few hundred feet off this road, up a gravel pathway leading to soldiers standing sentry, and a red barrier with a *STOP* sign. Next to the barrier there was a new building, the commander's office: it was white and flat roofed, inside the ceilings were tall, the floors tiled or carpeted, the rooms were spacious with open fireplaces, and a room upstairs had a balcony which viewed the downward sloping fields towards the city. This was the commander's office and the only dwelling made of brick in the camp. Behind it the Nissen huts were in three rows off the main camp road. This was where the refugees slept, ate and washed, alongside the seventy soldiers recently garrisoned. In the nearby fields there were few cattle, though you could see barns and farmhouses. Subject to quarantine, the refugees were forbidden to leave for one month. A barbed wire fence surrounded the camp.

Sandor's immediate concern was the English language. Apart from a smattering of German, Sandor knew only Hungarian. As soon as the quarantine restrictions ended, he could seek employment anywhere in the country, but Sandor knew that his chances of working as a mechanical engineer would be hindered if he couldn't speak the language. He was not intimidated by the prospect of learning another language, though he reckoned that he'd always have an accent, as rare is the interloper who sounds local. A woman upstairs from Sandor's Budapest apartment was the perfect example. She had come from Sarajevo when she was twenty-five, and fifty years later, though fluent in Hungarian, her accent still raised the flag of nationality and sent her back across borders, over rivers and lakes, landing her back home. In Austria a Red Cross official had given Sandor an English-Hungarian dictionary, he had started reading through the long columns of text, trying to memorise nouns, adjectives and verbs, looking at objects *table, chair, sky, cloud, field* and giving them their new name; but he knew that only when he was out there, standing in shops, offices or on factory floors would his command of the language develop properly.

Sandor looked to Kristina with envy. She was a young,

bright child, who was good at school. He believed that her ability to learn another language was far greater than his, and as she would be attending school soon, her English education would begin in earnest. But for now, school was in a hut and the teachers were refugees who thought English to adults and children alike. In the back row of class Sandor listened to one teacher talk her way around a map of Ireland: *Dublin, Cork, Limerick. Waterford, Wexford, Kilkenny.* Then the map progressed around the class, children traced the shape of Ireland, the intricate county boundaries, the blue lines of rivers, the smudge of lakes, and the islands that pimpled the ocean, and the mountains that scuffed the landscape like the dirty knees of children's trousers, and the ragged water-cracked coast of the west.

The teacher pointed out the Shannon Estuary between Loop Head and Kerry Head where the land widened as it sliced northwards. "Limerick City," she instructed.

And the class repeated, "Limerick City."

∽

Later that week there was quiet in the dining hut as Radio Éireann broadcasted a programme of Hungarian music dedicated to the refugees after which the news was translated by an interpreter in the camp. Among the refugees in Austria was a group of famous table tennis players who planned to tour Western Europe in order to raise money for Hungarian refugees. Their talent would be exhibited in all the major cities around Ireland and the newly formed Help Hungary Committee, an Irish organisation established to help the refugees, would benefit from these sporting events. Also, the rosary had been recited in Irish in Galway's Eyre Square to a gathering of people and a resolution of sympathy with the people of Hungary had been forwarded to the Department of External Affairs for transmission to the UN in New York.

When the news was over, the radio, which had been donated to the camp by a Red Cross officer from Limerick, was tuned to Radio Free Europe. In clear, unhurried speech, almost devoid of an accent except for a mild nasal twang which Sandor recognised as American, the broadcaster read letters of support and encouragement for the people of Hungary from exiled Hungarians around the world. Also, there was support from the USA as Washington said that it wasn't alone in condemning the horror which had been witnessed on the streets of Budapest where people had been killed for their love of freedom and democracy.

CHAPTER FOUR

Josef Horvath was twenty-five years old, had a dirty mess of brown hair, and in a croaky and scorched voice he explained to Sandor and Eva how he had crossed the Austrian border. He'd hired a guide, a Hungarian farmer who had extracted a considerable amount of money from him, but at the time of their departure, he didn't show up. "After waiting for him for three hours, we figured that he wasn't going to appear. Some of us speculated that he'd been arrested but I reckon that he was just a thief. Ten of us were left close to the border and as none of us had any money left to hire another guide, we decided to go it alone. We had an idea of which direction to take, we knew that we would be crossing a canal, but we ended up getting lost and wading through a tributary of the Einser Canal instead of the canal itself. So we crossed the small canal and thought that we had arrived in Austria, but we were still in Hungary. We only realised our mistake when we met some other Hungarians who told us where we were. In the end we came to the Einser and crossed into Austria, but we were freezing cold and soaking wet from wading through the wrong canal."

Horvath was treated for trenchfoot in Camp Eisenstadt and in Knockalisheen Camp he visited the medical hut where a number of people were suffering from illnesses typical of a winter flight of refugees: colds and influenza, trenchfoot and exhaustion. Horvath had been advised to rest, but he didn't like staying inside the huts. "If they didn't have stoves in the rooms, they'd be barns by any other name. And if I think they're bad, can you imagine what the women, children and elderly think?"

Horvath, who was nearly fluent in English, had spoken to some of the Irish soldiers in the camp. He asked them, if this was supposed to be an army camp, how come there wasn't any military equipment? "And they told me that nobody had lived in the camp for years. It was built during the Second World War and afterwards it was closed down. That's why there's no military equipment here. And that's why there's a funny smell in the huts, as they've been sitting empty for a decade. Nowadays the army only uses the camp for target practice in the surrounding fields. That's until we came along and some bright spark thought that it was perfect for us."

∞

A second plane of refugees arrived in Shannon Airport. Buses transferred them to the camp and Sandor welcomed the Varga family – a husband, wife and infant – into their hut. The army had fitted curtains around each bed to give privacy, along with cans of paint for the walls and two promises: lino for the floor and wooden partitions to divide each hut. Soon after the Vargas had arrived, the quartermaster spoke to them, entering the following details into his red ledger: name (Peter, Anna and Gábor Varga); sex (M,F,M); religion (Roman Catholic); hut number (thirty-three west).

Kristina didn't like sharing with another family. She didn't believe that all the huts had been filled thus forcing them to share and with an infant as well. Kristina demanded her privacy, she was getting older, eleven going on twelve.

Eva asked Anna how baby Gábor had been sleeping, she said without a problem, he was four months old and a pattern had been established. But some nights he screamed and Anna's calming, maternal whispers reminded Eva of the exhaustion of nursing Kristina at that age.

Anna apologised. It wasn't normal for Gábor to cry that much, it was the exception, most nights he was placid and tranquil.

Sandor didn't mind. He wasn't busy, he didn't have to get up for work, and with the baby in the hut and his nights interrupted, he slept late most mornings, sometimes until lunchtime, killing time until the quarantine restrictions ended, and he could start looking for a job.

∽

One afternoon Sandor was alone in the hut. There was a knock on the door. Outside stood an Irish journalist and a Hungarian interpreter. Sandor had seen the interpreter around the camp and she'd been in the airport when they had arrived. She was a small, plump woman with a round face and brown hair. She'd left Hungary before the war, moved to Spain and then settled in Ireland with her Irish husband. She lived in a small village outside Limerick. Her name was Lucia. She introduced the man as Tommy Gallagher, a freelance journalist. He was interviewing refugees in the camp and she wondered if Sandor would talk to him. Sandor agreed. Gallagher was dressed in a dark suit, white shirt and black tie, a rain coat, polished shoes and hat. Sandor guessed that he was in his late thirties, early forties. A notebook was produced from his pocket and Lucia started translating questions about the preliminary details of his life:

age, marital status, profession and place of birth. Then Sandor answered questions about the fighting in Budapest and whether or not he had taken part; about his family whom he'd left behind; about his religion; about his first impressions of Ireland and his expectations for his life here.

One question surprised Sandor. It concerned the Irish Red Cross and his dealings with them in Austria. Gallagher asked, "Can you recall if you were told that Ireland was a resettlement camp or a transit camp?" Gallagher discerned that Sandor was confused by the question and so it was rephrased, "Did the Irish Red Cross tell you that your stay in Ireland would be in a temporary transit camp before you were moved to another country or that you'd be settled permanently in this country?"

Sandor couldn't recall these definitions being used and so he told Gallagher that he'd come to Ireland to live, to settle permanently and that the officials hadn't given him the impression that he was going to be moved elsewhere.

Gallagher ended the interview by asking Sandor if there was anything else he'd like to add? Sandor walked over to his leather bag and produced two rolls of film, pictures which he'd taken in Budapest towards the end of the uprising. He suggested that Gallagher develop them for use in his article. Thankful for the films, Gallagher promised to return them in a few days.

Outside Sandor shook hands with Gallagher. Then he returned to his hut, to the sheets of paper full of English words gleaned from the dictionary as he tried to collect the vocabulary of his profession, the anatomy of the engine, but tiredness soon returned, he wasn't used to studying, and lying on his bed with his eyes closed, he drifted off to sleep while outside children kicked balls and ran noisily between the huts.

After ten days of living in the camp, sleeping in the hut, washing in communal showers, eating in the dining hut, spending afternoons playing football and evenings in the recreational hut, Sandor was bored. Added to this boredom was a feeling of claustrophobia, he was surrounded by people everywhere he went, the only place which offered peace was the recreational hut late at night when all had gone to bed. Down the hill the lights of Limerick intrigued him, he felt a desire to leave the camp and explore the city, and so he suggested to Josef Horvath that they sneak out of the camp one night. Although Horvath hadn't recovered completely from trenchfoot, he had little problem walking, and agreed to go.

Sandor was outside his hut smoking a cigarette. Although dark, he was mindful of the camp, the hills behind it, the slope towards the city, the few houses dotted around the fields. Horvath arrived on time and they moved quickly between huts. Most had their curtains drawn. Thin lines of smoke rose from the potbellied stoves ghosting towards a night sky clear and cold. Reaching the perimeter fence they looked around for guards though aware that they only manned the entrance. As the fence was old it was easily lifted off the hard, stony ground; they took turns crawling beneath it, careful not to dirty their clothes. Sandor was the first into the neighbouring field. Limerick burnt brightly in the distance. They moved swiftly across the land. Fields, uneven, bumpy, full of stones and frozen cow dung, were separated by crumbling stone walls and thick, thorny bushes. Soon their pace quickened, looking back at the camp, Sandor saw its floodlights gradually diminish.

They covered about two miles walking through fields and then joined the main road to Limerick. Soon, single houses appeared by the roadside, then an estate with similar sized gardens and symmetrical frontages. Outside a bar

Sandor asked Horvath to order him a bottle of beer as he spoke better English, and once they had ensured that their clothes were free of dirt from the fields, they entered. It was smoky and small. On the walls were a few pictures, faded and speckled with mould. The clean, new tiles on the floor were littered with cigarette butts and bottle caps. There was a group of men at the bar. Seats, which stretched alongside the walls and ran beneath the opaque windows stained with a crest of arms, were empty apart from a solitary man at a table. As the windows were raised on the front of the building and people couldn't see in, Sandor was reminded of synagogues that used a similar architectural technique to shelter those praying from outside.

Confidently Horvath walked towards the bar. Sandor felt as though they had entered a bar not on the outskirts of a city, but deep in the countryside. "Two bottles of beer please," requested Horvath. The barman asked a question which Sandor believed was related to the type of beer served.

Horvath replied, "Yes." As it was the first time Horvath had used Irish money which had been given to them as their Red Cross allowance, he placed coins on the counter for the barman to choose. After a cordial smile from the barman, and some interested glances from fellow drinkers, Sandor and Horvath stood awkwardly with their drinks in hand. Though it was obvious to the fourteen men at the bar that these new customers were Hungarian, Sandor and Horvath hoped to conceal this fact as their movement from the camp was still restricted by quarantine regulations.

There were no women in the bar. This was observed as they toasted their bottles. Sandor asked Horvath, who had travelled to Ireland as a single man, about women from his past. Horvath liked chain smoking, and after one cigarette was lit from another, he said, "I was married in Budapest but I was unhappy. We married young, I was eighteen and she was seventeen. I wanted to get out of the marriage and so did she. So when people started leaving the country, we both decided that it was a good time for me to go. So she stayed in the apartment and I came here."

After their third bottle of beer Sandor looked around for the toilet, and the barman, recognising this need in him, pointed towards the back of the bar. Once there, Sandor opened the only door, but it led to a yard where there wasn't a toilet. Inside, Sandor looked for a toilet door, but without luck. The barman, who had started cooking food on a small stove at the end of the bar, took the pan off the heat, walked over to Sandor and pointed outside. Again, Sandor failed to notice a sign for the toilet, he started thinking that perhaps he was more drunk than he actually felt. After standing in the yard for a couple of minutes, the barman returned and following a few words which Sandor couldn't understand, the barman walked over to the wall and pointed to it. "Ohh…" exclaimed Sandor and in English said, "…toilet."

Back inside, Horvath was talking to some men at the bar, Sandor saw a confused look on his friend's face as he tried to decipher their speech. The barman had finished cooking and was placing food on the counter for all to eat, he asked, "Are you Hungarian?"

"Yes."

"Are you staying up the road in the camp?"

"Yes."

"Knockalisheen Camp."

"Yes."

"The word Knockalisheen means The Hill of the Little Fort." Sandor understood a few words in this purposefully slow conversation. After lighting a cigarette he placed it in the ashtray as the barman pushed the plate of food towards him. With an enthusiastic flutter of his hand the barman encouraged him to eat. Sandor ate one of the salty snacks, "Thank you." By now Sandor and Horvath were surrounded by five locals, all of them attempting to be understood, vying for attention. Taking Sandor aside and offering him a cigarette even though one was already lit in his hand, a man said, "I work as a farmer. Pigs. What's your job?" the finger of his right hand was pointing at Sandor's chest, and with Horvath's help, he explained that he was an engineer.

More bottles of beer appeared on the counter. As Sandor and Horvath opened their wallets to pay, a loud chorus of disapproval came from the men, forcing them to put their money away. Sandor and Horvath said thanks, their bottles clinked with the others as they stood crescent-like around the bar.

One of the men asked, "Are you married?" The question was quickly translated by Horvath for Sandor who smiled and declared, "No." And then Horvath said, "My wife is in Hungary."

"Sorry to hear that. To be separated, that's terrible," all heads nodded sympathetically but Horvath said, "I left her there on purpose!" The men started laughing, "So that's the real Red Terror!"

Sandor, by now rather drunk, asked about Irish women and this caused more laughter from the men, and he was advised to go to the ballroom. One man said that Irish women were useless, nothing like the French.

At the toilet, Sandor looked at the sky, he saw the Belt of Orion, a constellation which was visible the night they had crossed the Einser Canal, an event which seemed immersed in history and a lot longer than four weeks ago. Sandor was amused at being in another country and removed from the rut which you invariably sink into at home. Back inside, Horvath said to Sandor, "We can only have one more bottle of beer as the bar is closing."

Soon after leaving the bar they were back in the countryside. With Limerick behind them, they followed their footsteps towards the camp, the cold, wintry air having a sobering effect. Twice Horvath pushed into a bush at the side of the road to relieve himself. Recognising the wall where they had crossed earlier, they jumped into a field. It was very dark. Lines like neon patterns danced in front of their eyes. As Horvath jumped over a wall stones fell behind him. A dog started barking. It was late, Sandor felt tired, the drunken high was beginning to wear off. He started to feel melancholy. His thoughts turned to his parents alone in their apartment and how far he was from them, scuttling across a field outside Limerick, a place he'd never heard of two weeks ago. Although he had reasoned his way out of leaving Budapest, it was what he had wanted to do, there was still a finality to his relationship with his parents which hitherto hadn't sunk in – quite possibly he'd never see them again. And if he did, when? Ten, twenty or thirty years' time?

When Sandor thought of his mother, he always imagined her as a willing audience, always full of praise, every smile a round of applause, her very presence, a standing ovation. Now he felt ashamed at the manner of their departure; abrupt, impatient, full of youthful energy disregarding the middle-aged emotion of his parents. He felt self-loathing and disgrace.

Horvath asked for the time and Sandor attempted to read his watch by pointing it towards the moon but darkness soaked up the minutes. Standing still, his bones became wind chilled.

Horvath asked, "Do you have any idea where we are?"

Sandor advised moving upwards as the camp was on the summit of a hill. "We can't miss the place," he exclaimed. "There are many huts."

Sandor looked for the road which they had taken to

Limerick, but it seemed to have disappeared, and though a car was sometimes heard, the search of headlights was too fleeting to mark the way. Any warmth which they had gathered in the smoky bar was swept away by the wind which rushed in off the Shannon Estuary. Over more stone walls and around thick bushes and denuded trees. For most of the journey the land had been rising slowly but now it levelled out, and Sandor, any feelings of drunkenness having left his body, declared, "We're completely fucking lost."

Horvath sat on the frozen ground, his hands tucked into his pockets, "I could fall asleep here." There was a drunken slur to his words which Sandor hadn't noticed before and when Horvath allowed his body to recline on the ground and close his eyes, Sandor kicked him gently on the soles of his feet telling him to get up. Sandor, guessing that lights in the near distance was a house, suggested that they call on a local farmer, ask for directions, even a lift, they had money and they could pay. Horvath agreed. Still suffering a little from trenchfoot, he just wanted to get to bed and give his mouldy toes a rest, "This walking isn't doing them any good."

This decision to seek help quickened their pace and they arrived at the house in a few minutes. It was 1.50 a.m. After jumping over a wall they landed on a gravel driveway. They saw a car with its window frosted over, there was farm machinery by the side of the house. A porch light was on. Horvath said, "Do you think we should disturb them?" Sandor pointed down the driveway, "Let's look at the road." They came to closed gates which they climbed over. Although the road was similar in size to the one outside Knockalisheen, there was no sign of the floodlit camp. Sandor said, "We either knock on the door or keep wandering around. But I don't want to spend the night outside."

They decided to knock on the door. A Christmas wreath hung on it. Sandor knocked loudly; lights switched on throughout the house. You could hear conversation, feet running the length of the bungalow. A man in a dressing gown, with a taller, though younger man, behind him, opened the door. "Can I help you lads? Is there a problem?"

Horvath came forward, "We are lost. We are looking for Knockalisheen Camp. It is late. We are sorry."

"Hungarian?" the man asked.

"Yes," said Horvath.

"You're not close. How long were you walking the fields?"

"One, maybe, two hours."

"Cold?"

"Yes."

"I'll drive you to the camp."

In the car Sandor tried to get his bearings. At times he saw the shine of Limerick, but Knockalisheen never came into view. As the journey was taking longer than expected, Sandor wondered how he had misread the fields and ended up so far from the camp. He had presumed that, as the camp was on an elevation, all he had to do was walk back up the hill.

They halted in a village. The man, without explanation, jumped out of the car shutting his door quietly. Sandor looked at Horvath who had fallen asleep in the back seat. A minute later two gardaí appeared. Sandor nudged Horvath telling him to wake up; as he did he looked confusedly at the gardaí. They exited the car, the man drove off. Inside the station the garda said, "Quarantine restrictions. You understand?" Horvath said, "Yes," and their details were taken down.

Later they were driven back to the camp. It was a short trip, at the *STOP* sign they were met by two soldiers who instructed them to return to their huts.

The following day they met McManus, the Irish Red Cross official. Sandor had seen him around the camp and had listened to his speech on the night of their arrival. A thin man, he had thick black-rimmed glasses and a bushy black beard streaked with grey. Although Sandor couldn't understand the man, he discerned a gentle, decent manner. They were seated in the only brick building in the camp, newly built, by the entrance. Originally it was the commandant's house and office, but McManus was living there now. Their feet rested on the black and white tiles of the kitchen floor. A kettle was brought to the boil on a stove, McManus poured tea and offered biscuits. Through Lucia, the Hungarian interpreter, McManus sympathised with the frustration which they must be feeling about being unable to leave the camp, but he assured them that it was only a matter of days before they were free. He explained that although charges could be brought against them for breaking their quarantine restrictions, they had been dropped.

"Technically," explained Lucia, "you are still guests of the nation. If this matter were pursued, you could lose that status and become aliens. But Mr McManus is amused. You wouldn't be the first to get drunk and lost in the fields around here."

∽

Later that week the scheduled press conference started fifteen minutes later than planned. Smoke filled the recreational hut; behind a table sat McManus, Commandant O'Mailey of the Irish Army and Lucia the interpreter. Journalist Tommy Gallagher was standing at the side of the table. McManus spoke first, the following translated: it was hoped that everybody had settled into the camp, that everybody was warm, was well fed and rested after the events of the last couple of weeks. His next point concerned the establishment of a camp council elected by refugees and all the positions staffed by refugees. On this committee one person would be elected as the camp representative. Any problems which might arise would be dealt with by the camp representative who would liaise with the authorities. "It'll be more efficient and somebody living in the camp would be more aware of any issues. In time, and in a similar way that all meals are now being cooked by refugees, it is foreseen that the camp would be run by Hungarians but under supervision of the Irish Red Cross."

Lucia informed the gathering that three thousand families around the country had offered to adopt Hungarian children. Four companies have offered to sponsor families but she wasn't sure how large the families could be or how many jobs, if any, were included in these offers. Over Christmas, many homes had invited families to join them for the celebrations, these invitations had come from all parts of the country and would be a good introduction to Irish family life.

Also, there was good news regarding quarantine: it had been reduced and in less than a week people would be able to come and go as they pleased – subject, of course – to immigration restrictions.

Sandor asked if immigration restrictions would affect their employment opportunities. She said that was a matter for the government and not the Irish Red Cross or the army. Regarding jobs, it was expected that the government would be making a statement on the future of the refugees soon and although the Irish Red Cross had yet to discuss employment matters with the trade unions it was hoped that once the quarantine restrictions were over, offers of employment would be made.

Sandor asked, "Have many offers been made already?" After discussing this with McManus, Lucia replied "No. But we are only starting to talk to potential employers."

The status of the camp was raised. A man said that he'd been informed in Austria that he'd only be in Ireland for a couple of weeks before his family would be flown to the USA or Canada. As he had no intention of settling in Ireland, he asked if preparations were being made to assist this onward journey, if any meetings had been held between the Irish Red Cross and the embassies. Through Lucia, McManus explained that Knockalisheen was always meant to be a resettlement camp and never a transit camp. On this point he was certain. Ireland had offered refugees asylum, "So that you can settle down in this country."

Josef Horvath said, "I agree with the last speaker. I have no intention of staying in Ireland because I was told in Austria that I'd be moved to another country. It was also explained to me that this was a transit camp and not a resettlement camp."

McManus disagreed, "The Irish have raised a lot of money in order to resettle you here. Let's be sure about one thing: this *isn't* a transit camp. It was always a resettlement camp."

Other people joined in the debate, at times the crowd became loud and quiet was demanded by McManus. It seemed to Sandor that many people believed that Ireland was a transit camp and not a resettlement camp, though he had always thought of it as the latter and had planned to stay here. After a few minutes, McManus announced that the press conference was over, and along with Commandant O'Mailey, departed the recreational hut.

Two nights later the crackle of donated gramophone records was replaced by the BBC news which said that the Soviet Union supported Premier of Hungary had demanded that Austria return the thousands of Hungarians who had fled and he accused the West of using these young men as slave labour in their capitalist economies. It was reported that the Hungarian economy was faltering, the workers were on a go-slow, mining production was running at an eighth of usual output. Gangs of people were employed in Budapest to restore the city to its former state: repairing tramways and electric cables, dismantling barricades and road blocks, cleaning streets and ensuring the safety of damaged buildings. During the uprising, while there had been reports of Russian fighter jets, most of the damage had been done by the thousands of Russian tanks which had ended the fighting, as one report said, the largest gathering of tanks since the Battle of Kursk during the Second World War.

That night saw heavy rain. Drops banged on the wooden roofs of Knockalisheen Camp. Another plane of refugees arrived, causing more pressure on the electricity generator and a failure occurred. As soldiers tried to restore power to the camp, people gathered around the potbellied stoves and lit candles. The huts creaked in the storm and when the wind blew, sheets of rain broke against them like waves against a storm-tossed ship.

CHAPTER FIVE

When the quarantine restrictions were over Sandor, Eva and Kristina went to Limerick. They were in awe of the bulbs bursting with solid reds and golden yellows and whites as white as the fake snow dusting the shop windows on the main street; for it was the first time Kristina had ever seen Christmas decorations; and many years since Sandor and Eva had witnessed this festive expression which had been banned under communism. Criss-crossing roads full of colourful bunting, pictures of cakes and candles, reindeer and Santa Claus, they stopped at a window depicting the nativity scene: life-sized figures, Mary, Joseph and the Three Wise Men with their gifts for the newborn King beneath the Star of Bethlehem.

It was a cold day full of rain; the descent of darkness came sooner rather than later; in the puddles on the potholed roads colour was reflected in the expanding ripples of diesel-dirt water; and when cars splashed pedestrians you'd hear them shout: wails of pity, cries of injustice.

There was little space on the packed footpaths and people crossed roads by jumping between cars and buses. Inside the shops the aisles were claustrophobic; the hard corners of shopping bags pricked your body like thorny bushes.

They held hands, Sandor, Eva and Kristina, their eyes smudged neon with advertisements for products which they'd never seen, their legs stop-starting, stunned by distraction, the sensual pleasure of the commercial touch. Eva scrutinised items. She spoke of material, craftsmanship, design. Sandor remembered their mother returning from Vienna, pre-war, with gilded costumes, speckled patterns and price tags which she boasted about. And she always had a present for one of their great aunts, a child's toy, and the great aunt would cherish it like the child-adult she was. Katie had explained to her twins when they were old enough to understand. When this great aunt was young, an accident had happened while she was swallowing food and she choked. The supply of oxygen was cut off to her brain. Her mental age was reduced from twenty-nine to eight. Sandor and Eva always saw this great aunt once a year, on Christmas Eve, sitting by the tree, quiet, remote, occasionally talking, and when she left, Sandor would fear her kiss goodbye, the blunted stare of her rust coloured eyes and her clumsy mouth wet and awkward.

In one shop they went upstairs to a floor full of men's clothes, and further upstairs to toys, where children queued nosily, waiting with their parents to meet Santa Claus who was housed in a small hut decorated with snow and ribbons and pictures of little men in green clothes, pointy ears and evil, elfish grins. When it was discovered that young Kristina was a Hungarian refugee, she was pushed to the top of the queue, and sitting on Santa's knee, he asked her questions which she didn't understand and gave her a present of a colouring book and pencils. Outside, Sandor looked at windows above shops on the main street and then alongside the river. Some were offices, others apartments. Sandor wanted to live in the city. He thought that it would be nicer than living in a housing estate like the one they had passed on their way into Limerick, with its grey bricks and smoky chimneys. And by a river too: to exchange the Danube for the Shannon. Now it was full of seagulls and noxious smells refreshed by a cold northerly wind, but in time, spring would waft above the sea, and on these trade winds, a wealth of warmth.

By mid-afternoon the sky was dark except for a sliver of light between clouds like a frozen fork of lightning and the sun started setting over the Shannon Estuary. Sandor and Eva felt tired and Kristina was thirsty. They rested in a hotel bar. Outside there were carol singers, a person in the centre of the group held a placard which read: 'Support Irish Red Cross. Appeal for Funds. Hungary'.

On their way home they passed King John's Castle, the only landmark Sandor had committed to memory from their approach to the city. It was grey and fat, its tower stacked like dirty coins about to topple. Quickly, the city dissolved behind them and the earth turned, twisting out of sight of the sun, and Limerick became a festival of light, its colourful billboards and neon signs sparring with the stars. The road to Knockalisheen Camp was a scant illumination of gravel and ragged bush, the darkness covering Sandor's eyes like his father's hands had once at Christmas time, just before the tree was unveiled. Sandor would sit on Frank's lap and Eva on Katie's. A neighbour would light the candles. There was the smell of matches and then Frank would loosen his grip ever so slightly on Sandor's eyes, the ring on his finger catching the sparkle of flame, and once free, Sandor would glide effortlessly towards the candles like a ghost hypnotised by light. But there was always a parental warning: *Don't attempt to light the candles without us, as you don't want to end up disfigured like the man across the street whose ears were so badly burnt in a house fire they had to be removed.* And with the image of him in mind,

Sandor would swear to God that his hands would never be led astray and climb the summit of the bookshelf where the matches were kept.

On one of the few days when Sandor had left his apartment during the uprising he took his camera to capture Budapest amid conflict. He had wandered the streets taking photographs of burnt-out tanks, smashed shops and buildings and a Russian helicopter overhead. On one street corner he took a shot of an overturned tram, the distinctive yellow body lying in a mess of uprooted cobblestones and electrical wire. He felt guilty taking some pictures: an apartment block had been damaged by Russian cannon, you could see into people's homes and what remained of their possessions: bookcases, chairs, tables and beds. Like a tribal warning dead Russian soldiers still lay in the streets, their bodies covered in lime. Photographing death was a rare and unnerving experience, it made him feel exploitative and guilty, but also charged his eye with an air of exclusivity.

These pictures were developed by Tommy Gallagher who knocked on Sandor's door one evening, and from his trench coat he produced an envelope containing the negatives and enlargements. Gallagher brought a copy of The Irish Press which he opened to show Sandor a couple of his pictures reproduced on the dirty-white newsprint. As Lucia wasn't there to translate, they spoke to each other in simple sentences, Gallagher expressing his gratitude for the photographs, Sandor full of pride at their use. And an amused Gallagher showed him an article which spoke of two refugees who had been picked up by the Gardaí for breaking the quarantine regulations.

Gallagher put on his hat and left Sandor with a bundle of newspapers, an archive of articles about the Hungarians arriving in Ireland, and though he couldn't read them properly, he looked at the photographs and the dominance of headlines across front pages. There were pictures of families sitting on steps outside their huts, the big white numbers, twenty three, twenty six, forty one, by their sides; mothers holding infants wrapped in swaddling clothes; little children perched high on parental shoulders their mouths soothered and silent. Another picture showed two children shaking hand to paw with the camp pet, a black and white sheepdog who lived in the commandant's house called Bimbo. Most people hadn't given their real names to journalists as they feared that if the newspapers got into the wrong hands, their families might face reprisal back in Hungary. In another photograph a group of windswept refugees walked across the runway at Shannon Airport waving and smiling at the photographers, the headline read: *HUNGARIAN REFUGEES HERE – Freedom fighters, elderly people and children seek sanctuary 4,000 miles from their homeland.*

Below that was a story about a couple and their baby. The baby's eyes shone pearly bright at the camera, and *due to the events in Hungary he has yet to be baptised.*

The couple had refused to give their names but Sandor recognised them as Peter and Anna Varga. One day Peter, who slept across the hut from Sandor, asked to speak with him. His voice was apprehensive. Peter was a large man. He was a foot shorter than Sandor, his chubby face was unshaven. He had narrow shoulders and his bulk was positioned centrally: fat hung from his jowl, breast and gut. Tousled brown hair spiked off a receding hairline darkened at the roots due to grease. He was thirty-five years old but looked forty, even forty-five. Sandor felt pity for him as he often did for the overweight. He had sunken eyes and the pasty white skin of the unhealthy. Peter asked Sandor if he would be his baby's godfather, he didn't know anybody else in the camp and didn't want to use a Red Cross representative or an Irish official.

Sandor wondered what he'd have to do? "In the church you renounce Satan, and maybe light a candle," Peter smiled.

The baptism was performed by Father Mikes, a thirty-one year old Hungarian priest who came to Ireland in 1949 after his seminary had been occupied by communists. After fleeing, he had spent time in Austria and England and then crossed the Irish Sea to live with fellow Jesuits in Dublin. He came down from his seminary in Rathfarnham Castle to take up the post of Camp Chaplain. He was a tall, good-looking man. His hair was cut short on the back and sides, beneath his cheekbones his skin curved inwards giving prominence to his lips. A dimple marked his chin. The chapel was in hut sixteen. Inside, it had the trappings of a church, the red glow of the lamp by the tabernacle, and candles sparkling on the few brass fittings. In Latin Father Mikes said, "I baptise thee, in the name of the Father, and of the Son, and of the Holy Ghost."

As instructed, Sandor made the sign of the cross upon Gábor's forehead. The baby shrieked, then twitched in his mother's arms, his legs kicking the shawl. His fingers were podgy, when his hands tightened into fists they looked like dumplings half eaten on a plate. Gábor's size was a knot from his father's genetic line. Peter told Sandor that he was the biggest in his family, it was an accident, he reckoned, as none of his brothers or sisters were overweight. He said that he was disappointed with the size of Gábor, he hoped that his podgy fingers would firm up and the fat would disappear. Sandor told Peter to think of the human traits; good and bad beating in his little heart, and his breath, which carried not a puff of sense, would one day make him laugh.

Unlike her husband, Anna was thin with a boyish

frame, flat chested, skinny legs, a body lacking definition. She had a pretty face, blue eyes nicely balanced above her narrow nose and dark hair hung low on her forehead. Sandor took pictures of the happy parents with their child; mother alone with child; father alone with child; and lastly the family with Father Mikes. Then Sandor instructed Peter on how to use his camera and a portrait was taken of godfather and godchild.

By mid-December 1956 it was announced that the further arrival of Hungarian refugees would be suspended until after Christmas. The last group of refugees to arrive brought the total to five hundred and thirty. Despite having raised enough money for one thousand refugees, apart from Knockalisheen Camp, the Irish Red Cross had yet to find suitable accommodation anywhere else in Ireland. When Christmas time arrived the Irish Red Cross organised for many Hungarians to spend the holidays with Irish families. Josef Horvath went to Dublin; the Vargas to Cork; and the Lovases to County Kerry.

At lunchtime John Murphy called to the entrance of Knockalisheen Camp, introduced himself to the soldiers on duty, and within five minutes, Sandor, Eva and Kristina had placed their bag in the back of his car and were speeding towards Limerick. John, a grey-haired man in his late forties, was dressed neatly in a suit, a camel-coloured coat, hat, scarf and gloves and drove his Mercedes with pleasure. It was Christmas Eve. It had been explained to Sandor by the Irish Red Cross that John was a Dubliner who spent his holidays in County Kerry and that was where he'd take them.

On leaving, the sky was dark with no sign of snow but a desire to rain was evident in the black clouds. Sitting up front, Sandor enjoyed the smell of upholstery, the polished wooden dashboard. He peered out the window going through Limerick, Saint John's Castle and O'Connell Street were now familiar sights, but quickly the road became unknown and Sandor looked for signposts detailing their route. For the first part of their journey the road remained close to the Shannon Estuary, as the car bumped along, Sandor explained to Kristina that Knockalisheen was across the water.

After two hours they stopped outside a bar in a small village. John turned to Kristina and said, "Toilet," a word which she understood and she replied, "Yes." Eva and her daughter went inside the bar while Sandor stretched his legs outside smoking a cigarette. John disappeared for a few minutes and arrived back with a bag of provisions which he placed in the boot. Back on the road it quickly became dark. Sandor wanted to talk to John, to express himself in the few English sentences which he knew, partly because he was his guest, but also to learn about their journey. John discouraged talking, not in any single gesture or statement, but in the concentration his eyes gave to the road.

Sunset was like a curtain drawn over the car windows bringing sleep to Kristina's eyes who stretched across the back seat using Eva's lap for a pillow. The roads were gravelly and full of potholes. At times the exhaust pipe scraped along the ground causing John to pass comment aggressively. The further they went from Limerick the worse the roads became. After filling up on petrol John showed the route to Sandor on a map. "We have a house," he said slowly. "Near a town called Waterville."

Soon Eva fell asleep. Sandor tried to stay awake as he felt that it would be rude for all of them to snooze. Four hours after they had left the camp, John became excited declaring that they had nearly arrived, and holding one hand in the air he said, "Five minutes." Carefully he drove the last few miles as the road became smaller, bushes scraping the side of the car like claws, the headlights shining on tight bends and steep descents. Coming to a halt outside large wooden gates, John yawned, smiled and then said, "Home."

Once the engine was switched off you could hear the sea lapping against a small beach. There was the damp smell of wintry vegetation. Wind brought tears to Sandor's eyes as he carried their bag into the house where they were welcomed by a woman and four children.

After Sandor left their bag in a room with two beds, John led him into a large sitting room where a Christmas tree sat in one corner, beneath which presents were piled. John collected pine needles which had fallen on the floor and flicked them on to the fire. Sandor sat in one of two leather chairs while John opened a bottle of wine which had been sitting in front of the fire. Before he poured Sandor a glass, he smelled the cork. From a silver case he offered him a cigar, which Sandor took. The wine was an elixir replenishing Sandor's body after the journey. John, with his shoes off and his feet in front of the fire, explained that he had left the house at eight in the morning and was now exhausted. Puffing on a cigar, sipping his wine, John appeared content and showed signs of relaxation. On the road certain drivers had angered him, but now his face was calm and the fire performed an amber dance on his grey hair. The cigar was new to Sandor, its heavy smoke was like a contagion to his lungs, many times he coughed, until John told him only to savour the smoke in his mouth.

When John asked about the camp he did so in slow, clear sentences. Sandor attempted to speak about the people who had left. Among the first to go were two Jewish families after the Jewish Representative Council of Ireland had sent a delegation from Dublin to take them under their care. Sandor had heard from Josef Horvath that they hadn't mentioned their faith to anybody, and had lied to the Irish Red Cross about their religion to enter Ireland but on their arrival they had immediately contacted the Jewish organisation. Sandor attempted to tell John this story but couldn't find the appropriate words and so he spoke about a man who had hired four weavers who had left the camp with their families. Sandor explained that another family had left the country altogether, a man of Swiss nationality arranged for his family to fly out of Shannon to Switzerland.

John explained that he knew many people in business and asked about the qualifications of the refugees. In a mixture of English, Hungarian and simple hand gestures Sandor spoke of miners, cobblers, barbers, lawyers, butchers, soldiers, postmen, tailors, an optician, accountants, civil engineers, motor mechanics, factory workers, plumbers and a pilot. With pride Sandor said that there were two sportsmen: a boxer and a football player.

John smiled and said that Hungary had beaten England recently. A toast was declared.

Soon, Meave, John's wife called them into the dining room. A large table had been set: knives, forks, glasses, side plates, baskets of bread, jugs of water, small plates of butter, candles and linen napkins.

John brought his hands together, his family looked down at the table and prayed. Kristina stared at the other children as she held her hands together in prayer. Recently, Eva had told Sandor that she had been worried about Kristina, she had been out of school for weeks and wasn't sure when she'd start again. When asked, the Irish Red Cross didn't know when or what school the children would attend. At the moment their education was still in the hands of voluntary teachers in the camp. Eva felt that Kristina needed to be around Irish children to learn the language; it was only then that she'd start learning English properly, and not by hanging around a camp surrounded by Hungarians. Still, Sandor thought that Kristina was learning the language better than Eva or himself and seated in-between the two girls (the Murphy children were composed of two girls aged ten and twelve and two boys aged fourteen and sixteen) she seemed to have a basic level of communication.

Sandor attempted to reply to questions put to him by the family, amusing comments from the younger children, observations learned at school from the older ones, while Meave ensured that there was enough food on their plates and wine in their glasses. Throughout the meal Sandor wished that he had more vocabulary to praise the meal of roast beef, potatoes, vegetables, and after the plates were cleared, cheese and chocolate cake. Meave asked Eva about the food in the camp, and with the help of Kristina, they gave sample menus and talked about Hungarian food and the Irish variations which the refugees had prepared. After the meal Sandor offered to take the plates into the kitchen but Meave insisted that he sit down. Cigars were produced, this time Sandor carefully held the smoke in his mouth without inhaling but a dizziness still came to his mind.

After the dessert Meave asked her girls to sing. Behind a polished black piano in the corner of the room they sat, the room was filled with the sound of carols. Encouraged by Sandor, Eva and Kristina sang a version of Silent Night in German:

Stille Nacht, heilige Nacht
alles schläft, einsam wacht
nur das traute hochheilige Paar
holder Knabe im lockigen Haar
schlaf in himmlischer Ruh'
schlaf in himmlischer Ruh'

The Murphys clapped loudly and glasses were clinked and the girls sang the hymn in Irish:

Oíche Chiúin, oíche Mhic Dé,
Cách na suan go héiri an lae.
Dís is dílse ag faire le spéis.
Glór binn aingeal le clos insan aer.
Críost ag teacht ar an saol.
Críost ag teacht ar an saol.

John complimented Sandor on his family, telling him that his wife and daughter were beautiful. After momentary confusion Sandor explained that Eva was his sister, not his wife, and that Kristina was her daughter. John was surprised, silent for a few minutes. Leaving the table he returned with a bottle of brandy. He poured the golden liquid into bulbous glasses, the heavy weight and hard edge of the tumbler sat nicely in Sandor's hand. Soon the children went to bed, the younger ones first, the older ones being granted concessions as it was Christmas Eve. Kristina stayed at the table beside her mother until the older boys went to bed, and then Eva took her sleepy daughter into their room. Maeve stacked plates beside the sink, John finished off his brandy and looked dreamily into the candle lights on the crumb full and chocolate-smeared table. Sandor, warmed by the brandy and the heat of the fire, asked if he could get some fresh air and went outside. He lit a cigarette. The smoke was cooled by the sea air. Walking to the edge of the garden he looked down on the small cove, smoke from the chimney following in his wake; occasionally the moon was revealed through the clouds; wind came in off the Atlantic in vicious bursts; water splashed angrily against the stony beach; an upturned, rotting boat by the pier gave shelter to a dog;

and Sandor, reflective after a good meal in good company, felt tears push in his eyes: this was charity and he was in receipt of it.

On Christmas morning, after a trip to mass (the priest welcomed the Hungarians to the ceremony), John cited tradition as the reason for the men to climb a nearby mountain. As Sandor hadn't the proper clothing with him, Meave ran around the house collecting jackets and boots, scarves and hats and then the women bid farewell to them. Sandor looked anxiously at the large mountain. Behind the house, the land shot upwards, it was a steep incline; once moving, his heart beat faster though he was glad that the others were just as challenged as he was. For the first hour, there was much talk between John and his sons, but soon after the conversation died out. Sandor regretted smoking and drinking too much the night before and pledged that he wouldn't indulge so much later on.

After two hours they reached the summit. Sandor was very tired, so were the others. He looked at the Atlantic Ocean, a vast, grey-blue mass of water; it was the first time he'd seen the sea so spectacularly. For a man who had known only landlocked Hungary, who had never seen an ocean from this height (the sixteen hundred feet of Farraniaragh Mountain), it brought to his mind the insignificance of dry land. John pointed at various islands, little pimples pricking the sea and he gave them names which Sandor forgot instantly; and the boys spoke of headlands, and of other islands which could be seen on a clear day. It was very cold and damp on the mountain. Sandor's nose ran as if he had a cold.

Sandor stood like a tripod holding his camera firmly in his hands and his legs stretched out. He took a couple of pictures: the sky, the sea and the bay where the Murphys' house was positioned.

After they rested for a few minutes, John pointed in the distance and said, "New York City – three thousand miles away." Then slowly, and with an air of importance, he asked Sandor, "Do you know how many people leave Ireland each year?"

Sandor didn't understand the question and he shrugged his shoulders. John continued, "You know, leave. To go to another country to live. Look for work. To leave their homes, their families."

On comprehending the question Sandor looked out to sea. He couldn't even guess as he'd never thought about it before. John waited a minute for Sandor to answer and said, "You have no idea, do you?"

Sandor's head swayed from side to side, "No."

"Over the last five years, two hundred thousand people."

Sandor asked how many people lived in Ireland?

John replied, "Nearly three million," adding, "it's a significant percentage. A census is about to be published and the amount who left this year is around forty thousand."

As they walked down the mountainside they talked about immigration, but due to the blustery wind and John's breathy, tired gasps for air, Sandor couldn't hear most of the conversation. Nevertheless, it turned Sandor's mind from the festivities and he decided that once they returned to Limerick, he was going to walk the length and breadth of the city in search of work, and he figured that, as he was a qualified mechanical engineer, he'd get a job.

It took them less than an hour to reach the sea. Looking back at the mountain Sandor felt pride in this athletic achievement, especially after the previous night's consumption. Like the wind on the top of the mountain, the sea was the dominant noise while walking beside it. John pointed to a house just inland beneath a bushy forest and explained that a famous Irish politician had once lived there. As John spoke, the boys started laughing. Sandor was amused as they jeered their father, their hands raised to their mouths in a gesture of yawning, "It's where Daniel O'Connell lived. He was like an Irish Kossuth or a Deák." These names of nineteen-century Hungarian politicians seemed incongruous being uttered by an Irishman. Sandor was impressed that John was aware of their existence. You never expect people from other countries to know characters from your history and Sandor thought of the books which lined the walls of John's house. Having no knowledge of Irish history, Sandor felt respect and admiration.

After walking along a path which ran close to the sea, up and down water soaked rock, beneath the naked remains of bushes and trees, they returned to the small bay and the house.

As Sandor changed his clothes in the bedroom, he spoke to Eva. Kristina was playing with the girls in the living room. Eva told Sandor that Meave had offered to arrange work for her as she knew people in Dublin in need of domestic staff. Eva tried to tell her of her experience as a teacher but she didn't understand. On a piece of paper Meave had written the address of a person whom she could contact. Though Eva had taken the name out of politeness, she insisted that she was overqualified to clean houses.

They had Christmas dinner and went to bed late. Before they did, Sandor insisted that the Murphy family pose for a photograph. The women sat on the couch, with the men standing behind them. After a few photographs Sandor thanked them, trying to explain in English that, if the pictures were good, he'd send them copies.

The next day John drove them to Knockalisheen Camp. Saint Stephen's Day was quiet as most of the children were still with Irish families around the country, and those who had stayed were exhausted from the celebrations which the

Irish Red Cross had organised. Sandor and Eva sat in the recreational hut which was littered with wrapping paper, boxes of sweets and listened to the radio. It was just under two months since they had left Budapest. Sandor remembered Stalin's statue and how, a few days after it had fallen, he'd been walking down a street and had come face to face with its severed head. He was amused at how he'd stroked the dictator's hair. It was a strange feeling; he felt a little perverted.

CHAPTER SIX

Josef Horvath returned from Dublin with his messy brown hair cut short and his trenchfoot almost cured. He had enjoyed his time in the capital and the Irish family with whom he'd stayed. "I have never drunk so much in my life. Each day the father of the house took me into the city and we walked from bar to bar with him paying for everything. The end result was that I spent one night throwing my guts up. I was scared to fall asleep in case I got sick and choked to death, and so I stayed on the floor beside the sink in my bedroom. When I didn't come down for breakfast, they sent the youngest child to get me. You should have heard her scream. She thought that I was dead, lying there on the floor.

"Anyway, the grandmother of the house, who was about eighty, walked me in circles around the garden, patting me on the back, feeding me soup. The family thought this was very funny and whenever anybody called to the house I could hear them talking about me getting sick and sleeping on the floor."

Eva asked about the house, "Was it big?" Horvath described a four-storey terrace home overlooking a square. At night the house was cold, there was a hole in his bedroom window and a stream of icy air circulated around the room. Downstairs, a huge Christmas tree sat in one of the windows which could be seen from across the square. At the front of the house there was a garden surrounded by heavy iron gates. Four houses on the square were boarded up, not in use.

"And Dublin?" asked Sandor.

"It's a lot smaller than Budapest. And poorer. Close to the city centre whole terraces are crumbling, falling apart, awaiting demolition. Many times I saw children running around in the city centre in their bare feet. But the places where the family took me were nice, the father was a professor at a university, Trinity College, and we had dinner there one night and listened to choral music."

Horvath hadn't spent all his time in Dublin being entertained. For a few afternoons, and with the help of the professor, he had walked around the city looking for work. Although he had no plans to stay in Ireland, he was still curious about its employment opportunities. He had trained as a baker, his last job had been in a hotel, his military service had been spent in the army kitchens. "I wandered all around Dublin calling into every bakery I could find and into the larger hotels, but there was nothing. As I learned my trade from a Jewish baker I called into a few Jewish bakeries, but they had nothing either. And it wasn't because they couldn't understand me as my English is good, one of the children in the family used to test me in the evening, she'd go over the same questions again and again as if I was in an interview."

Horvath stubbed out his cigarette and drank from a glass of water, his actions urgent and impatient. "I was fully prepared. I looked good. I had a letter detailing my experience, I wrote out some of the sample menus which I have been working on, the different types of cakes, pastries and chocolates, and the German and Austrian variations. But there's no work, that's what people kept saying to me. Again and again, no work. And that's the capital city."

Sandor said, "Perhaps it's a quiet time."

Horvath shrugged his shoulders, "Baking tends to be steady. People need bread and they need it everyday."

"Maybe it's different here?"

"No," replied Horvath. "The only difference is that while we're coming into the country, everybody else is going out because there's no work here. Thousands leave every year. I asked the professor, 'If so many people are leaving the country, what are we doing coming in?' and he replied, 'Well my friend, that's the sixty four thousand dollar question.'"

Sandor was confused, "What does he mean by that?"

"I'm not exactly sure," replied Horvath. "But it killed the conversation stone dead."

༄

"Sandor Lovas," was his introduction. "Maria Novak," was her reply but he didn't hear her properly due to the volume of the band, and when she repeated it, shouting loudly into his ear, little droplets of spit landed on his cheek and in his eye. He blinked, and for a few seconds his face became calm, then he repeated, "Novak?" and she smiled, "Yes."

And yes: she agreed to his suggestion of another drink, the bar was two tables at the end of the recreational hut, there was a lot of alcohol as one hundred pounds had been donated to the camp for the New Year's Eve celebrations. Through this crowded room Sandor made his way to the bar, the party reminding him of weddings as children were running around or sleeping in their parent's arms or stretched out like animals on coats bundled on the floor. Waiting his turn at the bar, he read his watch (11.27 p.m.), after finishing his cigarette, he looked back at the band as the singer took to the floor. A salsa group from Limerick had volunteered for the night. When the woman in the bright yellow, low-cut dress wasn't singing in front of her band, people cleared a space in the centre of the room where she danced. A group of children mimicked the extravagant gestures of the singer, waving imaginary dresses in the air, throwing each other around in clumsy circles, small bodies sliding across the wooden floor.

With drinks in hand, Sandor walked back to Maria, back to her tall body of five-foot eleven inches, four inches smaller than him, and back to her black, shoulder length hair. And back to her skin which was paler than the average Hungarian, making Sandor think of Russia and the large paintings of the steppe which he'd seen in an art gallery, pictures in which the sky was the dominant feature, an effulgent mass of cloud and morning sun, techniques which had inspired him to photograph the mackerel sky speeding across Pest one dull Saturday afternoon from his balcony.

Sandor felt self-conscious as they toasted their drinks. They spoke about Christmas. Maria and her parents had taken a bus to Galway and were met by a family holding a placard reading *Novak* who drove them for an hour to a farm. Maria, from Budapest, enjoyed the peace which the countryside carried in its spiky air, though it rained for most of their holiday. Their room, though warm and comfortable, had a metal roof which the rain banged on continuously, making sleep difficult.

Drinking faster than usual, Sandor nodded his head while listening to her, and his right hand, usually reserved for holding a cigarette, freed hair sweated to his forehead. Earlier Eva had encouraged him to get it cut in the barbershop which had opened in the camp, and he was now thankful for her advice, as perhaps something like the cutting of his hair would make Maria consider him just that little bit more. Perhaps, thought Sandor, as the band increased in volume and their conversation halted, attraction could be reduced to a matter so simple that you'd be embarrassed to admit it. But was there anything simple about the angle of Maria's cheekbones which framed the smooth, though not blemish free skin (two small moles just south of her bottom lip) or how her nose twisted slightly upwards? Sandor thought she was beautiful. And he imagined attraction as immediate and honest as the moment a camera opened its eyeful aperture and the world was imprinted on the photographic paper.

He read his watch: 11.42 p.m.

Soon it would be 1957. He imagined time, not as a continuum which grew as the years went by moving forward through the dates of history, but just one year, the four seasons repeated again and again. So this new year was not a new beginning as people thought, but the same beginning which happened every year when time set her clocks back twelve months and every living creature became trapped in this dubious advance.

At 11.52 p.m., Sandor asked Maria if she wanted another drink, which she did, so at the bar he ordered two bottles of beer as the singer attempted a few Hungarian words, a Christmas blessing, and when she stopped, the crowd cheered and the men in her band, between gulps of beer and cigarette drags, also applauded. Back with Maria, not in the same spot but a little closer to the bar and beneath a light bulb, Sandor looked into her eyes which had hitherto been concealed by shadow and cigarette fog, and when they weren't twitching from smoke, they became placid, perceptibly blue. Vivid.

Midnight passed.

Sandor greeted 1957 with a desire to sleep with Maria Novak. Soon the party ended and people returned to their huts, to their crowded shelters. Sandor enjoyed the release of emotion which she had inspired and he quickly developed an almost adolescent fascination for her, and because of the long, frustrating days of unemployment he was always trying to meet her when walking around the camp or sitting in the recreational or kitchen hut.

She liked to be distracted by him. Besides her parents, she didn't know many people in the camp and was happily taken on dates into Limerick where they'd sit over one or two drinks for long periods of time. Or when they were feeling wealthy, on the day of their Red Cross allowance, they'd go to the cinema.

Maria had worked as a nurse in Budapest and hoped to find a similar job in Ireland. When the uprising ended, it had been her father's idea to escape, and so her family of three had crept across the border and spent a couple of weeks in Eisenstadt. Maria agreed with her father; she wanted to leave Hungary, as to her mind it was time trapped and stagnant, a million miles away from the advances of the West and the bountiful lives which people seemed to lived there. Often her father had spoken of his regret at not leaving Hungary just after the war, before their lives had settled down again. So when the uprising occurred he viewed it not as a chance to rid Hungary of Soviet rule, but as their opportunity for escape. Why Mr Novak had decided to come to Ireland instead of America or Canada or Australia was simple; he liked the idea of the country, over the years he'd read books about the place, articles detailing its Celtic past and rugged countryside, stories of mythology and folklore. He was also keen to leave Eisenstadt quickly. Their family fitted the Irish Red Cross ideal – a professional Catholic man, his wife and child – and he was impressed with the small quota of refugees which Ireland was taking in and the immediacy of departure. Unlike her father, Maria had no interest in Ireland and had been surprised by his decision to come here, as she had thought that they were bound for North America.

But Maria appreciated the urgency of their situation and her father's desperation to settle down. While crossing into Austria they had been caught by border guards, forced to lie down on the cold earth at gunpoint, they had been robbed of what little money they had and all their valuables which amounted to a few watches and jewellery. Mr Novak had felt responsible for putting his family through this incident. Though they agreed that it could have been worse – there were stories of women being raped and people being shot by border guards – he longed to return his family to a normal, peaceful life. And Ireland, he had explained to Maria, was a neutral country, and though they weren't a very religious family, the idea of a Catholic state was appealing.

Sandor was jealous of Maria having her parents with her, the Novaks had remained intact, they had left as a family and had arrived in Ireland as a family hoping to continue their life here.

It had been a couple of weeks since Sandor had sent letters containing a cryptic message, prearranged with his father, to an American radio station which broadcasted into Eastern Europe. Late one night Sandor heard the message being read out among others by the presenter of Radio Free Europe while sitting in the recreational hut. *The Three Musketeers Have Arrived...A Baker's Dozen Is In The Oven...Green, White and Red is Red, White and Blue;* messages whose meaning was only known to a select few as families, separated by the Iron Curtain, tried to inform loved ones of their situation.

When Sandor's message *The Butterflies of Budapest Have Arrived* was read out, he imagined his parents sitting in their apartment, listening to the radio, their separation from their children now complete, this message carrying the indubitable fact that they had left Hungary and were not returning. And when the broadcast ended and the radio was switched off, in the quiet of the recreational hut, Sandor started wondering about the word *arrived*.

Yes, they had arrived and were no longer running across borders or staying in an Austrian camp hoping for a country to grant them asylum. Sandor couldn't deny the shelter which they had been given or the food which they ate; nor could he deny the generosity of the Irish people, the charity which financed the camp or the decency of people like the Murphy family.

As they'd left Budapest in a hurry, Sandor hadn't given their final destination much thought until they had reached Camp Eisenstadt. As far as he was concerned, they were heading for the West, and although Sandor didn't think that the West was a cohesive collection of bountiful countries where wealth was plentiful and material comfort unavoidable, he had thought that the western world which he'd discover would be more advanced than the Soviet bloc which he'd left. He had only seen a fraction of Ireland: Shannon Airport, parts of Limerick and a trip to County Kerry. Sandor couldn't claim to know the country, but his impression thus far was mixed. Perhaps it was the darkness of Knockalisheen Camp, the chilly nights and the damp days spent beneath perpetual cloud. Or the run-down parts of Limerick, the crumbling buildings, the old cars and the ill health which he'd seen on some of the faces of young and old alike.

The Butterflies of Budapest Have Arrived…

Sandor didn't want to judge Ireland on what little he'd seen of it, yet he couldn't help thinking that the place was somehow incomplete, that it didn't correspond to his idea of the West.

Sandor started to worry about his decision to come to Ireland. This sense of anxiety was painful, omnipotent. Any optimism he had felt was eroded. It was an emotional transaction, the exchange of expectation for disquiet. Leaving Budapest, crossing the border, the limbo of Eisenstadt and the quarantine in Knockalisheen, events which had distracted him from the essence of what he was doing: leaving one country for another. But now that he had arrived in another country, instead of feeling happy and relieved, Sandor started to worry about his choice. He felt a long way from home, from what he knew best and from what was familiar. After a couple of weeks in Ireland, Sandor felt like a man bled from the chamber city of Budapest on the Danubian vein.

CHAPTER SEVEN

It didn't take long for the five hundred and thirty refugees perched on top of a hill in County Clare to realise that Ireland was not the country of their dreams. By January 1957 the inhabitants of Knockalisheen Camp had become disillusioned by the lack of employment. Without work there wasn't a chance of getting out of the camp, a place which the Irish Red Cross had a budget for for three years. The idea of spending that amount of time in wooden huts in a remote part of Ireland surrounded by fields intensified feelings of abandonment and created, in some, a desire to protest against their situation.

It was not just statistics which Sandor Lovas and Josef Horvath had learned from others about immigration, but also the anecdotal evidence which the hundreds of refugees experienced when they left the camp, walked down to Limerick, enquired in shops, factories, hotels and garages. Others pawned their valuables for cash to get to Dublin, Cork and Galway, but these cities also lacked employment. Sandor had never thought that fleeing Hungary for the West was going to be easy, but he had assumed the following: when a country offered you asylum, it had *asylum* to offer. But how could Ireland offer him asylum when forty thousand people had already left due to unemployment in the past year?

Sandor had fled a country whose people were in exodus. Statistics were coming out of Hungary about the tens of thousands of people, some estimates were as high as two hundred thousand, now fleeing. But Hungary, reasoned Sandor, had an excuse. It had a failed uprising.

Still: Sandor felt a desire to better his situation, he felt responsible for his own actions, self-pity and depression were of little use when establishing yourself in a new country and so he became determined to get a job. After two weeks of walking the streets of Limerick he saw an advertisement in the paper. Although it wasn't a job advertisement, it concerned his trade: *Buckley Engineering Limited – Specialists in Machine Parts – Suppliers of Engineers' Tools.* Lucia, the plump Hungarian interpreter, agreed to accompany him to the factory and called the owner, Gerry Buckley, to arrange a meeting.

∾

In the camp one hut was reserved for donated clothes, bags of apparel sorted into piles for men, women and children. The smell of laundered clothes was as sharp as the odour of bleach which was used to clean the bathrooms. Sandor, a tall man of six-foot three, wasn't surprised that few items fitted him. Only two pairs of grey trousers were his size, a tag on the inside pocket referencing a Dublin tailor. He matched a jacket to make a suit and found a shirt and tie. He also found socks and a pair of leather shoes. There was a bag of underwear, clean smelling and ironed, but the idea of wearing them disgusted him, and so every second day he washed one of the three pairs which he brought from Budapest.

Sandor and Lucia left the camp and drove through Limerick towards the Shannon Estuary and to the far side of the city. Lucia said that Gerry Buckley employed many people, his was one of the busiest – if not the busiest – engineering company in Limerick, "You're lucky that he's willing to talk to you," her voice boomed above the car engine. It was the first time Sandor had been in a car since travelling back with John Murphy from County Kerry, he enjoyed speeding through Limerick, a place he was now used to walking around.

They parked outside Buckley Engineering. A sign pointing to the reception was pinned to a wall. Inside a woman asked their names and told them to wait. Gerry Buckley came out to meet them, a heavy-set man in dirty blue overalls and a clean shirt underneath. His moustache was tinged with amber, the colour of the hair on his head.

"Would you like a drink?" he asked.

They requested coffee. Gerry passed their request on to his secretary as they entered his office which overlooked the factory floor. Gerry sat behind his desk. "So tell me," he asked Lucia, "what is Sandor's English like?"

She replied, "Talk slowly and I'll translate from time to time. He understands more than he can speak."

"Okay." Gerry spoke of his interest in the recent events in Hungary and of how he supported Ireland's decision to help the refugees. Now that Ireland was a member of the United Nations Organisation, it had a moral obligation to help those who were less well off and in need of humanitarian aid, "You don't have to be a Christian to know that. There are some people in this country who are against the Hungarians coming, they say that we should look after our own before others and that there are enough people on this island who are in need, but I think that as a nation standing alongside others in the world, it is our duty to help those who are less fortunate. No matter how poor you are, there is always someone poorer."

Gerry's secretary carried a tray into the office. Outside you could hear the sound of welding. Gerry explained that he was involved in local politics and had donated money to the Help Hungary Committee, "But giving money is one thing. I think that it's more important that people can look after themselves."

Gerry asked Sandor about his qualifications. He spoke of his college education and the Budapest factory where he'd worked which manufactured engine parts for the aviation sector. Lucia spent five minutes translating this information. Gerry nodded his head, rubbing the amber reaches of his moustache, ensuring the biscuit crumbs were removed.

Then Gerry talked about his company. Presently they were working for a shipping firm which operated out of the Shannon Estuary. Also, farmers used him to manufacture machine parts. Sandor and Lucia were given a tour of the factory. Gerry rushed through the plant firing sentence off after sentence for translation. He was instinctively aware of obstacles in the way, his arm shielding Sandor and Lucia when passing machines.

Afterwards Gerry told Sandor to call him in ten days' time, "I might have something for you."

Sandor became filled with ambition. He imagined being able to work in Ireland, living in a nice apartment, having a few material possessions. When he considered his social class he imagined himself neither at the top or the bottom, but in the middle, where you had to work hard but the labour wasn't menial. He had seen the drudgery of the working classes in factories in Budapest, it wasn't a noble existence, and he was glad that his father had encouraged his career by helping him through university.

When paint arrived from the Irish Red Cross Sandor organised for their hut to be stripped of their belongings early one morning and for sheets to be draped over beds. Apart from Anna Varga, who was minding baby Gábor, all the occupants worked on the hut, sanding down the wooden walls; and when the winter sun shone its light became speckled with dust banished from the wood, and particles were suspended in the haze like hordes of insects floating dead in water. All windows were pushed open, the potbellied stove was lit and, by lunchtime, the yellow boards had turned a clean shade of white.

~

Despite Ireland's economic situation, Sandor was comforted by one aspect of Irish life, politically it was free. After he had been tortured, Sandor hadn't felt safe in Budapest as he was aware that the ÁVO could pick him up at any time and for any reason. He'd only been tortured once but it was enough for him to fear the state; but this feeling had been left in Hungary, as regardless of Ireland's economics, it was not a place of fear.

And so Sandor embraced this sense of liberty by organising a meeting in the recreational hut to find out what other refugees thought of Ireland, especially with regard to the confusion over the status of the camp, whether it was for transit or resettlement. He liked the idea of being the camp representative, a position that had yet to be filled, and even if the job wasn't paid, it was bound to have some benefits.

A large crowd gathered, Sandor stood at the front of the room. His first question concerned people's motivation for coming to Ireland.

Some spoke of their desire to get out of Austria as quickly as possible, they didn't want to spend winter in a refugee camp which was getting more crowded every day.

One man said, "We had heard that ten thousand refugees a day were flooding out of Hungary. How could we expect any help with so many people?"

Another thought that they were going to a transit camp in Ireland only to be moved on to Canada or the USA, "We believed that we'd be getting out quickly, but the Red Cross haven't told us anything. I thought that we'd be gone within two weeks, but now they are saying that we could be here for three years."

Sandor asked for a show of hands regarding those who had believed that they were going to a transit camp.

The majority of people raised their hands.

He asked, "And what did you expect to do here in the meantime?"

A woman replied, "I thought that I'd be given work and decent accommodation. I didn't expect to be stuck in a hut in worse conditions than in Austria."

Another woman agreed, "I remember being told that we'd be in an Irish camp for twelve days and then transferred to jobs and houses."

Sandor asked, "How many wanted to come to Ireland to settle?" A number of people raised their hands. One person adding, "I always liked the idea of Ireland, I always wanted to visit it. That's why I came. But what do some people expect? Instant riches? Anyway, what's the alternative?"

A man replied, "The alternative is that if the Irish Red Cross doesn't find us work, we'll have to leave the country anyway."

Sandor questioned the man, "Did you expect the Irish Red Cross to find you work?"

"Yes."

"What about looking for it yourself?"

"It's hard when I don't speak the language."

Sandor replied, "But you have to learn the language."

"But there aren't enough teachers or translators to help with the basic things: reading job notices, applications or preparing for interviews."

Sandor noticed Peter Varga raising his hand, "I am worried about our child. He might not be getting the correct vitamins or food."

Another said, "And schooling. Our children's lives are wasting away. They need to start attending school."

More voices were raised on this subject, "I agree with the last speaker, I have young children and I am worried about food. An adult diet can vary from time to time, but not a child's. I don't like the food they are feeding us. We need more green vegetables. As for schools, our children have been out of education for months and they need to go back as soon as possible."

Finally Sandor asked, "What about clothing?"

A woman said, "While we are getting clothes for ourselves, the better items are being siphoned off by the Irish. Some Christmas presents meant for us never actually got to us."

Another voice agreed, adding, "The Red Cross is not keeping us informed. We just want to be treated like human beings. If it's good or bad news, they should just tell us. At the moment they're not being helpful. We feel like we've been abandoned and left in the middle of nowhere."

∽

One Sunday morning, Sandor attended mass with Maria Novak. Father Mikes asked to pray for the Bishop of Killaloe as he'd donated six thousand pounds from his diocesan collection to the camp. Then he spoke about Austria, about the tens of thousands of refugees who had rushed over her border, and how she had given sanctuary to these Hungarians in their time of need. Austria, Hungary's old foe, didn't turn people back; in fact, it encouraged them to come even as the Russians tried to seal the border. Father Mikes spoke of six hundred and thirty eight refugees who had survived a recent snow storm and managed to cross the border safely. He believed that they'd be among the last to leave, to get out of the country in one piece, as the weather was appalling and the Russians were now in full control of the country. He asked his congregation to pray for those captured by the Russians trying to leave Hungary.

Continuing, Father Mikes said, "Let us pray for Cardinal Mindszenty. During the uprising he was freed from a communist jail after serving eight years on false charges. But now he is in exile with the delegation of the United States of America in Budapest. Recently he said that he was touched by the support of freedom-loving nations around the world, nations which, these days, are more and more dependent on each other. He said that the cultural world had unanimously supported the uprising and this was a much greater force than we possess as Hungary is only a small country.

"All over Ireland mass was being said for Cardinal Mindszenty, and The Irish Catholic newspaper believes that the heroic Primate of Hungary would be welcome to stay in Ireland if he left Budapest. In our prayers please think of Cardinal Mindszenty as he is a mighty weapon in our spiritual armoury."

Sandor remained seated as people queued for communion. The chapel was full, perhaps one hundred people in attendance. In one pew three generations sat together, elderly grandparents, their children and grandchild. Just below the alter Sandor could see the rotund shape of Peter Varga lifting up his bulky self, standing in line for communion while his wife Anna held baby Gábor in her arms. Sandor was impressed with the behaviour of his godchild, not a sound from his mouth, the quietest baby in the chapel, far quieter than some of the older children whose shrill voices bounced off the wooden walls.

That evening the camp experienced another electricity failure and so Sandor and Maria went to Limerick, and before they saw the river Shannon, they smelled it, an odour reminiscent of the Danube. At times that river stank too, effluent wafting slowly in the air, and like a bumbling swarm of bees, infesting the tall, breathy rooms of Sandor's apartment. And then the Danube would surge onwards like a great grey whale soiled by Budapest's smoke belching industry and residential sewers.

Arriving at the cinema, Sandor bought tickets for Othello, starring Orson Welles. They knew the story and weren't too dependent on language. Towards the end of the film Sandor lent towards Maria, careful not to distract the others seated around them, and in a whispering, conspiratorial voice he sought her opinion of Othello. Beneath the white, smoky light of the projector she smiled at him, and pointed a thin, hushed finger towards her mouth.

Afterwards rain quickened their return journey and within forty-five minutes they were home, a silent nod to the gardaí stationed beside the *STOP* sign. Maria lived in a hut near the entrance of the camp, and after talking for a few minutes, she kissed him on the cheek, they both smiled at each other and said, "Good night."

A few minutes later Sandor stood outside his hut smoking his last cigarette of the day, then a trip to the toilet, and afterwards, he entered his hut which was full of slumbering bodies, little Gábor sleeping peacefully beside his mother, the smell of burning wood pinched Sandor's eyes as he passed the stove. And alone in bed, he wished he could cross the camp to sleep with Maria and experience the simple pleasure of waking up beside her.

It was late afternoon. When Sandor entered his hut he could tell that Peter and Anna were having an argument. It wasn't something which he'd heard but how they reacted to his entrance; Anna looked up at him, baby Gábor in her arms, while Peter glanced over from beside the stove. Sandor wished that he'd stayed in the recreational hut. Crossing the hut quickly, he drew the curtains around his bed. Anna uttered some words. Peter seemed to agree with her. Baby Gábor started coughing. Peter offered to help with the child. Anna told him to stay where he was. Peter replied, "I'm only trying to help." The hut went quiet for a moment. Then the rustle of a leather coat, the noise of shoes, the door opening, closing.

Sandor wondered who had left the hut, but then Peter started talking, "Christ! Sorry about this, Sandor. She's so fucking...I don't know...unfair?" Peter was walking up and down the hut, his bulk weighing heavily on the floorboards.

Sandor opened the curtains, sat on the end of his bed. Bending down he picked up dirty clothes off the floor. Peter continued talking, "She thinks it's me. She thinks that it's my fault that I can't get a job. She finds it hard to believe that there isn't one single job out there," his arm flung towards the window, "for me."

Sandor replied, "Give it time. What else can you do?"

"That's what I keep saying to her. But she wants everything now. If we didn't have the baby she wouldn't be like this. She was never so anxious about things before. That's what happens when they become mothers." Peter was now sitting on a chair beside the stove. Its door was open and he was poking the embers with a small shovel. Sadness was a force which surrounded him. It was like the even heat from the fire. His hair was uncombed, his forehead smudged with coal dust. Sandor suggested that they go for a walk, get out of the hut, maybe get a drink in Limerick. Peter agreed. An hour later they were outside a pub. It had started to rain.

∽

A few days later Sandor was back in Limerick with Kristina, she was talking about school: when would it start? where was the school? would there be boys or just girls in her class? As he couldn't answer these questions he suggested that she enjoy her time off, it was inevitable that she'd be back in school soon, and once she was, she'd only be looking forward to her time off anyway.

As it was a sunny day Kristina asked him why he hadn't taken his camera. He shrugged and thought of the times they'd spent walking together when she was younger, and how he'd make her wait for the correct lighting conditions in the summer heat or the cold winter months, and during the walks she had showed an interest in photography, always asking about the camera, why he was waiting for the sun or for clouds to cover the sky.

They were seated on a bench opposite the Shannon. Sandor was awed by the idea of the ocean and the American continent – from Alaska to Argentina – had become an awareness in his mind like never before, to think that water lapping against Limerick could have once touched that expanse.

As Kristina continued talking about photography, Sandor recognised a man walking towards them. He had familiar features, a pudginess to his chin and cheeks and a yellow, but not an unhealthy, tone to his skin. His dark hair was neatly cut though dishevelled by wind and was thinning out on his forehead. He wore a black suit. He was tall, thin and walked with purpose, bullying the ground with his feet. When he greeted Sandor in Hungarian he recognised him as the doctor who had administered pills for his stomach on his first day in Ireland. His name was Dr Pader and he was in his late twenties.

After a few minutes of small talk, the doctor pointed to a building across the river, an apartment which he'd moved into with his wife and child. He asked them over for a drink and they walked to the apartment, from which there was a view of the Shannon. Dr Pader explained how they found their home, "After arriving here, Martha, my wife, collapsed from exhaustion and went to hospital. There she was treated by a doctor, who, after hearing that she was married to a doctor, offered us work in a research laboratory which is part of a private hospital in Limerick. And then the same doctor organised this apartment to rent." Dr Pader laughed, "My wife goes into hospital suffering from exhaustion and comes out with an apartment and jobs for both of us."

Sandor saw in Kristina's eyes a respect for the apartment, the large, clean and warm rooms, freshly painted but empty, apart from a few medical items on the table and two medical volumes on the bookcase. After unbuttoning her coat and placing it on the back of a chair, she sat on a small but firm couch, her curious fingers feeling the material. Dr Pader poured her a glass of lemonade, on a small saucer he placed chocolate biscuits, and he apologised for the poor taste of the coffee in advance.

Sandor asked, "Are you looking for work as a doctor?"

"I have to resit some exams in order to practice medicine here and that'll take about six months."

"Will you do the exams through English?"

"Yes. I have to, I have no choice. I have to learn the language first and then sit the exams." Sandor wondered if he would have to sit examinations in order to prove his qualification as a mechanical engineer. When he left Budapest he hadn't brought any documents to show where he had studied. Sandor sipped coffee which was a little too hot on his lips and asked, "Are you not worried about sitting exams in English?"

"I have no choice. I wanted to come here and work as a doctor and so I must sit the exams. Ireland has no idea of my medical qualification; they don't know anything about me, nothing at all." And with an arrogance to his voice, "You make serious decisions being a doctor. It's not like sweeping the road."

Soon the conversation turned to the fighting in Budapest. Dr Pader spoke of how he had missed most of the conflict as he had been working in the north of the country. "Last year I was transferred to the Czechoslovakian border, by the mountains. We spent the last eight months in the countryside." He looked at Kristina, "You might think that the huts are bad in Knockalisheen Camp, but you should have seen where we were living. There was no electricity in our village, and I had to look after two other villages, but not by car, motorbike or bike, but by horse. I spent the winter on horseback, and the nights sleeping beneath the biggest duvets you've ever seen."

Kristina answered, "No electricity?"

"Candles and open fires. We were so far away from Budapest that nobody bothered us. You wouldn't think that the modern world existed. We lived like kings, the patients giving us mountains of food."

After offering Sandor a cigarette he continued, "The ironic thing is that we, politically speaking, were almost beyond the control of the government as we were too far from Budapest and the village was so small, but the communal ideal was being played out in front of our eyes. People shared their food, nobody starved, but the difference was that we all knew our place. I was the doctor; the farmer was the farmer; and the peasant was the peasant."

Dr Pader said that he'd spent two days in Budapest during the uprising, his elderly father had died a natural death and they attended the funeral. Afterwards they jumped on a train, "And left my country. When I say *my country* I mean my mother's country. My father was a Serb, from Sarajevo, he was born a few streets away from where Franz Ferdinand was shot. And if you think about it, if that hadn't happened, we wouldn't be sitting here in this apartment overlooking the Shannon."

Dr Pader asked if they wanted another drink, they declined and he carried the empty cups and saucers to the sink. On the coffee table The Limerick Leader was open, in pencil words had been underlined, their translation defined in the margin.

"Kristina," Dr Pader's voice boomed from the kitchen. "How old are you? Eleven, twelve?"

"Eleven."

"The same age as my daughter. Would you like to come to Sinbad the Sailor with us?"

Kristina replied, "Yes, thank you. What's her name?"

Dr Pader returned to the living room, his wet hands holding a towel, "I decided the other day that from now on I'm going to call my daughter by the English translation of her name, which is Dawn. There are two types of immigrants: those who integrate and those who don't. I want to be the former." And ruffling Kristina's hair with his hand he said, "Be here on Saturday afternoon, no later than twelve."

CHAPTER EIGHT

Not everybody had to leave the camp in search of work. One day in the bad tempered month of January a businessman arrived in a van packed full of boxes. The boxes contained beads for the manufacturing of necklaces. They were carried into the recreational hut and stored in a corner. The owner of these boxes was an Austrian man who ran a company in Ennis, and when speaking to his female recruits, he addressed them in German, a language which most people understood to a certain degree.

He was adamant that the necklaces were of little value. "These are not expensive items of jewellery. The coloured beads have no value on their own and the individual necklaces are for the lower end of the jewellery market."

His labour instructions were simple, "Count out a specific amount of beads per necklace and follow a pattern depending on which necklace you are making. All patterns are explained on sheets of paper and the quantities of the beads too."

Anybody interested in making necklaces could work for him in the camp, and once a week he'd call on Knockalisheen to collect the finished articles and pay his workers.

Eva volunteered for the work. Although she had been a teacher in Budapest, due to her lack of English and the absence of work in Ireland, her confidence in her employment prospects were low. And she was becoming bored in the camp. She complained to Sandor, "What do we do all day? Sit around waiting for our meals, try to learn English or entertain our children who should be in school."

Maria Novak also started working for the Austrian, or the bead-man as he became known, and her reasons for doing so were the same as everybody else: lack of money and boredom. And so Eva and Maria joined the many women sitting on the floor on pillows brought from their huts, stringing beads together to the sound of music playing on a crackling speaker in the recreational hut.

Maria was glad to work for the bead-man as she didn't want to work for her father. Mr Novak was a carpenter, a master tradesman who honed his trade restoring antique furniture after the war. He created a small workshop at the back of his Knockalisheen hut, behind a curtain separating it from the inhabitants. He had only a couple of tools, second-hand ones which he'd bought in Limerick and he started creating small, ornamental objects, little holders for playing cards, small boxes for jewellery or other precious items, all of them polished and engraved with delicate patterns. Maria's father had asked her to walk door to door with him around Limerick to sell them, the idea being that a pretty, young woman would make a better salesman than him, but she'd declined. She would feel embarrassed standing on somebody's doorstep trying to sell his goods with her faltering, pathetic English, nor did she like the idea of wandering the city streets in the cold, dreary weather.

Although making cheap necklaces wasn't an example of Hungarian craftsmanship, it was encouraged by McManus, as he was interested in the Irish Folklore Commission and their plans for Knockalisheen Camp. It was envisioned that the talent in the camp, the tradesmen and skilled artisans, would create a bustling arts and crafts community producing goods reflecting their European origins which wouldn't compete with Irish goods already on the market. Space had already been reserved in Brown Thomas, a department store in Dublin, which would premiere the first of many such exhibitions. A notice had been hung in the recreational hut calling on artists to start working on their portfolios. On hearing that Sandor was interested in photography and had photographs in The Irish Press, McManus asked him to participate.

But Sandor was more interested in the meeting which he'd organised the other day when refugees had voiced their grievances about camp life. McManus insisted on having tea and coffee before any discussion took place, and a table was laid with cups and saucers, a plate of biscuits, a jug of water, sugar. Sandor ran through the items which the refugees had been concerned about. Lucia acted as translator, and Horvath was also in attendance. As Lucia translated she seemed disappointed by some of the comments which were being made. Regarding the quality of the food, she asked Sandor repeatedly if some people had not been exaggerating, "There is nothing wrong with the food, there's more than enough to eat and there's a good kitchen where it can be prepared by yourselves."

But Sandor said that it was a concern, especially among expectant mothers and parents of infants or small children.

When Lucia translated this point for McManus, his face portrayed a similar surprise, and pouring more tea into his cup, he exclaimed, "The food is good and plentiful!"

Then Sandor asked about the status of the camp, "In Austria many people believed that they were going to a transit camp in Ireland and that they'd be moving on to another country – America or Canada – soon after their arrival. But this doesn't seem to be the case."

McManus acknowledged that confusion had arisen but he didn't know why, "But as far as the Irish Red Cross is concerned, the money which has been donated by the Irish people was to allow one thousand Hungarian refugees to settle in Ireland. The Irish Red Cross was very specific about the amount of money needed per person for this resettlement and we have sufficient funds to last three years. This is the position of the Irish Red Cross, although it has been decided to admit only five hundred and thirty refugees and not the entire one thousand as initially planned."

Sandor asked, "Was the Irish Red Cross solely responsible for bringing the refugees to Ireland?"

"The Irish Red Cross collected the money and is linked to the International Red Cross, but the decision to bring refugees here was made by the Irish Government as only they can determine who gets asylum."

Regarding the employment of the refugees, it was explained to Sandor that the Irish Red Cross and various governmental departments were in consultation with trade unions and employers in order to secure work. Ireland had very high unemployment and it was important that the two hundred and fifty or so Hungarians able to work (around half of the refugees were children) would not upset the employment market. McManus thought that the Irish Folklore Commission had the right idea by encouraging the manufacturing of traditional crafts in the camp which could serve as a blueprint for a factory at a later date. But he understood that not every worker was a tradesman. Some had worked in banks, or like Sandor, in heavy industry. Horvath was a baker. Eva was a teacher. Maria was a nurse. Peter Varga had worked in a paint factory. Skills like these did not conform to the ambitions of the Irish Folklore Commission and they'd have to compete with Irish jobs, regardless of unemployment levels.

And these unemployment levels were huge. Journalist Tommy Gallagher explained to Sandor that, apart from the war years, 1956 was the worst year in the economic history of Ireland since the foundation of the state. Ireland had very few jobs, and the ones it had were well protected. This fact, Gallagher explained, could not be changed by the Irish Red Cross, an organisation which usually just helped those in distress such as the victims of floods or violent storms. Sandor informed Gallagher about the meeting which he had organised with the refugees, and through Lucia, told him of the concerns which they had, from the health and welfare of their children to unemployment. Gallagher wrote an article about these concerns, quoting Sandor at length. A few days later he arrived at the camp with the newspaper that contained the piece, and the pictures which Sandor had asked him to develop.

This time the pictures were of his trip to County Kerry. Two photographs were enlarged: one of the Murphy family after dinner, and the other was the view from the mountain climbed on Christmas morning. It took a few seconds for Sandor's initial, enthusiastic impression of his photographs to be reduced to disappointment. He always saw the errors, how the shot could have been made better by composition, lighting, printing or the ineffable quality which makes a great picture. Still: the pictures were good enough to be sent to John Murphy with a thank-you note for their hospitality.

Like in Budapest, Kristina joined Sandor on his photographic expeditions around Limerick. They'd leave the camp walking towards the city, taking pictures of the countryside, farmhouses and animals on the way. But it was the city which always entertained Sandor's eye. Whether surreptitiously taking portraits of people or the grand design and symmetry of Georgian buildings, he enjoyed the novelty of the subject matter as Ireland was the only country he'd visited outside Hungary. When they'd rest he'd point the camera at Kristina and she'd pretend he didn't exist as most of her eleven years had been spent with the giant snake eye of a lens staring at her. Sandor would encourage her to smile as it showed her age, for when her unsmiling face was isolated, when the wind blew her long, dark hair off her forehead, she appeared a few years older. As they wandered around the city, she'd discuss everything and anything with her uncle, oscillating between topics gleaned from her childhood years to the recent attempts at maturity procured from her mother.

Over the years there were occasions when Kristina's overeager fingers would reach for his camera, pawing the lens, and he'd have to get out his cloth, gently mist up the glass with his breath, polish its delicate surface, but now Sandor felt that she was old enough to hold the camera and take pictures herself. She snapped a picture from Thomond Bridge of Saint John's Castle across the water, and on the quays she took a picture of Smith's Garage, its large forecourt with a couple of petrol pumps out front. Sandor inspected the camera settings and waited while she took the picture, advising her to crop out the buildings behind it, the backs of terraces, a couple of crumbling structures.

A week later, when Gallagher gave Sandor an envelope containing his developed photographs, the journalist became very excited about the one of Smith's Garage, "If I were you, I'd go down to the garage and sell it to him. It'll look great on his wall. No doubt about it, he'd buy it."

So taking this advice, Sandor and Kristina returned to Limerick. In his hand he held the photograph. "Pretend that you're my daughter," Sandor instructed as they walked across the road. The forecourt was empty of cars and inside a man sat behind a desk reading a paper and smoking a pipe. He looked at Sandor, then looked at the forecourt.

Sandor smiled, "Hello, sir," and he began a speech which he'd prepared earlier, but the difference between reciting it in his hut and in reality was felt in the damp patches of sweat beneath his armpits and on his back. For a minute Sandor spoke about the photograph; opening the envelope with enthusiasm; watching as curiosity visited the man's face; a couple of words as Sandor placed the picture on the table; and advice not to touch the actual photograph for fear of fingerprints.

When Sandor finished his speech he felt vulnerable. While walking to Limerick, he had tried to predict how the man would react, the likeliest of comments and conversation which might ensue, but now he felt the full wash of intimidation.

The man complimented Kristina on the picture. Although she didn't know what he was saying, she smiled, lifting her wintry cheeks into the warm air of the garage. Placing his pipe down, the man studied the photograph as though it were an object in a glass case. He requested permission to hold it and angled it towards the light bulb hanging from the centre of the room, "It's an excellent picture. Leave it with me."

Sandor was confused. Slowly the man explained that he'd show it to Mr Smith, the proprietor of the garage, "Come back at lunchtime."

For the next two hours they walked around Limerick photographing business premises: Hayes Brothers Limited on Davis Street and Moloney's Garage on the Dublin Road, among others. Sandor preferred taking pictures of garages and stand-alone businesses rather than terrace shops, as they filled the lens without interruption from other buildings.

At lunchtime they went back to the garage. A different

man was behind the desk. He was young, in his early twenties. Sandor introduced himself and pointed to the picture which was on a shelf behind the counter. The man explained that Mr Smith was his father and that he wouldn't be back in the garage for two days, "I was on the phone to him and he knows about the picture. He'll see you then."

Two days later Sandor returned to the garage alone. Outside he cupped his hand in front of his mouth to check for bad breath. Casually he strolled into the garage. He didn't recognise the person behind the desk. "Mr Smith?" The man smiled. Above the desk on the shelf was the photograph. It had been framed. Mr Smith paid the amount which Sandor asked for, and as he handed over the money, he joked, "You're the first person in to me today and you're taking money!"

∞

Father Mikes had a loud voice. It was full of clear sentences, a natural public speaker, confident and forceful. Lying on his bed Sandor heard the priest talking outside, his voice seemed to form part of the architecture of the hut, like a central beam running the length of the structure. Sandor, content to remain behind the curtains drawn around his bed, didn't greet Father Mikes, but Peter and Anna Varga were happy to show the priest baby Gábor.

"See how he has changed, Father," enthused Anna as Peter suggested he go to the kitchen hut to get a drink. Father Mikes wasn't interested in coffee, but delighted in the good health of Gábor, "He's growing quickly."

Sandor heard a chair being positioned near the stove. The priest sat down. Sandor didn't hear him remove his jacket. That day the hut wasn't cold, but a little drafty. Father Mikes recalled the baptism with great joy, "I've baptised three other children since Gábor, but his will always be special as he was the first. I've also baptised a couple of adults and have a few weddings planned."

"Weddings?" asked Anna, "People who have met in the camp?"

"No," explained Father Mikes. "Couples who had married in registry offices back in Hungary. People who want proper weddings, a religious service. I hope you don't mind me asking, but were you married in a church?"

Peter spoke of their marriage. It was over a year ago and took place in a registry office in Budapest. He said, "We had to get married there. However, I know some people who married in a church but they lived in the middle of nowhere, the countryside, where the authorities turned a blind eye."

Father Mikes said, "Well, you won't have that problem here. Ireland is a Catholic country. It has also been very supportive of Hungary. When Cardinal Mindszenty was imprisoned, when the communists sent him to jail on the preposterous charges of espionage and currency smuggling among others, one hundred and forty thousand people demonstrated in Dublin. And obviously, the Irish have been very supportive since the uprising. You should bear in mind that it was the Catholic faith of Hungary which encouraged Ireland to give you asylum, the idea that a small Catholic country was being brutally dominated by the Russians. And because of this faith, you are free to marry in a church. In fact, it's essential. You must understand that by Irish standards, a marriage in a registry office isn't a proper marriage."

Anna asked, "And in what church are couples actually getting married?"

"Here, in the chapel in Knockalisheen."

"And do they have to get married in the camp?"

Father Mikes replied, "Because I am the camp chaplain, the camp chapel is my church. All of the religious ceremonies which I perform are in that chapel. Tell me, when are you considering getting married properly?"

Peter replied, "Soon."

Father Mikes asked, "You don't have a date?"

Anna's reply was unsure, "Not exactly."

"What's stopping you?"

"It's to do with the location," replied Anna. "When I have dreamed of a church wedding, I never imagined it taking place in a refugee camp. I always thought that it would be in a lovely old church in a pretty setting and afterwards we'd have a large reception with lots of friends and family. Also Father, you might think that I'm being too vain, but we don't have any cash to buy a wedding dress. What sort of wedding would it be if I didn't even have a dress?"

Father Mikes coughed, then continued, "Anna, if I were you I wouldn't be worried about a wedding dress. I'd be more worried about your son. You have a child born outside religious wedlock. And while that might be acceptable under communism, it's not acceptable here in Ireland. While people won't say anything to you here in this camp, they will once you leave it. Believe me, it will have repercussions. They will think of Gábor as a bastard. You must take my advice, 'When in Rome, do as the Romans do,' and get married as soon as possible."

Situated on the road to Limerick City, just before a bridge crossed the railway tracks, after a few bends sheltered from the sky by the heavy growth of trees, a plaque, not unlike a gravestone, rose out of the ground. On its heavy, cast iron front it noted a border, the point where County Clare ended and County Limerick began. Knockalisheen Camp was ten minutes north of this border. Limerick, forty minutes away by foot, was still an urban mass shielded from sight by rolling hills.

A rise in temperature melted frost, the thin sheets of ice which covered puddles became cracked with lines like those on Sandor's hands seeking warmth in his coat pockets. This early February promise of spring allowed the scent of damp bushes and decayed foliage composted by the roadside to waft upwards from the icy earth towards the yellow streaks of evening sky.

Sandor and Maria crossed into County Limerick. She suggested that they sit on the railway bridge and share a cigarette. As the sky darkened and the temperature dropped, he moved closer to her, their arms wrapped around each other for heat as much as intimacy. She was beginning to get a cold. Her upturned nose had a slight snivel. "I shouldn't really be smoking," she said flicking a butt on to the railway tracks. Soon after that they started kissing, their cold lips sweetened by smoke, and a warmth was released in Sandor's body, starting in his groin and moving upwards to his chest and heart. Sandor imagined sneaking down to the railway track, sheltering beneath the bridge, there was enough space either side in case a train came, and the layers of winter clothing which she was wearing, the heavy jacket, hat, scarf, jumper would be partly removed, and then her long woollen dress would be pushed upwards over her thighs, the imprint of the stone wall like a stencil on her flesh, and he'd drop to his knees to sink his head into her.

While sharing another cigarette she spoke optimistically of the future. Despite the camp and its problems, she'd rather be in Ireland than in Budapest. "What could be worse than being there now? Could you imagine the atmosphere, the failure of everything, the resentment of people going back to their lives and their work and everything being worse than a couple of months or even years ago."

When dark, they returned to the camp, to the recreational hut where Father Mikes had arranged for a projector to be set up. Before they settled into their seats Sandor and Maria went to the shop across the road from the camp and bought popcorn and chocolate. Some refugees were given credit in the shop, the owner's business having improved since they had come to the camp and the Irish Red Cross started paying out allowances.

Father Mikes spoke briefly about Singing in the Rain, how it was family viewing, and how, as the equipment and print were old, the quality wasn't too good. Sandor didn't think much of the film. He didn't like dancing and the songs were not to his taste.

When it ended the lights were switched on. Father Mikes, with the help of two others, dissembled the projector and rolled up the screen, and the recreational hut emptied of people apart from Sandor and Maria.

It always annoyed Sandor that he couldn't spend the night with Maria, instead they'd say good night and return to their respective huts, he'd lie in bed listening to the wind, at times gale force, banging unhinged doors and rattling electricity wires. And when the wind calmed, he'd expect to hear sounds from the camp or from the neighbouring fields, but instead he'd hear the blocked-nose breathing of Peter Varga sleeping at the far end of the hut. Sandor's body was too tall for the small blankets and his feet would be sacrificed to the icy air penetrating the wooden walls.

Nearly two weeks later, Sandor and Horvath still hadn't received a response from McManus regarding their meeting. Horvath wanted to leave Ireland as soon as possible, he had no intention of staying in the country and every hour of every day which passed he considered a waste of time. Sandor was also anxious; very few people had got jobs and Knockalisheen was beginning to resemble a village as opposed to a temporary camp. He didn't want to be trapped there for the three years which the Irish Red Cross had budgeted for, and so they came to the following conclusion: if the Irish Red Cross were unable to further their interests – get them jobs or visas – it was probably because they had little power to do so. McManus had said that the Irish Government was ultimately responsible for bringing them into the country and not the Irish Red Cross, and so Sandor figured that an approach to the government was necessary, "What is the Red Cross besides a charitable organisation which depends on the goodwill of people? How could they have power over the government or any influence on employers or trade unions? How can they create jobs or get visas from embassies?"

So one evening Sandor decided that they should organise a trip to Dublin and meet with government officials, and if nobody would speak to them, they'd leave a letter outlining their circumstances.

Horvath agreed and they made plans to go to Dublin. Sandor dictated a letter to him and he detailed in English the points which had been made to McManus, starting with the status of the camp (transit or resettlement) and ending with the lack of Hungarian-English interpreters to assist the refugees. Multiple copies of the letter were drafted as they decided to deliver it to as many government departments as possible. Lucia agreed to drive them to Dublin. Horvath collected money from other refugees to cover petrol expenses. To save money Horvath suggested calling on the Trinity College professor whom he'd stayed with over Christmas, but Sandor thought that it would be too much to ask so they decided to return on the same day.

The morning of their trip Sandor awoke at six to a cold hut. Standing in a vest and underpants he restocked the stove with logs as goose pimples covered his legs. He showered, shaved and dressed in the suit which he'd worn when visiting Gerry Buckley. Few people were in the kitchen. As there were no children, it was quiet. Horvath joined him at seven. They felt confident, powerful. Horvath spoke of a delicatessen in Dublin which stocked European food, salamis and paprika, which he'd discovered during the Christmas holidays, "We should stop there afterwards."

The sound of Lucia's Volkswagen Beetle rattled towards the camp, you could hear her changing gears, and then the calm in the air when the engine was switched off. She spoke to the gardaí who were on duty. A few minutes after eight they left. It was Horvath's first time in Lucia's car and he asked how long she'd had it for?

"Five years."

"A Beetle for five years?"

"Yes."

"And you work full time and your husband is also working."

"Yes."

"You'd think that if you were both working you'd be able to afford a better car." Looking at Horvath in the reflection of the rear-view mirror, Lucia said, "Some of you think too much."

They drove to Limerick and then on to the Dublin Road. Forty minutes later while driving through the countryside they came across a traffic jam. Sandor leant out the window. A sign read *Garda Checkpoint*. When their turn came to speak to the gardaí, Lucia rolled down her window. They were instructed to pull in to the side of the road. Lucia got out of the car. As she spoke to the Garda Superintendent, the other guard put the *Garda Checkpoint* sign into the back of his car. Although Sandor couldn't understand their conversation, from her facial expression he saw that Lucia was annoyed. She returned to the car. She sat in the front seat for a few seconds before speaking.

Sandor asked, "What's the problem?"

"We're being denied permission to go to Dublin. Notice has been served by the Department of Justice. We have to return to the camp, under police escort."

Lucia turned the car. Sandor asked, "Why?"

"I don't know, that's all they said."

"Are we not free to move? Quarantine restrictions have been over for weeks," stated Sandor.

Lucia said, "I know, but that's what they said."

Horvath said, "We should just keep going."

"What would that achieve?" questioned Lucia. "I think it's something to do with McManus."

Sandor thought about McManus's black-rimmed glasses, his salt and pepper beard, "Why would he stop us going to Dublin?"

"You're ignoring him, going over his head," she guessed.

"But how can he stop us moving?" repeated Sandor.

"The Department of Justice has responsibility for the camp," said Lucia. "And they run the police. The Irish Red Cross and the army just administer the camp. The police can do whatever they want to."

Soon they were back in Knockalisheen. Soldiers and gardaí were waiting for them at the entrance. Refugees peered out of their huts, standing on the steps, staring at this gathering of officialdom. Some started walking toward the *STOP* sign. After talking with the officials, Lucia told Sandor, "McManus will see you now."

They were ushered into the same room as before. Sandor told Horvath to keep quiet, not to say anything. "Don't show any anger," he advised, "as it will be used against you." Tea and biscuits were laid out on a table, they were encouraged to help themselves. Sandor, Horvath and Lucia sat down. Minutes later McManus entered the room. Pouring himself a cup of tea he spoke of being in Barringtons Hospital for most of the previous night. Sandor understood snippets of conversation, but waited until Lucia translated it in full. A Hungarian man had spent the last two weeks in hospital with a gangrenous leg, and after much deliberation, it had been amputated. "We're doing everything we can to organise a false leg. It'll be a long time before the poor man adjusts. But it couldn't be helped."

Sitting at the table McManus apologised for what had happened that morning, and speaking through Lucia he said, "I've been thinking about the demands which you spoke of and I feel that they're not representative of all the refugees. I have the impression that your demands are a little extreme, and that's the reason for what happened this morning. We have no problem with refugees making suggestions to us. In fact, it was our idea to establish a camp council to represent any issues which you might have. But we want to ensure that the demands accurately reflect the opinion of the majority of refugees."

Sandor thought about the meeting he had organised, the opinions which he'd heard. And yes: not everybody from the camp had been there, only a limited amount of people, and only a few of them had actually spoken. But the few seemed to reflect the many and the atmosphere was of disappointment.

McManus continued talking to Sandor, "And we're also concerned about you acting as a camp representative when you have not been elected to the position. When we decided that the camp was going to have a representative, we expected that person to be elected by the refugees. While you might have organised a meeting, it doesn't mean that you are the *actual* camp representative. You must be elected by a secret ballot. And only when you're elected as a camp representative can I meet you in that capacity. I apologise if this sounds strange to you as I'm aware that you've come from a communist society and are unfamiliar with democracy, but that's the process."

∽

That evening Sandor explained what had happened to Tommy Gallagher. There was anger in his voice as he tried to form sentences, to ensure that the correct meaning was being translated to Tommy's curious eyes and the swift movement of his pen. At times Sandor stopped attempting to speak English, yelling in Hungarian, "Fucking police! What are we – criminals? Am I a fucking criminal?" Although he knew Gallagher couldn't understand him, it still felt good to yell at an Irishman, to vent his rage at a citizen of this country.

Gallagher waited for Sandor to calm down. He had questions, and some which Sandor could not answer: the location of the Garda checkpoint, the station the police were from. And it took a few minutes for Gallagher to understand one question which Sandor asked, "Can anybody approach the government?"

Gallagher agreed in principle, but added, "You have to be somebody to be anybody, but you're nobody."

CHAPTER NINE

Gerry Buckley's amber moustache. That was what came to Sandor's mind when he phoned him from the camp. On a notepad Sandor had written English lines to help him with the conversation, and when Gerry came on the line, he was patient and helpful, telling Sandor to come down to the engineering plant on Dock Road at nine the next day. In the morning Sandor shaved and dressed smartly but not in his suit. He thought that the walk would take an hour and fifteen minutes, but he arrived in an hour. In his office, Gerry Buckley offered him tea. A small dog sat beneath his desk.

After tea, Sandor followed Gerry around the factory and was introduced to certain people and then they left the premises to visit a customer. Sandor waited in the car as Gerry delivered a box of machine parts. He felt like a child waiting for his father as he looked out over the river. Across the Shannon the land was green and some trees were full of leaves. They spent two hours driving around Limerick. Due to his weight Gerry found it difficult getting in and out of the car, the steering wheel pushing into his fleshy waistline, and when the front seat was relieved of him, the car felt lighter.

Around lunchtime Gerry stopped outside a house, "This is where I live." He introduced his wife. She was rather large and her hair was grey. She wore rings on her fingers. In the kitchen she prepared sandwiches. Sandor was careful not to get crumbs on his shirt. As man and wife spoke to each other, Sandor wondered what they were talking about. Afterwards they returned to the car. Mrs Buckley gave him a parcel which contained a cake. Sandor was surprised, "Thanks." In the car Gerry pointed to the cake and then to his own stomach, "She's terrible." Soon they arrived at the factory. Gerry told Sandor to go home, "And come back in the morning. I'll try to get you on the factory floor. If I can't, you'll come with me in the car."

Feeling confident about his future earnings, Sandor walked slowly through Limerick, inspecting shop windows, making financial calculations: in time he'd buy a suit, a lighter one for the summer. He bought a couple of newspapers. In the bar of The River Hotel he ordered a glass of wine and flicked through The Limerick Leader and The Irish Press; there was an article about Imre Nagy which he found hard to understand. There were also pieces about England, France and Egypt – the Suez Canal Crisis. He understood the word *atomic* and *vice-president* Richard Nixon. After another glass of red wine he indulged the fantasy of staying with Maria in a hotel, sharing a bath, drying each other with towels, and then having undisturbed sex throughout the night and again in the morning. It would be great to get out of the camp even for one night, to wake up in a room on their own, to be away from their claustrophobic huts, the endless talk of others, the lack of privacy. Sandor went to the toilet and in the quiet, clean cubicle he imagined that Maria was finishing her drink in the bar, a glass of white wine, and afterwards they'd slip upstairs to the perfectly heated hotel room. His sexual excitement was urgent, and taking advantage of the empty restroom, he relieved himself quickly.

After paying for his drinks, he gathered his newspapers and Mrs Buckley's cake, and returned to the camp.

In the morning Sandor went to the showers but they were busy. He waited in line as people washed and then shaved in front of a small mirror. He was feeling tired; baby Gábor had been crying during the night. Concerned that he might be late for work, he skipped breakfast and walked quickly to Dock Road. Sandor waited outside Gerry's office for forty minutes. When a man that Sandor recognised from the factory floor exited the office, he was ushered in. Gerry offered him tea and biscuits. Like the previous day Sandor spent the rest of the morning in the car. Gerry wasn't very talkative. They drove to Shannon Airport where a delivery was made, and then back to Gerry's house. His wife wasn't there. An old woman made sandwiches. As she placed ham slices on white bread, her fingers became yellowed with butter. Gerry listened to the radio, when it was switched off the kitchen became silent. After their sandwiches they went back to the plant. Sandor sat in Gerry's office for two hours, drinking tea, eating biscuits and attempting to read a newspaper. In the early afternoon, Gerry returned to his office and told him that he could go home, "Sandor, do you need money?"

Sandor laughed, "Yes." Gerry removed a couple of notes from his wallet and said, "I'll take it out of your wages."

Sandor took the money. Gerry listened patiently as Sandor asked him about working on the factory floor. "You don't like the driving," Gerry joked. "Any day now. We're just trying to make space for you, that's all."

∽

Sandor received a letter from John Murphy, the father of the family whom they'd spent Christmas with in Kerry. Sandor read it slowly. The handwriting was clear, the sentences, short and simple. John liked the photographs. One of them was placed in his Dublin office – *To remind me of the beauty of County Kerry*. In return for the photographs he enclosed two tickets for the opening of an art exhibition in Limerick - *With your eye you'd like it*. John asked about Kristina, if she had started attending school yet, and if she hadn't, he advised Sandor to contact him and he would see what he could do – *I know many people in Limerick*.

Sandor took Eva to the exhibition. She was excited about John Murphy's interest in Kristina's schooling as it was nearly three months since her daughter had attended any classes besides the improvised ones in the camp. Dawn, Dr Pader's daughter, had started attending a school in Limerick. Eva had enquired if Kristina could do likewise but her request was turned down as there weren't enough places. Kristina had wanted to attend the same school as Dawn and was disappointed by the refusal. For Eva, her daughter's education was her main concern while in Knockalisheen, she felt that she could spend time without working in a way that her daughter couldn't do without school, and she felt guilty about the education being denied to her. Anna Varga had told her of a new school opening in nearby Meelick, but that wouldn't be until next September, and by that time Kristina would have been out of school for nearly a year.

Outside the exhibition the windows were covered with condensation. A woman seated behind a desk took their tickets and gave them a programme. The room was packed and smelled of cigar smoke. A waiter carried a tray of drinks. Sandor took a glass of red wine; Eva, white. Another waiter carried a tray of sandwiches. Sandor had two glasses before they started looking at the paintings. It had been a while since he'd attended an exhibition. Eva, who had studied History of Art until she dropped out on becoming pregnant with Kristina, had always liked wandering around galleries, "They're quiet. People aren't encouraged to talk."

It was a small exhibition, they finished quickly and drank more wine. It was the third time Eva had been in Limerick that week. A few days ago she had gone to look at the shops and when it started raining she'd sheltered in a hotel, sitting over a cup of coffee for an hour waiting for the weather to clear.

It was in this hotel that a man who worked there had started talking to her. He was in his early thirties, black hair, slim, he smoked a lot and his face was a sun-shy colour. He introduced himself as Thomas. He knew a few Hungarian words gleaned from newspapers and made a great show of repeating these phrases over and over. The hotel lounge was busy but he was very attentive towards Eva.

The rain stopped around the same time as lunch ended, most people rushed back to their jobs, and Thomas, now free, sat down beside Eva for an undisturbed conversation of sorts. They spoke for an hour. He gave her free coffee and cake. Eva was entertained by him and enjoyed attempting to answer his questions in English. She told him that she had been a teacher in Budapest. They talked about the Hungarian uprising; about crossing the border; about Ireland. On leaving, Thomas asked her to call into the hotel the next time she was in Limerick.

A few days later Eva was in Limerick again and went to the hotel. Thomas, happy to see her, laid a table of coffee and cake and when the crowd petered out he came over and they talked. He seemed to be making more of an effort this time, aware of her trouble understanding him; his accent wasn't as strong and his sentences were simpler, more child-like in their construction. Any slang or colloquiums were removed from his speech. When Eva decided to go home, he offered her a lift in his car. She declined. Fifteen minutes later she was on the Thomond Bridge and the rain started pouring down. She quickened her pace and after five minutes of walking through diaphanous sheets of rain Thomas pulled in beside the footpath in his car. He said that he couldn't let her walk home in such a storm and felt obliged to collect her. Minutes later they were outside the camp. As Eva thanked him for the lift he asked her to go out with him some night. Eva wasn't surprised by this question; she figured as much when he'd come out to collect her. But she had her doubts about meeting him. She said she'd think about it. He replied, "If you want to, you'll find me in the hotel."

When she'd finished telling Sandor this story, he asked, "Do you like him?"

"He seems very nice."

"Then why don't you go out with him?"

Eva smiled, shrugging her shoulders.

~

It was late afternoon. Sandor had fallen asleep on his bed with one arm draped over his eyes blocking out the sharp light. On waking, he felt cold despite being fully clothed. He kicked off his shoes and pulled the blanket over himself. He felt very tired, disoriented by having such a deep sleep so late in the day. When the hut door opened, Sandor remained very still, as he didn't want to talk to anybody, preferring to remain undisturbed in his near slumbering state.

A voice called out, "Anyone here?"

It was Peter Varga. Sandor didn't reply. He felt sly hiding beneath his covers and behind the curtains surrounding his bed. He held his breath which increased his heart rate. Peter walked towards Sandor's bed, then turned around. Seconds later Peter drew the curtains around his own bed and took off his shoes. When settling on his mattress you could hear the sound of the springs being stretched. A pleasurable groan was released as he lay down on his bed.

Sandor felt himself falling asleep again. It was a beautiful feeling, giving in so willingly to this alternative state. Recently, he'd been sleeping a lot more than the seven or eight hours which he was used to. He was going to bed earlier and getting up later. He loved the escape it offered, the hours it wasted.

Sandor heard noises from Peter's bed: the opening of a belt, a fly being unzipped. Sandor listened as Peter's breath became more pronounced, heavy and the air carried the unseen rhythms which he was performing.

Sandor closed his eyes. He thought about sleep. He imagined it as being a dark room illuminated by fire.

An article by Tommy Gallagher discussed the Irish Red Cross and their worsening relationship with the refugees. In an interview, McManus said that certain disgruntled refugees did not reflect the true opinion of the camp but only the views of a number of "agitators and former communists".

When asked about Sandor Lovas being the representative of the camp, McManus said that a proper election must take place, and as the refugees had spent most of their adult lives under communism, he wasn't surprised that they were unfamiliar with the secret ballot system. An election would be scheduled and the result of it was subject to ratification by the National Executive of the Irish Red Cross.

In response to this Sandor was quoted as saying that certain officials in the Irish Red Cross were being unhelpful, and that the refugees wanted to be treated "like human beings and to be kept informed about our fate".

As for being accused of being a communist agitator, Sandor had said, "I risked my life escaping communism."

In summary Gallagher opined that there had been a lack of communication and this state of affairs had been created needlessly by "a hardening of hearts on both sides which has snowballed into ugly proportions".

∽

It sounded like a football being kicked. The windless winter air carried the dull thumping noise; it was repetitive and echoed around the wooden huts of the camp, a constant banging.

Another noise, however, was unmistakable. Glass smashing, sheets cracking like ice, shards landing on the ground.

Sandor was standing outside the recreational hut.

A man ran past him, "People are smashing up their hut!"

Sandor asked, "Irish people?"

"No, Hungarians. The people who live in it."

When Sandor arrived at the hut most of its windows were smashed. Beds and chairs were tossed around on the floor, though personal belongings were neatly stacked in one corner. Rubbish was scattered outside the hut on the gravel pathway. Paint, supplied by the Irish Red Cross, was poured on the ground. Sandor couldn't believe that the occupants would vandalise their own hut. He picked up large pieces of glass and, as he did, one of the people responsible appeared. Sandor didn't recognise him; a small, stout man with fair hair and a permanent grin.

Sandor asked him what had happened.

The man introduced himself as Frank Tóth. He said that it was a protest against the conditions in the camp, he was tired of living like an animal in a hut and eating substandard food. He was concerned about the health of his children and most importantly, getting out of the country. "They lied to us. They said that we'd be in Ireland for a few days and then we'd be off to the US or Canada."

"But why smash up your hut?" asked Sandor.

"A protest."

"This isn't a protest. This is destroying someone else's property. Who is this going to benefit?"

He was disappointed with Sandor's reply, "But they wouldn't let you go to Dublin. What are we supposed to do?"

Sandor asked, "And this is the only alternative?"

Sandor continued cleaning up the glass and stacked the empty paint cans by the side of the hut. With his feet he raked the gravel pathway to conceal the sight of white paint on grey pebbles. People started helping. Minutes later, the Gardaí and a few soldiers who had been stationed at the entrance of the camp, arrived. They had an interpreter with them. It wasn't Lucia. Sandor told them to talk to Frank Tóth and suggested that he should pay for the damage from his Irish Red Cross allowance.

With the threat of further disturbances in Knockalisheen, Gardaí established a small police station in the camp with staff from Killaloe.

Later that day Sandor decided to stand for election.

~

When the Irish Red Cross fixed a date for an election Sandor and three others, János Polgár, László Eper and Frank Tóth, stood for selection. In the recreational hut a ballot box was placed in the front of the room, between each window a number of small booths had been assembled offering the voter secrecy. Neither Sandor, nor the others, campaigned. Two hundred and fifty four people were eligible to vote.

After Sandor voted he went to work for Gerry Buckley. Gerry met him outside the plant and led him into his office. Tea was prepared by Gerry as the plant was closed for the day, even though it was during the week. Gerry explained that the staff were on a day's break because of a deal which he'd struck with the union, "Time off instead of a pay increase."

It was the first time Sandor had worked on the factory floor. The other times had been spent in the car. He was set the following task: to service an engine which powered a small conveyor belt used by a mushroom grower. After showing him where the tools and spare parts were, Gerry left him, "I'll be back in four hours."

Sandor was happy working, a familiar environment of oil and grease, spanners and chains. As he worked he kept an eye on a clock above the desk to ensure that he finished by Gerry's return. After an hour he went to the toilet. He walked around the factory alone, in the near dark, as most of the lights were switched off, including Gerry's office. It took him three minutes to locate the light switch for the toilet. There was no hot water in the tap and the room smelled of stale cigarettes. Graffiti was on the walls.

After cleaning the engine he put it back together. It started working and he felt a sense of wellbeing, happiness from his understanding of mechanics, the simplicity of each component part functioning in union. Gerry returned late that afternoon. He inspected Sandor's work and was happy. He gave him some money and told him to return on Saturday, "We're a little slow this week."

∽

McManus acted as the returning officer for the election. He stood on a chair in front of a crowded recreational hut. Sandor and the other candidates stood behind him. McManus spoke in English translated by Lucia. She had to shout loudly to be heard. McManus said that the purpose of the election was to elect a camp representative and a governing council. Sandor looked above the crowd and felt the prospect of shame, the possible humiliation of defeat.

Standing in front of people made him feel exposed, as though a shocking secret were about to be revealed about him.

McManus announced the results of the vote, starting with Frank Tóth. As he did Sandor made quick calculations to see what he'd have to get to win; but as the number of votes which the others received was small, before his vote was called he knew he'd won. McManus said, "As Sandor Lovas has received one hundred and fifty six out of two hundred and fifty four votes, I deem him to be elected as the camp representative."

There was a loud cheer from the floor. Victory made Sandor feel slightly embarrassed. Looking at the crowd he sought Maria and when their eyes met they smiled at each other. Later they went for a celebratory drink and then on to the cinema.

∾

The first request which Sandor entertained as camp representative came from Peter Varga. It was early morning, Sandor was lying in bed. Peter asked, "Can I talk to you for a minute?"

"Yes?"

Peter said, "I have a suggestion to make about the camp. It's to do with the food. As you know we're worried about the amount of vegetables which we are getting so I thought that we could grow our own. There's plenty of space between the huts for vegetable patches and it would only take a small amount of time each day to tend to them."

Sandor had no experience of growing vegetables, "Would it not take a long time?"

"For what?"

"For each vegetable to grow?"

"It depends on what we plant. Soon it will be spring. We could start sowing then and in a little while we could be eating certain crops."

Sandor asked, "How much will it cost?"

"Not much."

"Do you need equipment?"

"Garden tools. Soil. Seeds. Watering can. Ask the Irish Red Cross for the money. Once they make a small investment, it will save them in the long run. Spring is getting closer."

Later that week a Hungarian woman called to see Sandor. He recognised her accent as being that of an educated woman from Budapest. She was in her mid-forties and introduced herself as Julia Pinter. She had a narrow face, a dark complexion and her black hair was cut short. She wore jewellery. From a leather handbag she produced a packet of cigarettes and a prayer book. She offered Sandor a cigarette which he declined. She told him that she had come from a small village in County Tipperary. She had lived there for years with her husband, now deceased. She was visiting the camp for two reasons. Firstly, she wanted to see the conditions as she'd been following the story in the newspapers for the last couple of months. Secondly, she wanted to present the camp with devotional books which she'd organised.

Picking up a prayer book from the table she explained, "I organised the production of these books, all the prayers are in Hungarian with an English translation. I thought that it was necessary for the Presbyterians to have them. I was informed that Reverend Wilkinson ministers them in the camp, but he wasn't here this morning and so the guards instructed me to look for you. They only let me in when I showed them the books. Would you like one?"

Sandor explained that although he was raised a Presbyterian, he was out of practice. Julia said, "That's what I feared. And that's why I produced the books. Ten years of communism is all that it took to lose one's religion. Faith is very fragile."

When Sandor finished talking to Julia Pinter he escorted her to the camp entrance, and as he did, she spoke about the Irish Red Cross, "They are an excellent organisation which has only been in existence since the war. The Irish people respond to their call in an almost religious way. This might surprise you, but they aren't a humanitarian organisation. Their aim is not to lessen suffering because it is an impediment to human happiness, but because in each sufferer they behold, not a fellow mortal, but the Person of Christ.

"So I warn you Mr Lovas that the Irish are very patriotic about this organisation, as for many years this country couldn't have its own branch because it wasn't independent. And they're very proud of this independence. Very proud."

～

The next time Sandor saw Tommy Gallagher he was sitting on a wall outside the camp. Sandor was surprised to learn that Gallagher had been denied access, the Gardaí having informed him that journalists were no longer permitted. Gallagher had explained that he had friends in the camp and wanted to give them an envelope containing photographs but they said that friends weren't allowed either.

Later that day Sandor raised this point at the first meeting of the camp council, consisting of János Polgár, László Eper and Josef Horvath. Although Horvath hadn't ran for election, Sandor suggested he attend their meetings as he had a good command of English.

All agreed that it was unacceptable that Irish friends or journalists were barred from the camp as it was supposed to be their home.

In preparation for the meeting János Polgár had compiled the following statistics; by February 1957, out of five hundred and thirty refugees, one hundred and twenty two had left the camp. Thirty six (with twenty one dependants) had found jobs. Fifty four had moved into Irish homes. Four had left for England. Five had gone to Switzerland, and two were attending Irish boarding schools. Polgár explained that while the numbers seemed accurate, people were always coming and going from the camp, and the statistics failed to consider part-time workers. Polgár, a man in his late twenties from a farming background in eastern Hungary, said that the most depressing aspect of the statistics was that only one refugee, an engineer, had found work in Dublin, "And that's the capital city."

László Eper, a journalist from Budapest, said, "Perhaps the Irish Red Cross isn't doing enough. You'd think that more of us would be employed by now."

The organisation of the Irish Red Cross was discussed. As each county was a branch of the national organisation, Eper suggested that perhaps the Limerick branch was particularly useless, "Maybe useless is a bit too hard. Perhaps inexperienced. I think that we should appeal to the National Executive of the Irish Red Cross. A letter should be sent to Dublin and also copied to the newspapers. That way Dublin might put pressure on Limerick."

Sandor suggested that time be taken in drafting the letter. He said that the Irish people were losing sympathy with them, as newspaper articles had already questioned their gratitude.

For two days they worked on a letter. Lucia translated it. When all were satisfied, it was posted to the General Secretary of the Irish Red Cross Society and to newspaper editors.

The letter discussed the breaking down of confidence and cooperation between the refugees and the camp officials. It warned that disturbances in the camp would be unavoidable unless certain steps were taken. It requested that the refugees who wanted to travel to other countries should be told of the likelihood of leaving and what steps the Irish Government had taken so far. Although Sandor had wanted to come in Ireland, it was decided by the camp council to state, for greater effect, that:

> *All the refugees were under the impression that they were coming to Ireland first and then moving on to the USA or Canada. If this was the case, what replies have been received from the foreign governments concerned? If no conclusive replies have been received, this should be told to us, as at least we would know that something was being done on our behalf. The refugees understood that their time in Ireland would be a transitional stage before going to the country of their choice – but how long is this transitional stage going to last? And if the Irish officials do not know, then we should be informed of this straight away.*

The letter mentioned the concern which people had over the food and how unsuitable it was for infants, children and pregnant mothers. Overall, the letter said, the food was very good, there was a high percentage of meat, but it was stressed that it was not the type of food which they were used to, and they would be satisfied with meat twice a week if they could get more green vegetables for the adults and fruit for the children.

The subject of clothing was mentioned. It was requested that, for reasons of accountability, the clothing depot was handed over to the refugees for administration. They also requested that when representatives of the refugees wanted to go to Dublin or elsewhere at their own expense to see government departments or officials of foreign embassies that they would not be hindered in doing so by camp officials.

The letter continued:

The language difficulty has frequently given rise to misunderstandings between the camp administration and the refugees. Though many have volunteered with knowledge of German for part-time duty it is essential to have interpreters with a fluent knowledge of Hungarian on a full-time basis who will have the full confidence of the refugees.

One of the main causes of discontent is the delay in finding work. We are willing to work at anything, and the girls and woman among us are seeking employment as domestic staff even though they are not accustomed to such work.

However, whatever happens to us, we will always remember with gratitude the great generosity of the Irish people through their donations made to us and the hospitality which they have shown us in their homes.

But there is nothing worse than continuous uncertainty. In the future we hope that regular bulletins about our prospects will be given to us through the elected camp council. You will appreciate that however great the material generosity of the Irish people may be, a community of five hundred people living in political confinement without information as to their future, can be overcome by a sense of frustration, which grows as this time of uncertainty goes on. Under such conditions nervous tension arises, smaller frustrations seem large, major frustrations, unbearable.

Yours truly,
The Knockalisheen Governing Council.

Sandor liked translating articles about Hungary in the Irish papers. Slowly he learned how his country had been doing since the Russians had quashed the uprising. There was the mysterious whereabouts of Imre Nagy; he had sought asylum in the Yugoslav embassy in Budapest but reports now claimed that he was in the Crimea. Sandor read that Nagy had been captured leaving the embassy and was being detained in Romania. He thought about Nagy's rotund belly and chubby face and how, most likely, he would be executed by the Russians. And, no doubt, another man would soon die: a show trial was already underway for Major General Pal Maleter who had defected to the insurgents at the beginning of the uprising.

How strange, thought Sandor, that a couple of months ago he had demonstrated with thousands of other people for, among other things, the right to vote in free and democratic elections, but the only voting he'd done since then was in Ireland and the person elected was himself.

CHAPTER TEN

Correspondence between Sandor Lovas, Hut thirty-three west, Knockalisheen Camp, County Clare and John Murphy of Seaview, Marine Road, Dalkey, County Dublin, established that Kristina was still not in school. So John suggested introducing her to Principal Sister Carmel of Laurel Hill Convent School in Limerick, and on meeting her, he was instructed to present her with a letter of introduction.

Sister Carmel was a tall woman in her fifties. Her face was narrow and gaunt. She looked confusedly at Sandor and Eva as they handed her the letter; then her face broke into a smile and the lines around her eyes looked like cracked ice. They were asked to wait in an empty classroom. Sandor looked at the pictures on the wall, children's sketches and a map of Ireland. Kristina sat behind a wooden desk. She liked the school. A bell sounded.

When Sister Carmel returned she said that a place was available. She had a number of questions about Kristina. What was her level of schooling and grades in Hungary? What sports did she play? And most importantly, did she want to board in the school? Eva hadn't considered boarding as an option. She talked privately to Sandor about the advantages and disadvantages of boarding. Kristina might not like it; Eva would miss her daughter and her sudden immersion in an English speaking world might make her feel alienated.

As Eva was unsure, a compromise was agreed. If Kristina wanted to stay in school during the week she could, and if she didn't like it she could come home every day. When this was suggested to Kristina she said that she wanted to stay in the school. "I'm already sharing a hut with many others, it's the same thing."

Sister Carmel told Kristina that she could start next Monday, "Hold on and I'll get you a uniform."

Kristina became excited; Eva was relieved.

~

Sandor was thinking about the subjects which Kristina would learn, wondering about the differences between a Hungarian and an Irish education. Over the years, he had often thought about one lesson learned in school, the story of the Magyar tribes settling in the Transylvanian plains after wandering thousands of miles from the east, over a thousand years ago. Sandor, with his neutral-toned skin which seemed slightly paler due to his black hair, thought of his appearance as European – Central European – but somewhere in his sister's make up was what his teacher had spoken of in school, she seemed more connected to this dark-skinned race, who (and this scared Sandor as a child), if they hadn't started wandering to Europe from Asia all those years ago, might not have brought his European self into being. Staring fearfully out of his classroom window, he pushed his imagination to its geographical limit as he tried to imagine where he might have ended up if the Magyars hadn't reached Europe, his mind searching the globe for an alternative home, for it was impossible for his youthful self to imagine a world so cruel that it would exclude him.

On Monday, Sandor and Eva walked Kristina to school. Kristina looked pretty in her uniform. Sister Carmel met them at the entrance. Eva hugged her daughter and said that they'd see her on the weekend. Sandor hugged her too and told her to enjoy herself and make some friends. Kristina followed Sister Carmel into school, Sandor and Eva stood outside the building for a few minutes. Sandor didn't envy Kristina attending school, especially being the only Hungarian in an English speaking classroom.

It was a nice day. On the way back to the camp Sandor told Eva that John Murphy had said that the school was not only one of the best in Limerick but in all of Ireland.

It was late Thursday night, close to midnight. Sandor and Maria were in the recreational hut, all had gone to bed, the only sound was the wind outside and the occasional dog barking. The rain had stopped. Candle flame replaced electric light at midnight. They were sitting beside each other on the hard chairs. Sandor suggested they lie on cushions on the floor. As it was colder there, they moved closer together.

Sandor said it was a great pity that they couldn't share a bed. Maria agreed. The candle light on the table no longer coloured her face now shadowed by Sandor. There was a flatness to her chest when she rested on her back. He placed his hand on her waist, tucking it inside her blouse to access her warmth. On touching her skin she tensed from his cold hand. They started kissing. Minutes later Sandor opened the buttons on her blouse. He kissed her nipples and then moved his head towards her waistline, tickling her bellybutton with his tongue. She laughed, her stomach muscles tensing and then relaxing as he removed her skirt. He took off his trousers. She removed the last of her clothing and so did he. Along with the cushions these clothes formed a bed.

They continued kissing. After a few minutes she directed him inside her. She told him to withdraw in time, which he did. She finished him off with her hand. Soon, the euphoria of orgasm was overshadowed by an anxiety for their future. Recently, he'd been prone to bouts of panic. Sometimes he'd wake during the night and feel like he was slowly sliding on ice, a sense of unease. They'd only been seeing each other for just over a month but Sandor was in love with her. She had given meaning to his time thus far in the camp. She'd compensated for the disappointment of Ireland. Although they had only known each other for a short amount of time Sandor felt that due to the circumstances of their meeting, it had been more pressurised and had accelerated the relationship. If they had met in Budapest while living their former lives they wouldn't be eating three meals a day in the same room like they were in the camp, nor would they be faced with the same problems of work, accommodation, language and the worrying motif of the future.

Sandor was concerned about Maria's father, especially now that he wanted them to leave Ireland. Mr Novak, like Sandor, had wanted to come to Ireland. But now he wanted to leave for the USA as he felt that there was little chance of working in Ireland. Selling his wooden ornaments door to door had introduced him to many people who had given him the impression that there was little or no work for a man of his trade. For a carpenter to be in demand you needed a construction industry and there wasn't one, as people repeatedly informed him on doorsteps around Limerick. And so after a few weeks of selling his wares Mr Novak had decided that it was time to apply for visas and get out of the country.

With Mr Novak wanting his family to leave the country, Sandor felt that it could have one of the following consequences for his relationship. Either Maria left with her parents and he stayed in Ireland; or she stayed in Ireland; or he went with her. If she went with her parents their budding relationship would end along with its unrealised potential. If she stayed in Ireland, she'd have to be financially secure and have a job. No father would be willing to leave his only daughter behind in a state of penury; and even if she had a job Mr Novak might want her to leave Ireland for more security abroad. This possibility, however, hinged on visas being given to the Novaks and when that might happen was anybody's guess.

Sandor knew what he wanted from the future: the security of a job and life with Maria. He thought about Hungary, the routine he'd had there, his family, work and friends. He had taken so much for granted, especially how the bare essentials of life had been taken care of; there was always food, housing and employment. As a country, Hungary had offered that much. And as a result he had always thought that Western countries would offer more than that. But he hadn't counted on Ireland. Back home, he wouldn't have believed that he would be materially worse off in another country, as he had equated freedom with economic success, as if the former would beget the latter.

Although Eva had agreed with him to come to Ireland, ultimately, Sandor felt responsible for them being here as it was he who had heard the *Ireland, Ireland* announcement in Camp Eisenstadt. This regret he had in coming to Ireland fell as guilt on his shoulders; and it was with Peter Varga that this feeling of guilt was shared. Sandor knew of the Vargas' unhappiness as often he'd overheard them in the hut.

Peter was worried about Anna. She had always been a balanced person, her moods were steady and her company good, but recently she'd become moody. "Having a baby is bound to affect you but she has changed so much. Perhaps it's depression but how long are women supposed to be depressed after childbirth?"

Peter believed that there were many reasons for his wife's anxiety, a mixture of having a baby, leaving the support of her parents and family and arriving in Ireland. "It was the biggest mistake of my life coming here. I can't help wondering: if I hadn't picked this place, where on earth I would be? America? Canada? I think that we would be better off anywhere else but here.

"But how was I meant to know that Ireland had nothing to offer? I signed up as they were keen to have Catholic families, as after years of not being able to practise our faith, here was a country wanting to take us in because of it. But looking back I have to laugh at the preference which the Irish Red Cross had for Catholic families. It's bad enough trying to look after yourself, but trying to raise a family here is almost impossible. And Irish families are so large – it's strange, stupid and cruel. We might be Catholic but no Hungarian Catholic is going to have twelve kids without a way to feed them. What God wants to bring children into the world to starve or emigrate?"

Peter had believed that he was clever in choosing Ireland. "The queues for the other countries were so large that I thought that we were getting one up on everybody else. But looking back I should have guessed that the reason few were queuing to get into Ireland was that nobody had heard of the place. And why would they have?"

Apart from wanting to come to Ireland, it had been Peter's idea to leave Budapest in the first place, and while Anna had agreed with him, she would have been just as happy staying. "She thought that the benefits of leaving Hungary would be immediate and though we expected to be waiting around in camps and having problems settling in another country, we didn't think that we'd go to a country which was worse off than back home.

"So Anna keeps talking about Hungary as if it's the greatest place on earth and that we were mad to leave it in the first place. And I keep telling her that we *will* end up in a better country and that not everywhere in the West is like Ireland, soon we'll be in America or Canada, and our lives will be better.

"But I'm beginning to wonder myself. Questions keep going around in my head. What do I want from a country? What should I expect? But I don't have an answer. I'm at a complete and utter loss."

⁓

During the week Sandor received a letter from Julia Pinter, the Hungarian woman who had donated prayer books to the camp. She wanted to meet him. As she was an early riser, an appointment was scheduled early one morning.

On meeting they spoke about the mild weather. She made observations about the camp and they agreed that it was looking better. Over coffee, Hungary was briefly mentioned, and then she coughed clearing her throat and her eyes became focused, businesslike. "I am speaking to you as the camp representative but also as an engineer. I have a plan which you might be interested in."

Sandor nodded, "Okay."

"When I became widowed my late husband left me some money and for many years I have been wondering what to do with it. I have given some to charity and used some of it for personal purposes, helping my children and travelling in Europe. But as I still have a sufficient amount of capital I have devised a plan.

"I would like to invest it in Ireland, to help this country, the place where I have made my home and where I enjoy living. But I would also like to help the Hungarian refugees as I can't help thinking that, but for the grace of God, it could have been me.

"And so my plan is to kill these two birds with one stone by investing in Ireland and the refugees at the same time. I have an interest in engineering as that was my husband's profession and it's also an industry which Ireland lacks. Hungary is an industrial nation, Ireland isn't, and I think that it has to become one in order to survive.

"So I'm willing to invest my money in a factory which will employ skilled Hungarian workers who in turn can train unskilled Irish people. My plan has three elements. Firstly, I will invest money. Secondly, you — that's if you're interested — will source the workforce among the refugees. And thirdly, as I will ultimately be creating jobs for Irish people and not just refugees, I think that the government should support me. What I need from them is an empty building. It doesn't have to be big, as when the business grows we can expand. If they supply a building, whether it's an old one which is refurbished or a new one built from scratch, then everything should come together."

"What will we be producing?" asked Sandor.

"It's a specific type of electrical component. My husband obtained a patent for it a few years ago. In fact, he was given it by two Hungarians who had fled Budapest. They had stolen it from a factory there. He met them in London and they gave it to him for free. When you see the details, you'll appreciate its application. My husband was looking into this area before he died and had considered setting up a factory abroad as the necessary skills weren't in Ireland. My accountant is working on the project and getting the figures ready for a meeting with the Irish Government.

"If you are interested, you will have to compile a list of suitable workers, their education and skills. It doesn't matter if it's only a few people at first; we just have to show that we have the talent. Then, we'll meet the Irish Red Cross and the Help Hungary Committee, and with a bit of luck, the government will be willing."

Sandor agreed that it was a good idea and one which he'd like to be involved with. Julia said that she'd be in contact with him in a couple of weeks and asked him to start finding suitable people. Sandor knew who to pick from the camp, as there were a number of people who, like him, had passed through Budapest's Technical College.

If an engineering plant was established and he had a senior position there, Sandor thought that there would be many advantages. For a start it would be Hungarian owned and run, language wouldn't be a problem. And if Irish people learned engineering skills through them, refugees would be perceived as benefiting Ireland and not just being the recipients of charity.

Sandor was worried about the rain. It was the morning of the Varga's wedding and he had promised to take photographs. Dressed in his suit with his camera on the floor beside him, Sandor, along with the others in the chapel, waited for Anna to arrive. There was no music and the altar lacked any flowers. Peter, standing at the top of the chapel, was talking to Father Mikes. Peter looked relaxed. He was dressed in an ill-matched suit, a dark grey jacket and black trousers. His shoes were polished and his jowly face was cleanly shaven. When Anna walked down the aisle Sandor started taking photographs from behind the altar. She was wearing a white dress which had been donated for the day by a Limerick shop.

Father Mikes welcomed Anna to the chapel. She seemed a little nervous and the priest did his best to reassure her. Sandor returned to his pew, sitting beside Maria. After an hour Sandor become increasingly bored with the ceremony. Removing a small cloth from his pocket he cleaned his camera lens. Every few minutes he'd lean towards the window and examine the lighting conditions outside. Sometimes it seemed to be raining on one side of the chapel but not on the other. Sandor hoped that the rain would stop as he wanted to take all his photographs outside. There wasn't a decent building in the camp where they could pose for pictures.

Towards the end of the ceremony Sandor stood in the aisle, close to the couple, waiting for them to kiss, and once they did, they walked down the aisle, and he took many shots.

It took a few minutes for the rain to end. And when it did they walked to the far side of the camp where trees and bushes cloaked the perimeter fence and the horizon line was the distant curve of a rolling hill. For twenty minutes Sandor took photographs. The light was perfect; bright but without any direct sunlight, it was as if a light cloth had been placed over the sun.

When the pictures were developed Tommy Gallagher used a shot of the couple for a small article about the wedding.

༄

The camp council waited for a response to their letter to the Irish Red Cross. Sandor bought newspapers everyday, scanning the long columns of text, looking at pictures, searching articles for the words *Hungarian* and *refugee*.

The first newspaper to carry the story was The Irish Times. In an editorial the relationship between the Irish Red Cross and the refugees was discussed. For two hours Sandor and the council went through it word by word, breaking down the sentences, analysing its content.

A few lines of their original letter were quoted in the editorial:

People living in political confinement without information as to their future, can be overcome by a sense of frustration, which grows as this time of uncertainty goes on.

And The Irish Times commented:

These words frame the unspoken thoughts of a great number of Irish people.

Sandor was happy with The Irish Times. He imagined the Irish Red Cross in Dublin reading the editorial and paying more attention to their letter; and then Dublin would talk to Limerick and an effort would be made regarding their fate.

But not all newspapers were supportive. An editorial in The Limerick Leader read:

The Hungarian refugees at Knockalisheen would seem to have mastered the English language in record time judging by the lengthy fulmination on the conditions obtaining to the camp. The refugees, if they mean what they say, are dissatisfied with the army rations with which they are served; in other words, the food given to the army is not good enough for them. Did the Hungarians flee from a land flowing with milk and honey or are they being duped by some crafty agitators? It is hard to believe that the general body of refugees do not appreciate what is being done for them. It is also hard to believe that they are in effect accusing us of inhospitality. The Hungarians, as our guests, were received with open arms. The allegations made in their name sound unreal and unbecoming.

It was an unusually warm day. Sandor and Maria were walking through the fields, upwards behind the camp, over stone walls and flat slabs of cow manure, beneath trees, their branches still without leaves. Maria was sick of working for the bead-man. She wasn't used to the monotony of the labour but she needed the money. She wondered what was more boring: working for the bead-man or not working at all? "But the problem with that," she concluded, "is that my father would get me to work for him, walking door to door selling his ornaments. And I don't want to do that."

Beneath an oak tree, on its smooth, dry roots, they lay down. You could see the Shannon Estuary from this height and Limerick was a smoky mass of urbana. They were surrounded by fields; cows were dotted in the distance. They shared Sandor's last cigarette, and as the sun had yet to set, Sandor removed his camera. For a few minutes he pointed it at her but without exposing any film. Maria didn't mind having her picture taken; when looking at the camera she'd make the same face and ensure her black hair was removed from her forehead and tucked behind her ears. But she always kept her lips shut. Sandor believed that she didn't want to show her teeth because of a slight crack on her front tooth, a small grey line, hardly noticeable. He thought that her dark hair would translate well on to photographic paper as it contrasted nicely with her lightly-coloured skin.

Sandor took a few pictures, and as he did, he thought of the books which he'd seen in a library in Budapest, pictures of partial nudes: arms clasped around breasts; curved backs with prominent spines stretching down towards naked bottoms; the curvaceous body of a woman set against the strict architectural lines of a city; pubic hair bushing out of milky-white skin; nipples, like sand castles, close up and full framed. Sandor imagined Maria being stripped of her clothes, she'd be outside, perhaps in a field, it would have to be during the summer, and he'd take pictures of her from angles which concealed rather than revealed, but like those pictures which he'd seen, he'd leave a blurry breast or a glimpse of fuzzed hair, as you'd have to, he figured, to make it artful and worthy.

Maria took the camera from Sandor. He rested against the tree. He enjoyed having his photograph taken, he never complained about looking good or bad or stupid or ugly or young or old, he always looked just above the camera, and his eyes, slightly raised, appeared confident.

That evening they were invited to Dr Pader's for dinner. Sandor applauded his host for attempting to sit medical exams through English. This impressed Maria. She compared learning English to walking over monotonous scenery day after day, month after month, "I was never good with languages. In school I was hopeless at German."

Dr Pader replied, "For some people the ability to learn a language comes easier than others. You could say that it's a talent, a gift, like playing the piano or painting a picture. Why is it that some people can easily pick up five or six languages while others struggle to learn one? The curious thing is that everybody has the ability to learn their native language, but not everybody can learn a second one.

"Maria, if it makes you feel any better all you need to speak a language in everyday situations is a vocabulary of five hundred words and a couple of verbs. That's all. However, for the average student of a top university, their vocabulary would be between three thousand and five thousand words. And then there's Shakespeare; his complete works show a vocabulary of around twenty thousand words."

Dr Pader smiled, "But forget about Shakespeare. Just remember that the next time you're in Roches Stores and you're fumbling with your five or ten words, the person taking your money is probably only four hundred and ninety words ahead of you."

∞

The Irish Red Cross responded to the camp council's letter and press releases were sent to the national newspapers. It outlined the strategy of the Irish Red Cross, starting with:

Emigration. Through the offices of the government approaches have been made to the Canadian Government, but so far the Canadian emigration authorities will be unable to facilitate the refugees until the spring. An approach has been made to the US Government and information is awaited.

Employment. The Irish Red Cross has set up a special committee to co-ordinate with employers and employees' organisations and the Department of Industry and Commerce. The function of this committee will include the problems of employment for: persons for temporary employment outside the camp pending emigration; persons who wish to remain in Ireland in permanent employment. A list of the qualifications of refugees has been published and applications are now being examined.

Education. Arrangements are being made for children to attend local schools. It is hoped to obtain further full-time interpreters who will be competent to give adult classes in English. Language difficulty has frequently given rise to misunderstandings between the camp administration and the refugees. Whilst many have volunteered with knowledge of German or for part-time duty, it is essential to have people with a fluent knowledge of Hungarian on a full-time basis responsible to the administration who will also have the full confidence of the refugees.

> *Travel. With permission the refugees have been free to travel away from the camp, while visitors and the press have been free to enter the camp with permission from the Irish Red Cross.*

The letter finished by detailing the amount of money which had been raised. In a newspaper article an Irish Red Cross official from County Wicklow said that the refugees had no genuine complaints, and while it was true that one of the huts had a leaky roof, his own house had a leaky roof due to the recent rainstorms and many other roofs in the country were leaky. With regards to the food supplies, the adults were getting full army rations every day, and there were endless stocks of branded baby food, which, it seemed, the mothers would not use. As well as the army milk ration, one hundred bottles of milk were also given to the refugees which amounted to three times what regular soldiers receive.

The article reported that not all refugees supported the demands which the newly elected camp council had made. It quoted an anonymous man, originally from Budapest, "In Hungary we were glad to eat black bread, watered milk and, if we were lucky, two ounces of butter a week while workers only got sixteen ounces of meat a week. But here in Knockalisheen Camp we get two ounces of butter and twelve ounces of meat every day".

Mr Lee, assistant manager of a Limerick bottling plant, arranged to meet Sandor. Mr Lee explained, through Lucia, that a considerable sum had been spent on a modern extension to the factory and that this investment would create further employment in the city. To support the Hungarian refugees the plant wanted to employ one person with experience in a similar industry, if not the same. Sandor inspected the list of refugees and their qualifications. Tibor Kottek had worked in a similar plant in Györ and a job interview was arranged. Tibor, with Lucia's assistance, impressed Mr Lee and got the job.

Sandor, Lucia and Tibor were invited to a hotel for a celebratory luncheon in honour of the new extension. Local politicians and businessmen were in attendance. Before lunch the Very Reverend Francis Byrne blessed the factory and opened a shrine with a statue of Saint Joseph. He gave a speech, paying tribute to the factory and the workers. He spoke about Ireland, about the thousands of children in Limerick and how this new factory extension might prevent some of these children emigrating in future years. It was sad that so many had to leave. Nevertheless, he finished on an optimistic note, "Until such time as the large population could be absorbed at home, emigration is a tribute to the good family life and healthy fertility of our race."

CHAPTER ELEVEN

Sandor looked at the February sky. It seemed to vary every hour, sometimes every minute. Mornings of sunshine turned gloomy and wet. Clouds of every strength appeared, from little fluffs of near-transparent white to an entire sky dark and disturbing. Sandor noticed one constant feature of Irish weather though, wind. The elevated position of Knockalisheen Camp was exposed to a blustering force, there was rarely a day without the aggression of the air. Sandor compared the weather to Budapest's freezing winter, it was much colder than Ireland, though the Irish damp and windy climate made it more uncomfortable. Sandor counted nearly three months since their arrival last November and he longed for summer to put an end to his first Irish winter.

At the next council meeting the reply from the Irish Red Cross to their letter was discussed and Sandor agreed what he'd say when next talking to McManus.

Josef Horvath said, "It seems to me that the biggest complaint people have is the camp itself. If it were a nice place, people wouldn't mind staying here, but most people fear living here for any length of time. It just isn't fit for long-term accommodation." Horvath started laughing,

"The place was built for soldiers not women and children. Some of the huts are full of damp; hardly an environment for children. Okay, the Red Cross is supplying enough fuel to heat the huts, but you still have to get up during the night to restock the stoves and once the fire goes out the heat disappears immediately. It's not an efficient method of heating by any means."

Councillor László Eper had been reading the English newspapers in a library in Limerick as he thought that it was important to follow their compatriots' progress in other countries. He spoke of an article which detailed the success of eight hundred Hungarians who were living and working in the Derbyshire mines near Skegness in England. Their community, though small, was large enough to host the first Hungarian newspaper in England – Skegness-Hungarian News – and a letter had been published by a Hungarian who paid tribute to England for her generosity after the uprising. Also, an article reported that hundreds of Hungarians were being taught English by the East Midlands division of the National Coal Board. The absorption of Hungarian workers into the mines was not without its problems; objections had been made by some Nottinghamshire colliers about their employment and its implication for English workers. One union lodge had decided not to allow Hungarian refugees to work at their colliery for fear that they would get free housing before their English counterparts.

Eper also mentioned Austria. "Hungary is not the only country to suffer economically since the uprising. Austria fears that, due to the tens of thousands of refugees, some have put the figure close to two hundred thousand, currently in their country, they are at risk of bankruptcy and anarchy."

Other items for discussion came from János Polgár who spoke of a refugee family consisting of a man, wife and three children, who had been offered a house in Kimmage,

Dublin, where they would live rent free for one year in a property owned by the Irish Red Cross.

A few days later Sandor was invited to meet McManus. As Sandor waited he studied the black and white tiles on the kitchen floor and ate biscuits which had been laid out for the appointment. Lucia was the next to arrive.

During the meeting, Sandor mentioned Peter Varga's suggestion about growing vegetables, this was welcomed and money would be released for the necessary equipment. "Perhaps," suggested McManus, "we could get sponsorship from a shop or at least a discount."

They discussed the health of a teenage boy who appeared to have chest problems. McManus agreed with a doctor who thought that the boy was far too young to suffer from a coronary condition, and said that if the problem persisted then the boy would be sent to a Dublin specialist and removed from the Limerick hospital, "I have visited him a few times and it's awful to see a young man, not yet in his prime, suffer like this."

Sandor was assured that the boy would be seen by the best consultant in the country. As he had never seen the boy, Sandor asked about his parents. McManus told him that, "After fleeing the country he had been separated from them and arrived in Ireland alone. He has lost touch with his family, but is close to some adults in the camp."

Sandor asked about employment for the refugees.

McManus said, "We have talked to certain trade unions and they have concerns about Hungarian refugees upsetting the labour market. So we are trying to locate jobs for Hungarians in non-competitive areas."

Sandor worked his way through his points; one of the last concerned the employment which was created in the camp, "Would it be possible for all jobs currently held by Irish people to be given over to Hungarians?"

McManus finished his tea, "Certain jobs have already been handed over, cooking, for example."

"But when an Irish person was cooking they were getting paid for it, but we volunteer as unpaid labour for the same position."

"This will be considered."

Although Sandor didn't mention his meeting with Julia Pinter and her idea for a factory, he suggested to McManus that skills unique to Hungarians should be utilised for the benefit of Ireland. A rudimentary example of this was Mr Novak's wood cuttings, one of which McManus had purchased. Sandor said, "There are plenty of skills which are native to Eastern Europeans, talents which could be exploited in Ireland. Unlike Ireland, Hungary is an industrial nation and Ireland could benefit from this experience."

McManus replied, "This all makes perfect sense in principle."

The meeting ended and hands were shaken. Afterwards Sandor thought about what hadn't been discussed: the refugees who smashed up their hut, his election as camp representative, and the articles in the newspapers which had labelled Sandor as an "agitator" and McManus as "difficult".

∽

László Eper was talking about a story he read in The Times of London. In Newcastle upon Tyne, a group of Hungarian refugees were living in a hostel and the authorities decided to move some of them to another place in Northumberland. Many of the refugees were against this decision as they had made friends and some had met their fiancées in the first hostel and so in protest against the decision, they wrote to the authorities:

In the name of all the Hungarian refugees we inform you about a twenty-four hour hunger strike if there is no favourable decision taken in connection with our transfer.

Eper explained that the notice had been written yesterday, the date for the beginning of the hunger strike being last night, and as the newspaper was a day old, they wouldn't find out what had happened until tomorrow. "Also, there seems to be some contradicting stories about the refugees. It said in the refugees' statement that they all wanted to take action, but the paper reported that fighting took place between some of those who didn't what to strike and those who did, though nobody was hurt. It also reported that since the refugees came to England a small number of them had expected to transit to the United States or Canada. Some, it seems, are disappointed with English wages as nineteen refugees quit their work as cooks, waiters, carpenters and farm workers as they thought that they would be earning more money. One of the refugees said, 'When we left Austria we were told that there was big money in England but we have found that this is not so.'"

The next day Eper spoke about one thousand Hungarian refugees who had rioted in a camp in Metz, France, to protest against what they perceived as delays in admitting them to the United States and Canada. "Most of the refugees were young and they decided to smash up tables, chairs and windows in their camp. And regarding the hunger strike that took place in England, it seems that the council gave into their demands and it was called off. Their tactic seemed to have worked – they won!"

Sandor said, "The authorities wouldn't have backed down if an article hadn't appeared in the newspaper as it's embarrassing for the government to have a bunch of hunger strikers on their hands. But how serious were they about the strike? If they started to strike and the authorities did not respond, how many days would they have lasted?

Were they prepared to damage their health? This is perfect propaganda back home, the idea that Hungarian refugees have to starve themselves in order to get what they want."

Eper replied, "There are some in England who think that this strike and a few other minor disturbances by other refugees have been organised by ÁVO men acting as refugees in order to discredit the reputation of actual Hungarian refugees."

Josef Horvath, sitting at the table, said, "How about we forget the conspiracy theories and believe that a group of refugees wanted something and the only way which they thought they'd get it was by hunger striking. Perhaps they *were* acting spoilt as there are more reports from England about decent jobs than not, but in this case, it seems, that they've succeeded in their aims by hunger striking. And we got to ask ourselves – if it worked for them, maybe it would work for us? Perhaps they'd get us visas and we'd be out of here quicker?"

∼

Sunday evening. Kristina, dressed in her school uniform, was soon to be walked by Eva and Sandor to Laurel Hill Convent. It was her second week at school. She was the only refugee attending the convent, one of a few girls from another country. Most of her time was spent in a state of placid boredom as she didn't know what the nuns or the other children were talking about.

It was strange, she said, "They gave me books and when people were reading, they'd turn the pages for me to follow." She knew some words, but not many. Sister Carmel gave her an extra hour tuition every evening after games and before dinner, "The two of us sitting in a large classroom by ourselves and she'd help me to read. But last week we didn't do any extra work at all. Nuns kept on coming into the room and talking to Sister Carmel."

During the week Father Mikes called into the school and gave the nuns Hungarian-English translations of prayers. "I have been learning the Our Father, the Hail Mary, Prayers Before and After Meals and the Rosary."

Sandor asked if the nuns were friendly? "Yes. Very nice. But it is like..." Kristina stopped talking to collect her thoughts, "...it's like I'm sick. They keep making the Sign of the Cross on my forehead and praying for me."

Kristina liked playing games. On the pitch you didn't need much English. She was tall and could run fast, "One of the girls gave me all the sports clothes I need. Most of the girls are very nice and I have been invited to their homes." What she enjoyed most was the dormitory. It reminded her of the refugee camp in Austria; spacious with large iron radiators pumping out heat, and airy shower rooms. Apart from seeing her family she didn't like coming back to the refugee camp on the weekend, "The school is much more comfortable."

If Kristina hadn't been in boarding school Eva probably wouldn't have returned to the hotel to accept an invitation from Thomas for a night out. At various times during her life Kristina had enquired about her father and Eva had told her the story of his death during the war and how it had occurred just before her birth. And Kristina would always ask her mother, "Why haven't you found someone else to marry?"

"Life is not as simple as that," was her standard reply. Eva had always been worried about bringing a new man into their lives. She felt that Kristina had managed to have a good childhood in what could have been a bad situation. After the war many women raised children on their own as tens of thousands of Hungarian men had perished. Kristina's father had died a civilian death and since then she had felt lucky that her daughter had been raised in good circumstances among her family. Sandor had always acted as a cross between a father and the uncle which he was, while her parents doted on their only grandchild, always eager to help, freeing up time for Kristina to enjoy what little there was in postwar Budapest.

She had met a few men since the war. Two of whom she'd brought back to the apartment to meet her family, but for various reasons nothing came of the relationships, and she went back to being a single woman. But now Eva wanted to enjoy herself. With Kristina in school, she felt that she could start thinking about her life. She told Sandor, "It will be fun going out with an Irishman."

When Eva returned from her night out with Thomas, Sandor was alone in the hut. She told him about meeting Thomas outside his hotel, how they went to a bar and then on to the cinema. When the film was over, they had another drink and he drove her back to the camp. Thomas had four brothers and three sisters. His father had established a hotel in Limerick twenty years ago. Most of the family worked in the business apart from one of his sisters who lived in Dublin and worked as a nurse.

Eva said, "From what I could understand he didn't seem to like his family. He showed little or no interest in them and rattled off their details like a bunch of statistics. All he wanted to talk about was Hungary; he seemed fascinated with Budapest and its history. He told me that he had wanted to go to college but he'd been pressurised into joining the family business and though he felt lucky to have a job, he didn't like working in the hotel."

Eva felt very tired after her night out with Thomas. She found attempting to converse in what little English she knew, trying to make herself understood with a handful of words and a few verbs, using rudimentary sign language or resorting to pictures drawn on napkins, an exhaustive task.

A few days after their first date, Thomas called to the camp. As restrictions had been imposed on those entering it, a soldier fetched Eva and for a few minutes they talked by the entrance. At his suggestion it was arranged for Eva, Sandor and Maria to enjoy a meal in the hotel.

And so that evening was the first time when Sandor met Thomas – or Thomas Townsend, as he was introduced – and he saw in him an obvious affection for Eva. It had been years since Sandor had witnessed a man acting attentively towards his sister and he felt an immediate rush of suspicion. Sandor always liked having a single sister. She was there to listen to him and he felt that, after his father, he was the patriarch of the family.

During the meal Thomas was entertained by being in the minority. Whenever the inevitable bluster of Hungarian lasted for any length of time he looked at Eva for clues to their conversation. Maria enjoyed stringing her English sentences together for Thomas's benefit as she was more confident speaking the language when surrounded by Hungarians. Sandor had visited shops with Maria and on one occasion while struggling with the language she had broken into an uncustomary stammer. Most shopkeepers had patience but every so often a busy store owner would make her feel awkward without realising it.

After the meal a man pulled a chair over and sat at their table. Sandor recognised him as one of Thomas's brothers, but he couldn't guess if he was younger or older. There was the same light-coloured skin tone and dark hair, and when he laughed his eyes seemed to disappear amid wrinkles. Patrick was his name. Sandor sensed that Thomas didn't want his brother to join them, as he sat back in his chair and became less talkative.

Patrick started making suggestive statements, "So you are living for free in the camp." This made Thomas grimace, and though Sandor couldn't understand everything that was being said, he figured that it was hostile.

Sandor replied, "Could you speak slower, please?"

Patrick said, "You are living for free," and then he laughed, "living off my taxes. I am paying for all of you."

Thomas said, "Please Patrick, not now. These are my guests. I asked them here."

Patrick said, "They are my guests too. They get a fucking allowance every week for doing nothing. Can you imagine that! For doing fuck all." And again he repeated, "For doing nothing. Sitting on their holes all day long." Patrick wasn't drunk but he had a pedantic, laborious nature, prone to repeating himself as if he were talking to a child or training a dog. "So what do you have to say for yourselves?"

Sandor replied, "You are wrong."

Patrick was surprised by this challenge, "So you are not living for free?"

Sandor said, "The Red Cross pay us. Irish people pay the Red Cross. It's not a tax."

"What about the police, the army? Am I not paying them to keep you all under fucking control?"

Eva said in English, "We go. Thank you Thomas. We go."

Patrick was keen to get a reply to his question, "So my taxes are being wasted on people like yourselves while Irishmen and women are starving in this country. How does that feel?"

Again, Thomas apologised for his brother's behaviour. Patrick demanded an answer. Sandor said, "We were refugees invited here."

"So you think that it's perfectly okay for you lot to take food out of the hands of hungry Irish people?"

Sandor said, "We were asked to come here. We did not know that the place was poor." Sandor smiled, enjoying the argument, "We did not know that your country was useless."

Angered, Patrick replied, "Useless? You take our money and you call us useless. You deserve a good fucking beating."

Sandor stood up, encouraging everybody to do so. He was looking down on Patrick, "The people are not useless, just the country. You confuse people with their countries."

"Go fuck yourself."

Thomas, clearly annoyed, asked Patrick to leave the table, but he exclaimed that their family owned the hotel, "So they want to take over this place as well? Go back to your camp, back to your cow sheds."

Thomas offered them a lift back to the camp. While driving he kept repeating, "I'm so sorry. He's an awful man. And that's not what people think. Believe me, honestly. He's a one-off."

∽

As the weeks went by and winter gave way to spring, Sandor concluded that Ireland could absorb between sixty to one hundred Hungarians at the most. This estimate was based on the amount of people who had already got jobs, but failed to take into account whether these people were over or underqualified for their positions. Tradesmen were working as farm hands, teachers as domestic staff; people were prepared to work at anything in order to get out of Knockalisheen.

As Josef Horvath believed that Ireland was always meant to be a transit camp he wanted to go on hunger strike immediately. After four months he was still unemployed and figured that a strike was necessary to encourage the government to act. Horvath had given up on the Irish Red Cross. He believed that they were just the administrators of the camp but without any power. Yes, they were necessary for the day-to-day running but had little influence over the policy which had brought them to Ireland in the first place.

Although Sandor understood Horvath's impatience with Ireland, he didn't want to go on a hunger strike just yet. Just as Horvath wanted to get out of the country, there were many refugees who were happy to find jobs and settle down. Sandor wanted to protect the reputation of the people who imagined their future in Ireland. He believed that employers would be less likely to offer jobs to those perceived as trouble makers. Sandor said to Horvath, "Everybody in the camp will have to agree to go on a hunger strike. It can't just be a couple of people. And I don't think that the time is right yet."

"And when do you think the time will be right?" asked Horvath.

Sandor replied, "If Ireland can't absorb a few hundred refugees willing to work at anything after five months, then we should call a strike. But not before then."

If they were to go on hunger strike, Sandor was not looking forward to the day when he'd have to tell McManus, as he was beginning to appreciate the position of this Red Cross official. Ireland's preparation for the arrival of the refugees had been exemplary; money had been raised, accommodation, although rudimentary, had been found and the decision to bring in the Hungarians had been supported nationally. Nevertheless, consideration had not been given to what the refugees would actually do once in the country. But this wasn't a matter for the Irish Red Cross; their duty was to raise money for those in need, and it had been carried out flawlessly; in fact Sandor had thought that if they hadn't raised so much money the refugees wouldn't have been able to come to Ireland in the first place.

But behind the advertisements in the newspapers and the collection boxes in the streets and the recognisable white flag with the red cross upon it were people like McManus: a man in late middle-age working tirelessly for the charitable organisation which he loved, but who would never have guessed that when a decision was made to raise money last October, it would lead to a bunch of disgruntled refugees contemplating a hunger strike in his native county.

∞

Shortly after becoming camp representative Sandor had been introduced to a woman called Rita, a blonde, thirty-four year old from a small village in southern Hungary. While crossing the Hungarian border with her husband and child, she had become separated from them and had arrived in Austria without knowing whether her husband and child had crossed safely – and if so, where they were. She had spent weeks in Eisenstadt searching for her family but without success. When they were leaving Hungary, however, her husband had spoken of coming to England as he didn't want to leave Europe. Rita had mistakenly thought that Ireland was a part of England and it was only when she had arrived in Limerick that she was informed that her asylum in Ireland didn't grant her access to England.

Of the few belongings which she had taken from Hungary was a collection of letters, correspondence between herself and her husband from the war. He had spent two years fighting in Russia soon after they had married. She had the letters on her when she became separated from him but she'd lost them in the camp. On mentioning this to Sandor, tears came to her eyes and she silently sobbed. She believed that they had been stolen from her hut by someone who had believed that they contained money.

Sandor felt helpless listening to Rita. She complained

about the Irish Red Cross as she believed that they weren't doing enough to help find her family. Listening to her complaints, Sandor didn't know what to say, he knew nothing of the Red Cross and its capabilities, nor was he competent at counselling a distressed woman. It felt voyeuristic to be so close to a stranger's tears and his pity seemed cruelly counterfeit. Sandor explained to Rita that all refugees coming out of Austria would have been registered by the International Red Cross and details of the movement of people between countries would have been recorded.

Alerted by McManus, the British Red Cross had started searching for her family, he was in regular contact with them and kept Sandor informed. But McManus didn't expect much as the Red Cross was under severe pressure as the uprising had created the largest displacement of people since the war.

Sandor informed Rita of the levels of bureaucracy, how each country had its own Red Cross which dealt with national governments who in turn, dealt with the UN. Sponge-like bureaucracy soaking up thousands of people.

Although Rita had been informed by McManus that refugees could not move from Ireland to England, people in the camp soon realised that it was possible to make their way to Dublin and sail across the channel to Holyhead and on to London. It was some refugees' intention, including Josef Horvath, to make this trip to London in order to find work, as it was believed that the English customs presumed that everybody crossing the channel were Irish.

Rita was considering this option when Sandor learned that her husband had been located, not in England, but in Austria, and that a flight had been arranged for him to fly to Shannon. Sandor wasn't in the camp the night Rita was united with her family but the following morning she called to his hut to show gratitude. After thanking him profusely, she told him that in a couple day's time they were planning to go to London. "But I feel guilty about leaving the camp. You helped to unite us and now we're off to England," she said. "I feel I owe Ireland something."

∽

Sandor checked the number. He knocked on the door. A small woman opened it. He asked, "Are you Klara Glos?"

"Yes."

"And is your husband Béla in?"

"Yes, come in?"

Sandor entered the hut and was offered a seat beside the potbellied stove. Apart from a photograph hanging near the door, the hut was identical to every other hut Sandor had visited. Béla Glos was a small man. And like Klara, he had black hair and dark skin. They looked more like brother and sister than man and wife.

Béla picked up a bottle of beer, "Would you like a glass?"

"No thanks."

Béla poured himself some beer and stated, "You are here about the house."

"Yes. We can't understand why you aren't interested in taking the house. From what the Red Cross tells me, it's a great place, in a nice part of Dublin, it's in perfect condition, it's fully furnished and what's more, they are willing to give it to you rent free for one year. So why did you turn the offer down? You did visit the house, didn't you?"

Béla replied, "We spent a week in Dublin in the house. And as you say, it's a nice place."

Sandor said, "A lot of people would die for a place like that, and rent free."

"We were worried about getting work in Dublin."

"But the house is rent free for a year and the Red Cross will keep giving you an allowance."

"Yes, yes, I understand. But if we don't take it, some other people will," Béla replied. "The house won't be wasted."

"Perhaps," replied Sandor. "But we still want to know why you turned the house down. The Red Cross can't figure it out. What more can they do? They are offering you a start in this country and you throw it back in their faces." Sandor shuffled in his seat, "Did you not like Dublin?"

Béla looked at his wife. She shrugged her shoulders, "It's okay."

Sandor asked, "What about the people next door to the house. What were they like? Friendly? Hostile?"

Béla said, "They seemed fine. Friendly, I suppose."

Klara looked at her husband and then at Sandor, "We don't want to stay in Ireland."

Sandor's reply was tinged with anger, "But why turn the house down?"

She said, "We think that if we leave the camp we won't be able to get a visa."

Sandor asked, "Correct me if I am wrong: you want to leave Ireland to get a job and a decent place to live?"

"Yes."

"But the Red Cross has given you a decent place to live here; all you have to do now is get a job. And there's nothing stopping you applying for a visa if you are living outside the camp. You don't have to be unemployed and housed here to apply."

Béla replied, "But we have heard that we have to be living in the camp."

"Heard from who?"

"Other people in the camp."

Sandor sighed, "If that was the case – which it's not – and people follow your example, then this camp will never empty of people even if there's jobs and houses for everybody."

Béla replied, "But there's not. The place is useless."

Sandor stood up, ready to leave, "There is nothing useless about getting a free house for one year and an allowance to go with it. Most people would consider that very useful."

༄

McManus was sick with a cold. He was wearing a heavy woollen jumper, a large scarf was wrapped around his neck. His voice had been reduced to a whisper. He spoke slowly, explaining that the Austrian necklace manufacturer had decided to stop employing the women in the camp due to adverse business conditions. "I was talking to him earlier. He said that there just wasn't the market for his product any more. He liked the workers here and he's sorry that he can't use them. It's a blow to the camp." McManus coughed, then wiped his nose, "No more bead-man."

CHAPTER TWELVE

Sandor was in Gerry Buckley's office. He noted Gerry's haircut. His white moustache had been trimmed of its amber edges which gave his face a tidier, though older appearance. The haircut also made him appear fatter: the weight which hung from his waist now lacked a counterpoint without his longish hair.

Sandor understood that today, a Monday morning, he would start working on the factory floor. Up till now he had worked weekends or had spent time driving around in Gerry's car. Sandor consumed tea and biscuits as Gerry told him what work needed to be done, "You have to service an engine for the end of the week. That's the priority."

After their meeting, Sandor walked through the factory towards his desk observing other people's jobs; some worked on engines, others were making parts. Once at his desk Sandor started on a small engine, it was not unlike the one he had serviced for the mushroom grower.

Seconds later Sandor heard a man raising his voice, it was the same red-haired person whom he'd seen talking in Gerry's office on occasion. The man was trying to get the attention of all workers and within a few seconds most of them were looking at him except one or two who were operating loud machinery. Sandor stopped what he was about to start, trying to understand what the man was saying. Some workers looked at him and Sandor felt like a novice, unaware of what was happening, what factory ritual was unfolding. Perhaps it was company announcement? A notice concerning a staff member? When the man continued speaking, many of the workers started looking at Sandor and he thought that the man was telling them about him joining the company. This made Sandor feel awkward and uncomfortable. Then all the workers left the factory floor.

Sandor remained still, wondering what to do. Feeling alone on the deserted factory floor, he followed them. Presuming that they had gone to the canteen, he walked towards the only doors leading out of the plant, one of which went upstairs to Gerry's office. He walked through the other door, the corridor faintly illuminated by a dim bulb. Quickly, he arrived at the canteen, but it was empty. At the end of the corridor was another door leading outside. Once there he saw the workers standing in a circle listening to the red-haired man in the car park. He felt self-conscious joining the group and as he did the man started to waver in his speech. Then for a few seconds the man stopped talking altogether, people turned around looking at each other and then at Sandor. Again Sandor felt self-conscious, unaware if this was a break or a some kind company procedure. At a slower pace the man resumed speaking, but still Sandor couldn't understand a word.

"Sandor, come here," called Gerry while standing at the door of the factory. A confused Sandor left the workers and followed Gerry back inside. Gerry told him to go up to his office, which he did. Minutes later Gerry arrived with the red-haired man and told Sandor to wait outside his door.

Sandor heard Gerry and the man speaking. He couldn't understand what they were saying, but their voices were raised. Gerry's tone had an aggressive edge; he was shouting at the man. Though the man didn't shout back, his voice was more threatening; a loud, though solid, timbre. When the man left the office he passed Sandor but failed to look at him. Soon the sound of work resumed downstairs. Gerry appeared, "Get your coat."

Driving back to the camp Gerry explained that the trade union wouldn't permit him to employ any refugees and so he couldn't offer Sandor a full-time position but he could still come down on weekends. Sandor wondered what control Gerry exercised over his factory if he couldn't employ who he wanted to. Gerry said, "They are scared of losing their jobs. They think that if I employ one Hungarian soon I'll employ more. They want to keep the jobs which come up for themselves. They are also scared of the wages which I might be paying you. They don't realise that there's a lot to be learned from other people. They're too fucking stupid to know that."

Outside the camp Gerry told Sandor to come down on Saturday. From his shirt pocket he gave Sandor some money and sped off.

Sandor looked at the camp. There were fewer fires burning since the arrival of spring. He decided not to go to his hut and walked back to Limerick. He'd have to tell Maria and Eva about the factory but he wasn't in the mood to explain what had happened.

He felt sad and his melancholy soon turned into depression. He wanted to be alone. With Gerry's money he went to the cinema to see Moby Dick. Velvet seats soothed a body weighed down with disappointment. The darkness of the theatre offered him liberty. There weren't many people in the cinema, Sandor relaxed by hanging his legs over the seat in front of him, his shoes off, his jacket on. Throughout the film Sandor's mind drifted from what was on screen to what had happened that morning. He felt schizophrenic; a part of him was feeling enjoyment and reward from the film while another part was dampened by the actions of the red-haired man and his ability to deny him work. Images of the open sea offered him a perspective on life. He imagined a different reality, one in which he was working full time with another set of workers around him and another employer: Julia Pinter.

∽

Sandor told McManus about what had happened at Buckley Engineering. McManus expressed disappointment with the trade unions, "That they want to protect their jobs I can understand, but why the pretence of supporting the Hungarian people fighting the Soviets? It was only a couple of months ago that the dockers refused to unload cargo from Russian ships, but when they're asked to help refugees on their own soil, all the main unions have flatly refused to do so."

As suggested by Pinter, Sandor had compiled a list of suitable employees and McManus assured that he would bring all his influence to bear on the government. He thought it was perfect. It bypassed Irish trade unions as the jobs were being created from scratch; it was largely self-financing; it could help Ireland develop a new industry; and it could educate Irish workers in new skills. He enthused, "There are plenty of run-down buildings which could be used. And if we can't refurbish one, we could create further employment by building one."

"At the most," Sandor reckoned, "Pinter's factory might absorb eight to twelve people from the camp, which is a small percentage considering there is around one hundred and fifty adults left in the camp."

"Nevertheless," McManus said. "It's a model way of creating employment, although they'd still need around twenty-five factories of that size to employ the remaining refugees. And that," he joked, "is an industrial revolution."

∽

Sandor was lying on his bed trying to read the obituaries in The Limerick Leader, death had been on his mind, not his or anybody's he knew, just the notion of it, the finality which meets us all. These thoughts were prompted by the singing which he'd heard when passing the chapel. Familiar Presbyterian hymns breathing through open windows, some sung in Hungarian, others in English. For Sandor, all hymns spoke of death regardless of their subject matter, whether they were rejoicing in life, rebirth, Christ or nature, they all seemed to be bound by morbidity. Sandor didn't have the metaphysical confidence to call his lack of faith atheistic, but it was. Faith was something which he'd never experienced and because he hadn't, it was indeed mysterious. He was jealous of believers as they had the afterlife. Death, for him, was the infinity before the year 1927, the year of his birth, or when he had a good night's sleep, one too deep for dreams. As the pious language of The Limerick Leader obituaries was too difficult for him to understand, he was happily distracted by a knocking on the door.

Eva answered it. It was Father Mikes. After initial greetings, he asked about Kristina, "How is she getting on in Laurel Hill? Does she like the school?" He spoke about the religious ceremonies which would soon happen, communion and confirmation, and how Kristina would have hers in the camp with the other children and not in school.

Eva replied, "We're very lucky that she's in Laurel Hill."

Father Mikes agreed that Kristina was lucky to be attending any school, and such a good one at that, as it would be next September before the majority of children would properly start school. He explained, "Not far from the camp a new school is being built in Meelick. The nuns in charge are keen to take in refugees and the same nuns are going to help with the upcoming confirmations and communions in the camp."

Father Mikes started talking to Sandor about other aspects of the camp, jobs and visas and then he turned to Eva and spoke about a game of tennis which she had played. She was surprised that Father Mikes was aware that she had been playing tennis with Lucia, and Sandor thought that perhaps the priest wanted to play, as he was in shape, youthful, athletic.

The priest started to mumble, "You might think that this is a little strange but I have been requested to ask you not to wear your tennis shorts back to the court where you played last week."

"My shorts?"

"Yes."

"What is wrong with my shorts."

"There have been complaints."

Although Sandor hadn't seen his sister playing tennis, she had turned a pair of shorts into ones suitable for the sport. She used to play tennis in Budapest, it was a game which she liked and she was particular about the clothes required.

Sandor asked who had been complaining?

"People," said Father Mikes.

"But my shorts," continued Eva, "are like the ones which I wear at home."

Father Mikes shuffled in his seat, "While I understand your preference, some people think that they are unsuitable for the court, that's all."

"But they are the most comfortable clothes you can wear while playing tennis."

Again Sandor asked, "Who was complaining?"

Father Mikes said, "A person from the village where the game was being played."

"A man or a woman?"

"A member of the clergy."

Sandor asked, "A Catholic priest?"

"Yes."

"And he thinks that they are unsuitable?" asked Eva.

"Yes."

She continued, "Why was a Catholic priest looking at my shorts while I play tennis?"

Nervously, Father Mikes explained the geography of the small village. It was on a hill overlooking the Shannon Estuary, the tennis court was beside the priest's residence, and when Eva had been playing tennis, he noticed her.

Eva said she felt insulted. Father Mikes smiled apologetically, and he restated that it was the wishes of the local priest, and no, it's not the law, and no, she didn't have to pay any attention to him, but as he was the priest and it was his village, it would be wise to obey.

Father Mikes was surprised by the anger in Eva's voice, "I'm a twenty-nine year old mother. I can wear what I want when I'm playing tennis."

Father Mikes explained that the Irish were very modest in their dress sense and offence was easily caused. Eva replied that the Hungarian Olympic team wore similar shorts and they weren't considered indecent. What constituted modesty was discussed for a few minutes until Eva ended the argument by saying that she wasn't going to play tennis again, not because she couldn't wear her shorts, but because the idea of a man gawking at her body as she played tennis was disgusting, "It makes my skin crawl."

Father Mikes was glad that the subject had been resolved, "It's best not to cause anybody offence. As Kristina is very happy in Laurel Hill, I'm sure you'd want her to remain there."

Maria wanted to see Moby Dick so Sandor went back to the cinema for a second time. He loved the film. Most of the dialogue he couldn't follow, but it didn't matter as he liked the action, the small boats leaving the Pequod giving chase to the whale, the bloody realism of the harpoons spearing their backs, and how the mammals gradually came to a halt on the ocean but they didn't sink and were towed back to the Pequod where flesh was turned into oil. After Sandor had seen it the first time, Tommy Gallagher had mentioned that the beginning was shot in Youghal as it resembled America one hundred years ago. Many people in the county were thrilled that a small place in Cork was appearing on the big screen. Gallagher laughed derisively as he told Sandor, "Their villages are trapped in time and they're proud of it."

So Sandor looked for signs of Irishness, the slope of the countryside, the design of houses, national characteristics, a lightness to their skin, those weather-beaten faces. Maria was happy that Moby Dick got away in the end, but she thought it was horrific to see Captain Ahab strapped to him, bobbing up and down in the water on the back of the whale.

It was a cold morning. Sandor felt an icy draft through the wooden boards behind his bed. Wind ghosted through the window frames with ease. The curtain around his bed flapped sail-like in the damp air. Sandor gave himself five more minutes in bed. His sleep had been heavy. His eyes were locked together by a night of vivid dreaming, an intense experience of talking to his mother. He was back in Budapest, back in the apartment, back in their kitchen. It was late summer and she was warning him about car accidents. She had his full attention. She was angry with him, but he couldn't tell why. She was gripping his arm. He felt the authority of her touch. On waking, Sandor continued an imaginary conversation with her. It was one which he often had and it concerned his reasons for leaving Hungary. *All we want is a chance for a better life; to live in a country free of the Soviets; to experience freedom.* But there was a festering cruelty to these phrases: it was all about him, his life, his desire to escape, his will to a better life. Personal gain at his mother's expense. Guilt made him feel stranded and isolated. Such was its force, he imagined it physically appearing on his body like a scar, a blood-red rip of his skin, his own sinful stigmata marking his sinful life.

Sandor decided to get out of bed. He liked to move, to stretch his legs, bend his back, feel the reward of exercise. He dressed quickly and purposefully, picking his warmest clothes piled by the side of his bed. Others were getting up too. Conversation whispered like breathy animals behind the Vargas curtain. Eva's bed squeaked as she sat upright, pillows squashed between herself and the wooden walls.

Suddenly, Peter's voice started rising. It was a solid expression of power and force, his words being forged in the pit of his stomach. Sandor couldn't help but overhear. Anna was close to tears, her voice tremulous. There was a reedy quiver to her words which sounded like the fading notes of a violin. Sandor, laces tied, his breath carrying the last of his morning's yawns, wanted to open his curtains and leave the hut, but he felt trapped by a crying Anna and Peter's fervent defence. Sandor tried to catch every word being exchanged; baby Gábor's name was invoked with maternal command; Ireland was cursed; Anna spoke reverentially of Hungary; and Peter appealed for calm. He also appealed for time, "We need more, that's all." Anna disagreed. Enough time had been wasted. She accused Peter of squandering it recklessly, saying the word *time* like the poor utter *money*.

Calm slowly descended on them once the baby started crying and blame like dirty snow flakes tried to settle on the warring couple. Peter spoke of Anna's sleepless nights as if they explained everything and she defended herself by criticising his decision to come to this ragged soul of a country.

Then their argument flared up again. This time Anna attacked Peter's size, his physical bulk which she called lazy, useless and unemployable. Sandor felt for Peter being attacked. Peter didn't respond. As the sun shone through the far window, Sandor saw the cumbersome silhouette of Peter's body, motionless behind drawn curtains, his hands slowly moving to his sides as he sat down on their bed, while Anna turned to Gábor lying in his crib.

∽

It was late March. The last four months in Ireland had been the longest period of inactivity in Sandor's adult life excluding the war. It was not money which he missed nor was it living in a hut; it was the lack of activity, the feeling that his brain was slowing down, that days, weeks and months were being wasted, and wasting time was, as his father Frank would say, "The greatest waste of all."

When Sandor told Maria about Gerry Buckley and his lack of full-time work, she was disappointed, not just for him, but for them as a couple. Recently she'd been assessing their relationship and felt that they were drifting from day to day without a plan, "I could get pregnant and then what would we do?" Sandor hadn't given much thought to getting her pregnant; having sex with her was one of the only pleasures he had in the camp.

While Maria agreed that their employment prospects and visa applications for other countries would affect their relationship, she also believed that they could influence their fate. She told Sandor that she didn't want to pressurise him but she was being pressurised by her parents as to the seriousness of their relationship. The Novaks had come to Ireland as a family and her parents wanted to leave as a family but now that Maria was beginning a relationship with Sandor, they had started wondering about it and wanted to know what their daughter would do if they got visas for America. Maria had blindly presumed that most people in the camp would be transferred to the same country, the wooden huts and green fields of Knockalisheen in exchange for the wooden houses and manicured lawns of suburban America or Canada. But Sandor wasn't as confident as her. He felt that they were being thrown around, not wholly against their will but like debris falling through the air of countries, bureaucracy and charity looking for a place to settle.

Since the bead-man had stopped employing women in the camp, Maria had resumed her search for work and found a job as a domestic help with a large family, the O'Malleys. One day when Francis O'Malley, the father of the family, asked Maria if she knew anybody who could repair an old car engine, she recommended Sandor and he walked the four miles to work with her the following day, to a large country house in County Clare.

Sandor spent the day in a workshop on the grounds of the house and every hour or so Francis O'Malley came over to check his work. He always had a cigar in his mouth and though Sandor understood everything that the sixty-year old man said, he insisted on repeating his words as if Sandor were a child. When Sandor fixed the engine, O'Malley asked him to clean the drains at the front of the house. Sandor explained that he worked as an engineer and had little knowledge of drainage, but O'Malley said that all he had to do was climb a ladder and remove the dirt which had gathered there during the winter. Against his wishes Sandor climbed the ladder and spent a further hour cleaning the drains and ensuring that they were properly secured to the house.

Once finished O'Malley asked him to move some timber from one shed to another, which he did, and afterwards, it was late evening and the yellow sun was beginning to set, O'Malley asked for one more favour. Sandor was given a bag of kidneys to slice up for the many cats which slinked around the big old house. As Sandor did, Maria came into the kitchen tired from a day of cleaning floors, washing and ironing linen and supervising the younger children.

Maria's last job before she returned to the camp was serving dinner for the family. This involved carrying large trays from the kitchen upstairs to the dining room, placing them on a side table and then spooning out measured portions for the eight members of the family. Once the family was served, Maria and Sandor sat at the table. Francis thanked God and then requested Maria to say a prayer in Hungarian. As Maria didn't know any prayers in Hungarian and didn't want to offend her employer, she recited Humpty Dumpty in her native language, slowly talking her way through its verses with solemn proclamation.

As Maria wasn't particularly good at English, Francis was thrilled to have Sandor over to dinner for an evening and questioned him about Hungary. A book had been written about the Hungarian Catholic Primate Cardinal Mindszenty and chapters had appeared in an Irish newspaper. With interest Francis had cut out these articles and asked Sandor about the cleric.

Sandor listened to Francis surprised at how much English he now understood. Like one of his senses, he felt that the language had become a part of him. He wasn't deaf to English speech and the written word was alive and clear. Although he didn't understand every word in every sentence, he took in an overall meaning. Words weren't wasted on him anymore, no longer littered on the floor around him. But he knew that his use of language was far from perfect, his tenses were incorrect and certain phrases were repeated too often.

Sandor explained, slowly at first, that Mindszenty was a powerful man because sixty percent of Hungarians were Catholic and when he was released during the uprising, it was seen as a victory of religious freedom over communism.

Francis said that the Irish papers gave the impression that the uprising was not only against communist but for Catholicism, "But hadn't people supported Nagy who was a communist?"

Sandor said that there had been a misunderstanding in Ireland about the uprising; it was for communism but against Soviet communism, "Which makes me a Hungarian communist."

"And what is that?" asked Francis.

"I can only tell you what it isn't," replied Sandor and he spoke about the last twenty years of Hungary's history, years when the country supported the Nazis and then was occupied by the Nazis; how fighting between the Russians and the Germans destroyed large parts of Budapest; and then the last ten years of Russian occupation and exploitation. Sandor was tired of political extremes and said that while most people pitied Hungary at this point in time, not so long ago she had occupied other countries and forced her language and customs on them, places such as Romania and Slovakia. Sandor concluded by saying that all he wanted was to earn a living in a peaceful country free of any ideologues.

Later, when Francis dropped them off at the gates of Knockalisheen Camp, he told Sandor that he'd settle up with him at the end of the week as he was a little short of cash, "I'll give it to Maria." But when the week ended and Maria returned to the camp, Francis hadn't given her any money nor had he paid her for this week's work.

Annoyed, Sandor walked up to the house on Saturday morning but it was empty. Returning to the house the following afternoon, Sandor met Francis and again he told him to call back during the week, "I've no cash on me." Later that evening Maria told Sandor that O'Malley hadn't actually paid her for the last two weeks. He had promised to pay her but had come up with excuses or talked too quickly and thus confused her.

Sandor became concerned about this debt and suggested that she should stop working for him until he paid her in full. But Maria liked the family, she got a good meal in the evening, the children were nice, and they appeared to be, not only honest, but wealthy too. She said, "Let's wait till the end of the week and see what happens."

∽

On Saint Patrick's Day, Father Mikes told his congregation, which included Sandor, Maria and her family, about the historic links between Ireland and Hungary. In the time of Oliver Cromwell, Catholic Hungary gave sanctuary to hundreds of Irish exiles, one of whom was Bishop Walker Lynch of Clonfert who arrived in 1655. Of the few possessions which he brought with him was a picture of the Madonna and when he became Deputy Bishop of the diocese of Juarintim, he hung the painting in his church. "And years later on the 17 March 1697, the picture shed tears of blood for three hours as a way of manifesting heaven's solidarity and sympathy for the suffering of Irish people," explained Father Mikes.

CHAPTER THIRTEEN

Mr Casey, a Limerick publican, liked the photograph Sandor had taken of his bar. It was lunchtime, the pub was quiet. Mr Casey instructed Sandor to take a seat and offered him tea. Sandor's spirit was buoyed by this offer. If Mr Casey had no intention of buying the photograph, why the offer of tea: infallible logic. It was Sandor's experience that people not interested in buying a photograph were generally blunt, sometimes rude, and all eye contact and body language became minimal as if there was a chance that a physical gesture or a misspent word would form a binding contract from which escape was impossible. But a cup of tea at a bar counter, and a nice bar as well, the front door open, spring wafting in, the place was quiet apart from the occasional scream from a baby wrapped in a blanket and resting behind the counter. Mr Casey was old, bloated; his red face had the unhealthy pallor of a man who had spent a life indoors, shunning sunlight, pipe-smoked skin and a polished bald head.

Mr Casey talked about Arthur Griffith. Sandor understood most of the conversation and learned about this Irish politician who had been influenced by Hungary's relationship with the Austrian Empire. Mr Casey mentioned 1867;

this date brought Sandor back to his school days, a defining moment in Hungarian history, the year when the Austrian Empire became the Austro-Hungarian Empire and the Dual Monarchy was established, thus granting Hungary near independence from Austria. These facts had been implanted in Sandor's mind during school thus forming an inescapable and unforgettable mantra. Mr Casey was proud of his knowledge and was excited that a Hungarian man was sitting in his pub.

When asked if he'd heard of Arthur Griffith, Sandor said, "No." Mr Casey pointed at a picture behind the bar, a group of men, Griffith among them. Sandor looked blankly at the photograph and smiled.

Mr Casey explained that once Ireland had been faced with a situation similar to Hungary as both countries had been underdogs, but within different empires. Both wanted independence from a monarchy and Hungary had managed a form of separation in 1867 which had inspired Griffith. Mr Casey said that Ireland, except for the north, was separate from England, but this independence had its problems, "Maybe we'd have been better off with closer ties to the empire, like Hungary had with Austria."

"It depends on the empire," replied Sandor and explained that Hungary was now linked to a Russian empire which was the cause of all her problems. When Sandor declined another cup of tea, Mr Casey took this as a sign to discuss business. He cleared a space on the counter to further study the photograph, tilting it to catch the low wattage of the light bulb. While Mr Casey examined the picture the silence between them became uncomfortably long and was only broken by the old man mumbling words which Sandor couldn't understand and so he started to wonder if he'd make a sale. Through the open door Sandor witnessed a dog urinating against a car tyre. A bird lighted on the windowsill.

Sandor, made anxious by Mr Casey's deliberation, waited for an answer, realising that his earlier certainty might have been wrong. He felt humiliated by his over confidence.

Mr Casey argued over the price and Sandor accepted a reduction, the publican gave him the money and walked him outside, and once there, he suggested that if the weather kept up and the weekend was nice, Sandor should go swimming in the Shannon, "Up river, towards the power station."

As Sandor wasn't working for Gerry Buckley that weekend he suggested to Maria that they take this advice and spend a day by the river. So they packed a picnic of sandwiches and beer and walked along by the river away from the other people also enjoying this glimpse of summer. Maria looked younger with her black hair wet against her face, her twenty-four years seemed reduced to sixteen or seventeen, her upturned nose exhaled bubbles beneath the water, and when they stood still close to the river bank, goose pimples pricked her skin while Sandor rubbed her arms trying to remove them. And when they finished swimming, they moved away from the river to a clearing in the woods which trapped the sun.

They enjoyed being away from the camp, to indulge in an afternoon lying together in the woods, it was comfortable, quiet and free of people. Knockalisheen was an endless search for privacy, waiting for the communal huts to empty of people which only happened late at night and which only left them an hour or so of tired intimacy. At times they enjoyed sneaking around the camp looking for places to have sex, the risk of getting caught heightening their pleasure. It was a source of entertainment, to be in the packed recreational hut during the day and to point to places where people were sitting, a spot where only hours ago, in the early hours of the morning, they had been intimate. These public rooms became possessed with their sexual memory, Maria's diminished screams and his subdued sighs.

Later that day, when the sun started to set and the air cooled, they dressed their naked, suntanned bodies and exchanged the clandestine woods for the camp.

∾

In early April Sandor learnt of the death of a Hungarian boy in a Dublin hospital, the first refugee to die on Irish soil. McManus spoke of the sadness of the boy's life, he had been separated from his parents and ended up in Limerick and, despite the help of the best consultants in the country, had died a lonely death thousands of miles from his home and in a city where he didn't know anybody. Why God would do such a thing was certainly a mystery. McManus had just returned from Dublin where a small funeral mass had been said in the hospital and the boy was buried in Deansgrange cemetery, "A nice resting place in the suburbs of Dublin."

Although their problems were put into perspective by this untimely death, the business of the camp continued, and now that the trade unions had refused to deal with the refugees, McManus spoke of Julia Pinter's plan for a factory, "We should be hearing from the government soon enough. They have been thinking about it for two months now."

Regarding accommodation, McManus mentioned one or two houses available in Dublin thanks to the Irish Red Cross or corporate charity, but for the foreseeable future, Knockalisheen Camp would still be the principal residence for the majority of the refugees. Jobs, accommodation – and lastly – visas were discussed and McManus responded to Sandor's suggestion that the government pressurise embassies into giving preference to the refugees.

McManus replied, "You must realise that the government thinks that the refugees are equals in Irish society, and that you are free to do whatever you want. If that means leaving the country, you are welcome to and, like any other citizen, you can apply to the various embassies for a visa."

McManus asked Sandor to investigate a report that people had tampered with the electricity in order to provide huts with power after the midnight blackout.

Josef Horvath volunteered to investigate this claim and spent three nights spying in the camp. It was assumed that if somebody wanted to use electricity after midnight, they'd still turn off their lights like everybody else and only later switch the lights back on. And so Horvath left his hut an hour after midnight to walk around the perimeter of the camp, close to the barbed wire fence where he'd have a good view of the huts, some dark, others illuminated by candle light. Curtains of different strength were drawn across windows, but he could still see light behind them like late evening cloud warmed by the sun. Outside some huts he heard laughter or conversation too muffled to be understood. Quickly he could tell if candles were being used as their flames would flicker and dance behind the curtains; except candles enclosed in lamps, a vacuum of still, calm air. Horvath felt mischievous and bold sneaking around the camp, pressing his body against the wooden walls of huts, peering into the windows ascertaining light levels. One hut seemed brightened by the steady wattage of electricity. It was hut sixty three. He went back three nights in a row.

On the last night Horvath took Sandor. Above was a cloudless sky; the moon was a semicircle, standing upright and looking as if its other half had been chopped off with a knife. Sandor marvelled at its geometry and tried to recall his school science, the position of the sun, earth and moon. He was always amazed at the brightness of the sky, a brilliance of light hidden from him in Budapest. Hut sixty three was brighter than every other hut and the following day Sandor warned them to comply with the electricity rationing. When this had been solved, McManus mentioned the use of an illegal radio. It wasn't clear to Sandor why such a device was illegal and, unlike the misuse of electricity, he didn't think it was very serious and so he ignored it.

After a couple of weeks dating Thomas Townsend, Eva decided that she wasn't interested in him anymore. She told him outside his hotel and he walked her to the camp in a vain attempt to change her mind. It had taken a few short weeks for Thomas to become attached to her, weeks which she had found increasingly tedious due to the language barrier. Their conversations were limited; communication about basic items was a long, drawn-out affair, her scrambling to find the words, always aware that, as she was the foreigner, it was her lack of English and not his lack of Hungarian which was the problem. The Irish Red Cross had printed small drawings of ordinary items such as cigarettes, food, drink and clothing so the tongue-strapped refugee could have a pictorial aid and Eva had felt like carrying these signs with her when dating Thomas. Not that he didn't try his best to accommodate her; he was always a gentleman, forever trying to cleanse the conversation of misunderstanding, eager to learn a few Hungarian words and patient of Eva's introductory grasp of English. But this wasn't enough for her.

One night Eva and Thomas had gone to a bar with another Irish couple, and though they had tried to include her in their conversation, it seemed to her that she had spent the night alone. She felt uncomfortable sitting among others as they laughed at jokes and anecdotes while she remained silent, though wearing an expectant smile as the humour was slowly translated, holding back the natural flow of the conversation. Eva didn't drink like Thomas and his friends did, she wasn't used to drinking for its own sake or without food, and so by the end of the night the banter would become boisterous and most of the translation lost amid their drunken hilarity. That she was attracted to Thomas she didn't doubt; he was good looking and had many appealing qualities – generosity, charm – but for Eva, language was far too much of a barrier as it reduced two adults to speaking like children.

∾

Sandor wasn't too surprised by her decision as Eva had never enthused about him, but he was surprised on returning to the hut one afternoon – he and the Vargas weren't expected home until evening – to see Josef Horvath in bed with his sister. For a few seconds, before Eva could reach out to close the curtains around her bed, Sandor glimpsed her naked body sitting on top of Horvath. Quickly, Sandor turned around and left the hut. Outside in the warmish air, he felt as though he'd committed an indecent act and one which should cause him shame. He felt an urgent sense of confusion. It was the same feeling as when he'd witnessed adult nudity for the first time. It was a friend's mother, he'd opened the bathroom door and she was drying her overweight body and shouted at him to leave.

Sandor sat in the recreational hut knowing that Eva would come and talk to him and an hour later she arrived. She was sheepish, hangdog and the usually frank talk between brother and sister was stilted and awkward. Eva said that she had been seeing Horvath for a few weeks and she didn't think of it as an affair as she'd only been seeing

Thomas for a few weeks longer. When she had started seeing Thomas, Horvath had declared his love for her. At first Eva had thought that he was suffering from a momentary infatuation but he continued along in the same vein for a couple of weeks.

In an initial attempt at decency towards Thomas, Eva had turned down all of Horvath's advances, but as the weeks passed by she realised that a few minutes with Josef was a lot more entertaining than a night or two with Thomas. On evenings spent with Thomas she had found herself looking forward to talking with Horvath back in the camp, to rid herself of the linguistical shackles and to slip back into her native tongue. English, or her lack thereof, had suffocated her relationship with Thomas. When Sandor asked why she hadn't ended with Thomas before starting with Horvath, she said, "I know it was wrong, but I was enjoying myself. Kristina was in school during the week, I hadn't worked since the bead-man and I needed some distraction."

∾

"I understood some of what O'Malley was saying," said Maria almost choking her words. "He kept on repeating himself. I was standing in the kitchen, he came in and started shouting at me. I couldn't believe it."

She was sitting at the end of Sandor's bed. The hut was empty. Sandor tried to remain calm, his voice unnaturally gentle, "Did he threaten you?"

"No. It wasn't like that. He was just angry," Maria started crying, Sandor placed his arm around her. Sandor had been in O'Malley's kitchen and could imagine it happening: Maria at one end, Francis at the other, light coming in from the window. And how Maria would be fearful of him, the father of the house, a man used to disciplining his many children, aware of his threatening self, his intimating stance. Sandor wished that he'd been there, that O'Malley had tried this on the day when he'd fixed his engine, cleaned his gutters and fed his cats. Anger made Sandor's eyes water and his heart pound. He said, "Fuckers like him take advantage. They prey on the vulnerable. What did you say to him?"

"I told him that I didn't understand everything. I said that there was a mistake. But he called me a thief."

"A thief."

"Yes."

Sandor shouted, "He's the thief."

Maria continued, "He was holding a couple of silver knives and forks in his hands. He said that he was missing some and that I had taken them." She was tremulous and this furthered his anger. Sandor said, "He doesn't want to pay you. He owes you for a couple of weeks, not to mention one day for me, and he's using this as a way of cheating you."

Maria started coughing, she asked Sandor for a tissue to blow her nose. "I was scared standing in the kitchen. There were other people in the house but they couldn't hear what he was saying. I thought he was going to hit me, you know, like I was a child. I have seen him beating one of his kids before, belting them with a piece of wood."

Sandor replied, "I'm going to get the money out of him."

"How? Do you think the police are going to believe him or me?"

"I'm not going to go to the police. I'll approach him myself. I'll try to talk to him."

"There was no talking to him today. He just kept shouting. I was terrified."

Sandor said, "I'll try talking to him and I'll see what happens. Have you told your father?"

"No. I came straight here. I don't want to tell him. I don't want him involved."

"What will you say about the job?"

"I'll just tell him that it finished. That there's no more work."

Sandor, full of nervous energy, said, "I'll go there tomorrow. I'll see what he has to say."

∽

Sandor spent an hour on the steps of Francis O'Malley's house waiting for the farmer to return from Limerick. O'Malley's whereabouts was given to Sandor by one of his sons, a twenty-year old man working on the front of the house, painting the drains which Sandor had cleaned. The son was surprised that Sandor insisted on waiting for his father to return. Sandor explained that it was a long walk from the camp and he wanted to talk to him.

When the son had finished painting he returned the ladder and paint cans to the garden shed, the place where Sandor had worked on the engine. Just after six, O'Malley pulled into the driveway and stopped in front of the house. Sandor jumped up with anticipation. O'Malley looked at Sandor and muttered something beneath his breath which he couldn't understand, not because of his lack of English but due to a purposeful mumble on the farmer's part. O'Malley walked past Sandor without looking him in the eye and entered the house, the large door slamming shut behind him. Sandor waited for a few seconds before he knocked on the door, letting the ornamental knocker echo around the airy hallway. O'Malley opened the door, not fully, but with caution, as if he wanted to identify an unknown caller. He asked what Sandor wanted.

Sandor had practised in English an imaginary conversation with O'Malley and had decided on a strategy; he would attempt to resolve their problems with politeness and an appeal to human decency. So Sandor spoke of a misunderstanding which must have happened. Maria wasn't a thief; she hadn't stolen anything from the house, in fact, she was grateful for a chance to work for a nice family. O'Malley disagreed, not so much with words, but with his eyes glancing dismissively sideways and his nostrils flaring with intolerance. The door closed.

Sandor heard footsteps in the hall. O'Malley opened the door to reveal his three sons, all large, stocky individuals. He said that as Maria had stolen the objects, he should ask her for his money. Again Sandor attempted to reason with him, he spoke of a misunderstanding, perhaps the objects had been misplaced by Maria or another worker as she certainly hadn't stolen them, nor had she broken them by mistake and disposed of them secretly.

But O'Malley wasn't convinced. The objects weren't in the house and the only workers who'd access to his home had been Sandor and Maria, and it was far too great a coincidence that personal belongings had started to disappear since they'd been in his employ. "Now fuck off," and he shut the door.

Sandor retreated from the property walking down the road until out of sight of the house. He jumped a fence and sat behind a large tree aware that he was still on O'Malley's land. Anger made his chest tighten and his eyes water. He felt that they'd been badly wronged. He pitied Maria as she had worked more than him and had more to lose. He wondered if he should wait for another day and return tomorrow evening, or forget about O'Malley altogether.

Sandor felt at odds with his surroundings. His anger seemed ill-matched with such a beautiful evening. Lush green fields extended into rolling hills below which the sun was setting, the few clouds in the sky seemed illuminated by fading light bulbs, the air windless and warm. When the feeling of anger subsided Sandor became tired and closed his eyes. Quickly, he fell asleep, waking a few hours later. It was dark and he felt disorientated. He stood up and urinated against the tree. He decided to return to O'Malley's house, not by the front, but by the rear. He walked through the field until he was a few hundred feet from the back of the house and jumped a fence. Having been inside the house before, he knew the layout of the downstairs, the location of the kitchen, dining room and hallway. As all lights were switched off upstairs, Sandor figured that the family was dining downstairs.

He started walking towards the building. Not far from the house stood the workshop where he had repaired the engine. The door was open and he entered. He found a torch and pointed it to the ground. The engine was still sitting on a table. He found a hammer and a large nail and punctured the radiator. By the entrance stood a tin of paint and brushes were sitting in a jar of water. He removed one of them and carried the tin outside. The lighting inside the house hadn't changed; upstairs was still dark and the only lights on downstairs were the kitchen and dining room. Sandor hurried to the front of the house, and kneeling down behind O'Malley's black car he painted a word on the rear bonnet which Tommy Gallagher had often used to describe Irish politicians – *cunts*. He returned the tin of paint to the workshop, placed the brush back in its jar and exited the grounds through the back field.

By the second week in April Sandor was feeling optimistic. Julia Pinter had came to the camp a number of times informing him of her meetings with government officials as she promoted her factory plan. She'd been in two meetings with McManus and had been impressed with his enthusiasm; his opinions were eloquently put and heartfelt. Pinter believed that McManus had an intuitive grasp of her vision and how it would benefit, not only Hungarian refugees, but the country in general. She said, "He seems to believe in the project more than I do."

Sandor replied that that was because it was a last resort, the Irish Red Cross had been abandoned by the government and left to look after the refugees on their own, "It's like a failed marriage with the Irish Red Cross being left in charge of the children while the government has run off."

Sandor had noticed a change in McManus. When they met to discuss the day-to-day aspects of camp life, he appeared calmer, less concerned with the minutiae of the refugees' existence, as if he'd been reassured by a higher power or a spiritual vision that salvation was close to hand. Sandor enjoyed these meetings with McManus. They started speaking more about each other and less about the camp. McManus told Sandor about volunteering for the British Red Cross in London during the war, afterwards he'd returned to Ireland to work in Dublin and then in Limerick. He had considered joining a political party but decided against it. Charity appeared to have an honesty which politics lacked. Unlike political parties, the Irish Red Cross stood for an ideal which would last for as long as the organisation was around, something which he couldn't say about politics, "You could dedicate your life to a party and it could transform into something entirely different, an organisation abhorrent to you, and as you had supported it, you would have only yourself to blame."

McManus couldn't think of a political party with an ideal which had stood the test of time. Within a generation most parties changed; but charity was the purest ideal, a Christlike concept, understood by all and undoubtedly fair.

When asked about his politics, Sandor said that all he wanted was to keep a close eye on his contradictions.

∽

McManus addressed Sandor as soon as he walked into the room, "Do you know who has been talking to this paper?" In his hands was a small publication, a folded newspaper. Sandor read the title, The Church of Ireland Gazette. As he had never seen it before, he replied, "No."

"Well, somebody from the camp has," McManus was dismissive.

Sandor replied, "I don't know."

McManus scratched his beard. It sounded like a mouse beneath the floorboards. He started reading from the paper, "'*We trust that the Irish Red Cross will, before long, give a full account of its stewardship to date of the monies handed to it by people, rich and poor, all over the country.*' Can you believe that? They are accusing me of financial carelessness. And there's a subtle hint that the Irish Red Cross might have pilfered some of the cash destined for the refugees. Someone in the camp is spreading these rumours and I want to find out who it is."

Sandor had often heard refugees discussing the money which the Red Cross had collected and how it was being used. Some people liked to think that the organisation was working against those it claimed to be benefiting; but Sandor figured it was just talk, baseless rumour born out of the long days of boredom. "I don't know anybody who has talked to the newspapers about this," repeated Sandor.

"But why," continued McManus, "these allegations in the press?" Doubt covered his face, he looked suspiciously at Sandor, "Are you sure you don't know who might have spoken to the paper?"

"Yes."

"But it's," McManus tried to exercise diplomacy with his choice of words, "your type of paper."

Sandor was confused, "Why?"

"You're a Presbyterian, aren't you?"

"Yes."

"Perhaps you'd feel more inclined to talk to one of your own?"

Sandor pointed at the publication, "I don't know this paper," his voice was stronger, aggressive.

"Okay, okay," McManus became calm but only for a moment. Suddenly he exclaimed, "This is very serious. They are accusing me of mismanagement. They are calling for an official report. '*It is inevitable that in the stress of the first influx, inexperienced and harassed local officials would have made mistakes.*' And then they have the nerve to challenge the entire organisation, '*There is a tendency to regard this organisation as sacrosanct and immune from criticism, but, while we are very ready to acknowledge the good work it is doing and has done in the past, we hold that the country has a right to expect competence in any organisation to which it entrusts its good name and the expenditure of a considerable sum of money.*'"

McManus folded the newspaper, placing it on the table, "Does the camp really think like this, do people think that the Red Cross doesn't care about every penny that we raised?"

Sandor saw hurt in his eyes, disappointment mixed with resignation. McManus sounded sad and defeated, "I have been listening to the refugees since day one and I don't think that I have done a bad job. I'd like to see my critics run things differently. It's all well and good writing about something which you don't know anything about, but at the end of the day," he glared at Sandor, "I'd love to get my hands on the bastards who wrote this."

On a hot Monday afternoon Sandor was informed by letter that a meeting had been arranged between the Irish Red Cross, Julia Pinter, himself and two representatives of the Fianna Fáil Government. It would take place in Knockalisheen Camp and the government representatives would travel from Dublin for the day and present the attendees with their decision on the factory.

Sandor was on edge before the meeting. He didn't sleep well for two days and kept waking up during the night, twisting in his bed from around four to six or seven, always aware that his tossing and turning was disturbing the others in the hut. On the morning of the meeting he cut himself shaving, he told Maria that it was a bad omen. She told him not to be superstitious.

Sandor was the only member of the camp council to attend the meeting, and along with Lucia, he was the first to arrive at the commandant's house, the modern building at the entrance of the camp. In one room a large dining table had been set up for the conference. Lucia brought along a pen and paper and she sat beside Sandor. McManus arrived just before Julia Pinter and her accountant, an Irishman called James Fox. Sandor was surprised at his youth; he was the youngest person there, in his late twenties. Sandor had presumed that he'd be older, as he'd associated the understanding of financial matters with the wisdom of age. The government representatives arrived a few minutes past the arranged time, the tall, skinny one spoke of the time it had taken to travel from Dublin, while the smaller one refreshed himself with a glass of water. Both of them wore glasses, the same thick black frames as McManus. The tall man was called Brendan Toner. He had grey hair and was in his early sixties. The smaller man was bald and a little older, possibly sixty-five. He was a plump man and reminded Sandor of a Russian doll. His name was

David Butler. He carried files which he opened on the table, notes shared by the two men as they talked for the next forty-five minutes.

Sandor couldn't understand most of the dialogue, parts were hurriedly translated by Lucia, she'd quickly interpret and decode certain phrases, but most of the words spoken by these officials were devoid of meaning. So Sandor concentrated on the facial expressions of Julia Pinter, a face which registered surprise mixed with subdued anger for most of the meeting, occasionally breaking with a smile or a tense laugh. When her accountant spoke he seemed to be rejected by the officials the way a father might snub an errant son; at one point he pushed a piece of paper across the table to support an argument, but Brendan Toner refused to look at it. Instead he held his hands up in protest and repeated his claim, "The figures don't add up."

Sandor sensed a rift opening between Pinter and the officials. James sat back with a strained look on his face. Pinter's face flushed with submission. During the last part of the meeting McManus attempted to mediate between both parties and called on Sandor to speak about the refugees willing to work in the factory, how they were prepared to train Irish workers in their skills, expertise which could benefit the country as a whole.

But as the meeting came to a close McManus sat back in his chair, and like Julia Pinter and her accountant, his face became flushed by a mixture of anger and disappointment, rejection and despair.

When the meeting was over the officials were led out of the building by McManus and you could hear their car driving down the gravel pathway and accelerating once on the Limerick Road. Sandor realised that the factory proposal had been rejected, but he wanted to know why.

Julia Pinter had an edgy tone to her voice, angered by

the meeting, the controlled and educated patterns of her speech had become tangled and deformed.

She responded to Sandor rhetorically, "Why are they against my factory? Why don't they think that my money, your labour allied with a government grant for some premises won't succeed? It's very simple," Julia explained, "the government are convinced, and without properly listening to our proposal, that *'It just won't work.'*"

∽

Sandor was alone in the hut. It was Saturday afternoon, a light rain was sprinkling from the sky. He was looking out the window. There was a knock on the door.

It was Thomas Townsend. Sandor, surprised to see him, asked him to come in. He offered him a seat but Thomas said that he wouldn't be staying long. Sandor replied, "Eva isn't in the camp. I think she has gone to Limerick for the day."

Thomas replied, "That's not why I'm here."

Sandor, a little confused, replied, "Why are you here?"

Thomas smiled, "You Hungarians are very frank. It's a quality which I admire. Listen Sandor, I always liked you, not that we saw much of each other, but I feel that I can trust you. The reason I'm here is that I want to talk to you about your sister."

Sandor, who was sitting down, insisted that Thomas take a seat. "Okay, but I won't be staying long. You see Sandor," his voice was clear and sincere, "I love Eva. And I think that she hasn't given us a chance. I really love her. I think that we could have a future together. I could provide for her, care for her and Kristina. We could be happy together but for some reason she doesn't want to be with me." Thomas looked at Sandor, "Do you understand everything I am saying?"

Sandor understood most of it, "You love her."

Thomas was perfectly still. His black hair was neatly parted and he was cleanly shaven. He asked if he could smoke. Sandor nodded, "Of course." As Thomas lit up Sandor wondered how Eva would react to this visit, perhaps she'd be annoyed, angry, upset that Thomas was trying to use Sandor's influence over her.

Thomas asked, "Does she ever talk about me?"

After contemplation, Sandor replied, "No."

"You're twins, are you not close?"

Sandor raised his hands, palms upwards, as he answered the question, "Yes and no."

"Did she tell you why she finished with me? Was it because of my brother?"

"No."

"I can't understand why she won't give us a chance. We seemed to get on fine and then one day she ended it."

Sandor said, "Perhaps she has no love for you."

"Did she say that to you?"

"No."

"Then why do you think that?"

"Love," Sandor locked his hands together, "joins people."

Thomas leant towards the stove, flicked his cigarette inside it. He muttered aloud, "She doesn't love me."

Sandor heard a noise outside. Fearing that it was Eva he looked towards the door, but it didn't open.

Thomas started crying. Slowly at first, making a hurt and plaintive sound. He didn't attempt to hide his tears by resting his head in his hands or by rubbing his eyes with his fingers, instead he looked straight at Sandor, eyes red and wet.

Sandor stared at Thomas. He considered saying something, offering words of comfort, perhaps telling him that he'd talk to Eva. But Sandor felt little empathy for Thomas and so he didn't say a word. Thomas continued crying, tears rolling down his face, whimpering ever so slightly, his hands helplessly in his lap.

After two minutes of listening to Thomas cry, Sandor stood up and said, "I can't do anything."

Thomas wiped his tears, "I should go." Walking towards the door he said, "Sandor, I'm very sorry. Please don't tell Eva."

∽

After five months of living in Ireland, Peter Varga decided to go home to Budapest. A return trip had always been his last option, and one which his wife Anna had been hoping for for more than half their time in Ireland. They had been better off in Hungary, their standard of living was higher, he had a job and their extended families were included in the raising of Gábor. Ireland had failed them. Their flight home was arranged through the Hungarian embassy in London who also paid for it. Sandor wasn't surprised by Peter's decision. He was aware of their problems; trying to raise a child in the camp, the lack of privacy, bathrooms designed for soldiers and not for infants, the absence of a Hungarian speaking doctor, and most importantly, Peter's unsuccessful search for work. He had worked in a paint factory in Budapest, a job which he'd had for over ten years, but he couldn't find a comparable position in Ireland as most factories would only employ unionised labour.

Anna wasn't willing to risk waiting an unknown amount of time to move to another country. Gábor was nine months old and she thought that it could be months, if not years, before they were settled elsewhere. She didn't want to raise her child in a refugee camp. She wanted to be among family and friends.

"And at times I agree with her," Peter told Sandor. "All a young family wants is stability. And there's no stability here, and to uproot from this country to go elsewhere just means more instability."

Seated on the steps of their hut, the late April sunshine pressing against Peter's jowly face, his trousers dirty from working the allotment of vegetables which occupied the many hours of his day. He was a defeated man. A gamble which he'd hoped would benefit his family had failed. By escaping across the border he had risked their lives. By spending five months in Ireland plus another one in Austria, he had wasted their time, and the surprise and novelty of their new baby had been dampened by life in a refugee camp. "Although I think that in America or Canada I could get employed, Anna is not willing to risk another move."

When Sandor suggested that it might be dangerous for him to go home, Peter disagreed. The Hungarian embassy was encouraging exiles to return as the country needed workers.

"But you are right," said Peter. "Hungary isn't a free country. Movement is restricted, political corruption is rife, people are jailed without due process, but we think that we have nothing to fear by returning. Out of the tens of thousands who have left, I'm sure that there are some who have already gone back. And what's the government going to do? Arrest us all?

"My attitude is simple. I took a risk escaping Hungary and it failed. But what was I escaping? Before the uprising my life wasn't under threat, it only became dangerous when the fighting started. I was recently married. Anna was pregnant. I had a job, food and accommodation. In many ways I hadn't a bad life. Then the uprising came along and I thought that I could better it. We escaped. We became refugees. But for us it wasn't about fleeing persecution but getting a better standard of living. It was always about the money.

"So we're going home and who's to say that we can't live a happy life there? Since we left, every day I've asked myself the following question – what do I want from life? And the answer is two things: to work and to raise our child. You can't do one without the other and so we're going home."

Two weeks ago, against the advice of the Irish Red Cross, another couple had returned to Hungary. Sandor thought that, despite Hungary's economic need for returning exiles, families like the Vargas could be indicted for fleeing their country and jailed. Peter was aware of this but it was a risk which he was willing to take, "We risked our lives getting out of the country and now there's a minimal risk on our return. Anna understands what might happen and so do I. But the risk is small and nothing compared to my family's well-being."

Peter, who was looking a lot healthier than he had done on arrival in Ireland, weight lost from his body by the manual labour in his allotment, told Sandor of his amusement on hearing the Red Cross's advice. "The Irish Red Cross is responsible for me being here in the first place; they've had problems trying to get me a job in Ireland or a visa to get out of Ireland, and when I decide to go home, they object. Out of the refugees, about one hundred and thirty including children have left the camp and are in employment of some sort or are living with Irish families. Ten have gone to England and three have gone to Canada. By now the Red Cross has admitted that there's little or no chance of the rest of us finding employment in Ireland. That's hardly a success. So what do they want me and my family to do? Perish along with the rest of the country? Start decomposing in this very field? While I am thankful for their efforts, I am amused at their arrogance, that rotting away in an Irish field is preferable to any one of the millions of lives led back in Hungary. They call that advice. I call it propaganda."

Sandor spent a few hours with Peter, Anna and Gábor as they packed their belongings and prepared for their journey to Dublin, across the Irish Sea, a train to London and a flight to Budapest. Gábor was developing a childish face full of personality and charm, losing the appearance of an infant, and his laugh was a glimpse of his personality in the making.

In the days after their departure Sandor and Eva adjusted to the peace of their hut, with Kristina in boarding school and the Vargas departed, they hadn't enjoyed as much tranquillity since Budapest. They rearranged the hut; Eva moved her bed to the front and Sandor to the back. In-between was Kristina's bed and the potbellied stove which, due to the warm weather, was rarely used.

∾

People were shouting. Standing on a chair at the top of the recreational room, Sandor called for calm, urging people not to speak at once, his hands making gestures denoting the uselessness of this verbal onslaught. But they weren't interested in ordered conversation, an exchange of views and possibilities, instead they wanted a release, an expulsion of opinion and attitude.

The hut was packed, people spilled on to the steps outside and into the evening sunshine, the dusty camp roads and the smell of stewing meat from the kitchen. Only a week ago it had snowed, a climatic memory which seemed hard to believe on this pleasant evening.

"If you talk one at a time," yelled Sandor, "then we'll all be able to listen." But Sandor knew that his appeal was in vain, at least for a time, and he reckoned he'd have to stand in front of them until they calmed down. He didn't think that so many people would turn up to this meeting he'd convened, so many angry, aggressive people full of verbal taunts and useless antagonism.

Sandor decided that appealing to the crowd was useless so he attempted to talk to one person. He concentrated on a man standing a few feet away from him and when he had his attention, he called him over. Skin barely covered his protruding bones, sharp angles on his face, prominent forehead and his rolled-up sleeves almost revealed the mechanics of his elbows, the balls and sockets. He seemed surprised that Sandor was trying to get his attention. After looking around he moved forward, Sandor stepped down from his chair and asked, "What are you saying?"

When the man started talking, those close by stopped yelling. The man was convinced that a hunger strike was the best option, "There's nothing to lose by striking. Everybody wants to go on strike, we are all tired of this place, the camp, the country, the lack of anything. It's what people want."

When Sandor returned to the chair the crowd had calmed down a little. There was less shouting. Sandor detected an eagerness about the brief conversation he'd just had and he started speaking at the top of his voice, "I need a show of hands. How many people want to go on hunger strike?"

At the front of the room many hands shot up, at the back, however, people couldn't hear him. He repeated his question. More hands appeared. The room looked like an army rally, a regiment of saluting hands.

"And when do you want to strike?"

Those who heard the question were adamant. "Now!"

One person stepped forward. "We must strike against the government. They brought us here for no reason."

Another person added, "We have been here for five months already and look how many of us are still here. At this rate it could take years for all of us to go. Who the hell wants to stay here for that length of time?" The room cheered and so the man continued speaking, "I think you'll find that it doesn't really matter what the camp council says on this point, most of us are ready to strike immediately."

A loud cheer from the room, people started banging the wooden floors with their feet. It was a deafening noise. Although Sandor had been running the camp council for months, he never felt that he controlled anything, the job just brought him into contact with other people, sometimes for better, sometimes for worse. But now he felt challenged, a possible object of hate like the Red Cross and the Irish Government. Even if he was losing influence over the camp, Sandor believed that the authorities must not become aware of this, it was important that the camp was seen to be a governable force. If the camp didn't have a power structure the chances of the Irish Government dealing with it were reduced, and the Red Cross could use it against them.

Sandor said, "I support the idea of a hunger strike. And I will tell the Red Cross about it. But we have to have terms."

People started talking amongst themselves, others continued shouting at Sandor. He wasn't sure if they agreed or disagreed with what he had just said. One man made his way towards the front of the hut. Sandor recognised him as Frank Tóth; the man who smashed up his hut a few months ago thinking that it was a form of protest. He called for Sandor's attention. Sandor didn't like the man and waited until he was at his side before he acknowledged him.

Tóth said, "Here are our terms. Everybody goes on strike."

Sandor replied, "I agree."

Tóth continued, "No – everybody. Men, women and children."

Sandor asked, "Do you have children?"

"Yes."

"And you want to risk their health?"

"These are our terms."

"Whose terms?"

Tóth pointed towards the back of the hut. A group of men were staring at Sandor. Tóth said, "Ask the people if they want their children to go on strike?"

Sandor was reluctant to debate this topic as the room seemed hostile to him and tempers were heated. But Tóth insisted, "If you don't get up on your chair and ask them, I'll do it myself."

Sandor said, "Do you know what people will think if our children are on hunger strike?"

"They'll think we're serious."

Sandor called for hush. "This man wants our children to go on strike. Can we have a show of hands?" Tóth's crowd put their hands up and cheered loudly. They encouraged others to do so, people started looking around at each other, unsure of what to do. Sandor didn't know whether to give his opinion; perhaps the room would act against him.

As the room became quiet, Tóth started shouting, "They'll think we're serious if the children are on strike. Come on, a show of hands."

Gradually more hands rose. Soon there was enough support for Sandor to concede that, yes, the children would go on strike too.

Sandor turned to Tóth, "They'll think that we're barbaric."

CHAPTER FOURTEEN

When Sandor informed McManus of their decision to go on hunger strike he did so without the help of Lucia as he wanted the conversation to be short. Calling on McManus unexpectedly the day before the strike, the Irish Red Cross representative was surprised to see Sandor, and ushered him into his house. McManus told him to make himself a cup of tea and in a few minutes he'd be down to talk to him. A nervous Sandor sat at the table wondering how McManus would react to the news. When McManus entered the kitchen, Sandor, without recourse to any preliminary conversation, rose from the table and announced that a hunger strike would begin the following day.

McManus wore a short-sleeved summer shirt. His pale, hairless skin hung from his bones like skin from a chicken's neck. He continued to move around the kitchen, filling the kettle with water, placing it on the stove, removing a cup from the cupboard, then sitting at the table. As a response had not been forthcoming, Sandor repeated himself. "We are going on a hunger strike tomorrow. The majority of adults in the camp will not accept food and we won't be feeding our children either."

Again McManus didn't reply. Instead he looked at the black and white tiles on the floor and then towards the small breathy gasps of steam from the kettle. A sun-warmed dog the colour of toast wandered in from the back garden and sought shade beneath the table. Sandor felt a sense of déjà vu, an anxious swell of emotion, and like a smell which brought him back in time, he was reminded of leaving his parents six months before, the disappointment on their faces.

McManus replied, "I had hoped that you wouldn't." He got up from the table and went to the stove. In slow sentences, some of which were too quiet for Sandor to understand, McManus said that he'd been worried that something drastic like a hunger strike might take place. He had heard from his colleagues in England, mainland Europe and New York about the various protests by Hungarian refugees. "It seems to me that you're an unruly lot. The problem, however, is so simple that a child could understand. You have great expectations. You think that the West is one big picnic where jobs are everywhere and happiness is rife.

"And added to this delusion is a blindness to charity. You don't seem to realise what the Irish have done for you. It's very easy for a rich man to donate money and while it's always great to receive it, it's not as meaningful as when a poor person is charitable. You arrived in Knockalisheen Camp *after* the fact. You didn't see the collections, the people who went out of their way to raise money, old women giving part of their life's savings to the Hungarian cause, sportsmen melting down their medals into gold and silver to turn into cash for you, clubs and theatres putting on special events and shows. The whole country got behind Hungary and just because five months later you aren't living in some earthly paradise you throw it all back in our faces by going on strike.

"And a hunger strike is the worst form of strike as you are denying yourself what millions of people around the world are dying without. Your life is a gift from God and you have no right to play with the health of your body and regardless of what you think of the conditions in Ireland, you have healthy lives here, you always have enough food and your diet is among the best in the country as I know plenty of people who'd be grateful for three solid meals a day."

The tone of his voice rose slightly, "But what really sickens me is that if anything happens to you, if this hunger strike continues for any length of time, who will be rushing your ailing bodies to hospital? We will. And who will be looking after you in hospital? The same doctors and nurses who raised money to send penicillin to Budapest when the uprising started and when you arrived here with your illnesses, it was they who looked after you. The thing about a hunger strike is that it never happens where there's a shortage of food. It's the protest of the privileged."

Sandor remained silent while McManus was speaking. Most of the conversation he had understood and its content didn't surprise him, but as the strike had already been arranged he didn't feel any necessity to defend their decision and thus engage in argument. He planned, however, to get one point across, and when McManus stopped talking, Sandor said, "It's not a strike against you or the people of Ireland, it's against the government."

"And who but the people voted for the government?"

"But we feel that the government brought us here and then forgot about us."

"Forgot about you? Let me tell you that there are tens of thousands of people, not only in Ireland but in England as well, that would love to be in your position. Not only getting food, accommodation and a weekly allowance but having the Red Cross at their beck and call, looking after your needs, and just because your magical lives haven't materialised, you think that you've been hard done by."

Sandor felt a circular spin to the argument and one which he couldn't challenge, let alone win. He rose from the table and motioned towards the door signalling an end to their discussion.

But McManus continued, anger rising in his voice, "Some of you are just opportunists, using the uprising, the sacrifice of others to better your lives, but I can tell you that the Red Cross was never about ensuring the material wealth of your fellow man, we're not an organisation which guarantees nice jobs and nice houses, an organisation of alchemists who can transform tin and copper lives into gold.

"When Henry Dunant established the Red Cross nearly one hundred years ago, do you think he cared about the material quality of people's lives? Do you think that he was concerned about getting the victims of war nice jobs and houses? All he wanted was for people wounded in battle to be properly looked after, that they had doctors and nurses, shelter and food. Dunant had seen the effects of war, and it was the experience of witnessing the dead and wounded which inspired him to establish this organisation.

"And it's his vision to care for the suffering that inspires me and the rest of the Red Cross. We have cared for you and we'll continue to care for you, but we are not about providing great houses and jobs, but dealing with the essence of life, the true wealth of mankind – health," McManus stopped talking to catch his breath and Sandor walked towards the door.

McManus continued, "And it's this health which you are putting at risk by going on hunger strike. One hundred years ago when Dunant was wandering around Solferino in Italy, tens of thousands of soldiers lay dead and wounded, Frenchmen and Italians who had been fighting against Austrians and Hungarians.

"Yes, Dunant's desire to alleviate the suffering of your

fellow countrymen, among others, is the reason why I, nearly a hundred years later, work tirelessly to ensure that you have enough food, clothing and the hope of a healthy life. And just because the better life which you imagined hasn't matched the reality of this country, a country that has generously donated thousands of scarce pounds, it doesn't give you the right to risk your health. You weren't thinking about starving yourself to death when you wandered fearfully over the Austrian border six months ago in the freezing cold. You were more than happy to avail of what the Red Cross had to offer you in Eisenstadt.

"So before you leave I ask you to think about the Red Cross, about what we have done for you and about the money which the Irish have raised. And I implore you not to strike. While Dunant may have founded this organisation on the sight of dying Hungarians one hundred years ago, it's not a sight which I want to see in County Clare."

∽

Later Sandor called on Tommy Gallagher to inform him of the hunger strike. He hadn't been inside Gallagher's apartment before, large windows were open to the setting sun over the Shannon Estuary, window boxes full of flowers scenting the evening air. Thankful for a bottle of beer, Sandor, distracted by his meeting with McManus, was glad to be in the uncritical presence of Gallagher, a journalist whom Sandor felt was something of a friend.

Sandor told Gallagher that, as there were thousands of people from all over the world in need of charity in countries throughout Africa and Asia, not to mention all the poor and hungry in Ireland itself, the only motivation in bringing Hungarians into Ireland was ideological, "And not because it's a good action to take, but because Ireland needs a distraction."

In the slow pace of Sandor's carefully constructed English, words were put together like a jeweller stringing precious stones. Ireland was in no position to bring refugees into the country, it was obvious that there weren't any jobs or the chance of many in the near future, yet Ireland still wanted to offer asylum because the government realised that the people had found a country to pity more than themselves.

Angry, annoyed and a little drunk after two bottles of beer, Sandor believed that because Ireland's plan hadn't worked out, the country was now furious at them for being unhappy.

Gallagher, always the journalist, seemingly sympathetic to everything he heard but guarded about his personal beliefs, told Sandor that while he understood that the refugees felt they had to act he didn't think that a hunger strike was the best option. "For two reasons. Firstly, over a hundred years ago in Ireland, a famine cut the population in two between death and immigration, so the idea of forcing hunger on yourselves while having a plentiful supply of food won't win people over to your side. And secondly, the IRA have used the same tactic and you wouldn't want to be associated with murderers."

Sandor asked Gallagher about the last hunger strike which had happened in Ireland and he spoke about the Second World War when de Valera jailed some IRA men and three of them died on strike. "And that's the man you'll be striking against tomorrow."

Sandor drank from his third bottle of beer. He considered the idea of death. He believed that the Irish Government would react quickly to their strike because they were refugees. They were not in political opposition. Even though the hunger strike had been discussed by the camp council for a couple of months, Sandor had never considered ending his life or even damaging his health as he'd always thought that a strike would be short like the twenty-four hour one in England. During the war Sandor had seen people starve and he knew the lasting effects of hunger on your body, especially after twenty days or more. As the circumstances of their hunger strike were controlled, Sandor felt that they had a better chance of survival; people could leave anytime, the weather was mild, hospitals were close by and, hopefully, it would all end quickly.

Beneath a sea-blue sky, surrounded by lush green fields full of sun-still animals warmed by the near-summer weather, the huts of Knockalisheen Camp appeared empty and deserted like they had been six months ago, a piece of local history, a relic from the war and the threat of invasion. People weren't sitting on the steps of their huts or on the grass between them sunning themselves like they did when the weather was fine. The chapel was empty and the kitchen which turned out three meals a day was quiet; and so was the recreational room, a place where Father Mikes played films three days a week. The only refugees visible on that last Monday morning in April were a couple men walking around the camp ensuring that those who had volunteered to go on strike were adhering to it.

Children no longer played, their noise having been ominously silenced; Sandor believed that these people weren't sincere about threatening their children's lives and he'd heard that food had been secretly set aside for them.

The men on hunger strike occupied the hut which was used as a school, while the women and children stayed in their small homes. Only a handful of people had chosen not to strike. They stayed in their huts, keeping out of sight, aware that they were going against the wishes of the majority.

It had been organised for the camp council to meet journalists twice a day. And so at midday on the first day of the strike, they held a press conference near the entrance of the camp. Sandor recognised Gallagher but nobody else. A question was translated about the responsibility the camp council had for the lives and health of those striking. László Eper, speaking through Lucia, said that it had been the wishes of the majority of men to go on strike regardless of what the council had said, "It was decided last Friday. Five months of our lives have been wasted here, Knockalisheen is a lost colony of Hungarian refugees."

A journalist asked, "Have those who are against striking been put under pressure? I have heard accusations of bullying."

Eper replied, "No. That's a lie. People can do whatever they want. But nearly everybody is on strike."

"Is it true that the strikers are planning to cut down the electricity wires leading into the camp?"

"This is a peaceful strike and we don't plan to damage the camp in any way. In one local paper the camp council was referred to as the Gestapo; we are insulted by this term and everything which it represents."

Another journalist asked, "We have been informed that there are former communists on strike with you. Is there any truth to this?"

"Yes there are former communists on strike. But let me put this in perspective. Out of the three hundred and seventy one people remaining in the camp, three people have admitted to being former members of the Hungarian Communist Party. It has been suggested that these people are the ringleaders and are causing trouble in the camp, but none of these people are on the camp council or have anything to do with the day-to-day running of the camp.

"This strike is the result of a few things. The lack of jobs, decent accommodation and a promise which the Irish

Government had made in Austria regarding our transit to another country after arriving here. Five months later and this promise has been broken. It's false to think that this protest is being engineered by three former communist party members as we'd be on strike regardless of who is here."

Eper finished by talking about the solidarity among the refugees and how the strike was, "Until death." He hoped that the government would make contact with them sooner rather than later. He also said that they were in regular contact with the Irish Red Cross in case anybody's health was in danger.

On the evening of the first day, Sandor called on Maria. She was one of a few people not on strike as her parents were making preparations to leave the camp. After nearly five months of searching for work and selling his ornaments door to door, Mr Novak had been offered a job in Dublin to work for a construction company. For the last week he'd been in the capital and with the help of his new employer had found a house. As the new home was in need of repair, Mr Novak agreed to work off a month's rent by fixing it up.

Regardless of being in Dublin or not, he was against the strike and thought that it would do more harm than good. With her father in Dublin, Maria didn't want to leave her mother alone in her hut as one of a few people not striking. Mrs Novak was happy that her daughter wasn't on strike as after months of worrying about their lives, they finally had some good news with her husband's job.

Although Maria was not on strike, she wasn't against it as she thought that an act of protest was necessary. She felt that it was easy for her father to be against the strike as he had found work. Unlike most of the inhabitants of the camp, his luck was turning. Maria thought that whether she was on strike or not was irrelevant as all the refugees would be known as hunger strikers. If damage was done to their reputation, it would be felt collectively. Another person not striking wouldn't make a difference.

It was a warm evening and Sandor and Maria sat in the shade of the hut, out of earshot of Mrs Novak. It had been less than twenty-four hours since he had eaten and though tired after skipping three meals, a day of inactivity hadn't brought on much hunger, and he'd drunk a lot of water and smoked many cigarettes to suppress his appetite. What concerned Sandor most was Maria's future; her parents wanted her to move to Dublin. It was felt that the capital offered more opportunities than Limerick. She'd live in a house. Sandor would be free to visit and there was a spare bedroom where he could stay. Mr Novak had suggested that if Sandor considered looking for work in Dublin, he could live with them as well.

While Maria was happy that her father had found work in Dublin and was finally settling down, she wanted to leave the country. She didn't like Ireland. Although she hadn't visited Dublin, she hadn't heard many positive reports about the place. "I don't want to live here. I asked my father what would happen if in a couple of months he received a visa for Canada or America, and he said that he'd stay in Ireland. He's very excited about his job and feels that they have spent too much time in limbo and wants to settle."

Maria told Sandor about a conversation which she'd had with her father. She had sought his opinion about Sandor and herself going to another country if they got visas. But her father wasn't enthusiastic, in fact, he was annoyed and angered. "He thinks that it's one thing for us to be seeing each other within the confines of the camp, but quite another thing to leave the country together."

On the first night of the strike the camp council met a delegation from the Irish Red Cross led by McManus. Lucia talked for most of the meeting. She pleaded with them to call off the strike. She said that she loved the Irish, she'd been living here for many years and had married an Irishman. Last November, when she had heard that Ireland would take in refugees, she was thrilled. "Part of me wanted to be back in Budapest while the uprising was going on, to help in any way I could. I had felt so privileged living in Ireland, thousands of miles away from any danger.

"So when the Irish Government announced that they were taking in refugees I started receiving letters from friends, my husband's family and from people I barely knew who said that they were all supporting the Hungarians and agreed with the decision. People stopped me in the street to tell me how much money they were donating and how they were planning events to raise as much as they could. That so much was being done for my fellow countrymen was humbling – for what do the Irish know about Hungary?"

Lucia had contacted the Irish Red Cross and offered her services as a translator. Before the refugees had arrived, there was a handful of Hungarians living in Ireland but she had never met any of them as there hadn't been an occasion to bring them together. After spending years in Ireland she was now looking forward to spending time among her countrymen.

"How strange it was. All of a sudden to have a community of Hungarians a couple of miles from my house. And the chance to work among you, speaking Hungarian, a language which I rarely used. And being able to help you settle in another country after the uprising. I was overwhelmed by the generosity shown by the countries of Europe, Hungarians all over the continent were being helped. To be a part of this shared humanity, whether it was a donation by an old woman or thousands pledged by governments, it all served one purpose: to help people like you.

"I had thought that you'd be happy coming to a peaceful country where you would be looked after, given food and accommodation and a chance to get over the uprising. And for a while, for the first couple of weeks, everything seemed fine and I was proud of the work the Irish Red Cross was doing and it was great to see people recover from their ordeals. While the camp is basic, it's a lot better than nothing at all and the huts give each family a certain amount of privacy. But then it all started to go wrong.

"I know Ireland, I know the Irish. And like any other race they have their faults. They are full of talk. They lack efficiency. They don't always speak their minds. We are more direct. But there's nothing insincere about their desire to help you and now this help has been thrown back in their faces. How do you think it makes me feel to have people stop me in the street to ask about this hunger strike? People cannot understand it, they think that you are not only ungrateful but insulting. If you open your door to people in distress and then they start to protest at the condition of your house, what else are you going to think? Today someone said to me that he now understands why the Russians had sent tanks into Budapest as there's obviously no way of talking to a Hungarian.

"And while a hunger strike is bad enough, people can't understand why you want to starve your children as well. What have they done? Why risk their health? As adults you can do whatever you want, but why involve those who cannot choose for themselves? If you injure the innocent, that's not protesting but terrorising."

Later that night McManus addressed the school hut, "I appeal to you men of Hungary not to put your women and children in the frontline. We have missed the happy sight of children playing around the camp and we ask you to allow them to come out again. I know that as true men of Hungary you will continue this fight on your own." After this appeal, he explained that if the children weren't taken off the strike, the authorities might be forced to take action to feed the children under the Prevention of Cruelty to Children Act.

So: it was agreed to remove the women and children from the strike, but the men remained, one hundred and fifty of them lying side by side in the school hut. When the lights went off at midnight, most of them tried to sleep, sinking their heads into their soft pillows as their bodies lay on the hard wooden floors. A day without eating seemed to have strengthened Sandor's mind, giving it a clarity of thought hitherto absent. It had been a warm day and the windows were open to allow the fresh night air to circulate around the overcrowded room. Sandor was glad that the strike had been reduced to just the men. Earlier that day he had walked around the camp listening to women trying to comfort their distressed children, kids wondering why they hadn't had their breakfast and lunch.

Sandor felt misled by the eagerness shown by some people, the naivety of enthusiasm; on the second day of the strike the newspapers mentioned that a pregnant woman had volunteered to strike; Sandor thought it was ruthless to deny a baby food while in the womb, the life of the unborn being used for their aims. Other stories in the papers questioned the sincerity of the strike. It was reported that a local shop had sold out of basic goods in the run-up to it; perhaps food was being hoarded in the camp to sustain a fake protest?

A newspaper reported that McManus had found a document which had been circulated by the International Immigration Committee to the refugees in Austria, before they had left for Ireland. The document had explained that they'd be in Ireland for ten days in a transit camp and afterwards they could go to any country they wanted. McManus insisted that neither the Irish Government nor the Irish Red Cross had had anything to do with this document but it seemed to be the cause of the misunderstanding between the refugees and the authorities. "This might explain the confusion surrounding the status of the camp. But a hunger strike can't change that."

Sandor was quoted as saying that while the Irish Government might have brought them to Ireland in good faith, perhaps they were reluctant to let them go to another country as the government would be embarrassed by their failure to absorb so few refugees. "We went on strike and are planning to continue this strike because we don't want to be pawns in a diplomatic game. If the Irish Government made a mistake last October in bringing us here without any obvious future then they should accept responsibility and try to resolve the situation. You can't forget about three hundred and seventy refugees living in isolation and without a future. We should never have been brought here. Despite the generosity of the Irish people, it's been a mistake. And while we are thankful for this charity, how long can we live off the good wishes of the people?

"We will not stop our strike until the Irish Government talk to us about our future and stop ignoring our requests for a meeting. The elected council of Knockalisheen Camp appeal to the government before any of the weaker members are impaired by the strike."

As the second day pushed into the third the weather cooled. At 2.35 a.m., the school hut wasn't as warm as the night before, the sound of humbled conversations scratched the wooden walls as most men lay awake on the floor. And a tired, fully dressed Sandor surfaced from his makeshift bed to walk in the outside air, tempted by its soporific quality. A slow, sly throbbing ached his head. His stomach was a tight wall of skin, seemingly impenetrable. Smoking too many cigarettes during the day had covered his throat with a thick, soupy balm, uncoughable and unswallowable. Glass after glass of water rushed through a body unblocked by anything. He still tried to observe his evening routine of clearing his bowels though nothing was expelled. Sandor pondered his inners: even the dead shit, undertakers clear out life's last meal before a cork is squat into your cadaverous cleft.

Only a few stars were visible as grey cloud like rat fur squeaked across the sky. Sandor hadn't thought much about God since learning in school about Martin Luther nailing his ninety-five theses to the church door at Wittenberg. As a child he had imagined a man in black hammering away at the planks, drawing attention to himself with each blow of his hammer. Death as the ultimate effect of not eating had made Sandor aware of his own mortality. Some strikers were noticeably ill. Eyes had glossed over with a helpless, sick stare. Although it was the beginning of May, the refugees had spent a cold and damp winter in conditions far worse than back home, most of this time inactive, their bodies losing their natural strength while their spirits gradually eroded.

As bodies weakened, tempers flared, and people were easily agitated. An argument had caused two people to end their hunger strike. As they walked out of the hut they derided the strikers as deluded fools, "This is a fucking waste of time. What do you think you'll achieve?"

Soon after that had happened, Sandor called on Eva. She was glad that the women and children had been taken off the strike as she was in an unusual position: a mother with a child not living in the camp. Kristina had been in the camp on the weekend, but when the strike had started on Monday morning, she'd returned to school. She was confused by the whole affair. Her eleven-year old eyes seemed to disapprove of trouble and registered shock on hearing that nobody – men, women or children – would be taking their meals. Eva had assured her that nothing serious would happen and when returning to the camp next weekend all would be well.

But Kristina wasn't convinced and she left for school with the disquiet of the camp painted like make-up on her face. Eva wondered what the nuns would think of their strike. If they disapproved, as she was sure they would, could it affect Kristina's schooling? Perhaps the nuns would ask Kristina to explain it and she'd be left standing in a classroom with many eager eyes awaiting an explanation which wouldn't be forthcoming.

CHAPTER FIFTEEN

Tommy Gallagher was among a group of journalists attending the press conference on the third morning of the strike. He didn't ask many questions and jotted down a few remarks made by the hopeless sound of László Eper's voice speaking about a telegram they had sent to Éamon de Valera.

Standing by his side, however, Sandor knew that Eper wasn't feeling hopeless for that morning a letter had arrived from the Canadian embassy granting him a visa. Unlike most in the camp Eper had an advantage: a relative of his living in Canada had offered to sponsor his application. The pleasure which Eper felt on reading the letter among his fellow strikers was concealed by an act of facial subterfuge and the subtle placement of the envelope into his shirt pocket. Quietly he told Sandor about the offer and how in five weeks time he'd fly out to Canada at the Irish Red Cross's expense. Sandor's warmth of congratulation was sincere but he was jealous of Eper's departure. Eper had corresponded with the Canadian embassy to establish where his elderly cousin lived, as he'd never met him and was relying on the vague memory of his father who had mentioned him a few times. In the end, he had been located in Saskatoon and agreed to sponsor this long-lost cousin if he helped out on his farm.

Eper brought the press conference to a close by shaking hands with each journalist. They pocketed their notepads and pens. Gallagher approached Sandor to give him an envelope containing three enlargements of photographs of Limerick pubs. Cigarettes were easily lit in the still air.

Gallagher spoke about Gerry Buckley. It was a name which Sandor failed to recognise for a couple of seconds, a meaningless utterance to a tired man, but then Sandor's mind grabbed a hold of the name and Gerry's amber moustache asserted itself in his memory. In sympathetic tones Gallagher recalled Sandor's attempt at working in the plant, the journalist knew one of the workers, and he'd heard about the union blocking his employment.

Then Gallagher spoke about Julia Pinter's proposal for a factory and how the government had turned it down. "But what really happened was this: while you, Pinter and the Irish Red Cross were lobbying the government to get a grant for the factory, it turns out that Gerry Buckley was doing his own lobbying against it. I'm not saying that he put an end to it, but the amount of money which he donates to politicians carries some weight. Do you think he was going to let another engineering factory within seventy miles of his?"

∽

Suspicion, paranoia. Men started wondering who'd be the next to leave, to quit the hunger strike. Rumours circulated about some people wandering out of the hut on the pretence of going to the toilet and sneaking down to their wives and girlfriends and being fed. That their strike had lasted longer than the one in England caused concern. Theories and speculation about what might happen abounded; would they be left to starve to death on a hillside in County Clare? Would de Valera grant them a government audience? Perhaps the embassies of the United States and Canada would deny all hunger strikers visas due to the potential unrest which they might cause? Perhaps they'd all remain in the camp for the three years which the Irish Red Cross had budgeted for; three years of insufficient education for their children; three years of gradual absorption into the country which they were striking to leave.

And then there was talk of Peter Varga who had returned to Hungary. It was imagined that he'd be questioned by the ÁVO, a now strengthened ÁVO reasserting its power after the uprising, and details of the refugees who had escaped to Ireland would be passed on and their mothers, fathers, sisters and brothers would suffer.

Or perhaps they didn't need people like Peter Varga. Perhaps ÁVO spies were already working in Ireland. Perhaps they had been sleeping among them in the camp. Perhaps they had been taking notes, reporting back to Budapest and their relatives had already been rounded up?

∞

Sandor was lying in bed. Josef Horvath was sitting on a chair beside him, talking. Cups of tea were on the floor and like big bowls of dirty dandruff the ashtrays were full. Conversation moved slowly, shy of its conclusion. Cigarette smoke fell towards the open window. Sandor stared at the ceiling listening to Horvath talking about London. The small amount of money he'd managed to save would pay for a trip there when the strike was over. "We have a plan," Horvath said grouping himself with Eva. "We're going to leave Ireland at the beginning of summer. When the strike is over, I will go to London, find a job and a house. Once that's secure, then Eva will follow."

"What about Kristina?" asked Sandor.

"She'll come for the summer months and if we don't get her into an English school we'll send her back to Laurel Hill. Either way she won't miss any education."

Sandor wasn't used to Horvath being Eva's boyfriend. He felt that whatever he said to Josef would find its way back to his sister. And vice versa, their new confluence of hearts and minds. But regardless of his own feelings, Eva seemed happier than he'd seen her in months and Kristina had adjusted to Josef being a possible stepfather without question or debate.

But like a concerned father, Sandor had started to question Josef, examining the unshaven features of his face, his black hair shaped by invisible winds, and his age, he was a couple of years younger than Eva, four to be precise. Sandor thought about Josef's wife back in Budapest. He had used the uprising to clear out of the city and a loveless marriage, an arrangement which he claimed had been mutual but maybe he'd left her, maybe she had no idea that he was leaving. Perhaps she was all alone now. And say if they'd children too, one or two kids wondering about their missing father.

Then again, perhaps the dissolution of their marriage was by mutual consent as he claimed. Maybe Horvath had told Eva more than he'd told Sandor, complexities which a man wouldn't share with a friend, stories of catching his wife with another man or mental illness, depression, psychosis, details too deep for their friendship.

༒

And in Dublin, Dáil Éireann: the Minister for External Affairs, Frank Aiken, was being questioned about the refugees.

Was he aware of the anxiety which existed among those in Knockalisheen Camp with regard to their future? Had applications been made to his department by Hungarians for permission to go to Canada or the United States and would he arrange to have them admitted to these countries?

Yes, Aiken was aware, fully aware. But it wasn't necessary for any of the refugees to apply to his department for permission to go to Canada, United States or any other country. They were quite free to leave at any time. "We have simply given them asylum here for the period that circumstances compel them to remain with us, and already thirty one adults and thirteen children have left for other countries, their fares having been paid by the Irish Red Cross. It must be realised that we cannot unduly press other countries to admit refugees. It is for the government of each country to decide whom they shall admit. In fact, the governments of the United States and Canada are fully aware that a number of refugees here have expressed the wish to enter their territories, and the refugees have been kept fully informed through the Red Cross of the situation since their reception in this country."

Deputy O'Malley asked if the minister was aware that the refugees had actually asked the government to receive a deputation on the matter? And if so, what was his position?

Yes, he was aware that they had asked to see some member of the government but the deputy asking the questions would have to realise that they had been kept fully informed by the Red Cross authorities all the time.

O'Malley continued his questioning, "And is it definite that eventually all the refugees will be admitted to either Canada or the US?"

The reply was succinct, "That is a matter for those countries."

O'Malley said, "It should be made very clear to the Hungarians that Ireland has done all in its power to assist them, notwithstanding the fact that a large number of our own citizens are unemployed. They have never received a guarantee – or will the minister say that they did? – that they would get employment, and they are free to return to Hungary any time that they so wish. Furthermore, will the minister inform the Hungarians that while they are living in this country they will have to behave themselves in a reasonable manner?"

The Taoiseach, Éamon de Valera, rose from his bench. "The position in regard to these unfortunate people who are here in a strange country is that they do not understand the language. They do not realise that there are thousands of other refugees in other countries seeking to gain entry into the same countries that they wish to enter, that the position is not under the control of this government and that we are doing everything we can to assist them. We are doing our best to try and remedy the situation as far as they are concerned but they must be patient. We should understand these people, when one thinks of their background and so on, and we do understand them – at least the government does."

Jack McQuillan asked, "Why were they brought here under false pretences?"

DeValera replied, "I do not think that that is fair. I do not think they were brought here under false pretences."

McQuillan shouted, his words released like doves into the chamber, "It was a big show off to show what we could do!"

Mr W Murphy added, "These people were allowed in here very graciously and if I were in the government I would allow them to strike if on strike. We have a lot of people who have not got rashers and eggs for their breakfast but these people have them."

De Valera concluded, his voice aged, tired, "We have not passed through the trials which they have."

Sandor was thinking of his mother. He imagined her sitting in the living room, across from his father, gentle conversational gusts between their evening selves, dinner digesting in warm stomachs, the aroma of coffee blowing in from the kitchen. She could have been right about leaving Budapest. Maybe he did have unrealistic expectations. Perhaps she'd heard reports about returning exiles and was hoping that her family would be reunited. No doubt there were tales of appalling conditions in camps, how refugees were living like animals, how the West was mistreating people, the molestation by capitalists, the suffering of socialist children.

Sandor got on his feet. Sunlight was a sharp knife pointing towards his eyes. He hadn't showered in four days. He wanted to wash, to leave the school hut where they all slept. It smelled of sweating bodies, greasy hair and perpetual smoke. As he walked, Sandor moved between people careful not to step on wayward arms, stray legs, glasses of water and overflowing ashtrays.

It was May. Father Mikes had said that it was the month of Mary, Mother of Our Lord. Last night he'd tried talking to the strikers and they had reiterated their demand to meet a government delegation. Only then would they end their strike. Father Mikes said he would see what he could do. He hadn't sounded hopeful.

Sandor stood on the steps of the school hut. A big yawny breath was sent to the sky, to the deep-sea blue, the egg-yellow sun. Windless clouds threatened to fall down to earth.

The fresh air was water to Sandor's thirsty lungs. He stood in the sun for a few moments, taking in the view of the camp, the fields, the absence of people; then he placed his right foot on the first step, and as he did, he felt faint. He felt nervous, aware that something wasn't right. His weak hand gripped the handrail. He wished he'd stayed inside, the comfort of his pillow. He tried holding on to the handrail but he didn't have the strength. As he started falling, he wondered where he'd land. He knew that it would be one of two places: either on the wooden steps or the ground. His flailing hands searched for the handrail, but as he continued downwards, his left hand shielded his head as the other tried to break his fall.

∾

Slowly, Sandor became conscious of people talking beside him, familiar voices, unthreatening and concerned. He was resting on a soft mattress and a blanket covered his legs. There was an unfamiliar warmth to his head. A pulsing feeling too, like pressure being applied at intervals. And these intervals seemed connected to his breathing; the slower the draw of breath the slower the throbbing. This made Sandor feel in control of the pain, as if he could master it from behind his closed eyes.

He resented being awake. Sleep was the best drug, the purest form of release and relief. He wanted to rest, to lie undisturbed. He knew that if he moved he'd draw attention to himself. He was like a child with his fingers over his eyes pretending that he wasn't there.

It was the sound of Dr Pader's voice which inspired movement in Sandor's eyes. Water was offered to him, which he took. Sitting up, a pillow was placed behind him.

Dr Pader explained that he'd suffered a mild concussion. A bandage had been placed on his forehead. He didn't need stitches, only rest. There was to be no excitement. Sandor had been unconscious for a couple of hours. This passage of time was evident in the night sky beyond the dirty window panes of the medical hut. Along with a couple of other strikers, Sandor had been given a bed there. A nurse sat behind a desk sorting brown bottles of medicine. A lamp illuminated her sleight of hand.

Dr Pader was quick to warn Sandor. "It should be obvious to you why you fainted. While water can sustain life, your body is crying out for energy found in solids. Hunger striking is a nonsense. To deny yourself food for even a short period of time can do irreparable damage to your body. And that's just talking from a medical position. Personally, I think that you are biting the hand that feeds you. Just think about it, you'd really have something to strike about if Ireland stopped funding you people to the tune of three meals a day.

"But enough of my opinions. Do you want anything else? You should eat something, but I'm not going to force you. It's your choice. But try to drink as much water as possible and it wouldn't hurt if you put some sugar in it, anything to raise your energy levels."

Sandor didn't feel lonely with Maria seated beside him. Like the blanket spread over his legs and feet, she was pure warmth. One of her hands slowly massaged his head, careful to keep her fingers away from the bandage on his forehead. The medical hut was quiet. Only five of the fifteen beds were occupied. One man, who was in a lot of pain and waiting to be transported to a local hospital, was breathing heavily, his voice a coarse quiver hitting a note between exhaustion and pain.

Sandor was drifting in and out of sleep. When he'd wake, reality would confuse him, and he'd look to Maria for comfort and a sense of place. She was also in his dreams, not as a physical person, but like a spiritual essence, a presence which he adored and revered. That he'd found her in Ireland redeemed the country slightly. It had been good for something: love.

Later on that night when he woke she was gone. Sitting up in bed he drank a glass of water, wondering where she was. He felt childlike in his separation from her. Minutes later she returned. She smiled at him as she entered the medical hut. She was not alone, Josef Horvath was behind her. Sitting down beside Sandor he asked him how he felt. "I'm okay," replied Sandor.

"That's good. There's news," said Josef. "A delegation from the government has agreed to visit the camp. They are giving us what we want and people are happy. Everybody is tired of the strike, nobody thought that it would go on for four days."

Sandor felt spoilt lying in the medical hut. Compared to the school hut it was luxurious. He asked, "Who are you dealing with?"

"It's all going through McManus."

"When is the delegation going to visit the camp?"

"Within a week."

"If they are giving us what we are asking for, then what's the point in continuing?"

Josef said, "Frank Tóth wants to continue. He says that the government are trying to trick us. He wants the strike to end when the government actually shows up in the camp. But it's unrealistic, I think."

Sandor said, "We should just end now. If the government tricks us, we can go back on strike."

"I know."

Sandor smiled, "And now you can go to London."

"That's the plan."

∽

Daylight shone through the window. Sandor, sitting up in bed, ate from a breakfast tray straddling his body. Tea was hot and sugary, bacon was wrapped in buttery bread. Grease dribbled down his unshaven chin. Sandor ate slowly, it felt good working his way through the few items on his plate. Dr Pader had warned him about eating too quickly, he had been advised to build up his appetite slowly, over a couple of days. His body made an assortment of noises as food trundled through it, his stomach sounded like an echoey, underwater vault, and at times he felt a sudden jab of indigestion in his side, the painful passage of food through his innards.

Across the room from Sandor, the curtains, surrounding a bed, were opened. A man in his underpants was searching for his clothes. His movements were slow, delicately bending down as he peered beneath tossed sheets, awkwardly pulling back blankets, rummaging between pillows. Gradually, he pieced together his clothes, covering his skinny white body. Once dressed he parted his hair with a comb, a white line of scalp amid dark, frazzled hair. He scratched his beard at the base of the neck where the fuzzy hair joined the longer strands of chest hair. When ready to leave he looked down at Sandor and said, "We've won."

The man smiled, then lit a pipe. Sandor nodded and said nothing. The man left the medical hut. Sandor felt that he'd seen him before, but where? He finished eating and placed the tray on the floor. Then he remembered.

The baths of Andrássy Street.

❧

For two months after Sandor had been tortured he couldn't work. Days were spent in the local burn unit. Specialists treating the effect of boiling water on his skin. It was the first time he'd realised that skin was an organ in the same way that your heart or lungs or kidneys were organs. Skin was transplanted, sections of his back which had thinned out, and to Sandor's eyes, seemed transparent, that the doctors could peer inside him and see him as he truly was – a patchy bag of bones. Such was the scolding on his genitals that any stiffening of his penis caused him severe pain.

Between bouts of delicate dermatology, Sandor thought about Hungary, his fellow Hungarians and their fallen people, the bearded guard, for that's what he understood him to be. They shared the same country. Sandor could tell from his accent that he was from Budapest. Perhaps they lived near each other, attended similar schools, had common friends, had passed each other many times in the street.

But what was it in this man's personality that had led him to submerge Sandor in a bath of boiling water? Was it as simple as Russian influence over Hungary and Sandor was just one of thousands of people who happened to have said the wrong thing at the wrong time? Was Sandor unlucky in the same way that someone gets knocked down by a car or gets cancer?

At first, Sandor's blame had many targets, an obvious one being the Soviet Union. But Sandor didn't like being a part of history or an object for a statistician. Blaming history didn't satisfy him; history wasn't responsible for anything; to blame history removed blame from the individual. And as far as Sandor was concerned, history was the fault of individuals.

Sandor had always thought that he'd meet the bearded guard again. Perhaps on a bus or a train or they'd brush by each other on a tram. Perhaps a coincidence would arise whereby the guard would turn out to be a friend of a friend, and they'd be introduced to each other in a bar. Sandor felt that a meeting would eventually happen because of the emotion which he'd spent in the guard's company, the expense of his pain creating a bond.

So when he realised that the bearded guard had just left the medical hut, Sandor's initial feeling was one of affirmation, that his prediction had been correct.

But then he felt *fear*: a nauseous feeling in his stomach, the rattle of his kidneys. Suddenly the room felt hot, then cold, then hot again. He pushed off his blanket and looked at his legs. Then he peered out the window behind him, but he couldn't see the guard. Sitting up in bed, he looked out the window across the room, but no, the bearded guard wasn't there either.

Three other people were in the medical hut. They started looking at Sandor. One asked if he was okay? Sandor didn't pay any attention. The nurse was called. She rose from her desk and walked down to him, "Do you want anything?"

Sandor shook his head. He was still confused as to where the bearded guard had gone. He looked over at the bed which the bearded guard had vacated. He'd taken all his personal belongings. He wasn't returning.

The nurse saw that Sandor was confused. She asked, "Do you want your blanket?"

Sandor nodded. She picked it up off the floor. As she draped it over his body, he started to urinate, a slow discolouration of his sheets, the stingy, acidic stench of urine rising up to her face. She drew the curtains around his bed, "I'll get clean sheets and a towel."

CHAPTER SIXTEEN

They sat around the table. There were only two people Sandor hadn't met before, one was a representative of the government, the other was the Bishop of Limerick. The man from the government was middle aged, he'd arrived at the camp early that morning, he'd black hair, glasses, white shirt and black tie. His name was Michael Ryan. He read from a page which Lucia translated, "The Irish Government is glad that the strike has been called off and that there has been no serious injuries. It was a great pity and a cause of much sadness for all that it had come to this as the government has been doing its best for the refugees."

When Ryan finished reading the statement, the Bishop of Limerick spoke about his concern for people's health, especially the health of the children. "It brought me great sadness to hear that the younger ones were put on strike. But thank God it's all over and we're all meeting here as mature adults."

Then Ryan started speaking about the government's strategy. He seemed nervous, but efficient. "Firstly," he explained, "I'd like to make you aware of the following distinction. When a refugee leaves their homeland the first country which they arrive in is called the primary country of asylum. In your case, you left Hungary and arrived in Austria. Therefore, Austria was your primary country of asylum. While in Austria, Ireland offered you asylum, which made this country your secondary country of asylum.

"This is a very important distinction for the following reason. Even though you are still a refugee, once you are in a country of secondary asylum, in the eyes of the UN, you are in a different category to a refugee in a country of primary asylum. The reason for this is that countries of secondary asylum are generally in a better position to help refugees than countries of primary asylum. As the name suggests, countries of primary asylum are usually the first places where refugees arrive, whereas secondary countries are places where refugees have applied to go.

"As far as the UN is concerned, refugees in countries of primary asylum are the ones which require immediate attention. Usually, these countries are buckling under the strain of a sudden arrival of large numbers of people and therefore they are a priority for the UN. Once the refugees are in a country of secondary asylum, however, they are viewed as being in a much better situation as these countries can control the amount of refugees which they allow in.

"Since your arrival in Ireland, most of you have wanted to leave this country. A demand has been made by the camp council for visas to be produced for other countries but Ireland isn't in a position to give you visas. Therefore, when you apply for visas for other countries you are treated on the same level as any other citizen of Ireland. There is no special consideration given to the fact that you are refugees, because you are in a country of secondary asylum.

"Now, in order to help you leave Ireland, the Irish Government is approaching the UN with the following proposal. We want the UN to change our status from a country of secondary asylum to a country of primary asylum because of our high unemployment rate and the difficulty we have in absorbing you. If the UN agrees, then it will be just as if you have never left Austria and the same conditions will apply to you. In short, you'll be refugees with a primary-asylum country priority."

Sandor listened to the suggestion. There was a logic to it which he couldn't fault. They had ended the hunger strike because the government had agreed to meet with them, and with this proposal, they had gone further than just a meeting.

The Bishop of Limerick asked, "So will this put an end to any future hunger strikes?"

Sandor replied, "We'll see in a month."

∽

When Sandor called on Dr Pader he was alone in his apartment, his wife was out getting a confirmation dress for their daughter. Sandor sensed that Dr Pader wasn't impressed by religious ritual and his suspicion was confirmed when the doctor spoke of the absurdity of the upcoming ceremony, the parade of children through the grounds of Knockalisheen. "I asked Father Mikes to allow her to be confirmed with the other girls in her school but he insisted that she accompany the Hungarian children. So during this week when all her class are being confirmed in a church near her school, my daughter will be run up to the camp to be confirmed in a hut."

Sandor told him that a similar arrangement had been made for Kristina. Father Mikes wanted to make sure that the children understood what was happening to them. "I think he's going to explain everything before, a little course in Christianity, as most of the children don't know what he's talking about."

They were seated at the kitchen table. It was early afternoon. The smell of lunch hadn't vacated the apartment. A bottle of whiskey sat on the table, unopened. It was a present from Sandor to Dr Pader, a gesture of thanks for the medical attention.

Dr Pader talked about the strike. He said that he was always concerned, not with the motivation for the strike, but with people's health. "As I said to my wife on the first day of the strike, there will be casualties and I was right. About ten people collapsed and were moved to Barringtons Hospital. Some were in a bad way. But I don't think that there will be any long-term problems."

Sandor said that regardless of anybody's opinion of the strike, as a means to an end, it had worked. Yes, it was ruthless and toyed with people's health. "But we've already met with a government representative and we've been informed that next week we will be meeting a man from the United Nations."

"And what can he offer?"

Sandor explained the difference between primary and secondary asylum and the plan put forward by the government. "That's what the strike has done. It's focused their minds. We didn't know about this distinction a week ago. If we hadn't gone on strike, perhaps this detail wouldn't have come to light."

Dr Pader was unconvinced. "But look at you. You have enough to eat. You have a place to stay. While you haven't a job, what's to say that you won't get one in the future? How can you say that you are still a refugee? What are you fleeing? Where's this mysterious persecution? *You* have been the only risk to your life, not any government or war or political upheaval. The uprising was over months ago. Why should you deserve to be a refugee and replace one of the tens of thousands of people fleeing some war zone?"

Sandor replied, "Firstly, you don't know why I left Hungary. A country is a different place to each of its citizens. There are ten million Hungarians and therefore ten million Hungarys. But the reason I'm fleeing Ireland is simple. It's a nation of refugees. And what its citizens are fleeing is similar to what most people have fled since the dawn of time – poverty.

"Most refugees are economic. If this wasn't true, show me the hordes of people trying to get out of wealthy countries. And the reason why most refugees are economic is simple – poverty persecutes like no dictator could ever imagine."

As Sandor was leaving Dr Pader's apartment, he asked him for one last bit of help, "Can you remember who was in the bed across from me in the medical hut? He had a beard, tallish, from Budapest, I think."

Dr Pader tried to recall him as Sandor continued talking, "He lent me some money and I want to pay him back."

While thinking Dr Pader's hand gripped his jaw pushing his fleshy cheeks upwards, "Károly…Károly something or other."

"And what was wrong with him?"

"As far as I can remember it was exhaustion. But by the time I got to see him, he was doing fine."

∽

Later Sandor went to the camp council's office. He drew the curtains and turned on the light. Apart from a desk and four chairs, it was an uncluttered room with a potbellied stove in its centre. On the walls were newspaper cuttings, stories about Knockalisheen Camp, pictures of refugees. In the top drawer of the desk was a ledger. It was an exact copy of the army quartermaster's ledger which was used to list the refugees, their names, religion and the supplies which had been given to them on arrival. What happened to individual refugees was also noted: those who had left, where they had moved to, what companies had given them jobs or what countries had offered them visas.

Sandor turned each page taking note of every person called Károly. Back in Hungary it was quite a common name and to Sandor's surprise, there were only two listed in the camp: Károly Papp in hut twenty nine and Károly Szabó in hut fifty five.

It was now dark beneath a sky full of stars and the wishbone moon was tilting thin. It looked deceitful and cunning. Sandor peered out the window. He felt unnerved like he was full of bad news. He wondered if it was the man's real name? Once people had crossed the Austrian border they were whoever they said they were. Identities didn't matter as they were all refugees.

A few weeks ago McManus had asked Sandor to investigate the use of an illegal radio. And so on this pretence he started knocking on doors, talking to people about the radio, and if they'd heard of anybody using one.

Most people were happy to talk to Sandor. Since the end of the strike, the mood in the camp had been optimistic and change seemed to be on the way.

But nobody knew about an illegal radio. There was only one radio in the camp and that was in the recreational hut.

Károly Papp was a clean-shaven man with a two-year old child and a pretty wife. He was no more than twenty-five years old and that ruled him out.

That left Károly Szabó, hut fifty five.

∾

Sandor paused outside the hut for a moment before he knocked on the door. A woman in her early forties answered, Margaret Szabó. She had short brown hair, very straight, and her fringe arched around her forehead in a semicircle. She offered him tea, which he accepted. He sat on an old couch covered by a knitted blanket. Until recently, two families had lived in the hut, then one had moved out. Like most of the other huts which Sandor had visited, there wasn't much in the way of decoration. A small bookcase carried clothes and some personal effects. In one corner two beds had been pushed together to create a double. On a side table a wedding photograph stared out at the room. Sandor recognised Károly's face: the beard, the green eyes, the neat parting on one side of his head.

Sandor explained why he'd called. He spoke about McManus and the illegal radio. It was considered a serious matter by the camp authorities. He explained that since the strike the camp council and the Red Cross were trying to patch up their differences, "It would look good if we were seen to be co-operating."

Margaret said that she'd do anything to help, but she was not aware of anyone using such a device, "I'll ask my husband when he gets back. Perhaps he has heard something."

Sandor asked, "When would be a good time to call back?"

"It's probably best if he calls on you."

∽

On a drizzly morning, a car arrived at the camp. It contained Nicolas Wyrouboff of the United Nations High Commission for Refugees and Michael Ryan, a representative of the Irish Government. They were met by McManus at the entrance of the camp. After handshakes they entered McManus's office. Already seated at the table were Sandor, Lucia and László Eper. Wyrouboff was a man nearing middle age, in full health, a tall, lean frame with a touch of silver to his dark hair. He was cleanly shaven. His suit was well tailored. McManus introduced everyone and they sat down, drinks were offered, glasses of water, tea and coffee.

Sandor was impressed that an emissary of the United

Nations was visiting the camp. He felt that they were in the presence of a man of stature, a person of influence. For most of the meeting the attention was on Wyrouboff (earlier, McManus had diplomatically informed Sandor that his name was pronounced *Voroboff*).

Wyrouboff had a businesslike air to him which Sandor liked. There was little small talk and when he started speaking about the purpose of his visit it was in a matter-of-fact way. One of the first comments he made, in English and then translated by Lucia, was that he agreed with the Irish Government and felt relieved that the refugees had decided to come off the hunger strike. "There is little need for such action and I think that it must have happened due to some misunderstanding, because the Irish Government has been doing all it can to assist you. I think it's important that you see the Hungarian refugee situation as a European problem and one that puts an awful strain on most of the countries on the western part of the continent. The latest estimate is that one hundred and seventy thousand Hungarians have fled, which presents a great difficulty for some of the countries where they have arrived. Austria, for example, is under huge pressure and that's why the UN is grateful to a small country like Ireland to have taken any refugees at all. Our first priority was to get as many refugees out of Austria and then Yugoslavia, as she took in many too. I know you went on hunger strike because you feel that you have been forgotten, but believe me, this is not the case. It's just that it's a busy time."

He produced cigarettes from a case and offered them around. Sandor accepted one and McManus pushed an ashtray in his direction. Wyrouboff continued speaking after the gentle exhalation of smoke. "The UN has been trying to get as many countries as possible to help with the relief and we feel that Ireland's response has been a very generous one. But after saying that, I want to hear what you have to say in order to understand your problems."

Sandor spoke about the camp. He said that it wasn't suitable for long-term accommodation, many families were dreading next winter, "As you could imagine, the huts aren't great, especially if you have small children."

Wyrouboff said that the camp wasn't the worst which he'd seen and that the Irish Government was not at fault for housing the refugees here. "Obviously, it's not the Ritz. But good quality temporary accommodation is hard to find no matter what country you are in." Although McManus didn't respond immediately, he nodded his head with agreement and then he said, "We're trying to source new accommodation at the moment and we hope that, come winter, this camp will be closed."

Eper mentioned jobs, "People are very bored and penniless hanging around the camp all day long."

Wyrouboff sympathised with this situation but added that it was important for people to take up whatever work was offered, "I have been told that some people have turned down jobs, but I assure you that this only means less money for the individuals in question. It has been explained to me that people are fearful that if they take up work, they won't get visas. But I want to assure you that this won't disqualify you from getting a visa for another country."

Sandor replied, "Some people have turned down work, probably for this reason. But also because the work offered was not in their trade or profession. It has been our experience that the Irish trade unions have objected to us working in certain areas such is the lack of employment here."

Eper, clearing his throat, continued, "While jobs and housing are important, ultimately what most refugees want to know is when they are leaving this country." Eper smiled, "Some feel that this information is a military secret."

Wyrouboff was amused, "And if I had the answer to this secret, I'd reveal it to you." He said he understood that the refugees wanted to leave the country, but the UN could not guarantee when or to what country they would be going to, "You must be patient."

Eper replied, "Most people wouldn't have come here if they had known how long they'd have to wait."

Wyrouboff said that Ireland had kindly taken people last winter at a time when Austria was running out of money and couldn't support any more refugees, "There is the chance that you might have been worse off if you had stayed in Austria. You might not realise this now but Ireland has been doing you a favour."

Sandor said, "We understand the generosity of the Irish people and we are thankful for it. However, the difference is this: if we had stayed in Austria, we would have been in a country of primary asylum and we would have been given first preference for visas to other countries. But since we've arrived in Ireland, we have lost that status as we are in a country of secondary asylum. Is it possible that because of Ireland's poor economic situation it could be treated as a country of primary asylum?"

Wyrouboff said that he wasn't sure, it wasn't a matter which he could resolve immediately. "The problem is that you are in a better situation than in Austria despite what you think. On a day-to-day level you are not hungry or without accommodation. If you were still in Austria today, there is a chance that you would be. And therefore it's hard for the UN to give you primary asylum status on these grounds, because refugees in Austria are a lot worse off than you. It's as simple as that. But we haven't ruled it out and the Irish Government is in discussion with the UN about these issues."

The meeting ended on a sincere, optimistic note. Wyrouboff handed his card to Sandor and told him to contact him at any time, adding, "I was a refugee before. If you look at my name you'll know where I'm from."

Sandor read his printed name *Mr Nicolas Wyrouboff* and asked, "Russia?"

Wyrouboff replied, "You fled Khrushchev. We escaped Lenin. It was back in '23. We fled to France. I know what you're going through."

∽

The evening air was warm. It was close to summer. Sandor jumped over a crumbling wall and then turned to help Maria down from the stones threatening to avalanche into a small field wild with bushes and weeds. The dominant colours were the bright yellow of the gorse flowers on thorny bushes and the lush green of knotted grass, occasionally spoilt by the flat seal of cow dung. There was a thick smell, a bitter soupiness to the air, as if nature was working up a sweat providing for the life which she'd created since winter.

Cautiously they entered the ruins of an old cottage. Grey bricks and weed-woven windows, the remains of a door, rust coloured and hinged. There were two rooms in the cottage which viewed the hills, looking down on the wooden huts of the camp and then on to Limerick. Rubbish had been dumped in one of the rooms, sacks of broken timber and machine parts.

Sandor felt in awe of the cottage. He felt like he was in an old graveyard long forgotten, a colossus of grey stone, isolated from its ancestry, its now blurry lineage.

Sandor felt nervous excitement when Maria removed her clothes and his hands were free to move along her neck and down towards the white of her breasts, to the circular sprawl of her nipples. There was always a saltiness, a seaside taste to her chest, the horizon line of her breasts; and when her nipples firmed between his lips, Sandor became more confident, as if his instinct was being acknowledged by her body's gracious approval. He removed his shirt and placed it beneath them. They were just outside the cottage, hidden. He liked the air on his body, the tickling applause, the occasional insect buzz, the smell of sweat between them, a patina of pleasure on the surface of their skin. Careful not to hurt her head, Maria lay down slowly on their bed of clothes, and as she did, her breasts seemed to disappear, dissolving into the length of her body, and her nipples, still vocal and stiff, moved above her ribcage, a rack of protective bones that shielded a heart which Sandor heard beating.

When he finished moving his tongue around her chest he continued on to her neck, and back to her mouth. Maria paused to remove a hair shivering on her lower lip before their mouths met. Kissing always bemused Sandor. It seemed irrelevant, odd. Locking mouths, touching tongues. Perhaps it was a penetrative prelude, a hint of moisture.

Sandor teased his head away from Maria and moved towards her waist. He removed her skirt and then his own trousers. Being naked outdoors excited Sandor. That somebody might be watching inspired him. To Sandor's mind, nakedness among trees and shrubs seemed to be sanctioned by a higher power, the Old Testament, a resonance fecund in its praise for all God's creatures.

His body was still scarred from the torture. Skin on his back looked like badly ironed cloth, lined and veined. On his shoulder blades the skin was stretched and tight as if it could be shattered like a thin sheet of ice. Although it didn't hurt anymore, he was always careful, overly protective, avoiding direct sunlight and physical aggression. When Maria had asked about the scars on his back, Sandor had explained that it was the result of a work accident when hot engine oil had been spilt on him. He knew he'd tell her the truth, some time in the future when he was ready.

Maria told Sandor to lie down. She pushed his legs apart and knelt between them. Her hands rubbed his inner thighs. When he felt the warmth of her mouth, Sandor stretched back and opened his eyes to the blue sky. A few clouds passed, in their varied shapes Sandor saw outlines of people; beyond them, the nervy darkness of space.

It had been two weeks since they'd had any physical intimacy. In the tight sack of his balls each day was felt like a build up of sexual sediment, compact and unyielding. Sandor felt that release was imminent. By placing his hands on her head he gestured for her to stop, to move her mouth away from him. Maria smiled. She lay back down on their clothes. In the distance a dog barked. Maria wondered if people would find them. Sandor said he wasn't worried as the ruins of the cottage were isolated.

This time Sandor pushed her legs apart. He kissed her bellybutton, her pubic hair tickling his chin. Air drafted between his legs and vented over his balls. Maria wasn't as quiet as him. Slow at first, her breathing quickened as though she was short of breath, trying to stay afloat in water. Her hands held Sandor's head. Soon her muscles fully tightened and she told him to stop.

Sandor lay on top of her and she directed him inside. Soon she sensed that he was close. She gripped his back, tilting her head to the left to allow Sandor's face to fall above her right shoulder. Opening his eyes, Sandor looked at the pattern on the clothes which they were lying on. He withdrew in time, coming on her legs.

As Sandor put on his clothes he looked at his genitals, their flaccid state. How transitory was their strength, a couple of minutes of illusionary power before the clear, clean skin became wrinkled and shrivelled, the sexual season, swift and hasty. Urgency. That was the feeling which Sandor felt. Perhaps it was nature's way, there was nothing more important than the creation of life and so why would nature prolong sex? Behind this feeling was one of love. Pure love for Maria. It was generous and he reached out to hug her.

Sandor didn't think that another person could complete you. Growing up as a twin, he'd thought about this many times. Individuals were brought into this life whole and complete and you died that way; love wasn't about completing *yourself*. That would mean that we were all born flawed, and he never felt flawed.

Sandor wondered how long he'd feel sexually satisfied for, a couple of minutes, an hour, a day?

When dressed they lay on the ground. Neither of them spoke until Sandor turned to her and told her that he loved her.

She replied, "I love you too." He paused, coughed. "Will you marry me?" He wiped a tearful eye, "I don't have a ring or anything, but I love you and we can get that later on."

Sandor waited for her reply, counting the seconds. She accepted and they both started laughing.

∞

The confirmation procession moved through the camp, girls dressed in various shades of white, the boys in darkened tones of grey. Some hands carried large, homemade crucifixes, planks of wood held together with coarse twine, while others carried pictures of the Virgin Mary and Jesus Christ, portraits which tilted towards the blue sky before the weather turned as it always did in Ireland. Father Mikes led the procession while nuns from the local school walked alongside the children and their parents. Sandor stood on the sidelines, camera in hand, taking photographs of Kristina as she moved with the hymn-singing procession.

Over one hundred children of all ages were squashed into the camp chapel. In his priestly gown, a regal looking Father Mikes stood behind the altar. He spoke about the sacrament which he was about to perform; its purpose, significance and how he was pleased to offer religious guidance to the children, young adults who'd been denied this chance in their home country. "Atheism is worse than Devil worship because if you believe in the Devil you acknowledge God's existence and you might end up worshipping him. But if you believe in nothing, there's little hope for you."

The political situation in Hungary was mentioned. He offered prayers for those unfortunate souls who were being subjected to Russian rule, and the congregation went silent apart from the noise of children and the birdsong of babies.

Sandor sat beside Kristina, Eva and Maria. Kristina was one of the better dressed girls in the chapel as a Laurel Hill friend had lent her a dress that had only been worn once. Other girls were wearing homemade dresses that diligent mothers had spent weeks preparing, utilising whatever cloth was available or what could be afforded in local shops.

Last night, Sandor had listened to Kristina lecture her mother about the significance of being confirmed. Kristina was trying on her dress in the hut in order to show Eva, repeating what Sister Carmel had told them about the ceremony and being able to fully participate in other church rituals. Kristina was excited about the sacrament. She was impressed with the fuss which was being made of her, the style of the dress, the idea that she was approaching adulthood.

While Kristina was trying on her dress, Sandor told them about his marriage plans. Eva wasn't too surprised by his announcement; Kristina's excitement, however, was high pitched.

She asked Sandor about the ceremony. When would they be getting married? Would it be in Limerick? Could she get off school to attend? Could she be involved in the ceremony? Perhaps as a flower girl or a bridesmaid?

Sandor explained that no plans had been made as yet, but of course, they'd be sure to include Kristina, "You are family after all."

Maria's parents were happy with the news of their daughter's engagement. Mr Novak, who was in Dublin when he heard about it, promised a celebration in their new house.

Mrs Novak started making wedding plans. But Sandor was unsure about the ceremony. So was Maria. They agreed on timing, though, they wanted to get married as soon as possible. Once married Maria felt that she would be independent of her parents and they could do as they pleased.

"It sounds awful," said Maria. "But marriage is a great means to an end."

Gerry Buckley contacted Sandor asking him to work a couple of weekends. As he needed the money, Sandor obliged. After letting him into the factory, Gerry went home. In solitude, he laboured at his desk. Apart from the noise which he made, the factory was a quiet hulk of machinery, a sleeping mass of power and energy.

It was the first time he'd worked in the plant since Tommy Gallagher had told him that Buckley had lobbied against Pinter's factory proposal. Sandor wondered if this could be true? Could Buckley muster that power? Or was it a journalist's imagination?

After two hours of working Sandor went to the toilet, down the corridor and into the small, drafty room, a thick smell of bleach. Once finished, he returned to his desk but as he was ahead of time, he decided to have a cigarette outside in the sunshine, the warmth of the morning. The back of the factory looked on to the Shannon, a few boats passed, you could hear distant voices. The morning had heated up. It was too hot for him to fully enjoy his cigarette as it made him feel a little dizzy.

Sandor wished that he didn't need the money, that he didn't have to work for Buckley, that he could ask him about the factory proposal; and if it were true, that he'd lobbied against it, then Sandor could give him a piece of his mind.

He tried to imagine Buckley's power for it did seem contradictory, to be able to stop a factory being built, yet unable to give him a job in his own plant.

After a few minutes of sunshine Sandor returned inside. Being alone in the factory made him feel voyeuristic, ghost-like. He looked at the personal items lying around, old coats, work gloves and the clutter of everyday life, newspapers, sweet wrappers, empty bottles of milk, overflowing ashtrays. Many times Sandor had imagined himself working here, making friends, putting in a decent day's work. In this factory he had once seen a way of translating the nothingness of everyday into the glow of accomplishment.

Now, in its silent, vacated state, the factory appeared hostile. Sandor felt that he shouldn't even be there. He started going from room to room, from the plant to the canteen, to the reception and upstairs to Gerry's office, where he sat outside.

Sandor had met Gerry back in January. Although it was only five months ago, it seemed that this meeting had taken place years ago, as though Sandor's time in Ireland, every minute of every hour of every day, had been compacted and didn't reflect the normal calendar days and months. It was as if time behaved differently in Ireland.

Sandor pushed down the door handle to Gerry's office. It was open. Although he knew it was empty, he took his time entering, respectful of Gerry's absence. As Gerry was always in the office when Sandor had been there, it seemed strangely different without him, as though a large item of furniture was missing or a painting had been stolen. Sandor felt like a child invading a room out of bounds. Through a window, Sandor looked down at the desk where he was supposed to be working. He imagined owning the factory, keeping an eye on the staff. He wondered if the workers worried when Gerry's figure appeared at the window, his statesmanlike shadow, if it motivated them to work harder, quicker, to be perceived as diligent and industrious.

On Gerry's desk there were a couple of folders, a picture of his wife, some children. Sandor sat behind the desk, the squeak of leather beneath his work pants. He opened the top drawer: small change, a couple of stamps, a letter opener, a corkscrew, stationary. The next drawer contained a bundle of photographs. Sandor was impressed by the composition of certain shots which appeared to have been taken by newspaper photographers, pictures of Gerry with other men in suits, shaking hands. Gerry had the same broad smile in each photograph and there was always a neat trim to his moustache.

One drawer was locked. Sandor looked for a key in the other drawers. He found a bunch, but they were all too big for the little lock.

Sandor rose from the desk. On the wall there were pictures of the factory throughout the ages, the last fifty years. One photo had been taken from across the Shannon in the summer. Sandor loved the magical dance of sunshine on water, it reminded him of sparks, as though nature's power was intrinsically electrical.

Sandor wondered if he could make a connection between Gerry Buckley and Julia Pinter's factory proposal being turned down. Could Gallagher's suspicion be confirmed by a couple of minutes searching around Gerry's office?

Back in Budapest, those in the Communist Party had special shops, earned more money and looked after each other. There was a certain clarity, almost an honesty to their corruption. But Sandor wondered how it worked in Ireland, how were favours granted, how did influence smother the will of others?

Sandor heard footsteps on the factory floor. He looked at the light bulb hanging from the office ceiling even though he hadn't turned it on. Quickly he peered behind the desk to make sure that all the drawers were closed and that the chair was in the correct position.

"Sandor, Sandor," Gerry called out. The factory was quiet. Sandor edged towards the door. Then he heard footsteps barrelling up the stairs towards the office. Sandor moved behind the desk, then under it, wedging himself beneath the chair and the wooden panelling. His ear was squashed against his shoulder. He could hear his heart beating rapidly.

The door opened. Sandor wondered if Gerry could smell him. Perhaps the familiar odour of Gerry's office had been contaminated by his presence. Footsteps moved across the room. Sandor sensed their direction. Gerry went towards the window and stopped. A whistling noise came from Gerry's mouth, a form of thinking out loud, questioning Sandor's whereabouts.

Gerry left the office, shutting the door softly. Sandor remained still, holding his breath as if underwater. He was drenched in sweat. Gerry ambled downstairs, "Sandor, Sandor."

Sandor figured that Gerry would leave the building but he continued walking around the factory calling out Sandor's name. After a couple of minutes the footsteps and the calling stopped. A door was shut.

Sandor emerged from beneath the desk. He didn't stand

up. He crawled along the floor towards the door, raised his hand to open the handle and let himself out.

He was locked in the factory. The only window open was in the bathroom. Squeezing himself through it, he landed on the ground. Sneaking around to the front of the factory, he looked for Gerry's car, but it was gone. He decided to wait as he figured Gerry would return. And he did, with speed. Sandor explained to Gerry that he'd stepped out of the factory for a few minutes, he was ahead of schedule, and he needed to telephone the camp to give his sister a message.

Gerry smiled, "You should have used the phone inside."

Sandor said, "I didn't think I was allowed."

Gerry replied, "Of course you are." They went back inside and Sandor finished his job. Gerry never asked Sandor to work for him again.

∾

Outside the recreational hut you could hear the radio, the deep vibrations and warm timbre of the valves carrying the official news from Hungary, part of the Russian attempt to counter stations like Radio Free Europe. Sandor liked to listen to any radio station. It was comforting to hear the sound of American presenters, their soft, assured voices speaking in plain English, and he also liked to be reminded of Budapest by the Hungarian broadcasters.

Sandor listened as a Hungarian presenter asked those who had fled to return to their country, to leave the pretence of their lives in the West and to return home thus ridding themselves of any further exploitation. To support this appeal he introduced a few people who had returned. A man spoke of how, after spending months in Austria, he'd decided to go home as he felt disillusioned about his prospects in the West, "The Austrians always exploited the Hungarians, and nothing has changed."

A woman spoke of England, the pathetic conditions in the capital of that old, crumbling empire. France was also mentioned; a couple who'd left Paris because the opportunities which they had imagined did not exist.

And then to Ireland. Sandor recognised the voice, the same, soft speech he'd heard every day for months. It was Anna Varga. She spoke of the conditions which the refugees were forced to live in, how the government had left them in wooden huts abandoned in the countryside, how she was forced to raise her child like an animal in a barn, and how happy she was back in Hungary. She said, "Ireland is a lie. It's one big lie."

CHAPTER SEVENTEEN

Sandor recalled newspaper articles about the ÁVO spying on Hungarians in refugee camps. The idea being that they'd been sent from Hungary to discredit refugees in their host countries, to blacken their name thus making it more difficult for them to assimilate, and also to spy on people and to use the information gathered to threaten their families back home. Sandor hadn't thought much about this suggestion when he'd first heard it but now that Károly Szabó was living in the camp, he wondered if the bearded guard was actually working for the ÁVO.

From a propaganda perspective, Ireland had served the ÁVO well because of the difficulties the refugees were having settling down, and so there didn't seem to be any need for ÁVO disruption. Perhaps then, Sandor thought, Szabó was gathering information about the people in the camp. McManus's talk of an illegal radio: was this being used to transmit information?

But Sandor didn't believe that. Ireland had taken too few refugees for the ÁVO to care. Most likely, Sandor figured, Szabó had fled Hungary and the ÁVO. For one hundred and fifty hours during the uprising, just before the Russian tanks had returned to Budapest to quash the insurgents, the city had felt victorious. Szabó might have fled then in fear for his life, scared that a new government would round up former ÁVO men, or that the insurgents would hunt him down and kill him.

During the uprising Sandor had seen one such execution. It had happened on a side street in Pest, outside an old apartment block. A man was dragged downstairs by a group of civilians, some of whom carried guns. The man was accused of being in the ÁVO and was carried to a lamp-post where he was stripped of his clothing. Once naked, people took turns beating him with iron bars and kicking him as he desperately declared his innocence. After a while a rope was tied around the lamp-post and the man was strapped up by his feet; for the next twenty minutes he was beaten to death and afterwards left dangling with a sign at his feet saying *ÁVO Scum*.

When the crowd had thinned out Sandor went over to the body, his mind perverted by the idea of death and how a life had been suddenly and brutally ended. But he was also curious about the dead man's identity, as perhaps it might be the bearded guard. Fearfully Sandor edged towards the body. He was not afraid of the dead man but the crowd which surrounded him, their explosion of violence and unthinking savagery, the gut instinct of a group of people who now carried on with their lives, continuing to walk down the street, back to their homes, to eat and drink and spend time with their families. These individuals seemed to have shed their own identities when attacking the man, the group having absolved itself of any individuality.

Sandor looked at the bloodied and bruised face but he didn't recognise him, he was just some other ÁVO man or perhaps an innocent civilian mistakenly beaten to death. Had it been the bearded guard, had it been Szabó hanging from that pole, a part of Sandor would have enjoyed the sight of his dead body decorating the lamp-post, hanging beneath the yellow light which created a macabre halo on the dead man's head. And though a part of him would have been satisfied with revenge no matter how brutal it was, Sandor wouldn't have participated, he wouldn't have joined in, he wouldn't have murdered.

Szabó was alive, living in Ireland. And perhaps Szabó had chosen this country because there weren't so many refugees as the fewer links with his past, the better. Or perhaps he had picked Ireland because it was the furthest point from Hungary in Western Europe, miles away from the Soviet Union, as if there was another world war and the Russians managed to advance into Austria, Switzerland, France, Italy, Belgium and the Netherlands, if the Russians someday managed to sweep across Europe, Ireland would be the last country to fall.

Sandor felt awed by the power which he could have over Szabó's life: revenge was easy, he could tell others in the camp that a former ÁVO man was amongst them. Perhaps they'd attack him, his life would certainly be made very difficult, and most likely, he'd be run out of the camp. But this also made Sandor feel uncomfortable. Szabó's presence in the camp was an echo of the baths of Andrássy Street, a place which he'd thought he had left for good, a place he had travelled thousands of miles away from.

And at times this uncomfortable feeling turned to fear. One night Sandor awoke in the early hours, close to five. It was still dark outside which made him feel more anxious and agitated. Eva was breathing heavily at the end of the hut, sleeping deeply. For a little while Sandor wasn't aware of why he was worried and so he tried to recall his dreams but none came to mind. All he remembered was the four or five times he had woken up since going to bed. Gradually, however, he awoke fully, and as he did, Szabó came to mind. More specifically, Sandor wondered if Szabó was aware of their past association, was it possible that the bearded guard had recognised a former victim?

Sandor concluded that Szabó had recognised him. It was the safest assumption to make. Sandor was well known in the camp; Szabó had had months to recognise him. And surely that was the bearded guard's main worry; surely keeping his past quiet would have made him scrutinise every new face he saw, making sure that any link to the baths of Andrássy Street was kept secret.

But Szabó recognising him wasn't Sandor's main concern. He was more worried about Szabó realising that he'd recognised him, that Sandor had realised who the occupant of hut fifty five really was and that the former ÁVO man would be revealed. Then Szabó, thought Sandor, might silence him.

∽

When Josef Horvath came back from London, Eva decided that she'd return to the city with him in a matter of weeks. She was desperate to get out of Knockalisheen Camp. Once Kristina had finished school for the summer, the three of them would make the journey; train to Dublin, boat to England and another train to London.

Josef had spent three weeks in London. For the first two days he'd lived in a small hotel, a dingy old building near Victoria Station. Then, as he wanted to save his money, he slept rough on park benches and down alleyways. As it was summer, he didn't mind. Every third day he stayed in a hotel or a hostel to clean himself and wash the few clothes he had with him. After a visit to a Red Cross office, he got the name of a hostel where other Hungarian refugees were staying and he spent a couple of nights there. It was mainly women and children who were living in the hostel, waiting for their husbands to secure work in London or around England before they moved out to join them. Although work wasn't plentiful, there was enough; if you wanted to work you could. A lot of the men had started manual jobs while they were learning English, but as Josef was nearly fluent he started searching for a job in a bakery straight away.

"And it was relatively simple to get one," he explained to Sandor and Eva the night of his return. "I called to about fifteen bakeries and one owner told me of a vacancy in his cousin's shop. So I called out to the cousin and after spending an hour talking to him, he told me that he'd keep the job open for me for the next six weeks until I settled in the country." That Josef was Hungarian was the main reason why he had given him the job as the baker felt indebted to the country. "The man was in the air force during the war, and he was shot down outside Budapest. He parachuted out of his plane and landed near a small farm. On landing he fractured his ankle and found it difficult to walk. He was spotted by a farmer, the family took him in, cared for and hid him. The end of the war was only weeks away and once it was over, the family drove him to Austria where he met some English soldiers who brought him home."

So a day was set for their departure to London, towards the end of June. Although Sandor was happy for Eva, his only concern was for Kristina. If they didn't get her into a school in London by the next academic year, they were planning on sending her back to Laurel Hill. Eva said, "The worst outcome is that Kristina will return to a school where she has already spent a couple of months, and I'll only get to see her on school holidays until we find a school in London. As a worst case scenario, it's not too bad. She likes Laurel Hill and the children there. And if she has to return, she might only be there for a term or two, as we'll start looking for schools straight away."

Sandor agreed with his sister, it wasn't a bad option. And Eva was confident that she'd get work, maybe not as a teacher at first, but at least some job which would tide her over for a while, get her used to the routine of employment and be able to finance trips back to Limerick if Kristina were to stay in Laurel Hill.

Eva suggested to Sandor and Maria that they should go to London as well. It was an option which they had considered. Yes, England was close by, there were many opportunities there and since the uprising, a large Hungarian community had formed, but Maria had one problem with the idea: their status. As Ireland had given them asylum, technically, they'd have to apply to the English authorities for a work permit and this could take time. At least their presence in Ireland was legitimate. Maria didn't want to pursue an illegal life in England, even if, as Josef believed, English citizenship would be easy to obtain.

Sandor understood why Eva and Josef wanted to go to England as, even if their attempt failed, they could return to Ireland and to their present situation. But Sandor also agreed with Maria and her desire to have their papers in order, longing to be a citizen of another country and forgetting about her days of being a refugee.

With Eva moving to London, Sandor started thinking about their parents, especially Katie, as when they were leaving Budapest she had wondered what would happen to her twins if they became separated. Back then, Sandor had declared that it would never happen. Now it would, but it was for the best, as he imagined that Katie and Frank would like Josef Horvath. They would believe, as Sandor did, that his feelings for Eva were sincere and that their relationship was promising. Of course Sandor thought that

Knockalisheen Camp had influenced their affections for each other in the same way that his engagement to Maria had been influenced by their present situation. People were being pushed together. Decisions had been made which might not have been under normal circumstances. People were gambling with their futures, taking bets on where to live and with whom, as the possibility of being alone, without work, without family, without somebody to care for, was far too frightening.

Sandor started to feel his separation from his family as being almost complete. In the space of seven months he'd gone from being a single man living with his family in the only country where he'd ever lived, to settling temporarily in Ireland while awaiting transit to another as yet known country with his fiancée whom he'd only known for five months. Just as he had severed any links with his parents for the foreseeable future, all ties to Eva and Kristina would soon be cut, this last familial link, a bond of blood which he wouldn't experience until Maria, at some point, had his child. Despite his love for Maria he still felt a sense of loneliness, of being in-between two families, his own which he was leaving and the one which he would create with her. At times, he felt somehow disappointed by this talk of *family*, the mythology of bloodlines, for behind the creation of a family was just a risk which two people took, just a gamble.

∽

The following letter was prepared by the camp council so László Eper could post it to the Congress of the United States of America, Washington DC, on his arrival in Canada, therefore arriving quicker:

Dear Sirs,
Please excuse us for disturbing you in your great and responsible work which is certainly more

important than our own case. Nevertheless, we write to you as our main interest has been the USA over the past months.

During this time we have been waiting for news regarding your decision on Hungarian refugees. According to newspaper reports you were planning to decide after the Easter recess, but nothing so far has happened.

Our arrival in Ireland after our reception in Austria was a great disillusionment. We, who have never gone abroad and were blindly trusting the West, did not think that we would be misled by anyone. We hoped that we would be waiting with our children and families to go to America, but it is already the seventh month that – despite the undeniable goodwill and willingness to help of the Irish Government and the Irish people – we are being kept in unheatable wooden huts, on unhealthy food and without the possibility of schooling for our children.

The Irish are a very poor and unfortunate people with a population of nearly three million and ninety thousand are unemployed. Therefore finding employment is impossible and the Irish trade unions, most understandably, protest against our employment.

We are aware that the uprising fought by us at home was fought for a Hungarian cause and it is of little merit to the West. We, after the defeat, have taken upon ourselves the hardships of exile solely on these promises of help that the West had made to us during the uprising.

If you only knew the immense gratefulness and trust we felt when we arrived in the Free World! The enormous kindness of the Austrians and their great sacrifice made us believe that the free West, headed by the United States, understood and appreciated our fight. But we also know that two hundred thousand refugees are too many for you and we know that many of us have behaved unworthy and ungrateful. But if two hundred thousand Americans were locked up in camps in utmost hopelessness, would they behave differently?

We have to ask you the following. Your country is a great one, your people are charitable and they live in wealth. The Austrians are a small nation and are not wealthy. Yet, after tremendous sacrifices they were willing to accept thirty thousand refugees to settle there. You have accepted approximately thirty thousand and have given great material support, but we beg of you to assist those who are unable to start a new life in the countries where they presently are. Owing to our utmost hopelessness some of our fellow refugees have already returned to Hungary and will face the horror of retaliation from the communist government. Mr Wyrouboff, an emissary of the United Nations Refugees Committee, the Irish Government and the Irish Red Cross have admitted that there is no possibility of work for us in this country. Therefore, the only possibility is for us to go abroad.

We have experienced that not all promises are kept, even in the West. This experience might be the result of some irresponsible officials who brought us to Ireland. We ask you to not judge us for these bitter words. And we ask you to consider our case, this time not as administrative officials, but as good neighbours. We ask members of Congress who have children to consider our case through their paternal eyes.

Please take up the case of the Hungarian refugees and try to arrive at a just solution. We ask you to impress upon the governments of other countries to induce them to one further and last sacrifice. Hoping that our letter will be read and considered we hand it to a fellow refugee travelling to Canada to forward it to you in a speedy manner.

On behalf of the three hundred and seventy Hungarian refugees,
Yours truly,
The Knockalisheen Governing Council.

It was dark when Sandor was walking back to the camp. He'd been in Limerick trying to sell a photograph to a publican and the man had failed to show up at the arranged time. Sandor was tired of traipsing around Limerick trying to sell pictures. People liked talking, but not buying. It was as if he'd hours to waste and was free to talk to all and sundry.

With the photograph tucked under his arm, Sandor walked quickly. The entrance of the camp was seven minutes away. It was a warm evening. On Sandor's mind was a cigarette and a glass of cold water.

He heard a rustling sound in the bushes. Looking around he thought of animals, the cows ambling around the fields near the camp or perhaps a bird whose wings were muscling the thorny spikes of a roadside hedge.

He heard footsteps. As he turned around he felt a blow to his side, the claw of a metal bar on his kidneys that was quickly followed by a deadening weight to the back of his head.

Sandor stumbled and fell. The road had a gritty surface which scratched his hands and wedged itself into his forehead. A couple of words were shouted into his ear and then the footsteps departed, and Sandor was left lying in the centre of the road. Although he was in pain he heard the sound of a car and felt the urgent need to move. What hurt most was his forehead which was already wounded from falling while on hunger strike. He crawled towards the side of the road and rested in the long grass, his back against a mound of earth.

Sandor was so close to the road that when the car passed he felt he might be whipped up by the vehicle's slipstream or stoned to death by the onslaught of pebbles shot from car tyres. Sandor wondered if anybody he knew, if somebody from the camp, would pass by. He heard another sound, this time high pitched and whining, a motorbike. A dog was barking in a nearby field.

The throbbing in Sandor's head was painful, precise. The blow to his kidneys, however, spread agony around his insides, from his groin to his lungs, which were gasping for breath. He started spitting on the ground, and like a dog, warm trails of saliva hung from his mouth. After twenty-five minutes he got up and walked to the camp. Though unsteady on his feet, he was back in his hut in a few minutes. Eva's reaction was one of shock and she thought that he'd been run over. She went to the kitchen hut and returned with a bowl of hot water and daubed his forehead with a cloth.

By the time Maria arrived, although his forehead was clear of blood, a purple bruise had emerged above his eye. She also thought that he'd been hit by a car while walking home. She held his hands while sitting on a chair beside him. Her face was full of confusion and distress. Sandor, comforted by her presence, her sympathy, the alarm in her eyes, said, "There was no car. Just people."

"Who'd do such a thing?" asked Maria.

"Who'd you think?" Sandor looked at Maria with a rhetorical stare. "The person who attacked me gave me an explanation. When I was lying on the ground, he said, 'Don't fuck with the O'Malleys.'"

∽

The camp council received word from the Irish Government, a letter of reassurance. It mentioned Wyrouboff and how they had sent a letter to the UN requesting assistance for the speedy resettlement of the Knockalisheen refugees.

It spoke of Mrs Simone Delattre of the European Relief Services of the National Catholic Welfare Conference of America. Soon she'd be visiting the camp to take the details of refugees who were likely to qualify for admission under the present American regulations.

Other countries had been approached by the government, too. Australia had said that it would only take refugees who were sponsored by relatives or other residents there. As for Canada, she was struggling with many applications, not only from Hungarian refugees, but from tens of thousands of people from other countries as well. The Irish ambassador in Ottawa was trying to get their case specially considered; however, the rate of absorption of immigrants in Canada was relatively slow and no more would be taken until the fifty thousand Hungarian refugees already there were absorbed. Consideration would be given by the Canadian authorities to refugees sponsored by relatives or other residents.

As for South America, Argentina planned to take two thousand refugees from Europe but so far only six hundred had been admitted, while Brazil was willing to discuss taking some from the camp. Discussions were proceeding with the Chilean Government who had stated that they would take around one thousand refugees from Europe.

Bolivia said that while its capacity for accommodating immigrants was limited, it would take in refugees only if they'd settle in the tropical lowlands which the government was endeavouring to open up. Land would be given free, virgin soil recently cleared of forest around Santa Cruz.

And lastly, the Irish Government had recommended that the camp wasn't suitable for permanent accommodation, particularly during winter periods. Primarily because of the bleak and lonely location of the camp, morale would be very low and there might be disorders, further hunger strikes and suicides. Therefore, in principle, the government had decided that alternative accommodation should be provided for the refugees no later than October.

CHAPTER EIGHTEEN

When Mr Novak finished working on his rented house in Dublin, his wife moved from the camp, and they invited Sandor and Maria to come for an engagement dinner. Mr Novak was a tall man who liked to wear a hat to cover the few strands of hair on his otherwise bald head. Even during the heat of June, Mr Novak (he never encouraged Sandor to call him by his first name, Francis) allowed the sweat to drip down the side of his face as his camel-coloured cloth hat remained firmly in place. Now that Mr Novak and his wife Sarah were out of the camp, their attitude towards their future son-in-law changed a little and Sandor noticed Mr Novak becoming more paternal.

While the women prepared dinner, Mr Novak suggested to Sandor that they walk his new dog around the neighbourhood and so they left the terrace house in Clonskeagh and took a path alongside the river Dodder. Mr Novak was understandably happy to be out of the camp. He told Sandor how much he'd hated the place, how frustrating it had been for him, a middle-aged man, to be living in a hut without a job and trying to sell wooden ornaments door to door. He also spoke of his relief that now he'd have some money in order to pay for their wedding, "The last thing I wanted was for the two of you to get married in the camp. I saw a few people do that and I thought it was pitiful."

Sandor asked about his job, what was it like to be working in Dublin?

Mr Novak described the construction company, the project which he was working on, how he conversed with his employer through German, and how, in a couple of months, his boss was going to take on two more people, "One of them being an engineer. You should apply. I've told him about you."

The midday sky was blue like a hot flame. They sat on a bench overlooking the river. From his pocket Mr Novak produced a ball, splashed it into the river and ordered his dog, which he'd yet to name, to retrieve it. The black and white terrier swam against the flow of the river, at times the water brought the dog to a halt, his whitish head peering out of the current like a speckled stone. The dog lost the ball. Mr Novak questioned his pet's intelligence.

Over dinner Mrs Novak was confident of Sandor and Maria's employment prospects over the next couple of months. She was a small woman with wiry black hair and hands which fearlessly gripped hot plates straight from the oven. There was plenty of food and a bottle of wine. Mr Novak skilfully carved slices of chicken breast. Mrs Novak offered gravy.

After dinner Sandor examined Mr Novak's map of Dublin. It had routes marked in pencil, Mr Novak's bicycle trip to work and various journeys which he'd made around the capital. Sandor was looking for Mr Murphy's street, he remembered him talking about the suburb of Dalkey where he lived. It was at the bottom of the map, by the sea. Sandor, who had brought all his personal papers with him for fear of theft back in the camp, checked Mr Murphy's address and found his road on the map.

In the early evening Sandor and Maria sat in the back garden eating ice cream. Mrs Novak brought out blankets and laid them on the grass. Maria stretched out in the sun. Sandor remained in his chair and flicked through a newspaper looking for Tommy Gallagher's name on top of articles. The dog also stretched out.

Sandor slept in one of the three bedrooms in the house, alone. He missed Maria. In the time since the Novaks had moved to Dublin, he'd moved his few belongings into her hut and had become used to sharing a bed.

The next day Sandor and Maria, happy to spend time alone, set off for Dalkey early in the morning, making their way by bike to Sandymount train station. Again, the sun was a confident mass of heat bubbling in the sky. A stillness to the sweet air was occasionally sullied by car exhaust. Sandor peddled furiously as Maria sat on the saddle, her hands wrapped loosely around his waist, at times she tickled his sides causing the bike to swerve into the road.

On the train Maria spoke about her parents. They were convinced that she and Sandor would settle here, get jobs, live in Dublin, "They seem to be forgetting that we have applied for visas and have spent ages trying to get out of the place. But now that they've settled here, they want us to do the same. My father told me about a job which might be coming up in his company and he thinks that you should apply. I know that they think they're looking out for us, but I think they're meddling."

Sandor said that it was to be expected, that they were re-establishing their hierarchy, "The camp wasn't normal life. It must have been strange for your parents to be sitting around unemployed, without a house, while their daughter and her boyfriend were in exactly the same position. All their authority had been taken away from them. They're just making up for lost time."

Dalkey was a maze of small, steep roads. Marine Road, where Mr Murphy lived, was an exhausting hike which left them thirsty. But the view was spectacular; the sea was velvety calm, yachts gently pushed by the breeze, and in the distance, Howth sparkled on the horizon. A few cars past by as they caught their breath. Sandor felt the sun on his face, and he knew that he'd get a colour.

Soon they arrived at the house. It felt like a long time since he had been in County Kerry with John Murphy's family, the cold of winter seemed like another country. Sandor explained the location of the Murphy's holiday home to Maria, the proximity to the sea, the steep mountains behind, and how on Christmas morning they'd climbed for hours clearing their heads of alcohol and their lungs of smoke.

Sweat was a moist balm on Maria's face, beads rolled above her lip and on her forehead. She said, "I need a drink." She asked Sandor if it was okay for them to call unannounced. It was a point which she'd mentioned earlier that morning but Sandor had dismissed her concerns, "They're a nice family. It won't be a problem."

But after they opened the small gate, walked to the house, knocked on the door, and when one of the daughters opened it, Sandor realised that he'd made a mistake, that he had misjudged the situation, and that calling unannounced to the house had, in fact, been a bad idea. This realisation wasn't in anything that the young girl said, she looked confusedly at Sandor for a few seconds until she remembered who he was, and Sandor recalled how she, along with her sister, had sung around the piano in Kerry. But when Sandor saw her dress – the formal nature of her clothing, the careful combing of her blond hair – and beyond her the people gathered in the hallway, the dark colours everybody wore, a blackness which paled people's faces, their eyes reddened, their tears shedding for a family member. Sandor's gut reaction was that Mr Murphy had died. Seconds later Meave Murphy, John's wife, came over to the door, she smiled at Sandor and looked confusedly at Maria as if she was expecting Eva. He apologised for coming to the house as Meave explained that the family had bad news, that her husband was dead.

Sandor felt awkward and clumsy. He wished that he'd listened to Maria when she had suggested that they call ahead of time instead of taking it for granted that the family would happily entertain them. But Sandor had ignored Maria because of his affection for John Murphy. He had taken him in before and as he had explained to Maria, he had organised for Kristina to attend one of the best schools in the country. Sandor was drawn towards John Murphy like a child to a favourite uncle. After seven months in Ireland the two days with the Murphy family had been one of the highlights. To be taken in by a family, to be fed and entertained in their home, to be treated with respect and decency. And though the Murphys were being charitable towards them, their charity wasn't forced or blatant and it didn't seem motivated by self-reward or self-congratulation.

Again Sandor apologised for coming at such a bad time, he said that they'd been in Dalkey for the day and had decided to call, but as they made gestures to leave, Meave insisted that they come in and have a drink, food had been prepared, and she said that her husband would have liked him to be here, that they had all enjoyed Christmas.

"It was his heart you see," explained Meave. "It was weak, it runs in his family, his father was the same. Heart attacks. Both of them dead before they were sixty."

In the kitchen trays of sandwiches were laid out, bottles of wine and beer, jugs of water and orange juice. Sandor felt uncomfortable eating under such circumstances but a plate was quickly served and wine poured. Meave introduced them to the people in the room. Sandor was informed by an elderly man how John had worked for him for many years before he'd set up an insurance company himself and gone on to make a fortune.

A clock hung on the wall. Sandor decided that in approximately twenty minutes he'd make an excuse and they would leave. Maria was very uncomfortable, people were making conversation with her and she, in her faulty English, was attempting to reply. There was an awkwardness to her, from the sip of her drink to the wipe of crumbs from her lip, to how she tried to comprehend what these mourning faces were telling her. It was as if her lack of understanding was disrespectful.

Dressed like they had been on Christmas day, the two Murphy sons came over to Sandor, shook his hand and talked about climbing the mountain in Kerry, how their father had dragged them up there every year. There was a boyishness to their demeanour, the immortal belief of their teenage years. Sandor felt that they'd yet to appreciate what had happened to their father, that he was gone and that they were now the men of the house.

That John had died in summer made Sandor think that nature lacked soul, that all its beauty was false, that summer was a mirage, that life was hopelessly created and destroyed, that the whole enterprise was just death parading as life. Sandor felt like crying, but held his tears in. He mourned a lost opportunity for friendship, that his life could have been enriched by John's life. Sandor recalled sitting by the fire on their first night in Kerry. In his memory he noted something about him which he hadn't seen before, a paternalism, a glimpse of his own father; it was in the way he held his wine, the way he looked into his glass, as if it were prompting him, filling him, not with alcohol, but advice.

For a few ponderous moments John's death made Sandor feel closer to Ireland. That he'd lived here longer than he had, that he knew people who'd come and gone from here created a bond with the country, that he was no longer a Hungarian looking at Ireland from Knockalisheen Camp but just another person among the mourners at a funeral.

Meave Murphy was thrilled when Sandor explained that he was planning to marry Maria, her face beamed momentarily like the flash of a lighthouse, her eyes brightening with the memory of love and creation. Then Sandor felt boastful as if he was pitting his personal gain against her loss.

She said that John would have been happy for him, "He was very fond of you. He often wondered how you were getting on down in Limerick. He called you *The Magyer*. He even supported all that business, you know," her voiced trailed off looking for the words, as if what she was about to utter was tactless, "the hunger strike. He said that if you were involved it must be okay. And he knew de Valera would give in. He said that while it was okay for de Valera to starve his own country to death, he couldn't get away with starving a bunch of foreigners."

They stayed longer than Sandor had wanted to. On their way out, Meave took Sandor aside and asked him if he needed money. Sandor said that he was still unemployed, that he wasn't rich, but that wasn't the reason why he'd called to their house. Meave said, "Of course not! It's just that John had considered giving you some, but in the end he decided against it. Instead he donated some to charity. He thought that you'd be insulted if he sent you money directly. I told him that a gift of money wouldn't embarrass anybody. He thought that it would." Sandor declined the financial assistance adding that if he needed some money in the future he'd call her. Meave agreed, "That's a good idea."

∽

They were sitting at the dinner table. It was their last night in Dublin, they were returning to Limerick by train the following morning. Mr Novak was talking about aeroplanes, about an aspect of their design, the slope of their wings. Sandor was familiar with the topic from his engineering studies and he knew that Mr Novak was incorrect in what he was saying, but as he was a guest in his house and was marrying his daughter, he didn't want to challenge him. So he listened to what he knew was nonsense, feigning interest, showing false respect while Maria chatted to her mother.

His mind wandering, Sandor imagined his parents sitting at the table, that they had been transported from Budapest to this Dublin house on a summer's evening, the two families dining together, getting to know each other. Sandor imagined that the women would get along fine, mothers keen to see their offspring marry, to create children, to carry family histories down the generational line and he imagined his father making polite conversation with Mr Novak, two men trying to find common ground.

Since they had returned from Dalkey, Sandor hadn't been feeling good, his mood had been tainted by the funeral, his spirit darkened, at odds with the comfort of their meal. Though Mrs Novak had gone to a lot of trouble preparing dinner, Sandor found himself struggling to appear appreciative, he longed to be on his own, either upstairs lying on his bed or, back in Limerick, wandering around the small roads near the camp, pathways set quietly in the countryside, free of people, a landscape which had surprised him since his arrival, that the wintry hills had bloomed lushfully, shades of green against a blue sky.

Sandor's mood was one of rejection. He felt that his tolerance of people had diminished, that he was impatient of those close by. While listening to the Novaks, he started to see Maria as an extension of them, a couple of days in Dublin had lessened her individuality, she was being reduced to the status of their offspring, and they, a blueprint for her future existence. Sandor was amazed how he'd managed to keep his distance from her parents while in the camp, as he'd seen very little of them despite their proximity.

After dinner, as Mr Novak relaxed on a chair in the sitting room, Sandor suggested that he take the dog for a walk and as everybody else was tired from over eating, he happily spent time alone by the river.

And later that night when all were asleep, Sandor lay awake in bed in a room at the front of the house overlooking the road, his window open to the warm evening air, the sound of the occasional car passing and the talk of men, their heavy-heeled shoes clipping the footpath. He started to feel homesick. John Murphy's death had made him think of his own father's death, if statistics had any worth, it would be in the next fifteen to twenty years. Frank Lovas would be in his late sixties, early seventies, an obvious time to die. Sandor wondered what could happen to their lives, what political or historical change could come about that would see him living in the same city as his parents and bear witness to them in old age. As he couldn't imagine going home he started to feel guilty about events which had yet to happen. One of his parents standing over the graveside of the other, then being left alone in the apartment, and since their children and only grandchild had left the country, his mother or father would be relying on friends or neighbours for company and care.

But their friends were getting older too, they were dying already. Sandor imagined the loneliness of his mother, the pitiful sight of an elderly woman alone in her apartment, her husband dead and her children thousands of miles away. Or his solitary father, grey haired and ignorant of domestic matters, of cooking for himself, keeping the place clean. His absolute dependence on his wife now an established fact as witnessed in the dirt on the floors, the crinkled clothing he'd wear, how his well-fed face would thin out, how death would come to him silently in his sleep or by an accident, a trip on the stairs, or slipping while getting out of the bath, or by a flame being left on in the kitchen and starting a fire and the smoke clouding the apartment and smothering him.

Over the months Sandor had missed his friends and family, the routine of his life back in Budapest, and though it was a feeling of sadness, it was one which he could control. But now lying in bed somewhere in a city which he didn't know, with the family he was marrying into and had only known since the new year, he started to feel homesickness as an *illness*, that he'd caught a virus, and he wished that the experiences of the last seven months could be expelled from his body, that Ireland itself could be removed like faecal waste.

∽

Back in the camp, Sunday evening. Kristina was preparing for her last two days in school. She explained that as she wasn't fluent in English, she was exempt from the examinations which the other girls were doing, and while her classmates were silently scribbling in the large exam hall, extra English lessons were being given to her alone. And religious lessons too; it was a subject which Kristina enjoyed, a large children's Bible had been given to her, full of pictures of events which she'd never heard of before. The Great Flood, the Parting of the Red Sea, Moses receiving the Ten

Commandments, but the one which had the most impact on Kristina, the one which gripped her imagination more than anything else was the story of how Lot's wife turned into salt. That by moving your neck ever so slightly around to look at a forbidden sight could have such consequences made her question Sandor about how it felt to actually turn into salt, she quizzed, "And would you be able to turn back again?"

But Sandor didn't know. His memory of the Bible, what had stuck with him all these years, what had been imprinted on his mind since school, was the story about frogs. Kristina knew that story too, she didn't like the idea of frogs falling from the sky, to be rained upon by their leathery lick, and he told his niece that some of these stories had a basis in science, that perhaps they could be explained, not by God, but by nature. "Perhaps frog spawn got carried up in the air, that it somehow landed on a cloud, and when it fell, it gave the impression that it was raining frogs but it was only an extraordinary sequence of events," he suggested.

But Kristina wasn't interested in science. She liked God. She liked his miracles. She liked how crazy he was.

While Kristina had found her school lessons rather boring due to her lack of English, she had enjoyed her couple of months in Laurel Hill. She'd miss the school, the friends she'd made, the sports she played. And she'd miss the attention, the special consideration which the nuns gave her throughout the day.

A Limerick girl, one of her new friends, had invited her on holidays, two weeks in Donegal at the end of July, but Kristina had declined as she would be in London by then. So she'd told her friend, "Perhaps next year," and Eva hadn't contradicted this statement even though she knew that her daughter might be attending school in England by then. For Eva saw the pleasure which Kristina had in her routine, the potential of friendship and its reward. Eva told Sandor,

"I don't like misleading her, but one more move and then we're settled."

On a Monday morning Sandor received a letter, the words *Personal – Urgent* handwritten on the top left hand corner, so he sat down on his bed to carefully open the envelope, removing the letter with great care as though it were a valuable print. It was from Julia Pinter, she wanted to meet him. She'd be at the camp on Wednesday. She explained: since their last meeting there had been a development regarding her factory proposal which she wanted to discuss with him.

Sandor hadn't spoken to Pinter since the government had turned down her idea. That had been nearly two months ago. He wondered what could have changed. Although he didn't know Julia well, she didn't seem like a person who would waste his time. Perhaps she'd found another backer? An Irish businessman who'd heard about her proposal and was interested in investing in it? Or a man who owned suitable premises which were lying vacant in some part of the country and had made a deal with Pinter; perhaps she'd get free rent and he'd get a share of the business?

Tommy Gallagher had written an article about Pinter's proposal being rejected, businessmen and investors around the country would have seen it, perhaps there were like-minded people out there, entrepreneurs willing to take a risk, someone who had been impressed with Pinter's idea.

Sandor walked up and down his hut which was glowing in the morning sunshine. He started to feel excited, a nervousness in his heart. Sandor imagined a scenario since the rejection by the Irish Government, another investor stepping in, a wealthy man who saw the strength of Pinter's plan, a man who had seen potential where the government saw failure.

As Sandor became excited, ignited by the spark of ambition, he also felt cautious, the feeling that he'd been in this position before and nothing had actually happened. But then again, he reasoned, why would Julia Pinter contact him out of the blue?

∽

Sandor was talking to McManus. Since the hunger strike their relationship had improved, though both men were still a little wary of each other. Although the camp council had called off the strike, they still threatened to have another one in a month if nothing had been done, though Sandor knew that nobody's heart was in it.

McManus was straight talking, to the point. He told Sandor that the UN had decided that Ireland should be able to look after the Hungarian refugees. No special consideration would be given to Ireland, the refugees' status would not be changed. The government had received a letter from Mr Wyrouboff. McManus said, "This isn't the news you wanted, but you can't say that he didn't try. He came to the camp, spoke to us all. There's probably other reasons why the UN don't want to help you."

Reluctantly, Sandor agreed with McManus. No matter how bad you thought your situation was, there was always somebody else worse off. As refugees, the inhabitants of Knockalisheen Camp weren't suffering in the same way tens of thousands of others were. Sandor didn't feel anger towards Wyrouboff. Instead he felt thankful that the man had visited Ireland and listened to them.

McManus moved towards the kettle. He offered Sandor more tea which he accepted. A couple of months ago, a Garda Station had been established in the camp in response to a hut being smashed up. Sandor asked McManus how long the station would stay in the camp? He replied, "I haven't thought about that. Why do you ask?"

"There's fewer people in the camp."

"That's true," McManus trailed a finger down the side of his beard, "I'm sure the police will know when it's a good time to leave. They're from a nearby station. I don't think there's much need for them anyway." McManus joked, "Perhaps you have something to confess?"

Sandor smiled. McManus started discussing the Irish weather with particular reference to summer, usually a couple of months of disappointment, however, the months of October and May were generally good, "The summer hasn't been bad so far."

Sandor tried to convey the heat of Budapest, how he'd sit outside his apartment on the steps of the courtyard, shaded from the sun, "At times unbearable." And come winter, the weather would change, as children they'd slide down the snowy Buda hills, bodies radiating heat like smoke from train engines, mouths pumping warmth into the sub-zero temperature. Like a caterpillar the children would hold on to each other, a giant insect speeding downwards, pelted by snowballs.

McManus, his finished cup of tea placed perfectly on his saucer, a subtle suggestion that their meeting was over, replied, "Ireland doesn't really have seasons. Not in the conventional sense, anyhow."

Sandor left and wandered towards the Garda Station. It was in a hut like any other, there wasn't any official signage, just a small sign in Hungarian and English. He went inside. A couple of notices hung on the walls. A small table contained forms, applications for visas, correspondence from embassies. A garda was sitting in a chair reading a newspaper, "Can I help you?"

Sandor said he was okay, "Looking at the forms."

The garda nodded, his eyes returning to his paper.

Sandor looked at the garda with the awe of a child, that this youngish man with black hair was somehow invested with power and responsibility and the gift of knowing what was right and wrong and the ability to *act* and to *solve* and to *help*.

Sandor asked him if he was bored.

He placed the newspaper on the table in front of him, and smiling, he replied, "No more or no less than in the other station."

Sandor asked, "And you solve crimes?"

The garda looked at him quizzically, "Yes. Well not me personally, the detectives do. I'm in the station, dealing with the public. So if you need any help, just ask."

∞

Sandor imagined the following. He'd go to the police, tell them that a man living in the camp had tortured him in Budapest. Yes, a man living in the camp, the evidence was as clear as day in the marks on Sandor's back, the skin grafted in thin sheets over the frame of his upper torso, it was all very clear to see. Sandor would talk about the ÁVO, the power they had, infamous power, the whole world knew about them, and how he was just like many thousands, tens of thousands of people to suffer at their hands.

The police would be convinced. It was a plausible story, his wounds backed it up. But what then?

What if they called on Szabó's hut, took him in for questioning, sat him down, put forward Sandor's case, would he admit to it? Would he say, "Yes, I was in the ÁVO. Yes, I tortured this man."

Of course not.

Sandor played out the whole scene in his mind, the young garda standing behind an older man, a detective, and

Szabó saying, "I was a plumber in Hungary," or something else, "I was in the army."

Then what would happen? Could Sandor prove that Szabó was in the ÁVO? How would that be possible? It was just one man's word against another. How could Sandor expect the police to believe him and press charges.

No, it wouldn't work like that. Witnesses, juries, judges, courts of law, appeals, rulings, proof, evidence and then sentencing. Justice wasn't one man's word against another.

No, Sandor concluded, later, after he'd left the Garda Station, sitting on the steps of his hut, it was evening, the sun was an orange glow contemplating its descent, he was clutching a glass of water, smoking a cigarette, his shirt sleeves rolled up, a slight tan on his arms. He'd come to the conclusion, a very obvious one, but one which kept going around and around in his mind, "It happened in Hungary and there's nothing I can do."

Sandor was lying in bed with Maria. It was morning. He loved the moments before she awoke, when her black hair was tossed on the pillow, her breathing gentle and mellow. She had a sweaty smell carrying an earthy comfort.

Although the curtains were drawn, the sun still illuminated the room, a warm yellow glow, capturing dust in its shine. Yesterday's newspaper was open in front of Sandor but he wasn't reading it. His mind had become distracted while translating an article, and he was imagining the following – no, not imagining, fantasising about abducting Szabó. He'd be walking back to his hut, late at night, Sandor would be lying in wait, he'd been following Szabó's routine for a couple of days, he knew his each and every move. He knew what time he got up, what time he went to bed, what time he ate, what time he washed. Sandor knew that he'd be along any moment, any minute now. Then Szabó would appear, Sandor would walk up to him, they'd shake hands. Sandor would explain that he'd a problem in the camp council hut; he needed an extra pair of hands.

Szabó would agree, the two of them would go in.

Sandor would allow Szabó to enter first. Once the door was shut, Sandor would pick up a wooden bar or a hammer or any other hard object and whack Szabó on the back of the head.

Szabó would fall into Sandor's arms, unconscious.

Sandor would wait. Until late that night, when the camp was quiet, so quiet that he'd be able to drag Szabó between the huts to a part of the fence where he could slide Szabó under, and then he'd drag the unconscious body over fields, tumbling him down walls, Szabó's face getting scuffed-up a little, and after a while, they'd come to the ruins of the cottage where he'd proposed to Maria, and once there, he'd tie Szabó's hands together and wait until he regained consciousness.

Dawn. And that's when Sandor would talk to him, asking him about his past, what he did in Budapest, how long he worked for the ÁVO, and especially, had he recognised Sandor's face.

Perhaps hours, perhaps days, would pass.

Maybe Sandor would leave Szabó shackled in the ruins of the cottage for a week, depriving him of food and drink until the time came when Szabó realised that he was going to die unless he talked.

And then what?

He imagined Szabó admitting to his part in the ÁVO. He imagined Szabó recalling the morning of his arrest and being taken to the cell. He imagined him apologising for what had happened in the baths of Andrássy Street. He imagined remorse and forgiveness covering his face like the bruises which Sandor once had, and he imagined the absolute control and mastery over an individual who'd once exercised such power over him.

But what if Szabó never buckled and accepted starvation and gradually gave way to death after a couple of weeks?

What would Sandor achieve? Justice or murder?

As Maria stirred in bed beside him and reality returned, Sandor reckoned that something would trip him up. Perhaps Szabó had warned his wife about Sandor, that his life might be threatened while in the camp, if he didn't come home, call the police, tell them to question the camp representative.

When Maria opened her eyes and saw Sandor deep in thought, the newspaper lying on his chest like a dirty sheet, she asked, "Sleep well?"

Sandor, his faraway eyes still glossy, said, "Yes. Would you like some coffee?"

CHAPTER NINETEEN

A barrel of blood.

It was something Sandor had seen in Budapest a few days before the Russians returned. One of those optimistic days when victory was being discussed, when the Russians had withdrawn from Budapest, when people had thought that little Hungary had beaten the might of the Soviet Imperium, on one of those days, in the early afternoon, Sandor had visited a hospital.

He'd been walking around the city, his camera with him. He felt that the place needed documentation, he wanted to take pictures like the ones he'd seen of Budapest shot during the war. He went to a hospital, half ashamed of his voyeuristic sensibilities, his desire to take pictures of rooms full of the sick and dying, drips dangling from metal rods, nurses administering health. The hospital was packed, there were people everywhere, lying on stretchers, and on the floor. He walked through one crowded corridor, camera tucked beneath his jacket, towards an open back door on the ground floor, attracted to this location by the abundance of natural light.

Once there, however, he looked outside, distracted by a man driving a horse and cart. So surprised by this image, Sandor didn't try to capture it. Here he was in the centre of

Budapest, the city had been in conflict for nearly two weeks, and a man was entering the back of a main hospital on a horse and cart. In a country accent, the man called out to Sandor, "Is this where I can make a delivery?"

Sandor wasn't sure. He went back inside, a doctor appeared. He told him about the horse and cart. They returned to the rear entrance.

"Can I help you?" the doctor asked. Sandor was standing behind the doctor as the man started to explain. He'd come from a small village miles away from Budapest on behalf of villagers who wanted to donate blood to those wounded during the uprising. The man jumped down from his cart and opened a waterproof tarpaulin to reveal a large barrel. The doctor went over to examine it, the man continued, "And so we all got together and decided to donate blood because we'd heard that there was a shortage in the capital's hospitals."

As the barrel was rather large, the doctor asked Sandor to help lift it from the cart and the three of them carried it to the hospital door. Although the barrel was covered, you could hear the swishing sound of blood lapping against the wood. Once the barrel was safely inside, the doctor asked, "Tell me, was there any medical supervision when this generous donation was made?"

"No," the man explained. "We carefully cut ourselves and our wives bandaged us up. Nobody was injured. And only healthy people were allowed to donate."

"Okay," said the doctor. "Thanks."

The man returned to his cart and exited the hospital grounds, the sound of horseshoes on cobblestones quickly being erased by traffic. The doctor turned to Sandor, "Will you help me?"

They carried the barrel into a room off the corridor. Inside was a shower. The doctor asked Sandor to wait for a moment. Alone Sandor stood by the barrel of blood, the sound of humanity, from laughter to agony, in the corridor outside. The doctor arrived with a large crow bar and started opening the barrel. The blood didn't smell. Sandor expected a layer of filth or scum on top of it, but it was clean. Swashing around in the oak barrel, it could have been wine. The doctor motioned towards the shower and asked Sandor to help him pour it down the drain.

"Can you imagine the stupidity?" the doctor remarked as the blood splashed into the plughole. "They think that all their blood is the same. This is the shit that I've to deal with."

∽

Tommy Gallagher was standing with the sun behind his back. Sandor was sitting on the steps of his hut. They were smoking cigarettes as they talked about Nicolas Wyrouboff, Sandor explaining that the UN was not going to help them.

Gallagher said that it was a pity, "But what does Ireland expect? A couple of hundred people isn't very many, you'd think that they'd get it right and be able to look after them." Gallagher laughed, "But the thing about Wyrouboff is that the Irish Government didn't want him to come here in the first place. I know someone in the department. The government didn't invite him. He just decided to come on his own behalf. So when the government heard that he was on his way, they considered barring him from the camp. They were terrified of him, of what he might say. It was only after he arrived and everything went okay and he thought that the camp wasn't so bad that the government pretended that it had been their idea to bring him over in the first place."

∽

Sandor arrived early for his meeting with Julia Pinter. It was Wednesday morning and rain was pouring down on the streets of Limerick. He was dressed in his only suit which was too heavy for the summer. He'd sheltered from the rain with a large umbrella which he'd found in the camp. Sitting in the hotel reception, he wondered why he felt nervous. Although he wanted a cigarette, he didn't light up. He liked Julia Pinter and looked forward to seeing her. They had only met each other a few times, but he felt they'd shared experience. She reminded him of a certain type of woman back home from his youth, the wealthy wife of Budapest's rich, people he'd come across at various times, friends of his self-made uncle or mothers of certain children from school. Pinter was a glimpse of them, and of a time gone by, a city he couldn't imagine returning to.

A woman from the hotel bar asked Sandor if he wanted a drink. He explained that he was waiting for somebody, "Not yet."

Outside the rain was easing off. Sandor couldn't remember seeing such a powerful shower in all his time in Ireland, the water pummelling the earth like buckshot, each drop a little explosion.

Sandor started to feel thirsty. He requested a glass of water and it came with ice.

Julia Pinter arrived a few minutes short of her arranged time. After their greeting, they went to a room where people relaxed on large couches with newspapers spread over coffee tables. Julia spoke about the last time they'd met, when the government had turned down her factory proposal, "I was so disappointed by the whole affair. The two men from the government made me feel like I was a child, or worse, a stupid woman. I was so insulted by them. We had everything planned and they came along and ruined it all with their endless cynicism. Ireland is a complete mess. You can't blame the people. It comes from the top."

When the waitress appeared, Julia ordered, she spoke

rapidly and clearly, but with a heavy accent. As the waitress turned to leave Julia looked into space for a moment, then turned to Sandor who was finding it hard not to sink into the soft couch. She said, "I want to discuss something with you. As you can probably imagine, I became very disillusioned after the government turned down my offer. It was a most peculiar time for me. I have lived in Ireland for many years, I have made my home here, and I believed, perhaps not in my heart of hearts, but a belief all the same, that this country was a welcoming one. And so when the idea for this factory came about, I just took it for granted that the government would see the proposal the same way that I saw it. In short, an opportunity. But as you know, they didn't."

With subtlety the waitress placed a large pot of coffee on the table along with biscuits. When she was gone, Pinter continued, "I'm sure you can imagine the following. You have an idea. You can't get it out of your mind. You tell people you trust about it. Everybody agrees that it will work. And then you go to – in my case the government – and they turn your whole world upside down. It takes time to get over it. You know, the rejection I felt," she smiled a little and her voice hushed, "almost broke my heart. Then I thought that I was going insane, that I was dreaming up schemes, castles in the air, that I was living in a fantasy world. Or the worst feeling was that I was a wealthy widow – I make no apologies for that – but a widow who wanted to buy herself prestige or respect or to use her money to amuse herself while playing with the lives of others, lives like yours."

Sandor was surprised by her honesty, her openness. He felt that she was speaking to him as a confidant, that she was revealing a vulnerable side comprised of fear and weakness and anxiety. Though he felt charmed by her he wondered where this openness was leading to, and when she started talking about the purpose of their meeting, he realised that she'd told him about her angst, not to prove that she was an emotional being full of passion and self-doubt, but because she had been right all along, that her idea for a factory would, after all, be realised. "I had thought that an Irish businessman would come along and offer to invest in the factory, but this never happened. But I'll tell you what did happen."

She poured more coffee into Sandor's cup. Then she opened an envelope, removing a couple of sheets of paper. She gave them to him as she resumed talking. "What you see here is an offer from the Argentine embassy in Dublin. They're interested in the factory proposal. My accountant and I have had a number of meetings with them. They are willing to invest in the factory but in Argentina. There is a vacant factory close to Buenos Aires which they'll refurbish to our specification. In short, they are willing to do everything which the Irish Government won't. I am willing to go, take my money out of Ireland, invest it in Argentina, but I need you to come with me. It's the same deal as before, but in different country. My money, your labour along with other skilled workers from the camp and this time, backing from the Argentine Government."

Julia looked at Sandor as he finished his coffee. "What do you think?"

Sandor said, "It's a big difference from working in Ireland. I'll need time…I'm getting married…"

"In the letter it states that anybody you have personal relations with can come along."

"Yes, yes…but I'll need time…"

"A ship sails from Southampton in eight days. I need to know in four," Julia smiled. "I'm having a final meeting with the embassy next Monday in Dublin. You're more than welcome to come along."

Sandor knew that Maria was excited, but also troubled. Her face was shy to acknowledge the reality of Pinter's offer; the escape it promised, the end of camp life, the guarantee of work, and the adventure of going to Argentina, sailing for weeks across the earth, stopping in ports along the way, West Africa and Brazil.

Maria had just showered, her hair was wet. "But what will my parents think? They are convinced that we'll settle in Dublin, that we'll eventually get jobs there. I can't see them being impressed with us going to the other side of the world."

Sandor remembered last November, leaving his parents alone in their apartment, the upset on his mother's face, his father's disappointment and surprise, and at times over the last seven months, he had thought that perhaps they were right, that leaving Hungary had been a bad idea, that everything which they needed was there. Ireland had proved a waste of time, but Pinter's offer was redemptive, something good had come out of the place after all. "On one level your parents will understand," replied Sandor. "Of course they won't say that, but they'd probably do the same if in our position. Remember that your parents left their parents back in Hungary. People move, they always have and always will."

Maria said that she didn't want to stay in Ireland, "I never liked this place. Back in Austria when my father had decided to come here, I was surprised and so was my mother. We weren't interested in coming here, but he wanted to and he always gets his way. But to be honest, I never thought about going to Argentina. I have always thought that I'd go to the United States or Canada but not South America."

Sandor replied, "I think that it's the best offer we're likely to get. Okay, we might get visas for North America but I don't have any guarantee of work there. With Pinter,

I do. She is giving up her life here, too. That's how certain she is about the plan. As far as I can see, we have nothing to lose. But we must decide quickly. Pinter wants to know in four days."

∽

When Laurel Hill Convent closed for the summer, Sandor was reminded of his school days, the joy of the free months, but unlike him, Kristina was sad to leave the old convent. She'd made friends there and she'd enjoyed her position as the refugee child. The nuns had spoilt her with their spiritual care, eager to cleanse the parts of her soul hitherto exposed to communism; but there was a common decency there too, their care for Kristina went beyond the professional and when school ended for the summer, Kristina was not only sad to leave, but eager to return in September.

As soon as school finished Eva and Josef finalised their plans to move to London. As far as Kristina was concerned, they would only be spending summer in London, one of the greatest cities on earth. "You are very privileged to travel so much," explained Eva. "When I was a child, I hadn't seen half the places you have."

And so Sandor watched as Eva made the final preparations to leave. They were going early the following morning, their goodbyes were said the night before. Apart from one or two items, Eva's luggage hadn't increased since they'd left Budapest, and the only extra items Kristina had were religious books which the nuns had given her. Although Eva had only been in a relationship with Josef for a couple of months their togetherness had an air of authority. It was solid, strong and Sandor couldn't doubt Josef's love for her.

It didn't take long for Eva to finish packing. Afterwards they went for a meal in a cheap restaurant in Limerick. Much of the conversation concerned Sandor's meeting with

Julia Pinter. Eva thought that it was a good opportunity, too good to miss, "But you'd really be on the other side of the world. You could be there, quite literally, for ever."

Josef spoke of London as being advantageously located, "You never know what will happen in the future. At least with London, it's still Europe."

The evening passed quickly. Sandor, Eva and Kristina walked home side by side, leaving Maria and Josef in their wake. Sandor was aware of a truth which neither expressed, namely, that the uprising had destroyed their family, any unity which they once had was long gone, and now they were about to be scattered across the world. Future changes in their lives would be noted, not with each other's eyes, but by the solitary scratch of pen on paper.

Sandor was glad that Eva would marry Josef. If she had met an Irishman and stayed in Ireland, he felt that she'd always be at a disadvantage, she'd always be an outsider, and while he thought that love was love regardless, real communication, the subtlety of interaction which love was based on, was greatly helped by a common language. And for Sandor love was communication, pure expression, unfettered and free. To see Eva being absorbed in an Irishman's house, dealing with an Irishman's family and listening to an Irishman's friends would have made Sandor pity his sister, as ultimately, she'd lose something of herself.

Sandor hugged Kristina and told her to enjoy her time in London, "A great adventure."

Josef gave Sandor the address of the bakery in London where he would be working. Sandor said that they'd have to make a decision about Argentina in a couple of days. He'd let them know by post. They said their goodbyes.

When Sandor was back in his hut, lying on his bed with Maria, he placed his hand in his pocket and noticed that his wallet was missing. He remembered sitting on a bed in

Eva's hut. Quickly he rushed across the camp. After knocking on their door, he explained that he was missing his wallet. Josef started looking around the hut and so did Eva. Then Sandor saw it on the bed where he'd been lying. "There it is," he said. He picked it up, and as he left, he repeated, "Have a great trip."

Outside the hut, standing in the darkness, Sandor felt the full force of tears, his waxy eyes seemed to melt, to burn away, leaving a shivering world. He tried focusing on the huts across the road, but he couldn't. Instead their lights looked like they were reflected in water, and turning his head towards the ground, he tried to control his sobbing.

∽

In the days after Eva left the camp Sandor thought about family. Not his family, but *family* as it was discussed back in Budapest among the party faithful, theorists who attempted to fit all human interaction into economic models. Sandor recalled how husbands were exploiting wives; or how marriage was a capitalistic contract designed to keep property rights in a dynastic family; or poorer families were less exploitative as all members were forced to work and the wife was therefore equal to the husband. In these terms somebody was always exploiting somebody else. But what about loneliness and solitude? What about an emotional bond? Love like Sandor had for Maria, love which brought a sense of sublime calm to his heart when they were lying in bed together, nothing spoken, just a few comments here and there, observations about the minutiae of life. Sandor thought of the ignorance of these theorists. People engineering society, mutating it into something it could never be while attempting to remove what was human and good, decent and necessary.

∽

The taxi pulled up outside the Novaks. Sandor looked at the terraced building with trepidation as Maria paid the driver and he removed their bags from the boot of the car. Window blinds were parted, Mrs Novak waved at them from the house while Mr Novak greeted them at the door. Shaking Sandor's hand he said, "Good to see you. Good trip?"

Sandor replied, "Fine but my back is a little sore from the train."

Mrs Novak hugged her daughter, kissed Sandor's cheeks and then ushered them into her house. Sandor noticed subtle changes since their last visit, a number of plants dotted around the house, a painting above the fireplace, a mirror in the hall. The kitchen smelled of freshly baked bread, they were offered drinks in the living room. Maria had a small present, a box of chocolates which she passed around as her parents sat down. Windows were open and cars went by. In the back garden, the dog barked. Mrs Novak said, "He's not allowed in here anymore. Dirty little thing."

Mr Novak added, "The poor dog is driven mad by your mother. He's blamed for everything. But anyway, your trip to Dublin." Mr Novak looked at his daughter. "Your mother said that you were very secretive on the telephone." He was sitting up in his chair, his arms resting on his knees, his fingers intertwined. He was brimming with excitement.

It was Sandor, however, who started speaking. He spoke about Julia Pinter, a person Mr Novak had heard about, "The wealthy widow."

Sandor continued, "She has offered me a job."

"That's great." Mr Novak looked smilingly at his wife.

"But it's in Argentina."

Mr Novak sat back in his chair as Sandor explained, "A group of us have been offered work there. Pinter herself is going as well. A boat is sailing from England in a few days."

Mrs Novak asked, "You're not seriously considering going, are you?"

Maria said, "Yes."

Sandor added, "We think it's for the best."

Mr Novak replied, "But what about work in Dublin. I told you before that a job is coming up in my company. My boss knows all about you."

Maria replied, "We don't want to live in Ireland."

Mrs Novak said, "But what about us? Your family?" The living room went quiet, you could hear people passing by the house, and sounds from next door, the shouts of children, the scream of infants. Sandor didn't have an answer to this question, and neither did Maria, and so she started mumbling about opportunities, what Argentina could offer them, but Mrs Novak pressed her again, "What about us?"

Sandor felt Mr Novak's disapproving eyes. For it was he who was taking their daughter away, without him they wouldn't be having this conversation, and Mr Novak was quick to point this out, "Surely, Sandor, you can get a job elsewhere, some place which isn't on the other side of the world?"

"Since I came here, I've tried everything. Most people are having to go abroad in order to find work. You are the lucky ones, not many people have found work here."

Mr Novak replied, "Yes, but what's to say you won't get work in Ireland soon? You've only been here for a relatively short period. I'm certain that it's only a matter of time."

"Maybe you're right, I don't know. But I have tried everything since coming here. We think that it's a great opportunity for us to take."

Mr Novak started coughing. Then, with an authoritative air to his voice, asked, "Are you here to ask my permission to go?"

Sandor looked at Maria. She said, "It's not about permission, it's about what's best for us."

Mr Novak replied, "Maria, you are young. And Sandor, I know you are older, but you don't know everything. In fact," Mr Novak stood up, "would you mind leaving the room. I want to talk to my daughter."

Sandor stirred in his seat. Maria said, "We're engaged, he doesn't have to go anywhere."

Mr Novak asked, "Please, Sandor. I am Maria's father."

Sandor left the room. He stood in the small hallway looking out the window at the tiny front garden and the road. For a few minutes he could barely hear anything, Mr Novak's voice rumbled through the bricks and the heavy wooden door, but it was unclear. Then Sandor heard somebody crying but he wasn't sure if it was Maria or her mother. It was a plaintive, sobbing sound, female.

Sandor felt like a child having been sent to his room, and a feeling of hatred – almost a petulant, adolescent emotion – rose in his heart. He felt repulsed by Mr Novak and the way he used age to force an argument. Sandor moved to the door, his ear hovering inches from the wood. By the clarity of Maria's speech he reckoned that it was her mother who was crying. Mr Novak asked her about Sandor's influence and she insisted that she wanted to go, that she wasn't being led by him, "I never liked Ireland. It was your idea to come here. You never asked us for our opinion."

"I thought that it was best for us as a family," Mr Novak replied.

"No you didn't," countered Maria. "You had an idea of this place from all those books you read. The wrong idea, as it happens."

Sandor heard somebody rising from a chair. Quickly, he moved down the hall. Mr Novak appeared. He looked at Sandor, then walked through the kitchen to open the back door. When the dog started barking Mr Novak told him to be quiet. He passed Sandor in the hall without saying anything, slamming the front door shut.

Immediately, however, Mr Novak opened the door, "I should have known your type. Playing with people's lives in the camp, always thinking about yourself. If you loved my daughter half as much as you loved yourself, she'd be doing well. But she can't see through you," and he shut the door.

Sandor stuck his head into the living room, Mrs Novak was still crying, Maria was sitting on the couch beside her. Sandor didn't say anything, instead he waited until Maria noticed him, and when she did, she told him to go upstairs. "I'll be up in a little while," she said quietly.

A few days before László Eper's departure to Canada he arranged to meet Sandor in the camp council hut. It was after eight, Sandor had just finished his breakfast and walked over to meet him.

Eper had arrived early, he was sitting at the table opposite another man. As Eper started talking, Sandor didn't listen; instead he looked at the outstretched hand of the other man. Eper continued, "I'd like you to meet Károly Szabó. He's a friend of mine and somebody that I'd like to replace me on the council."

Sandor felt a wave of power sweep over him as he sensed in Szabó's eyes and the warm grip of his hand that he held something which Szabó wanted. But he also remembered Andrássy Street, how the tiles had felt as he lay on them all those years ago, how warm they were after the iced water. As the years passed Sandor had found it increasingly difficult to remember the exact details of his torture, it was as if his mind had censored the experience, but he never forgot the tiles on the basement floor and how his head had banged against them.

When Szabó spoke, he was amiable, friendly. And he was quite particular in his analysis of the camp council, talking about the Irish Government, the Red Cross and speaking highly of Sandor's efforts, "But it's still important for the council to exist because if it doesn't, who'll speak for us refugees?"

Sandor nodded. Eper spoke about Sandor's deal with the Argentine embassy, news which had delighted those who had originally planned to work for Pinter in Ireland. And while Sandor listened to these men who seemed to know each other well, their familiar conversational references and sense of humour, he wondered what had happened in the years since Andrássy Street. Abstractly, he thought of himself not as Sandor Lovas but as a subject for analysis, and why, he wondered, was Szabó now in pleasant conversation and not torturing him to death?

Szabó asked Sandor about the part-time jobs which he had while in the camp. And it was only when Sandor started talking that he realised how nervous he was, how his sentences were ill-formed, how he seemed to be mumbling his way through them. He listened to his voice as if it wasn't his own; it was as though it were being broadcast into the room by a speaker; a distant voice on a radio and something beyond his control. When Sandor stopped talking, Szabó asked him why he'd come to Ireland.

Sandor said, "A good question," and though he hadn't intended it to be a joke it was taken as one, and then he explained how quickly the Irish Red Cross had managed to get them out of Austria.

"To be left in Austria," replied Szabó. "That's what we feared. My wife just wanted to get the hell out of the place."

"And you? Why did you pick Ireland?" asked Sandor.

Szabó smiled. "It's a long, long way from Hungary." Then Szabó spoke about the problems since arriving, "I thought that we had left all problems behind. I thought that we'd be able to lead quiet lives."

Eper agreed, "That was the plan."

Szabó asked, "When are you leaving Ireland?"

"In a few days," Sandor replied. Eper looked at Szabó and said that they'd better be going. As they left the hut Szabó turned to Sandor, "I'll see you before then."

⁂

After sitting down for less than a minute, an excited McManus rose quickly from his seat, walked towards the window and peered out. Seconds later he turned to the table, "He's not here yet. That must have been some other car."

It was Sandor's final meeting as camp representative. János Polgár, the last remaining man on the council, was taking over his position. Sandor continued his conversation with Polgár, "Most of what you'll be doing is organising forms from embassies. Lucia will be helping people to complete their visa applications correctly."

A car pulled up outside. McManus said, "Okay, this is him. I'll return with him in a few minutes, and when we do, all of you stand up when we enter. I'm sorry if it sounds so formal, but please, show respect."

Minutes later you could hear McManus's reverential tones in the next room, his voice a mixture of respect and nerves, almost childlike. McManus entered the room, and like an adult wary of his brood, signalled to the table to stand up as Archbishop John Charles McQuaid appeared. Sandor looked at his slim face, his high forehead and the bright colour of his purple robes. It was a hot June day. Sandor looked for signs of sweat, but there weren't any.

Everybody was introduced. As McManus talked to McQuaid, Sandor's eyes fixed on the crucifix, a polished hulk of silver hanging around the cleric's neck. It wasn't a conventional crucifix as there were two perpendicular bars towards the top. Sandor remembered his father explaining the agony that this instrument inflicted on its victims: death by suffocation, and in Christ's case, in the savage heat of the Judean hills. Sandor had always thought that you'd bleed to death on the cross, but no, your body sags downward, your arms push against your shoulders which push against your windpipe, preventing the oxygen going to your lungs.

When everybody sat down McManus and McQuaid continued chatting for a few minutes, Sandor listening to their conversation but without understanding the quick patter of the cleric's accent.

McQuaid addressed the table, stopping every minute to allow Lucia to translate his words. "The main purpose of my visit is to discuss the National Catholic Welfare Conference of America, an organisation which will be able to assist your onward journey to the United States. Last week I was in discussion with some of their senior representatives and they are keen to receive applications from this camp. Regarding the amount of people they can take, at first, I think it will be one hundred and fifty. After my conversation with them last week, one of their representatives is scheduled to arrive here in the next couple of days."

McManus smiled, "That's great news. And this representative, do you know him personally?"

McQuaid replied, "In fact, it's a woman. Mrs Delattre." A few minutes later the party were walking around Knockalisheen, close to the perimeter fence where children were playing football, the loud clap of feet on leather. With Lucia's help, McQuaid spoke to Polgár for most of the time, Sandor strolling behind with McManus. When McQuaid was out of earshot McManus spoke about the cleric, unable to conceal his enthusiasm for the visit. "We were wasting our time with the government, we should have been talking to this man all along. A man of his word."

When McQuaid entered the recreational hut, a few

people stood up on seeing him, and the Archbishop walked over to them. McQuaid mentioned Cardinal Mindszenty, how he prayed for him everyday, how he was a source of inspiration.

And minutes later they were back where they had started, outside McManus's office at the front of the camp, the engine running in McQuaid's car. He shook hands with McManus, then turned to Polgár and Sandor, and in a clear, precise accent, a voice designed to be understood, McQuaid looked at the camp and the countryside beyond and said, "Leave it to me, I'll empty this place. Soon there will be nobody left."

When Eper left, Sandor met Szabó on his own. Immediately Szabó started talking about his first impression of Ireland. He'd never forget it, he said, "The wife and I arrived, it was pitch black and we couldn't see anything. It's strange, you arrive in another country in the dark and you have no idea what the place looks like. And what's strange is that you expect it to be so different, so removed from what you know, and so the next morning when we drew the curtains and looked at the surrounding fields we were surprised at how normal the country looked. It was just fields, houses, a city in the distance. What did I expect?" Szabó asked rhetorically, "I don't really know. My wife made one observation, she asked, 'Where is all the industry? Where are all the factories?' It was a good point. And do you know what I said?"

Sandor asked, "What?"

Szabó replied, "'Well, seeing as this is the West and everything is so advanced, all the factories are probably underground, kept out of sight.'" Szabó laughed, "And for a day or two, I actually believed it."

After a lull in their conversation, Sandor crossed his legs, folded his arms, and said, "Did you know Eper before coming to Ireland?"

"No. We met in the camp."

"He must like you. He really wants you to work on the council."

"He knows I'm interested."

"And he talked to Polgár as well. He's happy to work with you when I'm gone."

"I'm looking forward to it."

"As they both want you on the council, I've no choice. We're democrats."

Szabó looked quizzically at Sandor, "You don't want me working for the council?"

"I know what you did back in Budapest."

Szabó didn't flinch, just looked confused, "Know what?"

Sandor, now a little nervous, "The ÁVO."

"What about the ÁVO?"

"You were in it."

"Why do you think that?"

"Because I was there. Andrássy Street. The basement. The baths."

Sitting across from Sandor, Szabó remained calm, perhaps a little too calm, thought Sandor. He wondered about the signs of deceit, telltale gestures which gave away inner secrets: pupils dilating, a nervous twitch.

But Szabó remained perfectly still as he replied, "I have no idea what you are talking about. I was never in the ÁVO. I had nothing to do with them. I fled Hungary. I wanted to escape all of that. I think," Szabó moved, shuffling in his seat, "that you have got me confused with someone else." The hut was quiet for a moment, then Szabó continued, "But I know what you mean."

Sandor asked, "About what?"

"I've had dealings with the ÁVO," Szabó sounded sincere, as if Sandor was a confidant, "Well, not me, but my wife. She was," Szabó searched for words to express himself, "roughed up by them. And the man who was responsible, the man who did it to her, he lives in the camp. Well he used to until recently." Szabó paused, sat upright in his chair, "Whatever Josef Horvath has told you about his past, my wife will tell you another story."

For a few seconds Sandor wondered if this was true; but then he reckoned Szabó was deflecting attention from himself. Sandor replied, "If this is true, why didn't you approach Horvath?"

Szabó shrugged, "What could I do? My wife didn't want it mentioned. She said that we were free of Hungary now. And what would Horvath say? He'd just deny it. And then what could my wife do? Call the police? It would be her word against his, and in the end nothing would come of it. But I admit, it killed me that people like him weren't locked up. But what could I do? Take the law into my own hands? Revenge?" Szabó smiled, "People always confuse me for other people, but being in the ÁVO is a first. It must be the beard."

EPILOGUE

It was late evening when they arrived in the Argentine embassy. The building was in Ballsbridge, a short drive from the cheap guesthouse where they were staying. On arrival they were ushered into a meeting room were Julia Pinter sat at a table alongside her accountant and lawyer. A crowd of friendly faces and enthusiastic diplomats offered glasses of wine. Sandor looked at the walls; photographs of vineyards and waterfalls, the sprawling city of Buenos Aires, "Good air," as Julia translated.

There was a jovial and celebratory atmosphere as an Argentinian lawyer discussed the terms of their immigration. Contracts were passed around, forms signed and stamped which covered their visa requirements. Formalities took a short while and then the conversation returned to generalities. A diplomat expressed regret that they would arrive in Buenos Aires during the winter months and how in the southern hemisphere, spring started in September, "But the winter isn't too bad, just like an Irish summer."

After a few hours they left the embassy. As it was a nice evening, Sandor suggested they walk back to the guesthouse. Maria asked him, "Are you sure you know the way?"

Sandor was confident, "Yes, the taxi only drove down two or three roads." Pointing towards a bridge, he said, "It's that way." After fifteen minutes they started walking alongside a river, Sandor looked up at the trees, their green leaves blocking the orange glow of the setting sun. Children were playing in the river, splashing each other with water. As they walked by a row of cottages, you could smell food cooking. Outside, an old woman sat on a chair, her eyes closed to the sun, her hands holding a newspaper.

Sandor looked at his watch, it was 9.45 p.m. He was amazed at the bright colour of the sky. Back in Budapest, it would be dark by now. Stopping to light a cigarette, he realised the date, "Today's the longest day."

"Really?" She was waiting a few feet ahead of him.

"Yes," he said catching up with her, "that explains the sky."

FRIENDS OF PILLAR PRESS

Pillar Press

Sue Bowden. Andy Bowden. All That Glisters, Thomastown. Margaret Carey. Shem Caulfield. Maura Dieren. Gina O'Donnell. Eva Lynch. Murphy's Bar, Thomastown. Eoin McEvitt. Conor MacGabhann. Helen MacGabhann. Sean O'Neill. Brid O'Neill. Damien Wedge. Colm O'Boyle. Eileen O'Neill. Sean Mahon. Antoinette O'Neill. Aine O'Neill. Frank Neenan. James Hanley. Orla Dukes. Maeve O'Neill. Shane O'Toole. Debra Bowden. Tony Spooner. Elizabeth Cunningham. Richard McLoughlin. Kathryn Potterton. Cormac Buggy. Fiona Shannon.

To become a friend of Pillar Press please contact us at

Ladywell
Thomastown
Co. Kilkenny

Tel: 056-7724901   E-mail: info@pillarpress.ie